BARTIMAEUS

The Ring of Solomon

Also by Jonathan Stroud

Bartimaeus Books
The Amulet of Samarkand
The Golem's Eye
Ptolemy's Gate

Buried Fire
The Leap
The Last Siege
Heroes of the Valley

BARTIMAEUS

The Ring of Solomon

JONATHAN STROUD

Disney • HYPERION BOOKS
NEW YORK

First Edition
1 3 5 7 9 10 8 6 4 2

V567-9638-5-10227

Printed in the United States of America

Library of Congress Cataloging-in-Publication Data on file.
ISBN 978-1-4231-2372-9

Reinforced binding

Visit www.hyperionbooksforchildren.com

For Arthur,
with love

A Note on Magic

MAGICIANS

Since history began in the mud-brick cities of Mesopotamia more than five thousand years ago, rulers of great nations have always used *magicians* to help maintain their rule. The pharaohs of Egypt and the kings of Sumer, Assyria, and Babylon all relied on magic to protect their cities, strengthen their armies, and cast their enemies down. Modern governments, though cloaking the fact behind careful propaganda, continue this same policy.

Magicians do not have magical abilities themselves, but derive their power from the control of *spirits*, which do. They spend many years in lonely study, mastering the techniques that will allow them to summon these fearsome entities and survive. Successful magicians are consequently always clever and physically robust. Because of the dangers of their craft, they are also usually ruthless, secretive, and self-serving.

For most *summonings*, the magician stands inside a carefully drawn circle of protection, within which is a *pentacle*, or five-pointed star. Certain complex incantations are spoken, and the spirit is drawn from its far dimension. Next, the magician recites special words of Binding. If this is done correctly, the spirit becomes the magician's slave. If a mistake is made, the protective power of the circle is broken, and the unhappy magician is at the spirit's mercy.

Once a slave is bound, it must obey its master's instructions until its task is complete. When this time comes (it may take hours, days, or years), the rejoicing spirit is formally *dismissed*. In general, spirits resent their captivity, no matter what its duration, and seek any opportunity to do their masters harm. Most sensible magicians, therefore, keep their slaves for as short a time as possible, just in case their luck runs out.

SPIRITS

All spirits are formed of *essence*, a fluid, ever-shifting substance. In their own dimension, known as *the Other Place*, they have no solid form, but on Earth they must take some kind of definite guise. However, higher spirits are able to change shape at will: this gives them some respite from the pain that Earth's cruel solidity causes to their essence. There are five main categories of spirit.

These are:

1. *Imps*: The lowliest type. Imps are scurrilous and impertinent and their magic is humble. Most cannot change shape at all. Nevertheless they are easily directed and present no great danger to the magician. For this reason they are frequently summoned, and used for minor tasks such as scrubbing floors, clearing middens, carrying messages, and keeping watch.

2. *Foliots*: More potent than imps, but not as dangerous as djinn, foliots are favored by magicians for their stealth and cunning. Being reasonably adept at changing shape, they make excellent spies.

3. *Djinn*: The largest class of spirit, and the hardest to summarize. No two seem alike. They lack the raw power of the greatest spirits, but frequently exceed them in cleverness and audacity. They excel at shape-shifting, and have a vast arsenal of spells at their disposal. A djinni is the favored slave for most competent magicians.

4. *Afrits*: Strong as bulls, imposing in stature, and arrogant as kings, afrits are blunt and irascible by temperament. They are less subtle than other spirits, and their might frequently exceeds their intelligence. Monarchs throughout history have used them as vanguards in battle and as guardians of their gold.

5. *Marids*: The most perilous and least common of the five types. Supremely confident in their magical power, marids sometimes appear in discreet or gentle guises, only to suddenly switch to vast and hideous shapes. Only the greatest magicians dare summon them.

All magicians fear their spirit-slaves, and ensure their obedience by means of inventive punishments. For this reason most spirits bow to the inevitable. They serve their masters as efficiently as possible and—despite their natural instincts—remain outwardly zealous and polite, for fear of repercussions. This is what most spirits do. There *are* exceptions.

The Main Characters

JERUSALEM

Solomon	*King of Israel*
Hiram	*Solomon's vizier*
Khaba	*A magician—in service to King Solomon*
Ezekiel	*A magician—in service to King Solomon*
Various other magicians, servants, and wives	

MARIB

Balkis	*Queen of Sheba*
Asmira	*A captain of the guard*

THE SPIRITS

Bartimaeus	*A djinni*
Faquarl	*A djinni*
Beyzer Chosroes Menes Nimshik Tivoc Xoxen	*Djinn—in service to Khaba the Cruel*
Gezeri	*A foliot—in service to Khaba the Cruel*
Numerous other marids, afrits, djinn, foliots, and imps	

Map of Israel, Sheba, and Surrounding Lands, 950 B.C.E.

Tigris R.

Euphrates R.

Assyria

Mesopotamia

Great Sea

Damascus

Babylon

Uruk

Jerusalem

Eridu

Ur

Sumer

Memphis

Israel

Edom

Eilat

Gulf of Aqaba

Arabia

Egypt

Thebes

Arabian Desert

N

W

E

S

Nile R.

Nubia

Kush

Red Sea

Punt

Marib

Sheba

Hadhramaut

Himyar

BARTIMAEUS

The Ring of Solomon

Part One

I

Sunset above the olive groves. The sky, like a bashful youth kissed for the first time, blushed with a peach-pink light. Through the open windows came the gentlest of breezes, carrying the fragrances of evening. It stirred the hair of the young woman standing alone and pensive in the center of the marble floor, and caused her dress to flutter against the contours of her lean, dark limbs.

She lifted a hand; slim fingers toyed with a ringlet of hair beside her neck.

"Why so shy, my lord?" she whispered. "Come near and let me look on you."

In the opposite pentacle the old man lowered the wax cylinder in his hand and glared at me with his single eye. "Great Jehovah, Bartimaeus! You don't think that's going to work on *me*?"

My eyelashes quivered beguilingly. "I'll dance too, if you'll only step a *little* closer. Come on, spoil yourself. I'll do the Twirl of the Seven Veils."

The magician spoke with irritation. "No, thank you. And you can stop *that*, too."

"Stop what?"

"That . . . that *jiggling about*. Every now and then you— *There!* You did it again!"

"Oh, come on, sailor, live a little. What's putting you off?"

My master uttered an oath. "Possibly your clawed left foot. Possibly your scaly tail. Also possibly the fact that even a newborn

THE RING OF SOLOMON

babe would know not to step outside his protective circle when requested to do so by a wicked, duplicitous spirit such as yourself. Now, silence, cursed creature of air, and abandon your pathetic temptations, or I shall strike you sideways with such a Pestilence as even great Egypt never suffered!" The old boy was quite excited, all out of breath, his white hair a disordered halo around his head. From behind his ear he took a stylus and grimly made a notation on the cylinder. "There's a black mark there for you, Bartimaeus," he said. "*Another* one. If this line gets filled, you'll be off the special allowances list for good, you understand. No more roasted imps, no time off, nothing. Now, I've a job for you."

The maiden in the pentacle folded her arms. She wrinkled her dainty nose. "I've just done a job."

"Well, now you've got another one."

"I'll do it when I've had a rest."

"You'll do it this very night."

"Why should *I* do it? Send Tufec or Rizim."

A bright jag of scarlet lightning issued from the forefinger of the old man, looped across the intervening space, and set my pentacle aflame, so that I wailed and danced with mad abandon.

The crackling ceased; the pain in my feet lessened. I came to an ungainly standstill.

"You were right, Bartimaeus," the old man chuckled. "You *do* dance well. Now, are you going to give me any more backchat? If so, another notch upon the cylinder it shall be."

"No, no—there's no need for that." To my great relief the stylus was slowly replaced behind the aged ear. I clapped my hands vigorously. "So, another job, you say? What joy! I'm humbled that you have selected me from among so many other worthy djinn. What brought me to your attention tonight,

great Master? The ease with which I slew the giant of Mount
Lebanon? The zeal with which I put the Canaanite rebels to
flight? Or just my general reputation?"

The old man scratched his nose. "None of that; rather it was
your behavior last night, when the watch imps observed you in
the form of a mandrill swaggering through the undergrowth
below the Sheep Gate, singing lewd songs about King Solomon
and loudly extolling your own magnificence."

The maiden gave a surly shrug. "Might not have been me."

"The words 'Bartimaeus is best,' repeated at tedious length,
suggest otherwise."

"Well, all right. So I'd had too many mites at supper. No
harm done."

"No harm? The Watch reported it to their supervisor, who
reported it to me. I reported it to High Magician Hiram, and
I believe it has since come to the ears of the king himself." His
face became all prim and starchy. "He is not pleased."

I blew out my cheeks. "Can't he tell me so in person?"

The magician's eye bulged; it looked like an egg emerging from a chicken.[1] "You dare suggest," he cried, "that great
Solomon, King of all Israel, master of all lands from the Gulf
of Aqaba to the broad Euphrates, would deign to speak with a
sulphurous slave such as *you*? The idea! In all my years, I have
heard nothing so offensive!"

---

[1] Rizim had put the other eye out on a rare occasion when our master had made
a slight mistake with the words of his summoning. We'd additionally managed
to scorch his backside once or twice, and there was a scar on his neck where I'd
come close with a lucky ricochet; but despite a long career commanding more
than a dozen formidable djinn, the magician remained vigorous and spry. He was
a tough old bird.

"Oh, come, come. Look at the state of you. Surely you must have."

"Two more notches, Bartimaeus, for your effrontery and cheek." Out came the cylinder; the stylus scratched upon it furiously. "Now then, enough of your nonsense. Listen to me closely. Solomon desires new wonders for his collection. He has commanded his magicians to search the known world for objects of beauty and power. At this very moment, in all the wall-towers of Jerusalem, my rivals conjure demons no less hideous than you and send them out like fiery comets to plunder ancient cities, north, south, east, and west. All hope to astound the king with the treasures they secure. But they will be disappointed, Bartimaeus, will they not, for *we* will bring him the finest prize of all. You understand me?"

The pretty maiden curled her lip; my long, sharp teeth glinted wetly. "Grave-robbing again? Solomon should be doing seedy stuff like this himself. But no, as usual he can't be bothered to lift his finger and use the Ring. How lazy can you get?"

The old man gave a twisted smile. The black hollow of his lost eye seemed to suck in light. "Your opinions are interesting. So much so that I shall depart right now and report them to the king. Who knows? Perhaps he will choose to lift his finger and use the Ring on *you*."

There was a slight pause, during which the shadows of the room grew noticeably deeper, and a chill ran up my shapely spine. "No need," I growled. "I'll get him his precious treasure. Where do you want me to go, then?"

My master gestured to the windows, through which the cheery lights of lower Jerusalem winked and shone. "Fly east to Babylon," he said. "One hundred miles southeast of that dread city, and thirty miles south of the Euphrates's current course,

lie certain mounds and ancient diggings, set about with fragments of windblown wall. The local peasants avoid the ruins
for fear of ghosts, while any nomads keep their flocks beyond
the farthest tumuli. The only inhabitants of the region are religious zealots and other madmen, but the site was not always so
desolate. Once it had a name."

"Eridu," I said softly. "I know."[2]

"Strange must be the memories of a creature such as you,
who has seen such places rise and fall..." The old man gave a
shudder. "I do not like to dwell on it. But if you recall the location, so much the better! Search its ruins, locate its temples. If
the scrolls speak truly, there are many sacred chambers there,
containing who knows what antique glory! With luck, some of
the treasures will have remained undisturbed."

"No doubt about *that*," I said, "given its guardians."

"Ah yes, the ancients will have protected them well!" The
old man's voice rose to a dramatic pitch; his hands made elo-
quent fluttering gestures of dismay. "Who knows what lurks
there still? Who knows what prowls the ruins? Who knows
what hideous shapes, what monstrous forms might... Will you
stop doing that with your tail? It's not hygienic."

I drew myself up. "All right," I said. "I get the picture. I'll
go to Eridu and see what I can find. But when I get back I want
to be dismissed straight off. No arguments, no shilly-shallying.

---

[2] Eridu of the Seven Temples, the bone-white city, glittering in green fields. One
of the earliest cities of men. In its day its ziggurats rose high as falcon's flight and
the scent of its spice markets drifted on the winds as far as Uruk and the sea....
Then the river changed its course; the land went dry. The people grew thin and
cruel; their temples toppled into dust, and they and their past were utterly forgotten.
Except by spirits such as me. And, naturally—whenever their gold lust overcame
their fears—by magicians too.

I've been on Earth too long now and my essence aches like a moldering tooth."

My master grinned a gummy grin, stuck his chin toward me, and waggled a wrinkled finger. "That all depends on what you bring back, doesn't it, Bartimaeus? If you impress me, I may let you go. See that you do not fail! Now—prepare yourself. I shall bind you to your purpose."

Midway through his incantation the horn blew hard below the window, signaling the closure of the Kidron Gate. It was answered, farther off, by the sentries on the Sheep Gate, Prison Gate, Horse and Water Gates, and so on around the city walls, until the great horn on the palace roof was sounded and all Jerusalem was safe and sealed for the night. A year or two back I'd have hoped such distractions would make my master stumble on his words, so that I might have leaped forth and devoured him. I didn't bother hoping now. He was too old and too experienced. I needed something better than that if I was going to get him.

The magician finished, spoke the final words. The pretty maiden's body became soft and see-through; for an instant I hung together like a statue formed of silken smoke, then burst soundlessly into nothing.

2

No matter how many times you see the dead walk, you always forget just how rubbish they are when they really get moving. Sure, they look okay when they first break through the wall—they get points for shock value, for their gaping sockets and gnashing teeth, and sometimes (if the Reanimation spell is *really* up to scratch) for their disembodied screams. But then they start pursuing you clumsily around the temple, pelvises jerking, femurs high-kicking, holding out their bony arms in a way that's meant to be sinister but looks more as if they're about to sit down at a piano and bash out a honky-tonk rag. And the faster they go, the more their teeth start rattling and the more their necklaces bounce up and get lodged in their eyeholes, and then they start tripping over their grave-clothes and tumbling to the floor and generally getting in the way of any nimble-footed djinni who happens to be passing. And, as is the way with skeletons, never once do they come out with any really good one-liners, which might add a bit of zest to the life-or-death situation you're in.

"Oh, come *on*," I said, as I hung from the wall, "there must be *someone* here worth talking to." With my free hand I fired a plasm across the room, causing a Void to open in the path of one of the scurrying dead. It took a step, was sucked into oblivion; I sprang up from the stones, bounced off the vaulted ceiling, and landed nimbly on top of a statue of the god Enki on the opposite side of the hall.

To my left a mummified corpse shuffled from its alcove. It

wore a slave's robe and had a rusted manacle and chain about
its shrunken neck. With a creaky spring it leaped to snare me.
I yanked the chain, the head came off; I caught this mid-palm
as the body fell away, and bowled it unerringly into the midriff
of one of its dusty comrades, snapping its backbone with neat
precision.

Jumping from the statue, I landed in the very center of the
temple hall. From every side now the dead converged, their
robes as frail as cobwebs, hoops of bronze twirling on their
wrists. Things that had once been men and women—slaves,
freemen, courtiers, and under-priests, members of every level
of Eridu's society—pressed tight about me, jaws gaping, jagged
yellow fingernails raised to rend my essence.

I'm a courteous fellow and greeted them all appropriately.
A Detonation to the left. A Convulsion to the right. Bits of
ancient person spattered merrily on the glazed reliefs of the old
Sumerian kings.

That gave me a brief respite. I took a look around.

In the twenty-eight seconds since I'd tunneled through the
ceiling, I'd not had time to fully assess my surroundings, but
from the décor and the general layout, a couple of things were
clear. First, it was a temple of the water god Enki (the statue told
me that; plus he was featured prominently in the wall reliefs,
along with his attendant fish and snake-dragons) and had been
abandoned for at least fifteen hundred years.[1] Second, in all the
long centuries since the priests had sealed the doors and left the
city to be swallowed by the desert sands, no one had entered

---

[1] To my connoisseur's eye, the style looked late-Sumerian (c. 2500 B.C.E.), with just
a hint of Old Babylonian decadence, but frankly there were too many body parts
flying about for a proper critique just yet.

before me. You could tell that from the layers of dust upon the floor, the unbroken entrance stone, the zeal of the guardian corpses and—last but not least—the statuette resting on the altar at the far end of the hall.

It was a water serpent, a representation of Enki, fashioned with great artifice out of twisting gold. It glittered palely in the light of the Flares I'd sent forth to illuminate the room, and its ruby eyes shone evilly like dying embers. As an ancient work of art alone, it was probably beyond price, but that was only half the story. It was magical too, with a strange pulsing aura visible on the higher planes.[2]

Good. That was *that* settled, then. I'd take the serpent and be on my way.

"Excuse me, excuse me..." This was me politely ushering the dead aside, or, in most cases, using Infernos to strike them burning across the hall. More were still emerging, trundling forth from slotlike alcoves in each wall. There seemed no end to them, but I wore a young man's body, and my movements were swift and sure. With spell and kick and counterpunch I plowed my way toward the altar—and saw the next trap waiting.

A net of fourth-plane threads hung all around the golden serpent, glowing emerald green. The threads were very thin, and

---

[2] *The planes:* seven planes of existence are superimposed upon each other at all times, like invisible layers of tracing paper. The first plane includes everything in the solid, everyday world; the other six reveal the hidden magic all around—secret spells, lurking spirits, and ancient enchantments long forgotten. It's a well-known fact that you can reliably gauge the intelligence and quality of a species by the number of planes it is able to observe, e.g. top djinn (like me): seven; foliots and higher imps: four; cats: two; fleas, tapeworms, humans, dust-mites, etc.: one.

faint even to my djinni's gaze.[3] Feeble as they looked, however, I had no wish to disturb them. As a general principle, Sumerian altar-traps are worth avoiding.

I stopped below the altar, deep in thought. There *were* ways to disarm the threads, which I would have no trouble employing, provided I had a bit of time and space.

At that moment a sharp pain disturbed me. Looking down, I discovered that a particularly disreputable-looking corpse (who in life had clearly suffered many skin ailments and doubtless looked upon mummification as a sharp improvement to his lot) had snuck up and sunk his teeth deep into the essence of my forearm.

The temerity! He deserved special consideration. Shoving a friendly hand inside his rib cage, I fired a small Detonation upward. It was a maneuver I hadn't tried in decades, and was just as amusing as ever. His head blew clean off like a cork from a bottle, cracked nicely against the ceiling, bounced twice off nearby walls, and (this was where my amusement smartly vanished) plopped to earth right beside the altar, neatly snapping the net of glowing threads as it did so.

Which shows how foolish it is to go enjoying yourself in the middle of a job.

A deep concussion echoed across the planes. It was fairly

---

[3] A Trigger-summons such as this is always invisible to mortal sight, of course, but with time, faint residues of dust accumulate on the threads, giving them a ghostlike presence on the first plane too. This allows perceptive human thieves a chance. The old Egyptian tomb-robber Sendji the Violent, for instance, used a small squadron of trained bats to suspend tiny candles above patches of floor he considered dubious, allowing him to trace the delicate shadows made by the dust lines, and so pass unscathed between the traps. Or at least that's what he told me shortly before his execution. He had an honest face, but, well . . . trained bats . . . I just don't know.

faint to my hearing, but over in the Other Place it would have been hard to ignore..

For a moment I stood quite still: a thin young man, dark of skin and light of loincloth, staring in annoyance at the writhing filaments of broken thread. Then, swearing in Aramaic, Hebrew, and several other languages, I leaped forward, plucked the serpent from the altar, and backed hurriedly away.

Eager corpses came clamoring behind me: without looking I unleashed a Flux, and they were whirled asunder.

Up beside the altar the fragments of thread stopped twitching. With great speed they melted outward, forming a pool or portal upon the flagstones. The pool spread beneath the corpse's upturned head. The head dropped slowly down into the pool, out of existence, away from this world. There was a pause. The pool shone with the myriad colors of the Other Place, distant, muffled, as if seen from under glass.

A tremor passed across its surface. Something was coming.

Turning swiftly, I considered the distance to the shattered patch of ceiling where I'd first broken through: trickles of loose sand still spooled down into the chamber. My tunnel had probably collapsed with the weight of sand; it would take time to push my way back up—time I didn't presently have. A Trigger-summons never takes long.

I spun back reluctantly to face the portal, where the surface of the pool was flexing and contorting. Two great arms issued forth, shimmering green and venous. Clawed hands grasped the stonework on either side. Muscles flexed and a body rose into the world, a thing of nightmare. The head was human in semblance,[4] and surmounted by long black coils of hair. A

---

[4] See? How grotesque can you get? Yeuch.

chiseled torso came next, and this was of the same green stuff. The components of the bottom half, which followed, seemed to have been chosen almost at random. The legs, corded with muscle, were those of a beast—possibly a lion or some other upscale predator—but ended sinisterly in an eagle's splaying claws. The creature's rear end was mercifully cloaked by a wraparound skirt; from a slit in this rose a long and vicious scorpion tail.

There was a pregnant pause as the visitation pulled free of the portal and stood erect. Behind us, even the last few milling dead were somewhat hushed.

The creature's face was that of a Sumerian lord: olive-skinned and handsome, black hair coiled in shining ringlets. The lips were full, the squared beard oiled. But the eyes were blank holes torn in the flesh. And now they looked on me.

"It's . . . Bartimaeus, isn't it? *You* didn't trigger this, did you?"

"Hello, Naabash. Afraid so."

The entity stretched its great arms wide so that the muscles cracked. "Ohhh, now what'd you go and do that for? You know what the priests say about trespassers and thieves. They'll have your guts for garters. Or rather . . . *I* will."

"The priests aren't that fussed about the treasure now, Naabash."

"They aren't?" The blank eyes looked around the temple. "It does *seem* a little dusty. Has it been a while?"

"Longer than you think."

"But the charge still holds, Bartimaeus. Can't do anything about that. '*While stone stands on stone and our city lasts . . .*' You know the score." The scorpion tail juddered up with a dry and eager rattle, the shiny black sting jerking forward above his shoulder. "What's that you're carrying? Not the sacred serpent?"

"Something to look at later, when I've dealt with you."

"Ah, very good, very good. You always were a chipper one, Bartimaeus, always spoke above your station. Never known anyone get the flail so often. *How* you vexed the humans with your backchat." The Sumerian lord smiled, showing neat double rows of sharply filed teeth. The hind legs moved slightly, the claws dug into stone; I watched the tendons tensing, ready for sudden movement. I didn't take my eyes off them. "Which particular employer are you vexing now?" Naabash went on. "The Babylonians, I assume. They were on the up last time I looked. They always coveted Eridu's gold."

The dark-eyed youth ran a hand through his curly hair. I smiled bleakly. "Like I say, it's been longer than you think."

"Long or short, it matters not to me," Naabash said softly. "I have my charge. The sacred serpent stays here in the temple heart, its powers lost to common men."

Now, I'd never heard of this serpent. To me it just seemed a typical bit of tat the old cities used to war over, a kitsch little number in rolled gold. But it's always good to know exactly what you're stealing.

"Powers?" I said. "What does it do?"

Naabash chuckled, wistful melancholy suffusing his voice. "Nothing of consequence. It contains an elemental that will emit jets of water from the mouth when the tail is tweaked. The priests used to bring it out in times of drought to inspire the people. If I remember correctly, it is also rigged with two or three little mechanical traps designed to dismay robbers who meddle with the emerald studs upon the claws. Notice the hinges hidden beneath each one...."

I made a mistake here. Half lulled by Naabash's gentle tones, I couldn't help flicking a half-glance down at the serpent in my hands, just to see if I could spot the little hinges.

Which was exactly what he wanted, of course.

Even as my eyes moved, the beast-legs flexed. In a flash of movement, Naabash was gone.

I threw myself sideways just as the flagstone where I'd stood was struck in half by the sting-tail's blow. I was fast enough for that, but not enough to avoid the lashing impact of his outstretched arm: a great, green fist struck against my leg as I hurtled through the air. This blow, together with the precious artifact I held, prevented me employing my usual elegant keynote maneuver in such circumstances.[5] Instead I half rolled painfully across a convenient mat of scattered corpses and leaped to my feet once more.

Naabash, meanwhile, had righted himself with stately care. He turned toward me, bending low, his human arms pawing at the ground; then he sprang again. Me? I fired a Convulsion straight up at the ceiling above my head. Once more I jumped away, once more the scorpion tail drove straight through the flagstones; once more—but this time Naabash didn't get around to striking me as well, since the ceiling had fallen on him.

Fifteen centuries of accumulated desert sands lay atop the buried temple, so with the falling masonry came a pleasant bonus: a great silvery-brown cascade that plunged down in a torrent, crushing Naabash under several solid tons.

Ordinarily I'd have lingered awhile to jeer loudly near the rapidly spreading heap, but hefty as it was, I knew it wouldn't delay him long. It was time to leave.

---

[5] The Evasive Cartwheel ™ © etc., Bartimaeus of Uruk, circa. 2800 B.C.E. Often imitated, never surpassed. As famously memorialized in the New Kingdom tomb paintings of Ramses III—you can just see me in the background of *The Dedication of the Royal Family before Ra*, wheeling out of sight behind the pharaoh.

3

Dawn was at my back when I returned to Jerusalem. The
tops of the magicians' towers were already fringed with pink,
and the dome of Solomon's white-walled palace shone bright
like a new sun.

Farther down the hill, by the Kidron Gate, the old man's
tower was mostly in shadow. I flew to the upper window, outside which a bronze bell hung suspended, and rang this once,
as per my orders. My master forbade his slaves to come upon
him unawares.

The echoes faded. My broad wings stirred the cold, fresh
air. I hovered, waiting, watching the landscape melt into being.
The valley was dim and silent, a trough of mist into which the
road wound and faded. The first workers emerged from the gate
below; they set off down the road toward the fields. They went
slowly, stumbling on the rough stones. On the higher planes
I could see one or two of Solomon's spies going with them
—foliots riding the halters of the oxen, bright-hued mites and
implets drifting on the wind.

The minutes passed, and finally a charming sensation like a
dozen spear points plucking out my vitals heralded the magician's summons. I closed my eyes, submitted—and a moment
later felt the sour warmth of the magician's chamber pressing
on my essence.

To my great relief the old man was in his robes, despite the
early hour. A temple full of corpses is one thing; a wrinkly,
undressed master would have been another. He was standing

ready in his circle, and as before, all the seals and curse-runes were correctly in position. With the goat's-fat candles burning and the little pots of rosemary and frankincense repelling me with the sweetness of their stench, I stood in the center of my pentacle and regarded him steadily, holding the serpent in my slender hands.[1]

The moment I materialized I knew how badly he wanted it, not for Solomon, but for himself. His eye widened; avarice shimmered on its surface like a film of oil.

He did not say anything for a while, just looked. I moved the serpent slightly so the candlelight flowed alluringly upon its contours, tilting it to show him the ruby eyes, and the emerald studs upon the splaying claws.

When he spoke, his voice was coarse and heavy with desire. "You went to Eridu?"

"As I was ordered, so I went. I found a temple. This was inside."

The eye glinted. "Pass it to me."

I held back a moment. "Will you dismiss me as requested? I have served you faithfully and well."

At this the old man's face congealed with violent passion. "You *dare* try bartering with me? Pass me the artifact, demon, or by my secret name I swear I shall plunge you screaming into

---

[1] I'd chosen the girl's form again for continuity's sake, and also because I knew it irritated my master. In my experience most magicians can be discomfited if you choose the right form. Apart from the high priests of Ishtar back in Babylon, mind you. Ishtar was the goddess of love and war, so her magicians were unfazed by both pretty girls *and* gore-spattered monsters. This unfortunately eliminated most of my repertoire.

the Dismal Flame² before the hour is out!" He glared at me, eye popping, jaw jutting, thin white lines of moisture on his parted lips.

"Very well," I said. "Be careful not to drop it."

I tossed it over from one circle to the other, and the magician stretched out his clawing hands. And whether it was his single eye that did it, so that he had trouble judging distance, or his trembling eagerness, his fingers fumbled on the serpent: it danced between them and fell back toward the circle's edge. With a cry the old man snatched at it, clasped it against his wrinkled chest.

This, his first unguarded movement, was almost his last. If so much as the tips of his fingers had crossed above the circle, he would have lost its protection and I would have been on him. But (by a whisker) they didn't cross, and the pretty maiden, who for an instant had seemed just a *little* taller, whose teeth had perhaps grown just *slightly* longer and sharper than a moment previously, settled back in the center of her circle with a disappointed look.

The old man did not notice any of this. He had eyes only for his treasure. For a long time he turned it over in his hands, like a vile old cat playing with a mouse, cooing at the workmanship and practically dribbling with delight. After a while it was too revolting to bear. I cleared my throat.

The magician looked up. "Well?"

---

² *Dismal Flame*: a swift and painful expunction. In later periods, following its refinement by Zarbustibal of Yemen, it was known as the Shriveling Fire. It was the ultimate sanction for spirits who simply refused to carry out their master's commands, and its threat by and large ensured our (grudging) obedience.

"You have what you asked for. Solomon will reward you richly for this. Let me go."

He chuckled. "Ah, Bartimaeus, but you clearly have such a gift for this line of work! I am not sure I care to let such a skillful thief go. . . . You just stand there quietly. I must explore this most *interesting* device. I see small hinged studs upon the toes . . . I wonder what they *do*."

"What does it matter?" I said. "You're giving it to Solomon, aren't you? Let him investigate."

My master's scowl was expressive. I smiled to myself and looked out of the windows at the sky, where the dawn patrols were barely visible, circling at great heights, leaving faint pink trails of steam and sulphur in the air. Looked good, but it was all for show as much as anything, for who would seriously attack Jerusalem while Solomon had the Ring?

I allowed the magician to inspect the serpent for a while; then, still looking out of the window, said: "Besides, he'd be terribly cross if one of his magicians withheld an object of such power. I really wish you'd let me go."

He squinted up at me. "You know what this is?"

"No."

"But you know it has power."

"Even an *imp* could see that. Oh, but I forget—you're only a human. You can't see the aura it radiates on the seventh plane. But even so, who can truly tell? There were probably many such serpent statuettes made in Eridu. It's probably not the one."

The old man licked his lips; his caution fought with curiosity, and lost. "Not the what?"

"It's none of my business, and none of yours. I'm just standing here quietly, as ordered."

My master spat out a curse. "I revoke that order! Speak!"

22

"No!" I cried, holding up my hands. "I know what you magicians are like, and I don't want any part of it! Solomon on one side with that terrible Ring, and you on the other with... with..." The maiden shivered, as if with sudden chill. "No, I'd be caught up in the middle, and that wouldn't do me any good at all."

Blue fires leaped in the center of the magician's outstretched palm. "Not another second's delay, Bartimaeus. Tell me what this object is, or I'll pummel you with the Essence Fist."

"You'd hit a woman?"

"Speak!"

"Oh, very well, but it won't do you any good. It bears a passing resemblance to the Great Serpent with which the old kings of Eridu conquered the cities of the plain. That treasure contained a mighty spirit which was compelled to do its master's bidding."

"Its master being...?"

"Whoever held it, I suppose. The spirit was contacted by pressing a secret catch."

The magician considered me in silence for a time. At last he said, "I have never heard this story. You lie."

"Hey, of course I do. I'm a demon, aren't I? Just forget all about it and give the thing to Solomon."

"No." The old man spoke with sudden decision. "Have it back."

"What?" But it was too late; he had tossed the serpent back across the space, where the maiden caught it doubtfully.

"Do you take me for an idiot, Bartimaeus?" my master cried, stamping a wrinkled foot upon the marble. "Quite patently you planned to snare me with some trick! You egged me on to pry into this device, hoping it would seal my doom! Well, *I'm* not going to press any of these studs. But *you* will."

The maiden blinked up at the magician with her big brown eyes. "Look, this really isn't necessary——"

"Do as I say!"

With the greatest reluctance, I raised the serpent in my hand and considered the studs set upon the claws. There were three of them, each decorated with an emerald. Selecting the first, I pressed it gingerly. There was a whirring sound. At once the serpent emitted a brief electric shock that raddled my essence and set the maiden's long luxuriant hair standing up like a toilet brush.

The old magician hooted with laughter. "You planned that for me, did you?" he chortled. "Let this be a lesson to you. Well, and the next!"

I pressed the second stud. Swiveling on a set of hidden cogs and fulcra, several of the serpent's golden scales flipped up and egested puffs of tarry smoke. As with the first trap, long centuries had dulled the mechanism, and my face was only lightly blackened.

My master rocked back and forth with mirth. "Better and better," he crowed. "Look at the state of you! Now the third."

The third emerald had evidently been designed to let off a jet of poison gas, but all that remained after so many years was a faint green cloud and a bad smell.

"You've had your fun," I sighed, holding out the serpent once more. "Now dismiss me, or send me off again, or whatever it is you want to do. But leave me be. I'm fed up with this."

But the magician's good eye glinted. "Not so fast, Bartimaeus!" he said grimly. "You forget the tail."

"I don't see—"

"Are you blind? There is a hinge there too! Press that, if you will."

I hesitated. "Please. I've had enough."

"No, Bartimaeus. Perhaps this is the 'secret catch' you mentioned. Perhaps you will now get to meet this 'mighty spirit' of ancient legend." The old man grinned with cruel delight; he folded his spindly arms. "Or more probably you will find out yet again what it is like to attempt to defy me! Go on—no dallying! Press the tail!"

"But—"

"I *order* you to press it!"

"Righty-ho." *That* was what I'd been waiting for all this time. The terms of any summoning always include stringent clauses preventing you from directly harming the magician who brings you here: it's the first, most basic rule of all magic from Ashur to Abyssinia. Lulling your master into disaster through soft words and raw cunning is different, of course, as is striking if they break their circle or mess up the incantation. But direct assaults are out. You can't touch your master unless you're expressly commanded to do so by his own spoken word. As, rather pleasantly, was the case here.

I hefted the golden serpent and tweaked the tail. As I'd assumed, Naabash had not spoken falsely;[3] nor had the water

---

[3] Dissemblers as we sometimes are when conversing with humans, higher spirits almost always speak truth among themselves. The lower orders, sadly, are less civilized, foliots being variable, moody, and prone to flights of fancy, while imps just enjoy telling absolute whoppers.

elemental[4] trapped within deteriorated like the clockwork mechanisms. A bright, pulsing jet of water shot forth from the serpent's open mouth, glistening in the happy light of dawn. Since, by merest chance, I was holding the serpent directly facing the magician, the jet crossed the intervening space and struck the old codger full in the chest, lifting him off his feet and carrying him out of his circle and halfway across his chamber. The distance he went was gratifying, but leaving the circle was the crucial bit. Even before he landed, heavily and soggily, on his back, the bonds about me snapped and withered, and I was free to move.

The pretty maiden tossed the serpent to the floor. She stepped forward out of her constraining pentacle. Away across the room, the magician had been winded; he lay there helpless, flapping like a fish.

The maiden passed the goat's-fat candles, and as she did so every single one of them winked out. Her foot glanced against a bowl of ward-herbs; rosemary spilled upon her skin, which fizzed and steamed. The maiden paid no heed; her big dark eyes were fixed upon the magician, who struggled now to raise his head a little, saw my slow approach.

He made one desperate effort, wet and winded as he was. A shaking hand was raised and pointed. His mouth moved; he stammered out a word. From his forefinger a sputtering Essence Lance leaped forth. The maiden made a gesture; the spears of

---

[4] *Elemental*: most spirits incorporate within their essence two or more of the four elements (the finest djinn, naming no names, are perfectly balanced entities of fire and air). Those spirits formed of air, earth, fire, or water *alone*, however, are elementals—a different kettle of fish altogether. They entirely lack the finesse or charm that make a select few of us so fascinating, but compensate for this with raw, bludgeoning power.

lightning exploded in midair and shot off at random angles to strike the walls, the floor and ceiling. One gout plumed out of the nearest window and arced out into the valley to startle the peasants far below.

The maiden crossed the room; she stood above the magician and held out her hands, and the nails on her fingers, and indeed the fingers themselves, were much longer than hitherto.

The old man looked up at me. "Bartimaeus—"

"That's my name," I said. "Now, are you going to get up, or shall I come to you?"

The answer he made was incoherent. The pretty maiden shrugged. Then she bared her pretty teeth and fell upon him, and any further sounds he made were swiftly stilled.

Three small watch imps, drawn perhaps by a disturbance on the planes, arrived just as I was finishing. Wide-eyed and wondering, they clustered together on the sill, as the slender young woman got unsteadily to her feet. She was alone in the room now; her eyes glowed in the shadows as she turned to face them.

The imps sounded the alarm, but it was all too late. Even as the air above was rent with rushing wings and talons, the pretty maiden smiled and waved good-bye—to the imps, to Jerusalem, to my latest bout of slavery on Earth—and without a word was gone.

And that was the end of the old magician. We'd been together awhile, but I never got to know his name. Still, I remember him with fond affection. Foolish, greedy, incompetent, and dead. Now *that's* the kind of master worth having.

Part Two

4

King Solomon the Great of Israel, High Magician and Protector of his People, sat forward on his throne and frowned an elegant frown. "Dead?" he said, and then—more loudly, after a ferocious pause in which the heartbeats of four hundred and thirty-seven people skipped and jolted in anticipation—*"Dead?"*

The two afrits that sat before his chair in the form of gold-maned lions lifted their golden eyes to look at him. The three winged djinn that hung aloft behind the chair, carrying fruit and wines and sweetmeats for the refreshment of the king, trembled so hard, the plates and glasses rattled in their hands. High in the rafters, the doves and swallows dropped from their roosts, and dispersed beyond the pillars to the sunlit gardens. And the four hundred and thirty-seven humans—magicians, courtiers, wives, and supplicants—who were gathered in the hall that morning bent their heads and shuffled their feet and looked intently at the floor.

Rarely, even in matters of war or wives, did the great king ever raise his voice. Such occasions did not bode well.

At the foot of the steps Solomon's vizier bowed low. "Dead. Yes, Master. But, on a happier note, he got you a very fine antiquity."

Still bowing, he indicated with an outstretched hand the nearest plinth beside him. On it sat a serpent statuette of twisting gold.

King Solomon regarded it. The hall was silent. The lion-afrits blinked down at the people with their golden eyes, their velvet forepaws lightly crossed, their tails flicking occasionally on the stones behind. Above the throne the djinn hung waiting, motionless save for the lazy beat of their eagle wings. Out in the gardens butterflies moved like flecks of sunlight among the brightness of the trees.

At last the king spoke; he sat back upon the cedar throne. "It *is* a pretty object. With his last act, poor Ezekiel served me well." He raised a hand to signal to the djinn for wine, and since it was his *right* hand, a ripple of relief ran around the hall. The magicians relaxed; the wives began arguing among themselves; and one by one the assembled petitioners of a dozen lands raised their heads to gaze in fearful admiration at the king.

In no way was Solomon ill-favored. He had been spared the poxes in his youth, and though now into middle age, his skin remained smooth and creamy as a child's. In fifteen years upon the throne, indeed, he had not changed markedly, remaining dark of eye and skin, narrow-faced, with straight black hair hanging loose about his shoulders. His nose was long, his lips full, his eyes lined with green–black kohl after the Egyptian style. Above his splendid silken robes—sent as a gift from the magician-priests of India—he wore many wondrous treasures of gold and jade, sapphire earrings, necklaces of Nubian ivory, amber beads from far Cimmeria. Silver bangles hung about his wrists, while on one ankle rested a thin gold band. Even his kid-skin sandals, a dowry present from the King of Tyre, were studded with gold and semiprecious stones. But his long slim hands were naked of jewels or decoration—save for the little finger of the left, which bore a ring.

The king sat waiting as the djinn poured wine into his golden goblet; he waited as, with golden prongs, they added to it berries from the windswept Anatolian hills, and ice from the summit of Mount Lebanon. And the people gazed on him as he waited, basking in the glamour of his power, his radiance like the sun's. The ice was mixed; the wine was ready. On soundless wings, the djinn retreated above the throne. Solomon considered the goblet, but did not drink. He returned his attention to the hall.

"My magicians," he said, addressing a circle of men and women at the forefront of the crowd, "you have all done well. In a single night you have retrieved many fascinating artifacts from across the world." With a wave of the goblet he indicated the row of seventeen plinths before him, each topped with its own small treasure. "All are doubtless extraordinary, and will shed light on the ancient cultures that precede us. I shall study them with interest. Hiram, you may have them removed."

The vizier, a small, dark-skinned magician from distant Kush, snapped to immediate attention. He gave an order. Seventeen slaves—human, or in human form—ran forth and carried the golden serpent and the other treasures from the hall.

When all was still, the vizier swelled out his chest, took his staff by its ruby pommel, and banged it thrice upon the floor. "Attention!" he cried. "Solomon's council shall now proceed! There are several issues of great moment to bring before the king. As ever, we shall all benefit from the bounty of his wisdom. First—"

But Solomon had raised a lazy hand, and as it was the *left*, the vizier broke off at once, choking on his words and blanching.

"Saving your pardon, Hiram," the king said silkily, "the first business is already before us. My magician Ezekiel was killed this morning. The spirit who slew him—do we know its identity?"

The vizier cleared his throat. "Master, we do. From the remains of Ezekiel's cylinder, we have deduced the offender. Bartimaeus of Uruk is its favored title."

Solomon frowned. "Have I heard report of one with that name?"

"Yes, Master. Only yesterday. It was overheard singing a song of extraordinary insolence, which featured..."

"Thank you, I recall it." The king stroked his handsome chin. "Bartimaeus...of Uruk—a city two thousand years gone. So it is a most ancient demon. A marid, I assume?"

The vizier bowed low. "No, Master. I believe not."

"An afrit, then."

The vizier bowed still lower; his chin almost touched the marble floor. "Master, it is in fact a djinni of moderate strength and power. Fourth level, if some of the Sumerian tablets speak true."

"*Fourth level?*" Long fingers tapped upon the armrest of the throne; from the little finger came a flash of gold. "A *fourth-level* djinni has slain one of my magicians? With all due respect to the wailing shade of Ezekiel, this brings dishonor on Jerusalem —and, more importantly, on *me*. We cannot let such an outrage pass. An example must be made. Hiram—let the remainder of the Seventeen approach."

In keeping with the glory of King Solomon, his chief magicians were drawn from countries far beyond the bounds of Israel. From distant Nubia and Punt, from Assyria and Babylon, these men and women of power had come. Each, at a brief command, could summon demons from the air, raise whirlwinds, and rain death upon their cowering foes. They were masters of the ancient arts, and would have been considered mighty in their own lands. But all had chosen to travel to Jerusalem, to serve he who wore the Ring.

With a twirl of his staff, the vizier beckoned the circle forward; each magician, in turn, bowed low before the throne.

Solomon considered them awhile, then spoke: "Khaba."

Deliberate, stately, soft-footed as a cat, a man stepped from the circle. "Master."

"You have a somber reputation."

"Master, I do."

"You treat your slaves with appropriate severity."

"Master, I take pride in my harshness, and I do well to do so, for demons combine ferocity with infinite cunning, and their nature is vindictive and malign."

Solomon stroked his chin. "Indeed... Khaba, I believe you already have in your employment several other recalcitrant spirits that have recently proved troublesome."

"Master, this is true. Each loudly regrets its past audacity."

"Will you agree to add this wicked Bartimaeus to your roster?"

Khaba was Egyptian, a man of arresting appearance, tall, broad-shouldered, and strong of limb. His skull, like that of all the magician-priests of Thebes, had been shaved and waxed until it shone. His nose was aquiline, his brow heavy, his lips narrow, bloodless, tight as bowstrings. His eyes hung like soft black moons in the wasteland of his face, and glistened perpetually as if they were close to tears. He nodded. "Master, as in all things I follow your requirements and your will."

"Quite so." Solomon took a sip of wine. "See that Bartimaeus is brought to heel and learns respect. Hiram will bring you the relevant cylinders and tablets when Ezekiel's tower is cleared. That is all."

Khaba bowed and returned to his place among the crowd, his shadow trailing like a cloak behind him.

"With *that* settled," Solomon said, "we may return to other matters. Hiram?"

The vizier clicked his fingers. A small white mouse somersaulted out of the empty air and landed on his hand. It carried a papyrus scroll, which it unfurled and held ready for his inspection. Hiram studied the lists briefly. "We have thirty-two judicial cases, Master," he said, "that have been referred to you by your magicians. The plaintiffs await your judgment. Among the issues to be dealt with are a murder, three assaults, a marriage in difficulties, and a neighborly dispute regarding a missing goat."

The king's face was impassive. "Very well. What else?"

"As always, many petitioners from far afield have come to ask your aid. I have chosen twenty to make formal appeals to you today."

"I will hear them. Is that all?"

"No, Master. Word has come from our djinn patrols in the southern deserts. They report further attacks by brigands. Remote farmsteads have been burned and the inhabitants slaughtered, and there have been depredations on the trade routes too—caravans attacked, and travelers robbed."

Solomon shifted in his chair. "Who controls the southern patrols?"

A magician spoke, a woman of Nubia, dressed in a robe of tight-wound yellow cloth. "I, Master."

"Summon more demons, Elbesh! Track down these 'brigands'! Discover the truth: are they simple outlaws, or mercenaries working for foreign kings? Report to me tomorrow."

The woman grimaced. "Yes, Master... only—"

The king frowned. "Only what?"

"Master, saving your pardon, I already control nine strong, unruly djinn. This takes up all my energies. To summon yet more slaves will be difficult."

"I see." The king cast his eyes impatiently across the circle. "Then Reuben and Nisroch will assist you in this little task. Now—"

A tousle-bearded magician raised his hand. "Great King, forgive me! I too am presently somewhat stretched."

The man beside him nodded. "And I!"

Now the vizier, Hiram, ventured to speak out. "Master, the deserts are vast and the resources of we, your servants, are limited. Is this not a time when you might consider aiding us? When, possibly, you might—" He halted.

Solomon's kohl-rimmed eyes blinked slowly, like a cat's. "Go on."

Hiram swallowed. Already he had said too much. "When . . . perhaps you might consider using"—his voice was very faint—"the Ring?"

The king's expression darkened. The knuckles of his left hand gripped white upon the armrest of the throne. "You question my commands, Hiram," Solomon said softly.

"Great Master, please! I meant no offense!"

"You dare pronounce how my power might be used."

"No! I spoke without thinking!"

"Can it be you *truly* wish for this?" The left hand shifted; on the little finger a flash of gold and black obsidian caught the light. Below the throne the lion-afrits drew back their lips and made snapping noises in their throats.

"No, Master! Please!" The vizier cowered to the floor; his mouse sought concealment in his robes. Across the hall the assembled watchers murmured and drew back.

The king reached out, turned the Ring upon his finger. There was a thud of sound, a buffet of air. A darkness fell across the hall, and in the center of that darkness a Presence stood tall and silent beside the throne. Four hundred and thirty-seven people fell flat upon their faces as if they had been struck.

In the shadows of the throne Solomon's face was terrible, contorted. His voice echoed as if from a cavern in the earth: "I say to all of you: *Be careful what you desire*."

He turned the Ring again upon his finger. At once the Presence vanished; the hall was filled with sudden light, and there were birds singing in the gardens.

Slowly, unsteadily, magicians, courtiers, wives, and suppliants got to their collective feet.

Solomon's face was calm again. "Send your demons out into the desert," he said. "Capture the brigands as I requested." He took a sip of wine, and looked toward the gardens where, as so often, faint music could now be heard, though the musicians were never seen. "One other thing, Hiram," he said at last. "You have not yet told me of Sheba. Has the messenger returned? Have we heard the queen's response?"

The vizier had risen and was dabbing at a trickle of blood coming from his nose. He swallowed; the day was not going well for him. "Master, we have."

"And?"

He cleared his throat. "Once again, unbelievably, the queen rejects your offer of marriage and refuses to be numbered among your exquisite consorts." The vizier paused to allow the expected gasps and flutterings from among the assembled wives. "Her explanation, such as it is, is this: as the actual *ruler* of her nation, rather than the mere daughter of its king"—further gasps sounded at this juncture, and several snorts—"she cannot possibly leave it for a life of leisure, even to bask in your glorious radiance in Jerusalem. She deeply regrets this inability to comply, and offers her eternal friendship, and that of Sheba, to you and your people until, and I quote"—he checked the scroll once more—"'the towers of Marib fall and the eternal Sun goes out.'... Essentially, Master, it's another No."

The vizier finished and, without daring to look toward the king, made a great business of rolling up the scroll and stuffing it back into his robes. The crowd stood frozen, watching the silent figure on the throne.

Then Solomon laughed. He took a long draught of wine. "So *that* is the word from Sheba, is it?" he said. "Well, then. We will have to consider how Jerusalem responds."

5

Night had fallen and the city of Marib was silent. The Queen of Sheba sat alone in her chamber, reading from her sacred texts. As she reached for her wine cup, she heard a fluttering at the window. A bird stood there, an eagle, shaking flecks of ice off its feathers and regarding her intently with its cold, black eyes. The queen watched it for a moment; then, because she understood the illusions of the spirits of the air, said: "If you come in peace, step inside, and be welcome."

At this the eagle hopped off the sill and became a slim young man, golden-haired and handsome, with eyes as black and cold as the bird's had been and a bare chest studded with flecks of ice.

The young man said, "I bear a message for the queen of this land."

The queen smiled. "I am she. You have come far, and at high altitude. You are a guest of my house, and I offer you all I have. Do you require refreshment or rest, or some other boon? Name it, and it shall be so."

And the young man said, "You are gracious, Queen Balkis, but I require none of those things. I must speak my message and hear your answer. Know first that I am a marid of the seventh level, and the slave of Solomon, son of David, who is King of Israel and the mightiest of magicians now living."

"Again?" the queen said, smiling. "Three times I have received a question from that king, and three times I have given the same answer. The last occasion was but a week ago. I hope he has accepted my decision now, and isn't asking it a fourth time."

"As to that," the young man said, "you shall shortly hear. Solomon offers you his greetings, and wishes you health and prosperity. He thanks you for your consideration of his last proposal, which he now formally retracts. Instead he demands you acknowledge him as your sovereign overlord and agree to pay him an annual tribute, which shall be forty sacks of sweet-scented frankincense from the forests of fair Sheba. If you agree to this, the sun will continue to smile upon your domains, and you and your descendants will forever prosper. Refuse—and, frankly, the outlook is less favorable."

Balkis no longer smiled. She rose from her chair. "This is a most impudent demand! Solomon has no claim on the wealth of Sheba, just as he had no claim on me!"

"You may have heard," the young man said, "that Solomon is master of a magic ring, with which he can raise an army of spirits in the blinking of an eye. For this reason the kings of Phoenicia, Lebanon, Aram, Tyre, and Edom, among many others, have already sworn him fealty and friendship. They pay vast annual tributes of gold, timber, skins, and salt, and think themselves fortunate to be spared his wrath."

"Sheba is an ancient, sovereign nation," Balkis said coldly, "and its queen will not bend her knee to any foreign infidel. You may return to your master and say so."

The young man made no move, but spoke in conversational tones. "In truth, O Queen, is Sheba's prospective tribute *really* so terrible? Forty sacks among the hundreds that you harvest every year? That will not bankrupt you!" White teeth shone in the smiling mouth. "And besides, it is certainly a lot better than being driven in rags from your ravaged land, while your cities burn and your people perish."

Balkis gave a little gasp and took a step in the direction of the insolent creature, but held back when she saw the glitter in the blank, dark eyes. "Demon, you far exceed your duties," she said, swallowing. "I demand you leave this chamber on the instant, or I shall call my priestesses to snare you in their silver nets."

"Silver nets mean nothing to me," the spirit said.

It walked toward her.

Balkis backed away. In the cabinet by her chair she kept a globe of crystal that, on breaking, sounded an alarm that would bring her personal guards to her. But each new step took her farther from the cabinet and farther from the door. Her hand strayed to the jeweled dagger in her belt.

The demon said, "Oh, I wouldn't do that. Am I not a marid, who by my whispered word can summon storms and raise new islands in the sea? Yet, despite my strength, I am the least and most miserable of the slaves of Solomon, who stands supreme of all men in his glory and his pride."

It halted; Balkis had not yet reached the wall, but she sensed the bricks close behind her back. She stood erect, hand upon the dagger hilt, keeping her face impassive, as she had once been taught to do.

"Long ago I served the first kings of Egypt," the demon said. "I helped raise their tombs, which still remain as marvels of the world. But the greatness of those kings lies like dust before the power that Solomon now enjoys."

It turned away and with negligent steps crossed to stand beside the fireplace, so the remaining ice upon its shoulders melted swiftly and ran in rivulets down its long, dark limbs. It gazed into the flames. "Have you *heard* what happens when his will is crossed, O Queen?" it said softly. "I have seen it from afar. He wears the Ring upon his finger. He turns it once. The Spirit of the Ring appears. Then what? Armies march across the sky, city walls crumble, the earth opens, and his enemies are devoured by fire. He brings forth spirits uncountable, faster than thought, so the midday hour grows black as midnight with their passing, and the ground shudders with the beating of their wings. Do you wish to see this terror? Resist him, and it will surely come to you."

But Balkis had gathered herself; she strode toward the cabinet and stood there, stiff with fury, one hand on the drawer where the crystal lay. "I have given you my answer already," she said harshly. "Return to your master. Tell him that for a fourth time I refuse him, and that I desire no further messengers. That if he persists in his cruel avarice, I shall make him regret that he ever heard my name."

"Oh, that I *very* much doubt," the young man said. "You have hardly the sniff of magic about you, and Marib is no great center of sorcery or of arms. A final word before I start my long flight home. My master is not unreasonable. He knows this decision is hard for you. You have two weeks to change your mind. See there?" The demon pointed through the window, where the moon hung yellow behind the slender mud-brick towers of the city. "The moon is full tonight. When it has waned to nothing, have the forty sacks piled ready in the courtyard! If you do not, Solomon's army will take wing. Two weeks! In the meantime I thank you for your hospitality and your warming fire. Now here is a little blaze of my own. Consider it something to spur your thinking." It raised its hand: a bulb of orange fire swelled from the fingers, shot forth as a narrow bolt of light. The top of the nearest tower exploded in a flower of flame. Burning bricks tumbled into darkness; screams sounded across the gulf.

With a cry, Balkis lunged forward. The young man smiled contemptuously and stepped toward the window. A blur of movement, a waft of wind—an eagle flew out between the pillars, banked around the pluming smoke, and was gone among the stars.

Dawn came; thin gray veins of smoke still rose from the ruined tower, but the fire itself was out. It had taken the priestesses several hours to agree on the precise demon that should be summoned to fight the blaze, and by that time the flames had been quenched by water carried from the canals by hand. Queen Balkis had supervised this process, and seen the dead and wounded taken to their proper places. Now, with the city numb and quiet, she sat again beside the window of her room, watching the blue-green daylight stealing slowly across the fields.

Balkis was twenty-nine, and had occupied the throne of Sheba for something under seven years. Like her mother, the previous queen, she met all the requirements of that sacred station, and was popular with her people. She was brisk and efficient in court policy, which pleased her counselors; she was serious and devout in matters of religion, which pleased the priestesses of the Sun. And when the hill-men of the Hadhramaut came down into the city, with their robes weighed down with swords and silver djinn-guards, and the sacks of frankincense slung upon their camels' shanks, she met them in the forecourt of the palace and offered them khat leaves to chew, and spoke with them knowledgeably of the weather and the difficulties of tapping resin from the trees, so that they too were pleased and returned to their villages speaking highly of Sheba's wondrous queen.

Her beauty didn't hurt either. Unlike her mother, who had been strongly inclined to fat, and indeed in later years had required four young slaves to help her rise from the soft vastness of her couch, Balkis was slender and athletic and disliked assistance from anybody. She had no close confidants among her counselors or priestesses and made her decisions alone.

As was traditional in Sheba, all Balkis's personal slaves were women. They fell into two categories—the maidens of her chamber, who tended to her hair and jewels and personal hygiene; and the small hereditary caste of guards, whose duty it was to keep the queen from harm. Previous rulers had developed friendships with certain of these slaves, but Balkis disapproved of such notions and kept herself remote.

The dawn light reached the canals at last; the water flared and glittered. Balkis rose, stretched, and drank a draught of wine to loosen her stiff limbs. Within moments of the attack she had known in her heart the policy she would follow, but it had taken all night for her to analyze her decision. Now, having done so, she moved seamlessly from thought to action. Crossing the room to the little cabinet beside her chair, she removed the alarm globe and crushed the fragile crystal between her fingertips.

She waited, staring into the fire; within thirty seconds she heard the running footsteps in the hall beyond and the door spring open. Balkis, without turning, said, "Put away your sword, girl. The danger has passed."

She listened. She heard the sound of metal sliding in the leather sheath.

Balkis said: "Which of my guards are you?"

"Asmira, my lady."

"Asmira..." The queen gazed at the leaping flames. "Good. You always were the quickest. And the most skillful too, as I recall...Do you serve me in all things, Asmira?"

"My lady, I do."

"Would you lay down your life for me?"

"I would do so with joy."

"Truly," Balkis said, "you are your mother's daughter. One day soon, all Sheba will be in your debt." She turned then, and rewarded the girl with the full radiance of her smile. "Asmira, my dear, ring for the servants and have them bring us wine and cakes. I wish to talk with you."

When in due course Guard Captain Asmira left the royal chambers and returned to her little room, her solemn face was flushed and she was breathing hard. She sat for a while on the edge of her trestle bed, staring first at nothing, then at the old familiar cracks in the mud brick that ran from ceiling to floor. After a time her heartbeat slowed a little and her breathing quieted, but the pride that threatened to burst within her lessened not at all. Her eyes were filled with happy tears.

She rose at last and, reaching up to the high shelf set into the wall, brought down a wooden chest, plainly adorned with the symbol of the midday sun. Placing the chest heavily upon the bed, she knelt beside it, cast off the lid, and took from within the five silver daggers that rested there. They glinted in the lantern light as she picked them up, one after another, inspecting the edges, testing the weight. She set them neatly side by side upon the bed.

Balancing easily on the balls of her feet, she squatted low, reached beneath her bed, and drew out her traveling cloak, her leather shoes, and—this required an awkward moment or two of grappling in the remotest corners—a large leather drawstring bag, dusty with disuse.

Asmira emptied the contents of the bag upon the floor: two large, roughly folded cloths, oddly stained and charred; several candles; two lighting flints and tapers; an oil lamp; three pots sealed with wax; and eight small weights of carved jade. She considered the items awhile as if in hesitation, then shrugged, returned them to the bag, stuffed the silver daggers after them, tightened the drawstrings, and stood up.

Time was passing swiftly; the priestesses would be gathering in the forecourt to perform their summons, and she still had to visit the temple to get the Blessings of the Sun.

But she was ready. Her preparations were complete, and she had no one to say good-bye to. Unstrapping her sword, she laid it on the bed. Then she put on her shoes, picked up her cloak, and shouldered the bag. Without a backward glance she left the room.

6

High above the earth the phoenix soared, a noble bird much like an eagle, save for the reddish tint to its golden feathers and the iridescent flecks on the tips of its outstretched wings. It had a crest the color of brass, claws like hooks of gold, and jet-black eyes that looked forward and back across eternity.

It also had a narked expression and was carrying a quarter ton of artichokes in a big string net.

Now, the great weight wasn't the only thing that annoyed me about this job. The early start had been a pain in the plumage too. I'd had to set off shortly after midnight to get from Israel to the northern coast of Africa, where the finest wild artichokes grew, just so (and here I quote the specific terms of my charge) I could "pick the juiciest specimens in the crystal dews of dawn." I ask you. As if it made a blind bit of difference.

Digging up the wretched things had been tiresome enough as well—I was going to have soil stuck beneath my claws for weeks—and carrying them back fifteen hundred miles into a mild headwind hadn't been a picnic either. But I could cope with all this. What *really* stuck in my fiery craw were the amused chuckles and wry expressions I was getting from my fellow spirits as I neared Jerusalem.

Grinning broadly, they flitted past me through the air, splendid and warlike, carrying their shimmering spears and swords. They were off hunting for brigands in the desert wastes—a decent mission worthy of the name. Me? I trundled slowly north with my bag of groceries, wearing a forced smile and muttering salty insults under my breath.[1]

I was being punished, you see, and it frankly wasn't fair.

Ordinarily, when you kill a magician with a bit of honest trickery and escape back to the Other Place, you're likely to be left in peace for a while. A few years pass by, maybe a decade or two, and then finally another avaricious chancer who's learned a bit of old Sumerian and worked out how to draw a pentacle without too many wonky lines will locate your name, summon you back, and start your slavery anew. But at least when that happens, the rules are clear, and tacitly acknowledged by both parties. The magician forces you to help him get wealth and power,[2] and you do your best to find a way to nobble him.

Sometimes you succeed; more often than not, you don't. It all depends on the skill and judgment of both sides. But it's a personal duel, and if you score a rare victory over your oppressor, the last thing you expect is to be brought back instantly and *punished* for that victory by someone else.

Yet that was exactly the way things worked in Solomon's Jerusalem. Not twenty-four hours after devouring the old magician and departing his tower with a burp and a smile, I'd been summoned back to *another* tower farther along the city wall.

---

[1] Which I'm certainly not going to repeat here. Unlike some lesser djinn I could name, who rejoice in vulgarisms and inappropriate analogies, I'm a stickler for propriety. Always have been. Famous for it. In fact, you could tattoo what I don't know about good taste on the backside of a midget, assuming you hold him down hard enough to stop him squirming.

[2] Tomb-building, treasure-hunting, battle-fighting, artichoke-collecting... Outwardly different, maybe, but in the end all magicians' demands boil down to wealth and power, whatever they might *claim*.

Before I could so much as open my mouth to protest, I'd been raddled with a Spasm, Whirled, Pressed, Flipped, and Stretched, and finally given a good hard Stippling for my trouble.[3] You might think after all that I'd have been given a moment to pass a few acerbic remarks, but no. An instant later I found myself packed off on the first of many degrading missions, all specifically designed to break my carefree spirit.

It was a depressing list. First I was sent to Mount Lebanon to chip blue ice from its summit, so the king's sherbets would be nicely chilled. Next I was ordered to the palace granaries to count the grains of barley for the annual stocktaking. After that I was employed in Solomon's gardens to pluck dead leaves from the trees and flowers, so that nothing brown or shriveled might offend the royal eye. Then there followed an unpleasant two days in the palace sewers, over which I draw a slightly soiled veil, before a taxing expedition in search of a fresh roc's egg for the royal household's breakfast.[4] And now, if all that wasn't enough, I'd been saddled with this current artichoke-fest, which was making me a laughingstock in the eyes of my fellow djinn.

None of this broke my spirit, naturally, but it didn't half make me irritable. And you know who I blamed it all on? Solomon.

Not that he was the one who summoned me, of course. He was *much* too important for that. So important, in fact, that in the three long years I'd spent enslaved in the city, I'd scarcely set eyes on him. Though I'd hung about the palace a fair bit, exploring its mile-wide maze of halls and pleasure-gardens, I'd

---

[3] *Spasms, Whirls, Stipples,* etc.: punitive spells frequently employed to keep a healthy young djinni in line. Painful, tedious, usually nonfatal.

[4] Gourmet's note: one roc's egg, scrambled, feeds roughly 700 wives, provided you mix in a few vats of milk and a churn or three of butter. I had to whisk the thing as well, which gave me a sore elbow.

only once or twice seen the king in the distance, surrounded by a gaggle of squalling wives. He didn't get out much. Apart from his daily councils, to which I wasn't invited, he passed most of his time cooped up in his private apartments beyond the northern gardens.[5] And while he lolled about up there, pampering himself, day-to-day summonings were delegated to his seventeen top magicians, who dwelt in the towers strung along the city walls.

My previous master had been one of the Seventeen, and my new master was also—and this, in a nutshell, was proof of Solomon's power. All magicians are by nature bitter rivals. When one of them is killed their instinct is to rejoice. In fact, they're more likely to summon up the offending djinni to shake him heartily by the claw than to work any punishment upon him. But not in Solomon's Jerusalem. The king treated the demise of one of his servants as a personal slight, and demanded retribution. And so it was that—against all laws of natural justice —here I was, enslaved again.

Scowling furiously at my misfortunes, I drifted onward in the warm dry winds. Far below me my fiery shadow flitted over olive groves and barley fields, and dropped and skimmed down steep terraces of fig. Stage by stage Solomon's little kingdom rolled beneath me, until in the distance I saw the rooftops of his capital, scattered like glittering fish scales on its hill.

---

[5] It hadn't always been that way, if you could believe the stories. Long-serving djinn reported that in the early years of his reign, Solomon enjoyed regular banquets and masques and entertainments of every conceivable kind (though girning and juggling always featured prominently). Each night, garlands of imp-lights would illuminate the cypress trees, and roving spirit-globes bathed the palace in a thousand shifting colors. Solomon, his wives, and his courtiers would frolic upon the lawns while he worked wonders for them with his Ring. Times, it seemed, had changed since then.

A few years previously, Jerusalem had been a dowdy little town, not especially notable, and certainly not to be compared with capitals such as Nimrud, Babylon, or Thebes. Now, it vied with those ancient cities as a place of wealth and splendor—and the *reason* for this wasn't hard to guess.

It was all about the Ring.

The Ring. That was at the heart of it all. That was why Jerusalem flourished. That was why my masters jumped at Solomon's command. That was why so many magicians congregated around him in the first place, like bloated fleas on a leper's dog, like moths around a flame.

It was thanks entirely to the Ring he wore upon his finger that Solomon enjoyed his life of indolence and Israel its unparalleled prosperity. It was thanks to the Ring's sinister reputation that the once-great empires of Egypt and Babylon now kept their wary distance, and watched their frontiers with anxious eyes.

It was all about the Ring.

Personally speaking, I hadn't actually *seen* this benighted artifact close up—but then again, I hadn't needed to. Even from a distance, I understood its power. All magical objects emit an aura, and the more powerful they are, the brighter that aura is. Once, when Solomon had passed me in the distance, I'd briefly checked the higher planes. The flow of light made me cry out in pain. Something on his person glowed so fearsomely he was almost blotted out. It was like staring into the sun.

From what I'd heard, the thing itself wasn't actually much to look at—just a yellow band inlaid with a single gem of black obsidian. But stories said it contained a spirit of supreme power, who was brought forth whenever the Ring was turned upon the finger; merely *touching* the Ring, meanwhile, summoned a retinue of marids, afrits, and djinn to serve the wearer's will. In other words, it was a portable gateway to the Other Place, through which almost unlimited numbers of spirits could be drawn.[6] Solomon had access to this awful power on a moment's whim, and without personal danger. The usual rigors of the magician's trade were unknown to him. No fiddling with candles or getting chalky knees. No chance of getting fried, roasted, or plain old eaten. And no chance either of being murdered by rivals or discontented slaves.

In one place a slight scratch was said to mar the Ring; this was where the great marid Azul, taking advantage of an ambiguity in his master's phrasing, had attempted to destroy it while carrying Solomon by carpet from Lachish to Beth-zur. Azul's petrified form, worn ever thinner by the desert winds, now stood in lonely isolation above the Lachish road.

Earlier in his reign two other marids, Philocretes and Odalis, had *also* tried to slay the king. Their subsequent careers were similarly melancholy: Philocretes became an echo in a copper pot and Odalis a startled face etched into a floor tile in the royal bathroom.

----

[6] As well as all this, the Ring was said to protect Solomon from magical attack, give him extraordinary personal allure (which possibly explained all those wives cluttering up the place), *and* allow him to understand the language of birds and animals. Not bad, in short, though the last one isn't half as useful as you might expect, since when all's said and done the language of the beasts tends to revolve around: (a) the endless hunt for food, (b) finding a warm bush to sleep in of an evening, and (c) the sporadic satisfaction of certain glands.* Elements such as nobility, humor, and poetry of the soul are conspicuously lacking. You have to come to middle-ranking djinn for them.

* Many would argue that the language of humankind boils down to this too.

Many such stories were told about the Ring, and it was no surprise that Solomon lived a cushy life as a result. The sheer power and dread exerted by that scrap of gold upon his finger kept all his magicians and their spirits nicely in line, thank you. The threat of its use hovered over us all.

Noon came; my journey was at an end. I crossed high above the Kidron Gate, above the teeming markets and bazaars, and finally swung low over the palace and its gardens. In these last few moments my burden felt particularly heavy, and it was fortunate for Solomon that he wasn't at that moment promenading along his gravel walkways. If I'd seen him, I'd have been sorely tempted to zoom down and offload my cargo of ripe artichokes directly on his preening head, before chasing his wives into the fountains. But all was still. The phoenix continued sedately to its appointed landing site: namely a scrappy compound at the back end of the palace, where sour smells rose from the slaughtering sheds, and the gates to the kitchens were always open.

I descended swiftly, dropped my burden to the ground, and alighted, taking the form of a handsome youth as I did so.[7]

A band of imps scampered forward, ready to carry my net toward the kitchen. Stalking alongside came a plump djinni overseer, long papyrus scrolls in hand.

"You're late!" he exclaimed. "All banquet deliveries were due by noon!"

---

[7] It was the guise I'd worn when I was spear-bearer to Gilgamesh, two thousand years before: a tall, beautiful young man, smooth-skinned and almond-eyed. He wore a long wrapped skirt, necklaces of amethyst on his breast, and ringlets in his hair, and had about him an air of wistful grace that contrasted pungently with the foul detritus of the kitchen yard. I often used this form in such circumstances. It made me feel better somehow.

I squinted at the heavens. "It *is* noon, Bosquo. Look at the sun."

"Noon is precisely two minutes gone," the djinni said. "You, sir, are late. However, we will overlook it just this once. Your name?"

"Bartimaeus, bringing artichokes from the Atlas Mountains."

"A moment, a moment . . . we have so many slaves . . ." The djinni took a stylus from behind his ear and buried himself in his scrolls. "א—Alef . . . ב—Bet . . . Where's the ג scroll? These modern languages . . . there's no logic to them . . . Ah, here . . ." He looked up. "Right. Yes. Name again?"

I tapped a sandal upon the ground. *"Bartimaeus."*

Bosquo consulted the scroll. "Bartimaeus of Gilat?"

"No."

"Bartimaeus of Tel Batash?"

"No."

The scroll was unfurled still further. There was a long pause. "Bartimaeus of Khirbet Delhamiyeh?"

"*No.* Where in Marduk's name is that? Bartimaeus of *Uruk*, also known as Sakhr al-Jinni, famous confidante of Gilgamesh and Akhenaten, and—for a time—Nefertiti's most trusted djinni."

The overseer looked up. "Oh, it's *djinn* we're talking about? This is the foliot list."

"The *foliot* list?" I gave a cry of rage. "What are you holding *that* for?"

"Well, to look at you—Oh, hush. Don't make such a squalling. Yes, yes, I have located you now. You are one of Khaba's troublemakers, are you not? Trust me, your long-departed glories will count for little with him!"

Bosquo broke off to issue orders to the imps, while I restrained the urge to swallow him, scrolls and all. I shook my head grimly. The only good thing about the whole embarrassing exchange was that no one else had witnessed it. I turned away—

"Hello, Bartimaeus."

—to find myself standing face-to-face with a stocky, pot-bellied Nubian slave. He was bald of head and red of eye, and sported a leopard-skin skirt with a large machete tucked in the waistband. He also wore seven ivory torques about his thick bull neck, and a familiar expression of sardonic mirth.

I winced. "Hello, Faquarl."

"There you are, you see," the djinni Faquarl said. "*I* still recognize you. Your ancient greatness is not yet quite forgotten. And do not give up hope. Perhaps one day the Ballad of the Artichokes will be sung about the hearth fires too, and your legend will live on."

I scowled at him. "What do you want?"

The Nubian indicated over his swarthy shoulder. "Our delightful master requires the whole company to assemble on the hill behind the palace. You're the last to arrive."

"The day just keeps getting better and better," I said sourly. "All right, let's go."

The handsome youth and the short, squat Nubian walked together across the yard, and those lesser spirits we met, observing our true natures on the higher planes, hopped hurriedly aside. At the rear gate, vigilant demi-afrits with flies' eyes and the ears of bats noted our names and numbers, and checked our identities against further scrolls. We were ushered through, and presently came out on an area of rough ground on the edge of the hill, with the city shimmering below.

Not far away, six other spirits stood waiting in a line.

My recent assignments having all been solitary ones, it was

the first time I'd seen my fellow offending djinn together, and I scrutinized them closely.

"As revolting a group of ne'er-do-wells as have ever been assembled," Faquarl remarked, "and that was *before* you arrived. Not just hideous, either. Each and every one of us has killed or maimed his previous master—or, in the case of Chosroes, roundly insulted her with the harshest possible language. We are a grim and dangerous company."

Some of the spirits, like Faquarl, I'd known and disliked for years; others were new to me. All had adopted human guises on the first plane, their bodies in more or less correct proportions. Most had muscular torsos and sculpted limbs, though none quite as sculpted as mine; one or two had chosen bandy legs and plump, protruding bellies. All were dressed in the simple, rough-spun skirts of the typical male slave.

As we drew close, however, I noticed that even here each of the renegade djinn had subtly undermined his human shape by adding a small demonic detail. Some had horns peeping through their hair; others had tails, large pointed ears, or cloven hooves. The insubordination was risky, but stylish.[8] I decided to join in, and allowed two small ram's horns to curl out on my brow. Faquarl, I noticed, had given his Nubian an elegant set of nicely filed fangs. Thus beautified, we took our places in the line.

---

[8] Solomon's edicts dictated that ordinary human shapes were maintained at all times outside the palace walls. Animals were forbidden, likewise mythic beasts; grotesque deformities were out, too, which was a shame. The idea was to prevent the common people being startled by repulsive sights—such as Beyzer taking a stroll with his limbs on back to front. Or, admittedly, yours truly forgetfully popping out to buy some figs in the guise of a rotting corpse, thus causing the great Fruit Market Terror, fifteen deaths in the associated stampede, and the destruction of half the commercial district. Got my figs dirt cheap, mind, so it wasn't all bad.

57

We waited; a hot wind blew upon the hilltop. Far to the west, clouds were massing above the sea.

I shifted from foot to foot and yawned. "Well," I said, "is he coming or not? I'm bored, I'm knackered, and I could do with an imp. In fact, I saw some back in the yard that wouldn't be missed if we were quiet about it. If we got a little bag—"

My neighbor nudged me. "Hush," he hissed.

"Oh, come on, what's so bad about that? We all do it."

"*Hush,*" he snapped. "He's here."

I stiffened. At my side seven other djinn sprang to swift attention; we all stared glassily above our heads.

A figure in black came up the hill, his shadow stretching long and thin behind him.

7

His name[1] was Khaba, and whatever else he might have been, he was certainly a formidable magician. In origin, perhaps, he was a child of Upper Egypt, the quick-witted son of some peasant farmer toiling in the black mud of the Nile. Then (for this is the way it had worked for centuries) the priests of Ra would have chanced upon him and taken him away to their granite-walled stronghold at Karnak, where quick-witted youths grew up in smoke and darkness, and were taught the twinned arts of magic and amassing power. For a thousand years and more, these priests had shared with the pharaohs control of Egypt, sometimes vying with them, sometimes supporting them; and in the days of the nation's glory Khaba would doubtless have remained there, and by plot or poison worked his way close to the pinnacles of Egyptian rule. But the throne of Thebes was old and battered now, and a greater light shone in Jerusalem. With ambition gnawing in his belly, Khaba had learned what he could from his tutors, then traveled east to seek employment at the court of Solomon.

Perhaps he had been here many years. But he carried the odor of the Karnak temples still. Even now, as he clambered to the

---

[1] His *assumed* name, I mean—the name by which he was known in his comings and goings about the world. It was meaningless, in truth, a mask beneath which his true nature was protected and concealed. Like all magicians, his *birth-name*—the key to his power and his most precious possession—had been expunged in childhood and forgotten.

hilltop and stood regarding us in the brightness of the noonday sun, there was something of the crypt about him.

Up until that moment I'd only seen him in the summoning room of his tower, a place of darkness where I'd been in too much pain to assess him properly. But now I saw that his skin had a faint gray cast that spoke of windowless sanctuaries underground, while his eyes were large and roundish, like those of cavern-fishes circling in the dark.[2] Below each eye a thin, deep weal descended almost vertically across his cheek toward his chin; whether these marks were natural, or had been caused by some desperate slave, was a matter for speculation.

In short, Khaba wasn't much of a looker. A cadaver would have crossed the street to avoid him.

As with all the strongest magicians, his dress was simple. His chest was bare, his skirt plainly wrapped and unadorned. A long, leather-handled whip of many cords swung from a bone hook at his belt; about his neck, suspended on a loop of gold, hung a black and polished stone. Both objects pulsed with power; the stone, I guessed, was a scrying glass that allowed the magician to view things far away. The whip? Well, I knew what *that* was, of course. Just the thought of it made me shiver on the sunlit hill.

The row of djinn stood silently as the magician looked us up and down. The big, moist eyes blinked at each of us in turn. Then he frowned and, holding one hand above his eyes to shield them from the glare, looked again at our horns and tails and other extracurricular additions. His hand stole toward the whip, fingers tapped upon the handle for a moment . . . then fell away.

---

[2] They were unappetizingly moist, too, as if he was just about to weep with guilt or sorrow, or in pity for his victims. But did he? Nope. Such emotions were alien to Khaba's heart and the tears never came.

The magician took a short pace back, and addressed us in a soft and chalky voice.

"I am Khaba," he said. "You are my slaves and my instruments. I tolerate no disobedience. That is the first thing you need to know. Here is the second thing: you stand on the high hill of Jerusalem, a place held sacred by our master, Solomon. There shall be no frivolity or misbehavior here on pain of direst penalty." Slowly he began to walk to and fro along the line, his shadow trailing long and thin behind him. "For thirty years I have sent demons scampering beneath my whip. Those that resisted me I have crushed. Some are dead. Others yet live—after a fashion. *None* have gone back to the Other Place. Heed this warning well!"

He paused. His words echoed off the palace walls and faded.

"I notice," Khaba continued, "that in defiance of Solomon's edicts, you each flaunt some devilish accessory to your human forms. Perhaps you expect me to be shocked. If so, you are mistaken. Perhaps you think of this pathetic gesture as some kind of 'rebellion.' If so, it merely confirms what I already know—that you are too cowed and fearful to try anything more impressive. Keep your horns for today, if it makes you feel better, but be aware that from tomorrow I shall use my essence-flail on any who display them."

He took the whip in hand and flourished it in the air. Several of us flinched, and eight gloomy pairs of eyes watched the cords flicking to and fro.[3]

---

[3] *Essence-flail*: The favored weapon of the priests of Ra back in the old days of Khufu and the pyramids. Very good at keeping djinn in order. Theban craftsmen still make them, but the best are found in ancient tombs. Khaba's was an original —you could tell by the handle, which was bound in human-slave-skin, complete with faint tattoos.

Khaba nodded with satisfaction and returned it to his belt. "Where now are those arrogant djinn who caused such trouble to their previous masters?" he said. "Gone! You are docile and obedient, just as you should be. Very well, to your next task. You are brought together to begin work on a new construction project for King Solomon. He wishes a great temple to be built here, an architectural marvel that will be the envy of the kings in Babylon. I have been given the honor of fulfilling the initial phase—this side of the hill must be cleared and made level, and a quarry opened up in the valley below. You will follow the plans I give you, shaping the stones and dragging them up here, before—Well, Bartimaeus, what is it?"

I had raised an elegant hand. "Why drag the stones? Isn't it quicker to fly them up? We could all manage a couple at a time, even Chosroes."

A djinni with bat ears farther up the line gave an indignant squeak. "Hey!"

The magician shook his head. "No. You are still in the confines of the city. Just as Solomon has forbidden unnatural guises here, you must avoid magical shortcuts and work at human pace. This will be a holy building, and must be built with care."

I gave a cry of protest. "No magic? But this'll take *years!*"

The gleaming eyes gazed at me. "Do you question my command?"

I hesitated, then looked away. "No."

The magician turned aside and spoke a word. With a dull retort and the faintest smell of rotting eggs, a small lilac cloud billowed into existence at Khaba's side and hung there, palpitating gently. Lounging in the cloud, its spindly arms behind its head, sat a twirly-tailed green-skinned creature with round red cheeks, twinkling eyes, and an expression of impudent overfamiliarity.

It grinned at us. "Hello, lads."

"This is the foliot Gezeri," our master said. "He is my eyes and ears. When I am not present on the building site, he will inform me of any slackness or deviation from my commands." The foliot's grin widened. "They won't be no trouble, Khaba. Sweet-natured as lambs, the lot of them." Sticking a fat-toed foot down below its cloud, it kicked once, propeling the cloud a short way through the air. "Thing is, they know what's good for them, you can see that."

"I hope so." Khaba made an impatient gesture. "Time passes! You must get on with your work. Clear the brushwood and level the hilltop! You know the terms of your summoning: adhere to them always. I want discipline, I want efficiency, I want silent dedication. No backchat, arguments, or distractions. Divide yourselves into four work-teams. I shall bring the temple plan out to you presently. That is all."

And with that he spun upon his heel and began to walk away, the picture of arrogant indifference. Kicking an indolent leg, the foliot guided its cloud after him, making a series of rude faces over its shoulder as it did so.

And *still*, despite all the provocation, none of us said anything. At my side I heard Faquarl give a kind of strangled snarl under his breath, as if he longed to speak out, but the rest of my fellow slaves were utterly tongue-tied, afraid of retribution.

But you know me. I'm Bartimaeus: *I* don't do tongue-tied.[4]
I coughed loudly and put up my hand.

---

[4] Apart from *literally*, once or twice, when certain Assyrian priests got so peeved with my cheek they pierced my tongue with thorns and bound me by it to a post in Nineveh's central square. However, they'd reckoned without the elasticity of my essence. I was able to elongate my tongue sufficiently to retire to a nearby inn for a leisurely drink of barley wine, *and* subtly trip up several dignitaries as they strutted by.

Gezeri spun around; the magician, Khaba, turned more slowly. "Well?"

"Bartimaeus of Uruk again, Master. I have a complaint."

The magician blinked his big wet eyes. "A complaint?"

"That's right. You're not deaf then, which must be a relief, what with all your other physical problems. It's my work partners, I'm afraid. They're not up to scratch."

"Not...up to scratch?"

"Yes. Do try to keep up. Not all of them, mind. I've got nothing against..." I turned to the djinni on my left, a fresh-faced youth with a single stubby brow-horn. "Sorry, what was your name?"

"Menes."

"Young Menes. I'm sure he's a worthy fellow. And that fat one with the hooves over there might be a good worker too, for all I know; he's certainly packing enough essence. But some of the others...If we're cooped up here for months on a big job ...Well, the long and the short of it is, we just won't gel. We'll fight, argue, bicker...Take Faquarl here. Impossible to work with! Always ends in tears."

Faquarl gave a lazy chuckle, showing his gleaming fangs. "Ye-e-es...I should point out, Master, that Bartimaeus is an appalling fantasist. You can't believe a word he says."

"Exactly," the hoofed slave put in. "He called me fat."

The bat-eared djinni snorted. "You *are* fat."

"Shut up, Chosroes."

"*You* shut up, Beyzer."

"See?" I made a regretful gesture. "Bickering. Before you know it we'll be at one anothers' throats. Best thing would be to dismiss us all, with the notable exception of Faquarl, who, despite his deficient personality, is very good with a chisel. He will be a fine and loyal servant for you and work hard enough for eight."

At this the magician opened his mouth to speak, but was preempted by a somewhat forced laugh from the potbellied Nubian, who stepped smoothly forward.

"On the contrary," he urged, "*Bartimaeus* is the one you should keep. As you can see, he's as vigorous as a marid. He is also famed for his achievements in construction, some of which resound in fable to this day."

I scowled. "They don't at all. I'm hopeless."

"Such modesty is typical of him," Faquarl smiled. "His only drawback is an inability to work with other djinn, who are usually dismissed when he is summoned. But—to his abilities. Surely even in this backwater you will have heard of the Great Flooding of the Euphrates? Well, then. The instigator stands right there!"

"Oh, it's just like you to bring *that* up, Faquarl. That incident was totally overreported. There was no real harm done—"

The bat-eared Chosroes gave a cry of indignation. "No harm? An inundation from Ur to Shuruppak, so that only the flat white rooftops protruded above the waters? It was like the world was drowned! And all because *you*, Bartimaeus, built a dam across the river for a bet!"

"Well, I *won* the bet, didn't I? Get things in perspective."

"At least he can build something, Chosroes."

"What? My building projects in Babylon were the talk of the town!"

"Like that tower you never finished?"

"Oh come now, Nimshik—that was due to problems with foreign workers."

My work was done. The argument was going nicely; all

discipline and focus had vanished, and the magician was a satis-fying shade of purple. All complacency had gone from the foliot Gezeri too, who was gawping like a trout.

Khaba gave a cry of rage. "All of you! Be still."

But it was far too late. Our line had already disintegrated into a bickering melee of shaking fists and jabbing fingers. Tails whirled, horns flashed in the sun; one or two previously absent claws slyly materialized to reinforce their owners' points.

Now, I've known some masters to give up at this juncture, to throw their hands up in the air and dismiss their slaves—if only temporarily—just to get a bit of peace. But the Egyptian was made of sterner stuff. He took a slow step backward, his features twisted, and unhooked the essence-flail from his belt. Clasping it firmly by its handle and shouting out an incantation, he cracked it once, twice, three times above his head.

From each of the whirling thongs emerged a jagged spear of yellow force. The spears stabbed out, impaled us all, and snatched us burning into the sky.

Up under the hot sun we swung, higher than the palace walls, suspended on yellow snags of burning light. Down below us the magician spun his arm in looping circles, high and low, faster and faster, while Gezeri hopped and capered in delight. Around we flew, limp and helpless, colliding sometimes with each other, sometimes with the ground. Showers of wounded essence trailed behind us, shimmering like oily bubbles in the desert air.

The Gyration ceased, the essence-skewers were withdrawn. At last the magician lowered his arm. Eight broken objects fell heavily to Earth, our edges sloughing like pats of melting but-ter. We landed on our heads.

The dust clouds slowly settled. Side by side we sat there,

wedged into the ground like broken teeth or tilting statues. Several of us were gently steaming. Our heads were half-buried in the dirt, our legs sagged in the air like wilting stems.

Not far away, the heat haze shifted, broke, re-formed, and through its fractured strands the magician strode, his long black shadow flowing at his back. Wisps of yellow force still radiated from the flail, snapping faintly, fading slowly. On all the hill this was the only sound.

I spat out a pebble. "I think he forgives us, Faquarl," I croaked. "Look, he's smiling."

"Remember, Bartimaeus—we're upside-down."

"Oh. Right."

Khaba came to a halt and stared down at us. "This," he said softly, "is what I do to slaves who disobey me once."

There was a silence. Even I didn't have much to say.

"Let me show you what I do to slaves who disobey me twice."

He held out his hand and spoke a word. A glimmering point of light, brighter than the sun, floated suddenly in the air above his palm. Soundlessly it expanded to become a luminous sphere, cupped by his hand but still not touching it—a sphere that darkened now, like water filled with blood.

Within the sphere: an image, moving. A creature, slow, blind, and in great pain, lost in a place of darkness.

Silent, upside-down, and sagging, we watched the lost, maimed thing. We watched it for a long time.

"Do you recognize it?" the magician said. "It is a spirit like you, or was so once. It too knew the freedom of the open air. Perhaps, like you, it enjoyed wasting my time, neglecting the tasks I gave it. I do not recall, for I have kept it in the vault beneath my tower for many years, and it has probably forgotten the details itself. Occasionally I give it certain delicate stimulations just to remind it it is still alive; otherwise I leave it to its misery." The eyes blinked slowly around at us; the voice was just as level as before. "If any of you wish to become like this, you may annoy me one more time. If not, you will set to work and dig and carve as Solomon commands—and pray, if such a reflex is in your nature, that I may one day permit you to leave this Earth again."

The image in the sphere dwindled; the sphere fizzled and went out. The magician turned away and headed off toward the palace. His shadow trailed long and black behind him, skipping, dancing across the stones.

None of us said anything. One after another we toppled sideways and collapsed into the dust.

8

North of Sheba the deserts of Arabia stretched unbroken for a thousand miles, a vast and waterless wedge of sand and stone-dry hills, bordered to the west by the blank Red Sea. To the far northwest, where the peninsula collided with Egypt, and the Red Sea petered out at the Gulf of Aqaba, lay the trading port of Eilat, since ancient times a meeting place of roads and goods and men. To get from Sheba to Eilat, where their spices could be sold at great profit in the old bazaars, the frankincense traders traveled a circuitous route between the desert and the sea, winding through numerous petty kingdoms, paying tolls and fighting off attacks by hill tribes and their djinn. If all was set fair, assuming their camels remained healthy and they escaped major depredations, the traders could expect to arrive in Eilat after six or seven weeks in a state of considerable exhaustion.

Guard Captain Asmira made the journey in a single night, carried by a cone of whirling sand.

Outside the protective Mantle, in the howling darkness, the storm of sand grains scoured the air. Asmira saw nothing; she sat crouched with her arms clasping her knees, eyes tight shut, trying to ignore the voices that, from amid the whirlwind, continually screamed her name. This was a provocation on the part of the spirit that carried her, but otherwise the priestesses' strictures held firm. Asmira was neither dropped, nor crushed, nor torn asunder, but carried without harm; and set down gently just as dawn was breaking.

Painfully, by slow degrees, she uncurled herself and allowed her eyes to open. She sat on a hilltop, in the center of three perfect rings of sand. Small thickets of brush were dotted here and there, and razor-grass, and rocks that glinted in the rising sun. A little naked child was standing on the hillcrest, watching her with bright, dark eyes.

"There is Eilat," the djinni said. "You will reach it by late morning."

Asmira looked, and far away saw a yellow cluster of lights hanging smudged and distant in the lifting darkness, and close beside it a flat white line, thin as a knife-blade, separating sky and land.

"And that," the child added, pointing, "is the sea. The Gulf of Aqaba. You are at the southernmost point of Solomon's kingdom. From Eilat you can hire camels to take you to Jerusalem, a journey still of several hundred miles. I myself can bear you no farther safely. Solomon has established shipyards in Eilat, that he may control the trading routes along the coast. Some of his magicians are here, and many spirits, who will be vigilant against intruders such as me. I cannot enter the town."

Asmira was getting to her feet, gasping at the stiffness of her limbs. "Then I thank you for your help," she said. "When you return to Marib, please express my thanks also to the priestesses and my beloved queen. Say that I am grateful for their assistance, and that I shall carry out my task with the full vigor of my being, and—"

"Don't thank *me*," the child said. "I only do what I am forced to do. Indeed, were it not for the threat of the Dismal Flame, I would devour you in a twinkling, for you are a succulent-looking morsel. As for the queen and her minions, in my opinion your gratitude to them is equally misplaced, since they send you to a miserable death, while their backsides continue to expand at leisure in the soft luxuries of the palace courts. Still, I'll pass your regards on."

"Foul demon!" Asmira snarled. "If I die, it shall be for my queen! My nation has been attacked, and the Sun God himself has blessed my venture. You know *nothing* of loyalty or love of homeland! Begone from here!"

She clasped something that hung about her neck and spoke an angry syllable; a flashing disk of yellow light struck the djinni and sent it somersaulting backward with a cry.

"That was a pretty trick," the little child said, picking itself up. "But your power is thin, and your motives even thinner. Gods and nations—what are they but words?"

It closed its eyes; was gone. A gentle breeze blew away into the south, scattering the perfect rings of sand and making Asmira shiver.

She knelt beside her leather bag and removed from it her water-skin, a pastry wrapped in vine leaves, a silver dagger, and her traveling cloak, which she placed about her shoulders to keep warm. Her first action was to drink deeply from the skin, for she was very thirsty. Next she ate the pastry with brisk, efficient little bites, staring down the hill, planning her route toward the town. Then she turned to face the east, where the Sun God's disk was just pulling free of the Earth. Somewhere far away it settled on fair Sheba too. His glory blinded Asmira, his warmth fell on her face. Her movements slowed, her mind emptied; the urgencies of her mission loosened their hold upon her. She stood upon the hilltop, a slight, slim young woman, with gold light shining on her long dark hair.

When she was still very young, Asmira's mother had taken

her to the palace roof and walked her in a circle, so she could look out all around.

"The city of Marib is built on a hill," her mother said, "and this hill is Sheba's center as the heart is the center of the body. Long ago, the Sun God ordained our city's size and shape, and we cannot build beyond its limits. So we build upward! See the towers rising on every side? Our people live within them, a family to a floor, and when the need arises we build another level in fresh mud brick. Now, child, look beyond the hill. You see that all about us is green, while beyond lies yellow desert? These are our gardens, which keep us all alive. Each year snows melt in the mountains and run in torrents along the dust-dry wadis to irrigate our lands. Queens of the past cut the channels to irrigate the fields with water. Maintenance of these channels is their most important duty, for without them we die. Now look to the east—see that range of blue-white mountains? That is the Hadhramaut, where grow our forests. These trees are our *other* most precious resource. We harvest their resin and dry it . . . and what does it become then?"

Asmira had hopped and capered with excitement, for she knew the answer. "Frankincense, Mother! The stuff the hill-men stink of!"

Her mother had placed a steely hand upon her daughter's head. "Not so much jigging about, girl. A palace guard does not cavort like a dervish, even at the age of five. But you are right. This incense is our gold, and makes our people rich. We trade with distant empires far away beyond the deserts and the seas. They pay well for it, but they would steal it if they could. Only the great sands of Arabia, which an army cannot cross, have shielded us from their greed."

Asmira had stopped her spinning. She frowned. "If enemies

came here," she said, "the queen would kill them. Wouldn't she, mother? She keeps us safe."

"Yes, child. Our queen keeps Sheba safe. And we in turn keep *her* safe—the guards and I. That is what we are born to do. When you grow up, dear Asmira, you too must protect our blessed lady with your life—just as I have, and our grandmothers did before us. Do you so swear?"

Asmira was as still and serious as could be. "Mother, I do."

"Good girl. Then let us go down and join our sisters."

At that time the old Queen of Sheba had not yet grown too heavy to leave the palace, and was accompanied wherever she went by an escort of her guard. As its leader, Asmira's mother always walked right behind the queen, close as a shadow, curved sword hanging easily at her waist. Asmira (who particularly admired her mother's long and shining hair) thought her far more beautiful and regal than the queen herself, though she took care not to mention this to anyone. Such a thought was possibly treasonous, and there was a place for traitors on the bare hill beyond the water-meadows, where their remains were picked over by little birds. Instead she contented herself imagining the day when *she* would be First Guard and walk behind the queen. She went out to the gardens behind the palace and, with a severed reed stem, practiced savage swordplay, putting ranks of imagined demons to full and awful flight.

From the earliest age she joined her mother in the training hall, where, under the watchful eye of the wrinkled guardmothers, who were now too old for active service, the women of the guards daily learned their craft. Before breakfast they scaled ropes, ran around the meadows, swam in the canals below the walls. Now, their muscles readied, they worked six hours a day in the echoing, sunlit rooms, sparring with swords and twirl-staffs, dueling with knives and whirling fists, throwing disks and daggers into straw-stuffed targets across the floor. Asmira would watch it all from the benches, where the guard-mothers bound wounds and bruises in cloths lined with soothing herbs. Often she and other girls would pick up the little wooden weapons laid out for them, join their mothers in gentle play fights, and so begin their training.

Asmira's mother was the most accomplished of the women, which is why she was First Guard. She ran fastest, fought most fiercely, and above all threw the little shining daggers more accurately than anyone else. She could do this standing, moving, and even on the half-turn, sending the blade hilt-deep into any chosen target far off along the hall.

Asmira was mesmerized by this. Often she scampered up, holding out her hand. "I want a turn."

"You're not old enough," her mother said, smiling. "There are wooden ones that are better weighted, so you don't do yourself a mischief. No, not like that"—for Asmira had pried the dagger from her grasp—"you need to hold the point lightly between the thumb and forefinger...like so. Now, you must be calm. Close your eyes, take a deep, slow breath—"

"Don't need to! Watch this shot! Oh."

Her mother laughed. "Not a bad attempt, Asmira. If the target was six paces to its right and twenty paces nearer, you would have hit it square on. As it is, I'm glad I don't have slightly larger feet." She stooped and picked up the knife. "Have another try."

The years passed, the Sun God worked his daily passage through the heavens. Now Asmira was seventeen years old, light of foot and serious of eye, and one of four newly promoted captains of the palace guard. She had excelled during the latest rebellion of the hill tribes, and had personally captured the rebel chief and his magicians. She had several times been deputized for the First Guard in standing behind the queen during ceremonies in the temples. But the Queen of Sheba herself had never once spoken to her, never once acknowledged her existence—until the night the tower burned.

Beyond the window, smoke still drifted on the air; from the Hall of the Dead came the sound of mourning drums. Asmira sat in the royal chamber, awkwardly holding a cup of wine and staring at the floor.

"Asmira, my dear," the queen said. "Do you know who carried out this dreadful act?"

Asmira raised her eyes. The queen was sitting so close to her their knees almost touched. It was an unheard-of proximity. Her heart thudded in her chest. She lowered her gaze again. "They say, my lady," she stammered, "they say it was King Solomon."

"Do they say why?"

"No, my lady."

"Asmira, you *may* look on me when you speak. I am your queen, yes, but we are both of us daughters of the Sun."

When Asmira looked up once more, the queen was smiling. The sight made her a little light-headed; she took a sip of wine.

"The First Guard has often spoken about your qualities," the queen went on. "Quick, strong, and clever, she says. Unafraid of danger. Resourceful, almost reckless . . . and pretty too—I can see *that* for myself. Tell me, what do you know of Solomon, Asmira? What stories have you heard?"

Asmira's face was burning and her throat felt tight. Perhaps it was the smoke. She had been marshaling the water-chains below the tower. "I have heard the usual tales, my lady. He has a palace of jade and gold, built in a single night with his magic

Ring. He controls twenty thousand spirits, each more terrible than the last. He has seven hundred wives—and is therefore clearly a man of abominable wickedness. He—"

The queen raised her hand. "I have heard this too." Her smile faded. "Asmira, Solomon desires the wealth of Sheba. One of his demons carried out tonight's attack, and when the moon is new—which will be in thirteen days—the full host of the Ring will come here to destroy us all."

Asmira's eyes opened wide in horror; she said nothing.

"Unless, that is," the queen went on, "I pay a ransom. Needless to say, I do not wish to do so. That would be an affront to both Sheba's honor and my own. But what is the alternative? The power of the Ring is too great to withstand. Only if Solomon himself is killed might the danger pass. But *that* is almost impossible, since he never leaves Jerusalem, a city that is too well-guarded for armies or magicians to hope to enter. And yet..." The queen sighed heavily and stared out of the window. "And yet I wonder. I wonder whether someone traveling alone, someone with sufficient intelligence and skill, someone who *seems* harmless, and yet is not so—whether that person might find a way to get access to the king... And when she is alone with him she might—ah, but it would be a hard task indeed."

"My lady..." Asmira's voice quivered with eagerness, as well as fear at what she was about to say. "My lady, if there's any way that *I* can help—"

The Queen of Sheba smiled benignly. "My dear, you need say no more. I already know your faith. I know your love for me. Yes, dear Asmira, thank you for suggesting it. I do believe you can."

★   ★   ★

The rising sun hung low above the eastern desert. When Asmira stirred and turned to face the west again, she found the port of Eilat had become a clear white scattering of buildings, and the sea an azure strip, to which tiny white things clung. Her eyes narrowed. Ships belonging to the wicked Solomon. From now on she must take care.

She picked up the silver dagger from where it lay beside her bag and tucked it in her belt, pushing it out of sight beneath her cloak. As she did so, her gaze strayed high above: she saw the outline of the waning moon, still hanging frail and ghost-like in the blue. The sight gave her fresh urgency. Twelve days remaining! And Solomon was far away. Picking up her bag, she jogged swiftly down the hill.

9

"Watch where you drop those chippings," Faquarl snapped. "That last shower went down my neck."

"Sorry."

"And you might wear a longer skirt while you're about it. I'm afraid to look up."

I paused in my chiseling. "Can I help it if this is the current fashion?"

"You're eclipsing the sun. Move along a bit, at least."

We scowled at each other. I moved a grudging inch to my left; Faquarl moved a resentful inch to his right. We went on carving.

"I wouldn't mind so much," Faquarl said sourly, "if we could do this *properly*. A quick Detonation or two would work wonders on this rock."

"Tell that to Solomon," I said. "It's his fault we're not allowed to— *Ow!*" My hammer hit my thumb instead of the chisel. I hopped and pranced; my curses echoed off the rock-face and startled a nearby vulture.

All morning, since the dark-blue hour of dawn, the two of us had been toiling in the quarry below the building site, hacking out the first blocks for the temple. Faquarl's ledge was somewhat below mine, so he got the worst of the view. Mine was fully exposed to the rigors of the risen sun, so I was hot and irritable. And now my thumb was sore.

I took a look around: rocks, heat haze, nothing moving on any plane. "I've had enough of this," I said. "Khaba's not about,

78

and nor is that nasty little foliot of his. I'm having a break." So saying, the handsome youth tossed his chisel aside and slid down the wooden ladder to the quarry floor.

Faquarl was the Nubian again, plump, potbellied, dusty, and glowering. He hesitated, then threw his tools down as well. We squatted together in the shade beneath his half-squared block, in the manner of idling slaves the world over.

"We've got the worst job again," I said. "Why couldn't we be digging foundations with the rest of them?"

The Nubian scratched his stomach, selected a chipping from the rubble at our feet, and picked his delicately pointed teeth. "Perhaps because our master dislikes us most particularly. Which in your case isn't surprising, considering the lip you gave him yesterday."

I smiled contentedly. "True."

"Speaking of the magician," Faquarl said, "this Khaba: what do you make of him?"

"Bad. You?"

"One of the very worst."

"I'd say top ten bad, possibly even top five."

"Not only is he vicious," Faquarl added, "but he's arbitrary. Viciousness I can respect; in many ways I find it a positive quality. But he's just a little too quick with the essence-flail. If you work too slow; if you work too fast; if you happen to be nearby when he feels like it—every opportunity, out it comes."

I nodded. "Too right. He scoured me again last night simply because of a pure coincidence."

"Which was?"

"I made a gratuitous comedy sound effect just as he bent to retie his sandals." I gave a sigh and shook my head sadly. "True, it echoed off the valley walls like a thunderclap. True, several grandees of Solomon's court were in attendance and hurriedly changed course to get upwind of him. But even so! The fellow lacks humor—that's the root of the problem."

"Good to see you're still as cultivated as ever, Bartimaeus," Faquarl said blandly.

"I try. I try."

"But recreations aside, we need to be careful with Khaba. You remember what he showed us in the sphere? That could be either one of us."

"I know."

The Nubian finished picking at his teeth and tossed the chip away. We stared out together at the pulsating whiteness of the quarry.

Now, to the casual onlooker the dialogue above may seem unremarkable, but in fact it scores highly for originality as it featured Faquarl and me having a chat without resorting to (a) petty abuse, (b) contrived innuendo, or (c) attempted murder. This, down the centuries, was a fairly unusual event. In fact there were entire civilizations that had hauled themselves from the mud, mastered the arts of writing and astronomy, and decayed slowly into decadence in the intervals between us having a civil conversation.

We'd first crossed paths in Mesopotamia, during the interminable wars between the city-states. Sometimes we fought on the same side; sometimes we were ranged against each other in battle. This in itself wasn't a big deal—it was par for the course for any spirit, and a situation quite outside our control, since it was our masters who forced us into action —but somehow Faquarl and I seemed to rub each other the wrong way.

Quite *why* was hard to say. In many respects we had a lot in common.

First, we were both djinn of high repute and ancient origin, although (typically) Faquarl insisted his origin was a little more ancient than mine.[1]

Second, we were both zestful individuals, potent, resourceful, and good in a scrap, and formidable opponents of our human masters. Between us we had accounted for a great many magicians who had failed to close their pentacles properly, misspoken a word during our summonings, left a loophole in the terms and conditions of our indentures, or otherwise messed up the dangerous process of bringing us to Earth. The flaw in our feistiness, however, was that *competent* magicians, recognizing our qualities and wishing to use them for their own ends, summoned us ever more frequently. The net result was that Faquarl and I were the two hardest-working spirits of that millennium, at least in our opinion.

If all that wasn't enough, we had plenty of shared interests, too—notably architecture, politics, and regional cuisine.[2] So, one way or another, you'd have thought that Faquarl and I would have gotten along fine.

---

[1] By his account, Faquarl's first summoning was in Jericho, 3015 B.C.E., approximately five years before my initial appearance in Ur. This made him, allegedly, the "senior" djinni in our partnership. However, since Faquarl also swore blind he'd invented hieroglyphs by "doodling with a stick in the Nile river mud" *and* claimed to have devised the abacus by impaling two dozen imps along the branches of an Asiatic cedar, I regarded all his stories with a certain skepticism.

[2] In my view the people of Babylonia were the tastiest, owing to the rich goat's milk in their diet. Faquarl preferred a good Indian.

Instead, for some reason, we got up each other's noses,[3] and always had.

Still, we were generally prepared to put our differences aside when faced with a mutual enemy, and our present master certainly fit that bill. Any magician capable of summoning eight djinn at once was clearly a formidable proposition, and the essence-flail didn't make things any easier. But I felt there was something more to him even than that.

"There's one odd thing about Khaba," I said suddenly. "Have you noticed—"

Faquarl gave me a sharp nudge; he tilted his head slightly. Two of our fellow workers, Xoxen and Tivoc, had appeared down the quarry path. Both were trudging wearily and rested spades upon their shoulders.

"Faquarl! Bartimaeus!" Xoxen was incredulous. "What are you doing?"

Tivoc's eyes gleamed nastily. "They're having a breather."

"Come and join us if you want," I said.

Xoxen leaned upon his spade and wiped his face with a dirty hand. "You fools!" he hissed. "Don't you remember the name and nature of our master? He is not called Khaba the Cruel because of the fond generosity he shows to skiving spirits! He ordered us to work without breaks during the hours of light. By day we toil, by night we rest! What is there in this concept that you don't understand?"

"You'll have us all in the essence-cages," Tivoc snarled.

Faquarl made a dismissive motion. "The Egyptian is just a human, imprisoned in grim flesh, while we are noble spirits—I'm

---

[3] Or snouts. Or trunks. Or tentacles, filaments, palpi, or antennae, depending which guise we were in.

using the term *noble* in the loosest possible sense, of course, so as to include Bartimaeus. Why should *any* of us toil for Khaba? We should work together to destroy him!"

"Big talk," growled Tivoc, "but I notice the magician is nowhere in sight."

Xoxen nodded. "Exactly. When he appears, you'll both be chiseling at double speed, you mark my words. In the meantime, shall we report that your first blocks are not quite done? Let us know when they're ready to be dragged up to the site."

Wheeling around, they minced out of the quarry. Faquarl and I stared after them.

"Our workmates leave much to be desired," I grunted. "No backbone."[4]

Faquarl picked up his tools and rose heavily to his feet. "Well, we're just as bad as them so far," he said. "We've been letting Khaba push us around too. The trouble is, I don't see how we're going to fight back. He's strong, he's vindictive, he's got that cursed flail—and he's also got..."

His voice trailed off. We looked at each other. Then Faquarl sent out a small Pulse that expanded around us, creating a glowing, green Bulb of Silence. The few faint noises from the hill above, where the spades of our fellow djinn could distantly be heard, became instantly muffled; we were alone, our voices insulated from the world.

Even so, I leaned in close. "Have you noticed his shadow?"

---

[4] To be fair, a few of them were all right. Nimshik had spent a good while in Canaan and had interesting points to make about the local tribal politics; Menes, a youngish djinni, listened attentively to my words of wisdom; even Chosroes grilled a mean imp. But the rest were sorry wastes of essence, Beyzer being boastful, Tivoc sarcastic, and Xoxen full of false modesty, which in my humble opinion are three immensely tiresome traits.

"Slightly darker than it ought to be?" Faquarl muttered. "Ever so slightly longer? Responds just a *little* too slowly when Khaba moves?"

"That's the one."

He made a face. "Nothing shows on any of the planes, which means a very high-level Veil's in place. But it's *something*, all right—something protecting Khaba. If we're going to get him, we first need to find out *what*."

"Let's keep an eye on it," I said. "Sooner or later, it'll give itself away."

Faquarl nodded. He flourished the chisel; the Bulb of Silence burst into a scattered shower of emerald droplets. Without another word, we went back to our work.

For a couple of days activities proceeded quietly at the temple site. The top of the hill was leveled, scrub and brushwood were cleared away, and foundations for the building were dug. Down in the quarry, Faquarl and I produced a good number of top-quality limestone blocks, geometric, symmetrical, and so cleanly finished the king himself could have eaten his breakfast off them. Even so, they didn't meet with the approval of Khaba's odious little overseer Gezeri, who materialized on an outcrop above our heads and tuttingly inspected our work.

"This is poor stuff, boys," he said, shaking his fat green head. "Lots of rough bits down the sides need sanding. The boss won't accept 'em like that, oh dear me, no."

"Come closer and show me exactly where," I said pleasantly. "My eyesight isn't what it was."

The foliot hopped down from the ledge and sauntered over. "You djinn are all the same. Big bloated sacks of uselessness, I call you. If I was your master, I'd riddle you with a Pestilence each day just on princip—Ay!" Further such pearls of wisdom from Gezeri were in short supply for the next few minutes, as I industriously sanded down the edges of the blocks using the side of his head. When I'd finished, the blocks gleamed like a baby's bottom, and Gezeri's face was flattened like an anvil.

"You were right," I said. "They look much better now. So do you, as a matter of fact."

The foliot pranced from foot to foot with fury. "How *dare* you! I'll tell on you, I will! Khaba's got his eye on you already! He's just waiting for an excuse to plunge you into the Dismal Flame! When I go up and tell him—"

"Here, let me help you out with that." In a philanthropic spirit, I grabbed him, tied his arms and legs in a complex knot, and with an impressive kick, punted him high over the quarry walls to land somewhere on the building site. There was a distant squeak.

Faquarl had been watching all this with urbane amusement. "Bit reckless, Bartimaeus."

"I get the flail daily anyway," I growled. "Once more won't make any difference."

But in fact the magician seemed too preoccupied now even to do much scouring. He spent most of his time in a tent on the edge of the site, checking the building plans and dealing with messenger imps sent from the palace. These messages carried endless new instructions for the temple layout—brass pillars here, cedar floors there—which Khaba had to instantly incorporate into the plans. Often he came out to double-check his changes against the work that had been done so far, so whenever I was up dragging a block onto the site, I took my chance to study him.

It wasn't very reassuring.

The first thing I spotted was that Khaba's shadow was *always* at his heels, trailing behind him along the dirt of the ground. It remained there regardless of the position of the sun: never in front, never to the side, *always* quietly behind him. The second thing was even odder. The magician seldom emerged when the sun was at its zenith,[5] but when he did, it was noticeable that while all other shadows were reduced almost to nothing, *his* was still long and sleek, a thing of evening or early morning.

Though it more or less corresponded to its owner's shape, it did so in an *elongated* sort of way, and I took an especial dislike to its long, thin, tapering arms and fingers. Usually these moved in conjunction with the movements of the magician, but not always. Once, as I was helping push a block toward the temple, Khaba observed us from the side. And out of the corner of my eye I seemed to see that, though the magician had his arms crossed, his shadow's arms now resembled those of a praying mantis, folded hungrily and waiting. I turned my head swiftly, only to find the shadow's arms crossed normally, just as they should have been.

As Faquarl had observed, the shadow looked the same on each of the seven planes, and this was ominous in itself. I'm no imp or foliot, but a strapping djinni with full command of every plane, and ordinarily I expect to be able to see through most magical deceptions going. Illusions, Concealments, Glamours, Veils, you name it—by flipping to the seventh plane they all disintegrate before my eyes into obvious layers of glowing wisps and threads, so that I see the true thing beneath. It's the same

---

[5] He preferred to keep to his tent and let foliots in the shape of Scythian slave boys wave palms above his head and feed him sweetmeats and iced fruit. Which I suppose is fair enough.

with spirit guises: show me a sweet little choirboy or a smiling mother and I'll show you the hideous fanged strigoï[6] it really is.[7] There's very little that remains hidden from my sight. Not with this shadow. I couldn't see past its Veil at all. Faquarl didn't have any better luck, as he confided one evening by the campfire. "It's got to be high level," he muttered. "Something that can fox us on the seventh isn't going to be a djinni, is it? I think Khaba's brought it with him from Egypt. Any idea what it could be, Bartimaeus? You've spent more time there than I have lately."

I shrugged. "The catacombs at Karnak are deep. I never got far in. We need to tread cautiously."

Just *how* cautiously was brought home to me the following day. There was a problem with the alignment of the temple porch, and I'd shinned up a ladder to assess things from above. I was concealed in a narrow cleft between two blocks and fiddling with my cubit rod and plumb line when I saw the magician pass by me on the hard tamped earth below. A small messenger-imp approached from the direction of the palace, a missive in its paw, and intercepted him; the magician halted, took the wax tablet on which the message was impressed, and read it swiftly. As he did so, his shadow, as was its wont, was stretched out long on the ground behind him, though the sun was almost at its height. The magician nodded, tucked the tablet in a belt-pouch, and proceeded on his way; the imp, with the aimless vapidity of its kind, meandered off in the opposite direction, picking its nose all the while. In so doing it passed the shadow; all in an instant

---

[6] *Strigoï*: a disreputable subclass of djinni, pallid and nocturnal, with a predilection for drinking the blood of the living. Think succubus, but without the curves.

[7] Not always. Just sometimes. *Your* mother is absolutely fine, for instance. Probably.

there was a blur of movement, a single sharp snapping noise, and the imp was gone. The shadow flowed away after the magician; just as it disappeared from view, its trailing head turned to look at me, and in that moment it didn't seem the least bit human.

With slightly shaking hands, I completed my measurements and descended stiffly from the porch. All things considered, it was probably best to keep away from the magician Khaba. I would lie low, do my jobs effectively, and above all not draw attention to myself. That would be the best way to keep out of trouble.

I managed it for four whole days. Then disaster struck.

10

The port of Eilat came as a surprise to Asmira, whose experience of cities was limited to Marib and its sister town of Sirwah thirty miles away across the fields. Crowded as they often were, especially on festival days, they maintained at all times a certain *order*. The priestesses wore their golden kirtles, the townsfolk their simple tunics of white and blue. If men from the hill tribes were present, their longer robes of red and brown made them easily identifiable from the guard-posts. With the single cast of an eye a guard could appraise a crowd and assess the dangers within.

In Eilat, it was not so simple.

Its streets were broad and the buildings never higher than two stories. To Asmira, used to the calm, cool shadows of Sheba's towers, this made the city oddly formless, a hot and sprawling mass of low whitewashed walls that merged disconcertingly with the ceaseless tide of people that passed among them. Richly garbed Egyptians stalked along, amulets gleaming upon their breasts; behind came slaves carrying boxes, chests, and scowling imps in swinging cages. Wiry men of Punt, bright-eyed, diminutive, with sacks of resin teetering on their backs, wound their way past stalls where Kushite merchants offered silver djinn-guards and spirit-charmers to the wary traveler. Black-eyed Babylonians argued with pale-skinned men over carts of strangely patterned pelts and skins; Asmira even spotted a group of fellow Shebans come north on the grueling frankincense trail.

Up on the rooftops, silent things wearing the shapes of cats and birds watched the activity unfold.

Asmira, standing at the gates, wrinkled her nose with distaste at the unregulated magic of the magician-king's domain. She bought spiced lentils from a kiosk set into the city wall, then plunged into the throng. Its turbid flow engulfed her; she was swallowed by the crowd.

Even so, she knew she was being followed before she had walked a dozen yards.

Chancing to glance back, she noticed a thin man in a long, pale robe detach himself from the wall where he had been leaning and move after her along the road. A little later, after two random changes of direction, she looked again and found him still in sight, dawdling along, staring at his feet, seemingly entranced by the clouds of dust he kicked up with every casual step.

An agent of Solomon already? It seemed unlikely; she had done nothing to draw attention to herself. Unhurriedly Asmira crossed the street under the white heat of the day and ducked beneath a bread-seller's awning. She stood above the baskets in the hot shade, breathing in the scent of the piled loaves. Out of the corner of her eye she saw a pale flash move among the customers at the fish stall alongside.

An old and wrinkled man sat hunched between the bread-baskets, chewing toothlessly on his khat. Asmira purchased a thin wheat loaf from him, then said: "Sir, I need to travel to Jerusalem as a matter of urgency. What is the quickest way?"

The old man frowned; her Arabic was strange to him, and barely intelligible. "By camel train."

"Where do the camels leave from?"

"From the market square beside the fountains."

"I see. Where is the square?"

He pondered long, his jaw moving in slow, circular movements. At last he spoke. "Beside the fountains."

Asmira's brow furrowed, her bottom lip protruded in vexation. She glanced back toward the fish stall. "I'm from the south," she said. "I don't know the town. Is camel train *really* the quickest way? I thought perhaps—"

"Are you traveling alone?" the old man said.

"Yes."

"Ah." He opened his gummy mouth and emitted a brief chuckle.

Asmira gazed at him. "What?"

Bony shoulders shrugged. "You're young, and—if the shadows of your shawl don't conceal unpleasant surprises—goodlooking too. Plus you're traveling alone. In my experience, your chances of leaving Eilat safely, let alone reaching Jerusalem, are slim. Still, while you yet have life and money, you might as well spend freely; that's my philosophy. Why not buy another loaf?"

"No, thank you. I was asking about Jerusalem."

The old man stared at her appraisingly. "The slavers here do very well," he mused. "I sometimes wish I'd gone into that trade..." He licked a finger, stretched out a hairy arm, and adjusted the display of flatbread in a nearby basket. "Ways to get to Jerusalem? If you were a magician, you could fly there on a carpet. . . . That's quicker than camels."

"I'm not a magician," Asmira said. She adjusted the leather bag across her shoulder.

The old man grunted. "That's lucky, because *if* you flew to Jerusalem on a carpet, *he'd* see you by way of the Ring. Then you'd be taken by a demon and carried off, and subjected to all sorts of horrors. Sure I can't interest you in a pretzel?"

Asmira cleared her throat. "I thought perhaps a chariot."

"Chariots are for queens," the bread seller said. He laughed, his mouth gaping like a void. "And magicians."

"I'm neither," Asmira said.

She took up her bread and left. A moment later a thin man wearing a pale robe pushed aside the customers of the fish stall and slipped out into the day.

The beggar had been working his patch outside the bazaar since dawn, when the tide had brought new ships into Eilat's quays. As always, the merchants had heavy purses tied at their belts, which the beggar attempted to lighten in two complementary ways. His roars and pleas and pitiful exhortations, together with the proud display of his withered stump, always awoke sufficient revulsion to earn some shekels from the crowd. Meanwhile his imp, loitering among the bystanders, picked as many pockets as it could. The sun was hot and the business good, and the beggar was just thinking of departing to the wine shop when he was approached by a thin man wearing a long, pale robe. The newcomer scuffled to a halt, staring at his feet.

"I've found a mark," he said.

The beggar scowled. "Toss a coin first, *then* tell. Got to keep up appearances, haven't we?" He waited till the newcomer obliged. "So, spit it out," he said. "What is he?"

"Not a 'he'; a 'she,'" replied the thin man sourly. "Girl came in from the south this morning. Traveling alone. Wants to go to Jerusalem. She's off haggling with the camel traders now."

"Got much, you think?" the beggar said, squinting up from the corner where he sat. He waved his stick angrily. "Move away from the sun, curse you! I'm lame, not blind."

"Not so lame either, from what I hear," the thin man said,

stepping a few paces to the side. "Her clothes are nice enough, and she's got a sack with her that warrants a look too. But she'd fetch a good price *herself*, if you get my meaning."

"And she's on her own?" The beggar stared off along the street; he scratched the stubble of his chin. "Well, the caravans don't leave until tomorrow, that's a given, so she'll stay in town tonight whether she wants to or not. There's no hurry, is there? Go and find Intef. If he's drunk, knock some sense into him. I'll go to the square, keep watch, see what's going on." The beggar rocked back and forward twice and, by leaning on his stick, stood up with sudden swift agility. "Well, get off," he said savagely. "You'll find me in the square. Or, if she moves, wherever you hear my call."

He swung his stick, and, with a series of limping jerks, set off along the road. Long after he was out of sight, his cries for alms could still be heard.

"I *could* sell you a camel, girl," the merchant said, "but it would be unusual practice. Send your father or your brother; I will drink tea with them and chew khat and make such arrangements as are meant to be made between men. And I will berate them politely for allowing you out alone. The streets here are not kind to girls, as they ought to know."

It was late afternoon, and the peach-and-orange light refracting through the fabric of the tent struck lazily upon the carpet and the cushions, and upon the merchant who sat among them. A pile of clay tablets, some old and hard, others still soft and only partially covered by the merchant's marks, rested at his side. Laid out carefully in front of him was a stylus, a tablet, a cup, and a jug of wine. A dangling djinn-guard hung from the roof above his head, twirling gently to the movements of the air.

THE RING OF SOLOMON

Asmira looked back at the closed flap of the tent. Business in the square was ebbing. One or two shadows moved swiftly past. None of them was familiar to her: none dawdled, head down, staring at its feet. . . . Still, evening was coming; it would not do to be out alone much longer. Far off she heard a beggar's whining call.

She said, "You will make the arrangements with me."

The merchant's broad face did not alter. He looked down at his tablet, and his hand strayed to the stylus. "I'm busy, girl. Send your father."

Asmira gathered herself, forced her fury down. This was the third such meeting she had had that afternoon and the shadows were growing long. She had twelve days before the attack on Marib, and the camel ride to Jerusalem would take ten. "Sir," she said, "I have ample payment. You need only speak your price."

The merchant compressed his lips; after a moment he set down the stylus. "Show me this payment."

"How much do you need?"

"Girl, I am expecting the gold traders in from Egypt in the next few days. They too will seek transport to Jerusalem and will buy as many camels as I can provide. From them I will get little pouches of gold dust, or perhaps small nuggets from the Nubian mines, so that my mustaches will curl with excitement and I will close up my tent for a month and make merry in the Street of Sighs. What can you show me in the next five seconds that will make me give up one of my fine, dark-eyed camels to you?"

The girl reached inside her riding cloak; when her hand reappeared, it had something the size of an apricot stone glittering in the palm.

"It is a blue diamond from the Hadhramaut," she said. "Shaped and sanded into fifty facets. They say the Queen of Sheba wears one similar on her headdress. Provide me with a camel and it's yours."

The merchant sat very still; peach and orange light moved upon the surface of his face. He looked toward the closed tent flap, from where the sound of the marketplace was muffled. The tip of his tongue ran between his lips. He said, "A man might wonder whether you had more such things..."

Asmira moved so that the front of her riding cloak fell open; she rested her fingers on the dagger hanging loosely at her belt.

"...but to me," the merchant continued heartily, "such payment is more than adequate! We can make immediate arrangements!"

Asmira nodded. "I'm so glad. Give me my camel."

"She is going down Spice Street now," the thin man reported. "She's left the beast at the square. They're equipping it for tomorrow. Not sparing any expense either. A canopy and everything. She's got money in that bag of hers." As he spoke, he played with a long strip of cloth, twisting it between his hands.

"Spice Street's too busy," the beggar said.

"Ink Street?"

"Good enough. Four of us should manage it."

It was true what Asmira had told the bread seller. She was not a magician. But that did not mean she was innocent of magic.

When she was nine years old, the senior guard-mother found her as she was practicing in the yard. "Asmira, come with me."

They went to a quiet room above the training hall, where Asmira had never been. Inside were tables and cabinets of ancient cedarwood, their half-open doors revealing stacks of papyrus scrolls, clay tablets, and pottery shards notched with signs. On the center of the floor two circles had been drawn, each containing a five-pointed star.

Asmira frowned and pulled a lock of hair back from her face. "What's all this?"

The senior guard-mother was forty-eight years old and had once been First Guard of the queen. She had put down three tribal insurrections in the Hadhramaut. She had a thin white sword-scar slashed across her wrinkled neck and another across her forehead, and was regarded with awe and veneration by the sisterhood. Even the queen herself was said to speak to her with some humility. She looked down at the scowling girl and said mildly, "They tell me your training is going well."

Asmira was looking at a papyrus scroll laid out on the table. It was covered with an ornate and densely written script—except in the middle, where a sinister figure, half smoke, half skeleton, had been sketched with a few deft strokes. She shrugged.

The guard-mother said: "I have seen you with the knives. I could not throw as well as you when I was your age. And nor could your mother."

The girl did not look at her, nor change expression, but her bony little shoulders stiffened. She spoke as if she had not heard. "What's all this magical stuff, anyway?"

"What do you think it is?"

"Ways of summoning demons of the air. I thought it was forbidden. Only priestesses are allowed to do it, the guard-mothers say." Her eyes blazed. "Or were you all lying?"

In three years the senior guard-mother had had cause to beat the girl innumerable times for truancy, disobedience, and cheek. Now she only said, "Asmira, listen. I have two things to offer you. The one is knowledge, the other is this...." She held out her hand. Between the fingers hung a silver necklace; on its end, a pendant shaped like the sun. When the girl saw it, she gave a little gasp.

"I do not need to tell you that it was your mother's," the senior guard-mother said. "No, you may not have it yet. Listen to me now." She waited till the girl had raised her face: taut, hostile, tamping its emotion down. She said: "We did not lie to you. Magic is forbidden to everyone in Sheba but the priestesses of the temple. Only *they* may summon demons in the ordinary way. And it is right that this is so! Demons are wicked, deceitful things, dangerous to all. Think how volatile the hill-tribes are! If every chieftain could raise a djinni whenever he argued with his neighbors, there would be a dozen wars a year, and half the population dead! But in the hands of the priestesses, djinn can be put to better purpose—how do you think the reservoir here in Marib was built, or the walls of the city, for that matter? Each year they help repair the towers, and dredge the water-channels too."

Asmira said, "I know this. They do the queen's work, just as the men must labor in the fields."

The senior guard-mother chuckled. "This is so. Djinn are in fact much like men—provided you treat them sternly, and do not give them an inch of room to work you ill, they have several worthwhile uses. But here is the thing. Magic is useful to the guards also, and for one good reason. Our duty, the whole purpose of our being, is to protect our sovereign. We rely on our bodily skills for the most part, but sometimes that alone is not sufficient. If a demon attacked the queen—"

"A silver blade would deal with it," the girl said shortly.

"Sometimes, but not always. A guard needs other defenses

too. There are certain words, Asmira, certain magical Wards and incantations, which can temporarily rebuff a lesser demon's power." The senior guard-mother lifted the necklace so that the sun pendant swung slowly, catching the light. "Spirits hate silver, just as you say, and charms like this give force to the uttered spell. I can teach you such things, if you wish. But to do so, we will have to summon demons to practice on." She gestured around at the cluttered room. "This is why we have special dispensation to learn such techniques here."

"I'm not afraid of demons," the girl said.

"Asmira, summoning spirits is perilous, and we are not magicians. We learn basic incantations, so that we may test our Wards. If we are hasty, or careless, we will pay a dreadful price. Lesser guards do not need to understand these skills and I will not force you to do so either. If you wish, you can leave this room now and never return."

The girl was gazing at the little twirling sun. Its light flashed in her eyes like fire. "My mother knew these skills?"

"She did."

Asmira held out her hand. "Teach me, then. I will learn."

As she walked back to the inn where she was to spend the night, Asmira stared up between the darkened buildings at the glittering expanse of stars. As she watched, a light streaked in the heavens, flared briefly, and went out. A shooting star? Or one of Solomon's demons spreading terror to other lands?

Her jaw clenched; her nails dug into her palms. It was another *ten days* before she would reach Jerusalem—and that was without the sandstorms that might delay the caravan. Ten days! And in twelve the Ring would be turned and devastation brought upon Sheba! She closed her eyes and took a long breath in and out, as she had been taught to do when emotions threatened. Her training worked; she felt herself grow calm.

When she opened her eyes, there was a man standing in the road in front of her.

He held a long strip of cloth between his hands.

Asmira halted, looking at him.

"Softly," the man said. "No struggling." When he smiled, his teeth were very white.

Asmira heard footfall on the road behind; glancing over her shoulder, she saw three other men hastening close, one of them a cripple, a crutch wedged under his arm. She saw the ropes, the sack held ready, the knives tucked neatly in their waistbands, the glints of moisture in their smiling eyes and mouths. On the cripple's shoulder, a small black impling crouched, flexing its dirty yellow claws.

Her hand moved toward her belt.

"Softly," the man with the cloth said again. "Or I'll hurt you."

He took another step, then sighed, fell backward. Starlight glinted on the dagger blade protruding from the center of his eye.

Before he hit the ground, Asmira had swiveled, ducked beneath a clutching hand, and pulled the knife from the waistband of the nearest man behind her. Dancing aside from the stumbling assault of the third, who sought to loop a coil of wire about her head, she killed both men with rapid blows and turned to face the fourth.

The cripple had halted a few yards distant, his face slack with blank surprise. Now he gave a long, low snarl and snapped his fingers. The impling beat its wings and launched itself at Asmira with a cry. Asmira waited till it was close, then touched her silver necklace, spoke a Ward of force. The impling exploded in a ball of flame that spiraled away and burst against a wall in a shower of angry sparks.

Before the fires faded, the cripple was away along the street, stick tapping frantically upon the stone.

Asmira let the soiled knife fall to the ground. She turned and walked back to her bag, crouched, loosened its ties, and removed a second silver dagger. Flipping it in her fingers, she looked back along the road.

The beggar was a long way off now, head down, rags flying, lolloping and bounding, swinging himself forward with great sweeps of his stick. In a few more steps he would be at a corner and out of sight.

Asmira took careful aim.

Shortly after dawn the following day, those emerging from their houses on the corner of Ink and Spice streets made a gruesome discovery: four bodies sitting neatly against a wall, their seven legs stretched out side by side into the road. Each man had been a well-known slaver and vagrant of the district; each had been killed with a single strike.

At roughly the same moment, a camel train of thirty riders set out from Eilat's central square on the long journey to Jerusalem. Asmira was among them.

II

I blame Beyzer for the incident. It was his turn to keep watch, but his spot in the cypress was a tad too comfy, what with the noonday heat and the smell of resin and the nice plump implet he was using as a cushion. Dozing gently, Beyzer didn't notice Solomon's approach. This took some doing, partly because the king was pretty tall, and partly because he was accompanied by seven magicians, nine court officials, eleven slaves, thirty-three warriors, and a robust percentage of his seven hundred wives. The rustling of their robes alone made a noise like a storm-lashed forest, and since on top of this you had the officials shouting at the slaves, the slaves waving their palm leaves, the warriors rattling their swords, and the wives squabbling continuously in a dozen languages, Solomon and his entourage were hard to miss. So even without Beyzer, the rest of the temple workforce managed to stop in time.

Which left just me.

Thing was, I was at the end of the line; I was the one hefting each half-ton block out of the quarry, chucking it into the air, catching it by a corner on an outstretched finger, spinning it stylishly, and then punting it on to Tivoc, who was waiting by the temple. Tivoc would then pass the block on to Nimshik, Faquarl, Chosroes, or one of the other djinn who were hovering around the uncompleted walls in a variety of outlandish guises.[1]

---

[1] Most of them winged. Faquarl's were leathery, Chosroes's feathery, and Nimshik's ashimmer with the silver scales of the flying fish. Xoxen, as ever, had to be different;

After that: a quick toss into position, a hasty aligning spell, and Solomon's temple was a block nearer completion. Took about thirty-five seconds, quarry to wall-top. Lovely. A work-rate any employer would be chuffed with.

Except Solomon, that is. No. *He* didn't want it done like that.[2]

You'll notice that conditions at the building site had altered markedly since the first few days. Back then, with Khaba and Gezeri close at hand, we'd been doing everything painstakingly, while keeping human form. But then things changed. Perhaps reassured by our compliance, and with the temple now progressing well, the magician stopped visiting the site so often. Shortly afterward Gezeri departed too. To begin with, through fear of the flail, we remained on our best behavior. On the second day, still left to our own devices, our resolve wavered. We took a swift vote among ourselves and, by a majority of six to two,[3] approved a change of work practices with immediate effect.

We promptly set up our lookout and spent our time in a mixture of loafing, gambling, imp-tossing, and philosophical debate. Occasionally, when we needed the exercise, we'd whip

---

he bounded up and down beside the porch on a pair of giant frog's legs, which meant that most of his blocks were hopelessly out of true.

[2] Heaven knows why he was so fussy about this temple job. Early in his reign his host of spirits had jerry-built most of Jerusalem for him, throwing up new housing districts in a day or two, hiding their slapdash workmanship with strategically placed Illusions. They'd spent a bit longer on the palace itself, admittedly, and the city walls only wobbled if you pushed *really* hard, but this temple Solomon wanted done without any magical sleights of hand, which in my view kind of defeated the point of using djinn.

[3] Tivoc and Chosroes voted against: Tivoc because of a complicated argument involving certain subtleties in clause 51(c) of his summoning; Chosroes because he was just plain chicken.

a few stones magically into position, just to make it look like we'd been doing something. It was a definite improvement in our daily grind.

Unfortunately, it was during one of these brief spasms of activity that Solomon—having never chosen to visit us before —decided to drop by. And it was thanks to Beyzer that I didn't get the alarm.

Everyone else was fine, thank you very much. As the royal entourage came clanking, jabbering, and mincing to a halt, my fellow workers were safely back in human form, standing about meekly carving things with their chisels as if butter wouldn't melt in their smug little mouths.

And me?

Me, I was still the pygmy hippo in a skirt,[4] singing lusty songs about Solomon's private life and tossing a giant stone back and forth through the air as I climbed out of the quarry at the edge of the site.

Immersed in my ditty, I didn't notice anything amiss. As usual, I flexed a warty arm and tossed the stone.

As usual, it sailed across in the sweetest of arcs to the corner of the temple where Tivoc stood.

Or in this case didn't stand, since he'd long since bowed and scraped and made shuffling way for Solomon to inspect the porch. And with Solomon had come his magicians, court officials, warriors, slaves, and wives, each crowding close to bathe in the royal presence.

They heard my singing. They craned their heads around.

---

[4] *Hippo in a skirt*: this was a comic reference to one of Solomon's principal wives, the one from Moab. Childish? Yes. But in the days before printing we had limited opportunities for satire.

They saw the half-ton stone being lobbed toward them in the sweetest of arcs. They had time for maybe the briefest of lamentations before it squished them flat.

The hippo in a skirt slapped its hand over its eyes.

But Solomon just touched the Ring on his finger that was the source and secret of his power. The planes trembled. And from the earth jumped four winged marids in emerald flame, who caught and held the stone, one at each corner, a few inches from the great king's head.[5]

Solomon touched the Ring again, and from the earth sprang nineteen afrits, who caught the exact same number of his wives mid-swoon.[6]

Then Solomon touched the Ring a third time, and from the earth leaped a posse of sturdy imps, who caught the hippo in the skirt as it was quietly slipping away into the recesses of the quarry, bound it hand and foot with thorny bonds, and dragged it back through the dirt to where the great king stood, tapping his sandaled foot and looking rather tetchy.

And despite my trademark bravery and fortitude—famous from the deserts of Shur to the mountains of Lebanon—the hippo swallowed hard as it bumped along the ground, because when Solomon got tetchy, people tended to know about it. He had the wisdom stuff as well, it's true, but what really got results when he wanted something done was his reputation for no-holds-barred homicidal tetchiness. That and his cursed Ring.[7]

---

[5] A *bit* showy, that. You only need a middling djinni for a stone that size.

[6] Again, do you *need* an afrit to catch a wife? No, except maybe in the case of the one from Moab.

[7] I suppose I should have been glad he'd only *touched* the thing and not *turned* it. It was when the terrible Spirit of the Ring was invoked that things were supposed to get *really* nasty.

The marids placed the block of stone gently on the earth before the king. The imps swung me across so that I came to an undignified halt, slumped against the stone. I blinked, sat upright as best I could, spat assorted pebbles out of my mouth, and attempted a winning smile. A low murmur of repulsion came from the watching throng, and several wives fainted again. Solomon raised a hand; all sound cut off.

This was the first time I'd got close to him, of course, and I must say he didn't disappoint. He was everything your typical trumped-up west Asian despot could aspire to be: dark of eye and skin, long and glistening of hair, and covered with more clattering finery than a cut-price jewel stand at the bazaar. He seemed to have an Egyptian thing going too—his eyes were heavily made-up with kohl just like the pharaohs'; like them, he existed in a cloud of clashing oils and perfumes. That smell was another thing Beyzer should have noticed in advance.

On his finger something shone so brightly that I was almost rendered blind.

The great king stood over me, fingers toying with the brace-lets on one arm. He breathed deeply; his face seemed pained. "Lowliest of the low," he said softly, "which of my servants are you?"

"O Master-may-you-live-for-ever, I am Bartimaeus."

A hopeful pause; the regal countenance did not change.

"We haven't had the pleasure before," I went on, "but I'm sure a friendly conversation would benefit us both. Let me intro-duce myself. I am a spirit of notable wisdom and sobriety, who once spoke with Gilgamesh, and—"

Solomon raised an elegant finger, and since it was the one with the Ring on it, I kind of snatched back as many of my words as I could and swallowed them down sharpish. Best just be quiet, eh? Wait for the worst.

"You are one of Khaba's troublemakers, I think," the king said musingly. "Where *is* Khaba?"

This was a good question; we'd been wondering it ourselves for days. But at that moment there was a flurry among the courtiers, and my master himself appeared, all red of cheek and glistening of pate. He had clearly been running hard.

"Great Solomon," he panted. "This visit—I did not know—" His moist eyes widened as they alighted on me, and he gave a wolfish cry. "Foul slave! How dare you defy me with such a shape! Great King, stand back! Let me admonish this creature—" And he snatched at the essence-flail in his belt.

But Solomon held up his hand once more. "Be still, magician! Where were *you* while my edicts were being disobeyed? I shall attend to you presently."

Khaba fell back, slack-jawed and gasping. His shadow, I noticed, was very small and inoffensive now, a small dark nub, cringing at his feet.

The king turned back to me. Ooh, his voice was soft then. All gentle and luxurious, like leopard fur. And just like a leopard's fur, you didn't want to rub it the wrong way. "Why do you mock my orders, Bartimaeus?"

The pygmy hippo cleared its throat. "Um, well, I think *mock* is putting it a trifle strongly, O great Master. *Forget* might be better; and less fatal."

One of Solomon's other magicians, nameless, portly, face like a squashed fig, riddled me with a Spasm. "Cursed spirit! The king asked you a question!"

"Yes, yes, I was getting to that." I squirmed against the stone.

"And a cracking question it was. Beautifully put. Succinct. Probing…" I hesitated. "What was it again?"

Solomon seemed to have a knack of never raising his voice,
never speaking quickly. It was a good political technique,
of course; it gave him an aura of control among his people.
Now he spoke to me as to a sleepy babe. "When completed,
Bartimaeus, this temple shall be the holiest of places, the center
of my religion and my empire. For that reason, as set out with
great clarity in your instructions, I wish it built—and I quote
—with 'the utmost care, without magical shortcuts, irreverent
acts, or bestial shapes.'"

The hippo in the skirt frowned. "Goodness, who'd do any
of that?"

"You have disregarded my edict in each and every way. Why?"

Well, a number of excuses came to mind. Some of them were
plausible. Some of them were witty. Some of them offered a certain pleasure in the use of language while at the same time being
blatantly untrue. But Solomon's wisdom thing was catching. I
decided to tell the truth, albeit in a sulky monotone.

"O great Master, I was bored and I wanted to get the job
done quickly."

The king nodded, an action that saturated the air with jasmine
oil and rosewater. "And that vulgar song you were singing?"

"Um—which vulgar song was that? I sing so many."

"The one about me."

"Oh, *that* one." The hippo swallowed. "You mustn't pay
any attention to such things, O Master, etcetera. Ribald songs
have *always* been sung about great leaders by loyal troops. It's a
mark of respect. You should have heard the one we invented for
Hammurabi. He used to join in the choruses."

To my relief Solomon seemed to buy this. He straightened his back and stared hard around him. "Did any of the other slaves violate my orders too?"

I'd known this one was coming. I didn't exactly look toward my companions, but somehow I could sense them shrinking back behind the crowd—Faquarl, Menes, Chosroes, and the rest—all of them bombarding me with silent, heartfelt pleas. I sighed; spoke heavily. "No."

"Are you sure? None of them used magic? None of them changed form?"

"No . . . no. Just me."

He nodded. "Then they are exempt from punishment." His right hand moved left, in the direction of the dreaded Ring.

I'd been putting it off, but it was clearly time for a brief loss of dignity. With a strident expression of woe, the hippo lurched forward onto its wrinkly knees. "Do not be too hasty, great Solomon!" I cried. "I have served you faithfully and well until today. Consider this block of stone—see how I've shaped and squared it most exactly. Now look at the temple—witness the dedication with which I'm pacing out its dimensions! Measure it, O King! Three score cubits, I was told, and three score cubits it shall be, and not a rat's-arse more!"[8] I wrung my forefeet together, swaying from side to side. "My mistake today is just a symptom of my excess energies and zeal," I wailed. "I can turn these qualities to your majesty's good, if only you spare my life. . . ."

Well, I'll omit the rest, which involved a great many sobs,

---

[8] *Rat's-arse*: technical term this, corresponding to about ¹⁄₁₅th of a cubit. Other units of measurement used by the djinn during this period were "camel's thigh," "leper's stretch," and "the length of a Philistine's beard."

random gesticulations, and guttural cries. It wasn't a bad performance: a number of the wives (and several of the warriors) were sniffling by the end, and Solomon himself looked smugger and more self-satisfied than ever. Which was pretty much as I planned it. Thing was, just by looking at him, I could see Solomon modeled himself on the big boys—the kings of Assyria and Babylon way to the east, tough potentates who didn't get out of bed without a defeated enemy's neck to step on en route to the bathroom. Thus my snivelling appealed to his imitative vanity. I thought I'd swung it at the last.

The great king coughed. The hippo stopped mid-bawl and eyed him hopefully. "Your ridiculous display of overacting has entertained me," Solomon said. "I shan't need my girners or my jugglers tonight. As a result I shall spare your meager life" —here he cut short my torrent of gratitude—"and instead put your 'excess energies and zeal' to proper use."

Solomon paused at this ominous juncture to select a variety of sweetmeats, wines, and fruit from an attendant's silver tray. Several of his nearest wives fought subtly but viciously among themselves for the honor of feeding him. The hippo, gritting its teeth with unease, shook a few flies out of its tufted ears and waited.

One pomegranate, five grapes, and an iced date-and-pistachio sherbet had passed the royal lips before the king held forth again. "O meanest and most despicable of my djinn—and don't look around so blankly, I'm talking to *you*—since you find your work here so dull, we shall give you a more stimulating occupation."

I bowed my head to the dirt. "Master, I listen and obey."

"So then. South from Jerusalem, across the Desert of Paran and the Desert of Zin, my trade road runs; on it travel merchants from Egypt and the Red Sea, from the Arabian interior, even—though more rarely than we might wish—from mysterious Sheba itself. These merchants," he went on, "carry myrrh, frankincense, precious woods and spices, and other riches that bring prosperity to the people of Israel. In recent weeks it has come to my attention that many caravans have met with disaster; they have not gotten through."

I grunted wisely. "Probably ran out of water. That's the thing about deserts. Dry."

"Indeed. A fascinating analysis. But survivors reaching Hebron report differently: monsters fell upon them in the wastes."

"What, fell upon them in a squashed-them kind of way?"

"More the leaped-out-and-slew-them kind. These monsters were huge, hideous, and terrible."

"Well, aren't they all?" The hippo considered. "My advice is to send those four off to investigate." I indicated the marids from the Ring, who were still hanging about on the seventh plane, quietly arguing about the succulence of the nearest wives.

Solomon gave a feline smile. "Most conceited of my spirits, it is *you* who must investigate. The attacks are clearly the work of bandits, who have powerful magicians among them. So far my troops have been unable to trace the instigators. You must search the deserts, eliminate them, and discover who is behind this outrage."

I hesitated. "All on my lonesome?"

The king drew back; he had come to a new decision. "No, you will not be on your own. Khaba! Step forward!"

My master did so, fawning, supplicating. "Great King, please! I can explain my absence—"

"No explanation is required. I gave you strict instructions to keep a close eye on your servants, and this you failed to do. I blame *you* for this djinni's misdeeds. Since neither you nor your group is worthy of working on this temple a moment longer, you shall all depart into the deserts tomorrow and not return until the brigands are found and brought to heel. Do you understand this, Khaba? Well, man? Speak up!"

The Egyptian was staring at the ground; a muscle in his cheek throbbed steadily. One of the other magicians suppressed a chuckle.

Khaba looked up; he bowed stiffly. "Master, as always I follow your requirements and your will."

Solomon made an ambiguous gesture. The interview was over. Wives darted forth offering water, sweetmeats, and vials of scent; slaves wafted palms; officials unscrolled papyri with plans of the temple precincts. Solomon turned away, and the gaggle of humanity departed with him, leaving Khaba, the hippo, and the seven other disgraced djinn standing silent and disconsolate on the hill.

12

Returning to his tower at speed, Khaba descended by secret ways to his cellar workroom, where a doorway of black granite stood embedded in the wall. As he approached, he spoke an order. Soundless as thought, the spirit residing in the floor spun the door ajar. Khaba passed through without breaking stride; he spoke another word and the door shut fast behind him.

Blackness enfolded him, incalculable and absolute. The magician stood there for a time, enduring as an exercise of will the silence and the solitude and the relentless pressing of the dark. Gradually, soft noises started in the cages: shuffles, faint mewlings of things shut long in blackness, the anxious stirring of other things that anticipated light and feared its violence. Khaba luxuriated in the plaintive sounds awhile, then stirred himself. He gave a fresh command, and all along the ceiling of the vault, the imps trapped in their faience globes made their magic flare. Eerie blue-green radiance filled the chamber, waxing, ebbing, deep and fathomless as the sea.

The vault was broad and domed; its roof supported at intervals by rough-hewn columns that cut across the blue-green haze like the stalks of giant underwater reeds. Behind his back the granite door was one block among many on an immense gray wall.

Between the columns stood an assortment of marble plinths and tables, chairs, couches, and many instruments of subtle use. It was the heart of Khaba's domain, an intricate reflection of his mind and inclinations.

He threaded his way past the slabs where he conducted his experiments of dissection, past the preservation pits, acrid with the taint of natron, past the troughs of sand where the process of mummification could be observed. He skirted between the ranks of bottles, vats, and wooden piping, between the pots of powdered herbs, the trays of insects, the dim, dark cabinets containing the carcasses of frog and cat and other, larger things. He bypassed the ossuary, where the labeled skulls and bones of a hundred beasts sat neatly side by side with those of men.

Khaba ignored the calls and supplications from the essence-cages in the recesses of the hall. He halted at a large pentacle, made of smooth black onyx and mounted in a raised circle on the floor. Stepping into its center, he took up the flail that hung loosely at his belt. He cracked it once into the empty air.

All sounds from the cages stilled.

In the shadows beyond the columns, on the margins of the blue-green light, a presence made itself known by a deepening of darkness and a clattering of teeth.

"Nurgal," Khaba said. "Is that you?"

"It is I."

"The king insults me. He treats me with disdain, and the other magicians laugh."

"What do I care? This is a cold, dark vault, and its occupants make for dismal company. Release me from my bonds."

"I shall not release you. I wish something for my colleague Reuben. It was he who laughed the loudest."

"What do you wish for him?"

"Marsh fever."

"It shall be done."

"Make it last four days, worsening each night. Make him lie awash in his misery, his limbs afire, his body chilled; make his eyes blind, but let him see visions and horrors during the hours of darkness, so that he screams and writhes and cries out for aid that never comes."

"You wish him to die?"

Khaba hesitated. The magician Reuben was weak and would not retaliate; but if he died, Solomon would surely take a hand. He shook his head. "No. Four days. Then he recovers."

"Master, I obey."

Khaba cracked the flail; with a clattering of teeth the horla swept past him and away through a narrow aperture in the roof; sour air buffeted the margins of the pentacle and set the caged things howling in the dark.

The magician stood in silence, tapping the whip slowly against the palm of his hand. At last he spoke a name. "Ammet."

A soft voice at his ear: "Master."

"I have lost the favor of the king."

"I know, Master. I saw. I am sorry."

"How shall I regain it?"

"That is no easy matter. Apprehending these desert bandits would seem to be the first step."

Khaba gave a cry of rage. "I need to be here! I must be at the court! The others will seize the chance to speak with Solomon and further undermine me. You saw their faces on the hill. Hiram could scarcely keep from crowing with joy as he watched me squirm!" He took a deep breath and spoke more quietly. "Besides, there is my *other* business to attend to. I must continue to observe the queen. "

"Do not be distressed about *that*," the soft voice said. "Gezeri can report to you in the desert as well as anywhere. Besides, you have given too much time to your . . . secondary affairs these last few days—and see where it has gotten you."

The magician ground his teeth. "How was I to know that the preening fool would choose today to inspect his cursed temple? He might have given me some warning!"

"He has the Ring. He is not beholden to you or anyone."

"Ah! You think I do not *know* that?" Khaba gripped the flail tightly; his curling fingernails dug deep into the ancient human leather. He bent his head forward to let something stroke the back of his neck. "How I wish...I wish..."

"I know what you wish, dear Master. But it is not safe to express it, even here. You have glimpsed the Spirit of the Ring —you have seen how terrible he is! We must be patient, have faith in our abilities. We will find a way."

The magician took a deep breath, drew back his shoulders. "You are right, sweet Ammet, of course you are. It is just so *hard* to stand there and watch that vain, indolent—"

"Let us inspect the cages," the voice said soothingly. "It will relax you. But Master, before we do, I crave a word. What of Bartimaeus?"

Khaba gave a piercing cry. "That vile djinni—if it wasn't for him we wouldn't be cast out of Jerusalem! A *hippopotamus*, Ammet! A hippopotamus on Temple Mount!" He paused, reflecting. "And wouldn't you have said," he added slowly, "that in face and form it bore a certain resemblance to—"

"Fortunately for us," the soft voice said, "I don't think Solomon noticed."

Khaba nodded grimly. "Well, I have whipped Bartimaeus soundly for his sins, but a whipping is not enough! The flail is too good for him."

"I quite agree, Master. This is the last straw. He abused Gezeri a week ago; he has caused frequent dissension among the djinn. He deserves a proper punishment now."

"The Inverted Skin, Ammet? The Osiris Box?"

"Too lenient...too temporary..." The voice grew urgent. "Master," it beseeched, "let *me* deal with him. I hunger, I thirst. I have not fed for so, so long. I can rid you of this irritant, and satisfy my cravings at the same time." There was a wet, smacking noise behind the magician's head.

Khaba grunted. "No. I like you hungry; it keeps you alert."

"Master, *please*..."

"Besides, I need all my djinn available and alive while we comb the deserts for these outlaws. Stop your whining, Ammet. I will give the matter thought. There will be time enough to deal with Bartimaeus when we return to Jerusalem...."

The voice was truculent, resentful. "As you will..."

Khaba's posture had previously been tight and hunched, tense at the indignities fate had thrust upon him. Now he jerked upright, his voice newly hard and decisive. "In a moment we shall make ready to depart. First, however, there is the other matter. Perhaps we will have positive news at last...."

He snapped his fingers, spoke a complex string of syllables. There was a distant chime of bells. The imp-globes shivered against the ceiling of the vault, and drapes on some of the larger cages ruffled to and fro.

The magician peered out into the darkness. "Gezeri?"

With a sharp odor of rotten eggs, a small lilac cloud materialized in the air beside the pentacle. Sitting atop the cloud was the foliot Gezeri, who today appeared as a large green imp with long pointed ears and a pear-shaped nose. He made a series of complex and faintly facetious salutes, which Khaba ignored.

"Your report, slave?"

The foliot affected an attitude of matchless boredom. "I have been to Sheba as you 'requested.' I have wandered through its streets unseen, listening to the people. Be certain I let no whisper pass me by, no muttered comment go unheard!"

"I am sure of it—otherwise you would burn in the Dismal Flame."

"That was my thinking too." The foliot scratched its nose. "In consequence I heard a lot of dreary nonsense. The *lives* you humans lead! The *things* that preoccupy your doughy little minds! Are you not aware of how *brief* your span is, how small your place is in this vast universe? Yet still you worry about dowries, tooth-rot, and the price of camels!"

The magician smiled bleakly. "Spare me the philosophy, Gezeri. *I* worry about none of those things. Here is my concern: what is Queen Balkis doing?"

Gezeri shrugged his bony shoulders. "In a word: nothing. Nothing out of the ordinary, I mean. Far as I can make out, she's doing her normal round—meditating in the temples, meeting merchants, hearing representations from her people: all the usual sort of queenly claptrap. I've sniffed about behind the scenes, eavesdropped on all and sundry. What have I come up with? Naught. There's no sign of any response at all."

"She has five days left," Khaba mused. "Five days... You are sure there has been no buildup of troops? No increase in defenses?"

"*What* troops? *What* defenses?" The foliot gave its tail a derisive twirl. "Sheba's not even got a proper army—just a bunch of skinny girls who hang about the queen. And the priestesses haven't put so much as a second-plane nexus around the palace. An *imp* could stroll right in."

The magician stroked his chin. "Good. Clearly she intends to make the payment. They all do, in the end."

"Yeah, well, that being the case," the foliot said, lounging deep into its cloud, "why don't you dismiss me? I'm fed up with all this summoning long distance. Ooh, it gives me such headaches as you wouldn't believe. And swellings in the *strangest* places. Here, take a look at this one. . . . It's getting uncomfortable to sit."

"You will return to Sheba, slave," Khaba snarled, averting his eyes, "and keep watch on what occurs! Be sure to let me know if you notice anything untoward. Meanwhile, I will shortly summon you again, swellings or no."

The foliot scowled. "Must I? Frankly I'd prefer the building site."

"Our work there is done for the present," Khaba said stiffly. "Solomon has . . . ordered us elsewhere."

"Ooh, got cross with you, has he? Fallen a wee bit out of favor? Tough luck!"

Khaba's lips narrowed to nothing. "Mark my words," he said, "one day there will be a reckoning."

"Oh, *sure* there will," the foliot said. "Tell you what, why not make it now? Why not nip up to the king's apartments tonight and pinch the Ring while he's asleep?"

"Gezeri . . ."

"Why not? You're quick, you're clever. You could kill him before he had a chance to turn the Ring. . . . Well? What's stopping you?" It chuckled lazily. "Give it up, Khaba. You're scared like all the rest."

The magician gave a hiss of outrage; he spoke a word and clapped his hands. Gezeri squeaked; the foliot and its cloud imploded and were gone.

Khaba stood rigid and furious in the blue-green shadows of his vault, staring into nothing. There would come a time when all those who belittled him regretted their folly most profoundly. . . .

There was a whisper in the darkness. Something stroked his neck. Taking a deep breath, Khaba swept the issues from his mind. He stepped down from his circle and crossed the floor toward the essence-cages. Time enough, before departing for the desert, for a little relaxation.

13

On the day of the Spring Festival the religious ceremonies had taken twice as long as normal, and the little girl was bored. She waited till the guard-mothers were kneeling to the Sun God, with their big old backsides raised to heaven, and cautiously looked around. The other girls were busy praying too, eyes tight shut, noses pressed against the stone. As the drone of their ritual chanting swelled to fill the air, the little girl got up, tiptoed past them all, and clambered out of the window. She ran across the flat roof of the training hall, skittered along the wall beside the palace gardens, and dropped like a cat into the shadows of the street. Then she smoothed out her dress, rubbed her shin where it had scraped against the brickwork, and pattered down the hill. She knew she would get a beating when she returned, but she didn't care. She wanted to see the procession.

They were throwing orange blossoms from the tower tops, and the people of Sheba had been covered with them like snow. All along the streets they waited—townsfolk and men of the hill-tribes alike—waiting patiently for their queen. The little girl did not wish to stand at the front of the crowd, in case she was crushed beneath the chariot's great wheels, so she scrambled up the wooden steps to the nearest guard-post, where two slim women with swords at their belts stood watching the crowds below.

"What are *you* doing here?" one said, frowning. "You ought to be in training. Get back up to the hall, quickly."

But the other ruffled the girl's cropped dark hair. "Too

late for that. Listen—here they come! Sit down and stay quiet, Asmira, and perhaps we won't notice you."

The little girl grinned and sat cross-legged on the stone between their feet. She leaned her chin on her fists, then craned her neck out; she saw the royal chariot come rumbling through the gates, pulled by its team of straining male slaves. The throne it bore was golden like the sun, and on it—vast and splendid, dressed in bright white robes that made her vaster still—sat the queen herself. She was like a painted statue, stiff and immovable, her round face white with chalk, staring straight ahead without expression. On either side marched guards with naked swords; behind filed the priestesses in a solemn line. On the chariot itself, just behind the throne, the First Guard stood smiling, her dark hair glistening in the sun.

Into the city the procession came. The people cheered; blossoms fell from the towers in new cascades. High on the guardpost, the little girl grinned and jiggled. She waved both hands.

On the far side of the narrow way, in the shadows of the nearest tower, there came a burst of yellow smoke. Three small winged demons, with scarlet eyes and whipping tails of sharpened bone, materialized in midair. At once the guards beside the girl were gone into the crowd. Those beside the chariot also started forward, swords readied, daggers pulled from sleeves.

Screams sounded, the crowd scattered. The demons darted through the air. One was struck simultaneously by seven silver blades and vanished with a cry. The others spun aside on leather wings, sending loops of fire down upon the advancing guards.

The little girl watched none of this. Her eyes were fixed upon the halted chariot, where the queen sat silent, staring straight ahead. The First Guard had not left her post; she had drawn her sword and stood calmly beside the throne.

And now the real attack began. Three hill-men stole out of the melting crowd, ran toward the unprotected chariot. From within their robes they drew long, thin knives.

The First Guard waited. When the quickest assailant leaped toward the queen, she ran him through before his feet touched the ground. His falling weight pulled the sword out of her grasp; letting it go, she turned to meet the others, a dagger springing to her hand.

The others reached the chariot; they jumped up on either side of the throne.

The First Guard flicked her wrist—one was struck; he fell away. In the same instant she threw herself across the queen, blocking the final knife-strike with her body. She collapsed upon the royal lap, long black hair falling loose about her head.

The other guards, having dealt with the demons, discovered the danger behind them. In a moment the third assailant had died from a dozen wounds. The guards surged around the chariot, dragged the bodies clear.

Orders were given. The slaves pulled on the ropes to the rhythm of the whips, and the chariot continued on. Blossoms cascaded onto empty streets. The queen stared straight before her, white-faced and impassive, the lap of her robes stained red.

The body of the First Guard lay in the shadow of the city gate while the line of priestesses shuffled by. After they were gone it took several further minutes for shocked attendants to return to clear the street, and even then no one noticed the little girl sitting high upon the guard-post, watching as her mother's body was carried up the hill.

Asmira opened her eyes. All was as it had been just before she slept. The tasseled shadow of her canopy swaying upon the camel's back. The line of beasts ahead of her, stretching into nothing. The creak of the poles and the soft steady tread of pads on stone ... Heat scoured her mouth; her head ached. Her clothes were a wet cocoon.

She moistened her lips with her waterskin, ignoring the temptation to drink deeply. Nine days in the desert, and three since fresh water, and still the road went on. All around was a land of desolation and absence, of bleached hills fading to the edge of vision. The sun was a white hole in an iron sky. It warped the air into slices that danced and shimmered and were never still.

Always, when she dozed during those endless desert days, Asmira found herself beset by whirling dreams that looped, repeating, stinging like blown sand. She saw the Queen of Sheba smiling in her chamber, pouring her more wine. She saw the priestesses on the palace forecourt, with the djinni raised and waiting, and all eyes on her as she bade farewell. She saw the Temple of the Sun and its eastern wall, where the icons of dead champions were displayed and her mother's figurine shone so beautifully in the morning light. She saw the empty niche beside it that she had coveted so long.

And sometimes ... sometimes she saw her mother, the way she had always seen her, for eleven frozen years.

That evening the camel train halted in the shelter of a sandstone ridge. Brushwood was gathered, a fire lit. The master of the caravan, who had some magical knowledge, sent forth imps to survey the rocks and give word if anything drew near.

Afterward he approached Asmira, who was gazing at the fire. "Still here, I see," he said.

Asmira was stiff, weary, and weighed down with impatience

at the tedium of the journey. Nevertheless, she managed a smile. "Why should I not be?"

The master was a large and jaunty man, twinkly-eyed and broad of chest. Asmira found him somewhat disconcerting. He chuckled. "Each night I check to ensure everyone is human still, and not a ghul or fetch! They say that once a camel-master rode into Petra with thirty traders in his train; as he passed beneath the city gates, each rider's cloak fell empty to the ground, and, looking back, he saw the way for miles behind littered with picked bones. All the men had been devoured, one by one!"

The guard-mothers had told Asmira that story too, about a trader of Marib. "A folktale," she said. "Nothing more."

The master took out his djinn-guard and shook its silver bells fervently. "Even so, vigilance is essential. Deserts are dangerous places and not all is what it seems."

Asmira was staring at the moon. It was a thin crescent now, and shone bright above the ridge. The sight gave her a sharp knot in her stomach. "We made good progress today," she said. "Will we reach Jerusalem tomorrow?"

The camel-master adjusted his paunch slightly and shook his head. "The day after, if all goes well. But tomorrow evening I shall relax, for by then we will be drawing near the city. No desert demons will dare attack us under good Solomon's kind and watchful eye."

In the firelight Asmira saw the towers of Marib burning. The knot in her stomach broke asunder. "Good?" she said harshly. "Kind? These are not descriptions *I* had heard of Solomon."

"Indeed?" The camel-master raised his eyebrows. "What have you heard?"

"That he is a cruel warlord, who threatens weaker nations!"

"Well, there are many tales told about him," the camel-master

124

admitted, "and I dare say not all of them are to his credit. But you will find many in this company who believe differently than you; they come to Jerusalem to seek his charity, or ask him to sit in judgment on difficult matters. No? You do not believe me? Ask them."

"Perhaps I will."

As night descended and the flames rose high, Asmira fell into conversation with the person sitting beside her at the fire. He was a spice merchant bound for Tyre, a young man, bearded, with a quiet and courteous manner. "You have been very silent, miss," he said. "I have scarcely heard a word from you all journey. Might I ask your name?"

Asmira had long ago decided to avoid all mention of her real name and nationality, and had spent much of the journey devising an alternative. "I am called Cyrine."

"Where do you travel from?"

"I am a priestess of the Temple of the Sun in blessed Himyar. I travel to Jerusalem."

The merchant stretched his boots out nearer to the flames. "Himyar? Where's that?"

"South Arabia." Himyar was in fact a small coastal kingdom west of Sheba, notable for goats, honey, and its general anonymity, which is why Asmira had chosen it. She had never been there, and she doubted many other people had either.

"What is your business in Jerusalem, to have come so far?"

"I wish to see King Solomon. Our kingdom needs his help." Asmira fluttered her eyelashes a little, and sighed prettily. "I hope it will be possible to gain audience with him."

"Well, Solomon has daily councils, they say, where he listens to anyone who comes." The merchant drank deeply from his wineskin. "Couple of farmers near Tyre, they had a beetle plague a year ago. Went to Solomon. He sent his demons; they killed the beetles. Problem solved. That's what having a magic ring can do for you. Want some wine?"

"No, thank you. Daily councils, you say? You think I could get in?"

"Oh yes. Pretty girl like you, I'm sure there's every chance." He gazed out into the dark. "I suppose, what with you coming from Arabia, you've not stopped here before."

Asmira was thinking about what to do when she arrived in Jerusalem. She would go to the palace and request immediate audience at the next day's council. They would bring her before the king. And then, when she was standing before him, and they were waiting for her to make some groveling request, she would step forward, throw back her cloak and . . .

Expectation burned like fire across her chest; her palms tingled with it. "No," she said absently, "I've never been to Israel."

"No, I mean *here*." He gestured to the sandstone ridge above. "This place."

"Never."

"Ah!" He smiled. "You see atop that spur, where a single column of sandstone rises? That's a famous local landmark. Know what it is?"

Asmira roused herself, looked up. The column was certainly peculiar, its strata bulbous and contorted, with several stunted protrusions at the summit. As she looked, the sun's last rays, running like scarlet water down its flanks, almost seemed to give it form . . .

"That, they say, is the afrit Azul," the merchant said. "A slave of Solomon in the early years of his reign. He tried to destroy the magic Ring, or so the story goes, and such was the result.

Turned to stone and never moved again!" He turned aside and spat into the fire. "Good thing too, I say. Look at the *size* of him. Must be twenty-five feet tall."

Asmira stared at the lowering pillar, conscious of a sudden numbness in her bones. She shivered; the night seemed newly chill. The rock rose up *so* high. It seemed almost to merge into the stars. And what was that? Could she see the traces of a vast and brutal face among the shadows near the top. . . . ?

No. The wind and sand had done their work. The undulating surface no longer held expression.

Drawing her cloak around her, she shuffled closer to the fire, ignoring further questions from the merchant at her side. Her stomach had turned to water, her teeth felt loose in her mouth. The fierce exultation in her heart had gone, snuffed out as if by a giant hand. All at once she truly understood the implications of what she was about to do. The scale of the transformed demon, its solid, blank immensity, brought home to her what all the fireside tales had not: the sheer contemptuous power of the man who wore the Ring.

On the morning of the tenth day, the camel train reached a place where the sandstone hills pressed close upon the road. The upper reaches of the cliffs were bathed in sun; down in the gorge, where the camels walked, the light was gray and cool.

Asmira had slept badly. The wave of fear that had broken over her the night before had drained away, leaving her dull and sluggish and irritated with herself. Her mother would not have reacted so to a simple lump of stone, nor would the queen expect it of her champion now. She sat hunched upon the camel, weighed down with gloomy thoughts.

The gorge grew tight about the road; on the right-hand side

the slope had collapsed into a mess of stones. Listlessly surveying the desolation, Asmira caught sight of something small and
brown perched among the boulders. It was a desert fox, with
large, black-tufted ears and gleaming eyes, sitting on a rock,
watching the camel train go by.

Her camel slowed to negotiate the rough ground, and for a
moment Asmira came level with the fox. She was right alongside
it, just a few feet away. If she had wished, she could almost have
leaned out from her couch and touched it. The fox showed no
fear. Its round black eyes met hers.

Then the camel moved on, and the fox was left behind.

Asmira sat very still, feeling the slow swaying of the camel
under her, listening to its tireless pad, pad, pad amid the silence
of the gorge. Then, with a gasp, she took her whip from its
holster in the saddle and, wrenching on the reins, forced her
camel onward at a run. Her sluggishness was gone; her eyes
were bright. Her hand sought the dagger hilt beneath her cloak.

The master was four camels farther up the gorge, and Asmira
drew level only with difficulty.

"Speed up! We need to speed up!"

The master stared. "What is it? What's the matter?"

"Your imps—set them loose! Djinn too, if you have them
—there's something here."

He hesitated only a moment, then turned to shout an order.
As he did so, a ball of blue-black flame hit his camel from the
left-hand side. There was an explosion of dark blue fire; the
master and his camel were blown horizontally across the road
and dashed upon the rocks. Asmira screamed, throwing up
her hands against the buffet of burning air. Her camel reared
in terror; she fell back, almost plunging from the saddle, then
swung out sideways, clinging to the reins. Her outstretched hand

caught hold of a pole upon her canopy; she hung to it, half-dangling above the ground. The camel plunged and bucked. Craning her neck desperately from where she hung, Asmira glimpsed dark forms wheeling in the sky. Bolts of fire rained down upon the road.

Other explosions sounded, and screams and panicked shouts. Buffets and echoes rebounded through the gorge, seeming to come from every side. Smoke blocked her vision. Her camel sought to turn, but another explosion behind made it lurch back toward the cliff. Pulling savagely on the reins with one hand and wrenching at the pole with the other, Asmira drew herself upright, narrowly escaping being crushed against the stones. Grasping the pommel of her saddle, she brought the silver dagger from her belt.

Somewhere amid the smoke, black shapes thudded down to land upon the road; men and animals screamed in pain and terror. Asmira clung to her maddened camel, staring all around. Wresting control of it at last, she backed away through swirling darkness to press close against the shelter of the overhanging walls. Here she crouched, while bolts of fire went ripping past, and the shouts of the dying sounded, removing two more daggers from her bag. She pulled the silver necklace from her robes, let it hang loose upon her breast.

Movement in the smoke, a silhouette: something inhuman questing near. Asmira took swift aim and loosed a dagger. There was a gargling cry, a brief, dull flash. The shape was gone.

She held another weapon ready. Time passed; the smoke began to lift.

A second shape came bounding up the road. As it drew level, it paused; the head had turned. Asmira, stiffening, raised her knife in readiness; her blood beat against her ears.

The cloud parted. A creature with a reptile's head burst forth, a bloodied scimitar whirling in its three-clawed hand.

Asmira clutched her necklace and spoke a Ward of force. Yellow disks of light shot down and hit the creature, which flinched back, but did not retreat. It looked up at her, grinning, and slowly shook its head. Then it bent its legs and sprang at her, mouth gaping pinkly in delight.

14

Peace and quiet. That's one thing to be said for deserts. They give you a chance to get away from the everyday pressures of life. And when those "everyday pressures" consist of seven furious djinn and one apoplectic master magician, a few hundred thousand square miles of sand, rock, wind, and desolation is exactly what you need.

Three days had passed since my uncomfortable encounter with Solomon back at Jerusalem; time enough, one might reasonably feel, for water to run under bridges, tempers to become soothed, and bad moods to ease gently into calm introspection.

But had they? Not a hope.

Khaba was livid, of course—that was to be expected. The king had belittled and humiliated him in front of his peers, and his cushy existence at the palace had been replaced, for the moment, with bandit-hunting on the open road. Though it's true he wasn't exactly slumming it—he traveled by flying carpet, complete with cushions, grapes, and a chained foliot holding a parasol, and at night slept in a black silk tent complete with couch and incense bath—you could see he felt it deeply, and blamed me.[1]

The curious and disconcerting thing, though, was that

---

[1] You could tell this by the little evil looks he flashed, and his overall *froideur* when I passed by. Subtle clues, yes, but I'm a sensitive sort and I spotted them. The regular occasions when he shook his fists and cursed my name by all the death gods of Egypt only served to back up my theory.

beyond a few initial scourgings back on the building site, Khaba
hadn't actually *punished* me much for my misdemeanor. This was
so out of character that I found myself getting jumpy; I kept
expecting his wrath to fall upon me when I least expected it,
and as a result expected it all the time. I watched him and his
shadow obsessively, but nothing nasty came my way.

Meanwhile, my fellow djinn were cross with me as well,
indignant that the safe and predictable routines of life at the temple had been replaced with combing the arid badlands in search
of dangerous djinn to fight. I tried to argue that outlaw-killing
was far better suited to our ferocious talents than building work,
but was by turns shouted down, insulted, and plain ignored.
Xoxen, Tivoc, and Beyzer refused to speak to me at all, and the
others were decidedly snippy. Only Faquarl, who had loathed
the quarry, showed any disposition to sympathy. He contributed
a few acerbic comments, but otherwise left me alone.

The first two days were uneventful. Each morning Khaba
emerged from his tent, berated us soundly for our failings, uttered
random threats, and packed us off in all directions. Each evening,
having crisscrossed the skies from dawn to dusk, we returned
empty-handed to face his censure. The desert was large and our
enemy elusive. The brigands, whoever they were, lay low.

On the afternoon of the third day I was the phoenix again,
flying high above the southern trade routes. The town of Hebron
had passed beneath, and Arad. Not far to the east I caught the
mirror flash of the great Salt Sea, where bones of ancient cities
lay bleaching by the shore. Ahead rose the mountains of Edom,
gateway to yet vaster wastes, and at their feet a low, dark purpled
mass: the waterless desert of Zin.

The spice road here was a thin brown vein in the dirt, spooled between the lifeless ridges. If I followed it long enough, I would arrive at last at the Red Sea, and the trading depots where caravans converged from Egypt, Sheba, even distant Nubia and Punt. But *my* business lay close by.

As I circled, my dark eye flashing as it turned against the sun, I caught an answering gleam below. It came from a track just off the main highway, a path winding toward a village in the hills. The gleam was definite, and warranted investigation.

Down I dropped, enjoying the wind in my plumage and the simple freedom of the air. All in all, things weren't *so* bad. I was alive, I was aloft, I was away from that wretched building site. True, I had some "monsters" to track down and slay, but when you're a swashbuckling djinni of more than average talent who's survived the battles of Qadesh and Megiddo, and who (more to the point), has been cooped up in Jerusalem with some of the most irritating entities ever to squeeze inside a pentacle, a bit of a scrap is precisely what you need.

I was too late for the scrap *here*, though. It had been and gone.

Even while I was in the air, I could see the devastation on the little track. The ground was charred and blistered, and stained with something dark. Fragments of cloth and wood had been strewn over a wide area. I smelled old horror: spent magic, sundered flesh.

The gleam I'd seen turned out to come from a broken sword blade lying on a rock. It wasn't alone. Parts of its owner lay nearby.

As I landed, I turned into the handsome young Sumerian, dark-eyed and watchful. I stood and looked around. The remains of several carts were clearly visible, their wood split and blackened, their wheels smashed. The rocks of the cliffs on either side had sad, limp things scattered on them. I didn't look closely. I knew what they were.

One of the victims was lying in the center of the road, a splintered shield beside him. His arms and legs were spread out casually, almost as if he slept. I say *almost* advisedly, since he lacked a head. He, like his colleagues, had been robbed as well as murdered—the contents of the carts were gone. This was bandit work for sure, and it was recent. I guessed I was one day behind them at the most. They might still be near.

I walked a little way up the winding track, listening to the wind whispering in the rocks, studying the ground. In general the dirt was too hard and compacted to reveal footprints, but in one place, where something—perhaps a waterskin—had been punctured and the dirt made briefly wet, I found the deep impression of a triangular, three-clawed foot. I bent low and studied it a while, then rose and turned to go back the way I'd come.

And froze.

Below me, the track curled off to the right, following a steady gradient down. Twenty or thirty yards away, just beyond the area where the attack had happened, it disappeared from view behind the valley wall. The cliffs on the left-hand side were abrupt and sheer, and brightly lit from above by the noonday sun. Every detail upon them—each rock, each fissure, the slow pink twist of the tangled strata—was picked out for me in perfect detail.

As was Khaba's shadow.

The outline of his bald head was thrown in sidelong silhouette upon the sunlit cliff. I saw the smooth dome shape, his long, beaked nose, the jut of his bony chin; his bulky shoulders and upper arms were visible too, but his lower half was lost in the tumbled rocks of the valley floor. It was as if the magician himself stood just out of sight around the bend in the road, facing uphill toward me.

I stared at the apparition. The head upon the rocks stayed perfectly still.

I took a slow step back, and immediately the head began to flow forward around the curve of the cliff, rippling over its contours like dark water. As it came, it grew; and now its long thin arms rose into sight, with its long, thin shadow-fingers stretching out toward me.

My backward steps were somewhat faster now; I stumbled on the uneven ground.

Still the shadow grew and stretched—a long, black arch with clutching hands, its face elongated, its chin and nose protruding to grotesque proportions, its great mouth opening wide, wide, wide...

I gathered myself, stood fast; I let flame ignite between my fingers.

There was a flapping noise in the air above.

The shadow started; the questing fingers drew back in doubt. At incredible speed it fled back across the cliffs, shrinking, reducing, returning to its original position. Now it shrank still further and was gone.

Someone coughed behind me. Spinning around, a Detonation flaring at my fingertips, I saw a broad, plump Nubian lounging on a rock, studiously brushing flight-ice off his arms with taloned fingers while regarding me with detached amusement. He wore wings in the traditional style of Mesopotamian djinn—feathered, but split into four like those of beetles.

"Bit jumpy, Bartimaeus?" Faquarl said.

I gazed at him dumbly. Wheeling round again, I stared back

along the road. The cliffs were quiet and still—silent planes of light and shadow. None of the shadows had familiar form. None of the shadows moved.

The blue fire coursing between my fingers fizzled and went out. I scratched my head uncertainly.

"Looks as if you found something interesting," Faquarl said.

Still I didn't say anything. The Nubian walked past me, surveying the devastation on the road with a few sweeps of his practiced eyes. "Not like you to get put off by a little bit of blood and sand," he remarked. "It's not pretty, admittedly, but it's not exactly Qadesh, is it?[2] We've seen worse."

I was still shaken, looking all around. Except for a few scraps of fabric flapping pathetically among the rocks, nothing stirred anywhere at all.

"Doesn't look like anyone survived. . . ." Faquarl came to the mutilated corpse in the center of the road and nudged it with a sandal. He chuckled. "Now then, Bartimaeus, what have you been doing to this poor fellow?"

I came to life then. "That was how I found him! What are you suggesting?"

"It's not for me to judge your little habits, Bartimaeus," Faquarl said. He stepped close and patted me on the shoulder. "Calm down, I'm only joking. I know you wouldn't devour a dead man's head."

I nodded tersely. "Thank you. Too right."

---

[2] *Battle of Qadesh*: Major engagement between the Egyptians under Ramses the Great and the Hittites under King Muwatallis back in 1274 B.C.E. Faquarl and I had fought in separate divisions of the pharaoh's armies, and helped carry out the final pincer movement that drove the enemy utukku from the field. Many great deeds were done that day, not all of them by me. Two centuries later, the battlefield was still a blackened waste, a field of bones.

"You prefer a juicy buttock, as I remember."

"Quite. Much more nutritious."

"Anyhow," Faquarl went on, "the wounds are clearly old. Been lying there the best part of twenty-four hours, if I'm any judge of dead men."[3]

"The magic's cold too," I said, surveying the scattered debris. "Detonations, mainly—fairly high-powered ones, though there were a few Convulsions here and there. Nothing too sophisticated, but very brutal."

"Utukku, you think?"

"I'd say so. I found a footprint: bulky, but not big enough to be an afrit."

"Well, we've got a scent at last, Bartimaeus! I'd suggest going back to tell our master right away, but let's face it—he's unlikely to want to hear anything from *you*."

I glanced about me once more. "Speaking of Khaba," I said quietly, "I had an odd experience just now. When you came down, you didn't happen to see anything else here with me?"

Faquarl shook his gleaming head. "You seemed just as isolated as ever, if slightly more jittery. Why?"

"Only I thought I had Khaba's shadow after me—" I stopped myself, cursed. "Not thought, *know*—it was creeping after me along the gorge. Just now! Only when you turned up, it scarpered."

Faquarl frowned. "Really? This is bad."

"Tell me about it."

"Yes, it means technically I may have saved you from a nasty fate. *Please* don't tell anyone about this, Bartimaeus. I've got a reputation to maintain." He rubbed his chin meditatively.

---

[3] He was.

"Odd, though, that Khaba should move against you out here," he mused. "Why not back at camp? Why the secrecy? It's an intriguing little problem."

"I'm glad you feel that way," I snarled. "Personally speaking, it's a bit more urgent than that."

The Nubian grinned. "Well, what can you expect? In all honesty, I'm surprised you've survived this long. Khaba's got a grudge against you after that hippo debacle. And then, of course, there's the ongoing issue of your personality. That's two good reasons to bump you off for starters."

I stared at him askance. "My personality? Meaning what?"

"How can you even ask the question? I've been around the ziggurat a few times, Bartimaeus, but I've never known a spirit like you. Ghuls[4] are bad enough, skrikers[5] likewise—they may all have appalling habits, but by Zeus, at least they don't talk out of turn so loudly, or cheek their betters the way you do. Let's face it; just the sight of you is enough to drive any reasonable spirit insane."

Whether it was my recent shock, or the smug expression on his face, my temper snapped. Blue flames flared between my fingers; I stepped in fury toward him.

Faquarl gave an indignant snort. Shards of green lightning crackled about his pudgy hands. "Don't even *think* about it. You haven't got a chance."

"Is that so, my friend? Well, let me tell you—"

I halted; my fires died suddenly away. At the same time

---

[4] *Ghul*: a lowly class of djinni, a frequenter of cemeteries, a devourer of unburied morsels.

[5] *Skriker*: an unpleasant subtype of imp, with large flat feet and creeping tread. Follows travelers in lonely places, whispering and calling, and drives them to their death.

Faquarl let his hands fall back. We stood silent on the road, facing each other, listening hard. We could both detect the same sensation: an almost imperceptible shivering on the planes, with every now and then a faint, decisive thud. It was familiar and it was not far off.

It was the noise of djinn being summoned.

As one, we leaped into the air, our quarrel forgotten. As one, we changed. Two eagles (one plump, unsavory; one a paragon of avian grace and beauty) rose up between the cliffs. We circled high above the wastes, which shimmered brown and white beneath the sun.

I checked the higher planes, where colors are more muted and less distracting, and gave a caw of triumph. Away to the south, distant luminosities moved upon the ground. The lights —evidently those of several spirits—were closing in on where the spice road passed among some barren hills.

Without a word the eagles banked their wings. Side by side, we shot south toward the road.

15

Soon afterward two bearded travelers could be seen trudging forth upon King Solomon's highway. One was young and handsome, the other thick-set and disheveled; both were stained with the sand of many miles. Each wore a dyed wool robe and had a heavy pack slung across his shoulders. They supported their steps with staffs of oak.

Trudge, trudge, hobble, hobble—that was Faquarl and I doing our best to project an aura of human vulnerability. To cloak our actual potency, we'd made the change on five planes, and used Glamours to shield our true natures on the other two.

Shoulders drooping with weariness, the men scuffed southward through the dust and watched the dark hills draw in on either side. Here, as we'd judged while still aloft, were cliffs and overhangs that offered opportunity for ambush, if you were that way inclined.

Faquarl and I had decided on an ambush of our own.

Somewhere above were the hidden djinn we'd glimpsed from afar, but for the present we saw no sign of them. Everything was still, save for two vultures drifting slowly in and out of view against the sky. I snatched a look at them. Genuine, as far as I could tell. I lowered my gaze; on we went, step by weary step.

In the middle of the range of hills, the cliffs receded a little and the road entered a wider defile, surrounded by scree slopes topped with jagged spurs of basalt.

For the first time, the lonely and ever so vulnerable travelers stopped. Faquarl made a pretense of fiddling with his pack. I pulled at my beard, looked all around me with narrowed eyes. Quietness.

Grasping our staffs more tightly, we set off again along the way.

From behind, somewhere remote among the cliffs, came a tiny rattling of stones. Neither of us turned our heads.

At our backs sounded a skittering of pebbles, louder, halfway down the scree. Faquarl scratched his bulbous nose. I whistled tunelessly as I walked along.

A heavy thud sounded on the road, the click of claws on rock. Still we trudged on, weariness itself.

And now came the rasp of scales. The stench of sulphur. A sudden swath of darkness filling the ravine. A cackle of demonic—

All right, now *was* probably the time.

Faquarl and I spun around, beards jutting, staffs raised, ready to attack—and saw nothing.

We looked down.

There at our feet stood the smallest, most rubbish foliot we'd ever set eyes on, frozen guiltily mid-path with one foot raised. It wore the terrifying guise of a shrew in a baggy tunic. In one furry paw it carried a weapon that resembled a toasting fork.

I lowered my staff and gazed at it. It goggled back with its big brown eyes.

On all seven planes the shrew looked the same, though to be fair on the seventh it *did* have a set of fangs. I shook my head in wonder. Could *this* be the hideous monster that had carried out such rapine on the desert road?

"Hand over your valuables and prepare for death!" squeaked the shrew, flourishing its fork. "Make haste, if you please. There is a camel train approaching the other way, and I wish to dispose of your bodies and join my fellows."

Faquarl and I glanced at one another. I held up a hand. "Please, if I may: one question. In whose name do you act? Who summoned you?"

The shrew's chest swelled. "My master is employed by the king of the Edomites. Now hand over your goods. I don't want blood all over them."

"But Edom is a friend to Israel," Faquarl persisted. "Why should its king seek to rebel against great Solomon?"

"This would be the same Solomon who demands a vast yearly tribute from the king, so that his treasury is emptied and his people groan beneath the burden of their taxes?" The shrew gave a shrug. "Were it not for the Ring he wears, Solomon would find Edom rising against him in war. As it is, we must be content with simple banditry. Well, so much for international relations; we come now to your sad demise. . . ."

I smiled negligently. "First, a detail. Check out the planes." So saying, I made a subtle change. On the first plane I was still a dusty traveler leaning on his staff. On the higher planes, however, the man was gone, and I was something *other*. Faquarl had done likewise. All at once the shrew's fur went gray and bristled stiff and upright on its body. It shivered so violently that its fork began to hum.

The shrew sidled backward. "Let's talk about this. . . ."

My grin broadened. "Oh, I don't think so." I made a gesture; my staff was gone. From my outstretched hand a Detonation roared. The shrew sprang sideways; the earth at its feet exploded in crimson fire. Mid-leap, the shrew jabbed its fork; from the tip came a frail green shaft of light that raked across the ground, stabbing Faquarl's toe unpleasantly. He hopped and cursed, threw up a Shield. The shrew hit the ground with a squeak and darted away. I peppered its wake with a string of Convulsions that sent avalanches tumbling up and down the gorge.

The shrew sprang behind a boulder, from where its paw protruded at intervals, wielding the toasting fork. Further green bolts rained down on us, hissing and spitting against the edges of our Shields. Faquarl sent a Spasm whirling; the boulder shattered, became a heap of gravel. The shrew was blown backward, fur smoldering. It dropped its fork. With a high-pitched oath, it leaped for the scree and began to climb.

Faquarl gave a cry. "You go after it—I'll cut it off on the other side."

Hands smoking, robe and beard whipping around me, I vaulted onto a tumbled slab, jumped to an adjacent ledge, bounded up the slope from stone to stone. With my feet hardly touching the rocks, I quickly homed in on the desperate blur of brown that zigzagged ahead of me up the scree. Lightning crackled from my fingers; it drove down into the earth, propelling me upward even faster.

The shrew reached the top of the slope, and for a moment was outlined furrily against the sky. At the last instant it ducked away; my Detonation missed it by a whisker.

From my back I sprouted wings—each feathered, pure white, divided in two like those of a butterfly.[1] They flexed into life; over the buttery crest of the dust-dry hill I soared, so the sun's warmth burst upon my essence. Down below me was the shrew,

---

[1] Bit of a contemporary look, this: it was the latest thing in Nimrud that century. The white feathers were a drag during combat—they didn't half show up stains —but made you resemble a celestial being: fearsome, beautiful, cold, aloof. This was particularly useful when out hunting humans, who were often so busy gaping at you they quite forgot to run.

stumbling, plunging down an undulating ridge of ground. Not far beyond I saw a rough encampment of tents, four of them set in a little hollow, surrounded by store-piles, the blackened remnants of a fire, three bored camels tethered to an iron post, and many other spoors and scatterings.

The owners of all this were three men (presumably the Edomite magicians, though to be honest all the tribes of the region looked the same to me), clad in robes of brown and caramel, with walking staffs in hand and dusty sandals on their feet. They stood in the shadow of the tents, as still as statues, in postures of calm attention, looking away from us toward the opposite side of the ridge, which abutted another curve of the desert road.

The shrew's yelps alerted them: spinning around, they saw his tumbling approach and, farther off, my implacable, avenging form hurtling from the heavens.

The men cried out; they scattered. One cried out a spirit's name. From the ravine beyond came an answering call, deep and urgent.

Now things were getting interesting.

Down from above I plunged, giving vent to all the pent-up fury of my slavery. From my fingers a succession of fiery bolts strafed left and right into the ground. Stone shattered, dirt and sand burst against the bright blue sky. The shrew was hit finally in the center of his furry back, blasting him into a thousand plaintive motes of light.

Two hulking shapes rose from the gorge beyond. Both, like me, were winged in the bifurcated Assyrian style; both, like me, wore human bodies. *Unlike* me, they had chosen rather more exotic heads, the better to spread terror to their victims on the road.

The nearest, an utukku with a lion's face, carried a bloodied spear.[2] His comrade, whose head resembled that of an unpleasantly jowly, loose-skinned monitor lizard, preferred a scimitar; with horrid cries and feathered wings beating at the air, they flew toward me at speed.

I would kill them if I had to, but I preferred to kill their masters.[3]

The Edomite magicians had each acted according to his nature. The first had panicked, spinning this way, then that, before finally tripping over his trailing robe and falling into the side of the nearest tent. Before he could regain his balance my Detonation expunged him in a ball of flame. The second stood his ground: from a bag beside the fire he drew a long, thin tube of glass. As I swooped toward him, he broke the tube against a rock and pointed the broken end at me. A cord of oily black substance emerged, swung lazily back, then darted out like a fisherman's cast in my direction. I projected a Dark Node, which caught the center of the smoky cord and, with a rude sucking noise, pulled it inward into nothing. After the cord came the glass tube and the magician who held it: in the blink of an eye they too were sucked into the Node, which promptly ingested itself and so vanished.

Upon the death of the Edomite, which came a few short

---

[2] Clearly the shrew, whatever its many faults, had not lied to us. Other travelers were currently being waylaid below.

[3] This is a generally sound principle. When forced into sudden battle with another spirit, you have no way of assessing their character. They may be repugnant and loathsome, or genial and pleasant, or any combination in between. The only certain fact is that they would not be fighting you were it not for the charge put upon them, and thus it makes sense to expunge the master and spare the puppet. In the case of the utukku, of course, it was safe to assume they had the morals of two ferrets fighting in a bag, but even so, the principle remained.

moments after his disappearance into the Node,[4] the lion-headed utukku gave a joyous cry, became a resinous vapor and dissipated on the wind. The lizard-headed utukku, clearly the servant of the third magician, still remained; flourishing his scimitar, he interrupted my flight path with a series of violent hacks and thrusts that I struggled to avoid.

"Why couldn't you have killed my one?" the utukku said, slashing at my midriff.

I spun aside, darted, rolled over in midair. "I'm doing my best. Would you mind not trying to impale me in the meantime?"

The utukku dodged my Spasm; slashed with the scimitar. "It doesn't work that way."

"I know."

Evading the next attack by inches, I careened to the left and banked close to Earth; shooting between two tents, I rose again, scanning the ridge for the third magician, and was just in time to catch a flash of brown and caramel beginning a hurried descent into the ravine.

With murderous intent, and the utukku laboring behind, I followed the Edomite over the lip of the ridge, drifting like a hawk or other raptor following its mouse.

There he was, slipping and scrabbling down among the rocks, his robe hitched up about his knees, his sandals torn away. His face was tilted downward, fixed in concentration on the slope. Not once did he look over his shoulder: he knew his death followed hard behind him on bright, white wings.

Beyond and below him, on the road, I glimpsed several other

---

[4] This curious time delay always occurs in such cases. I sometimes wonder what, in those fleeting seconds, the victim's consciousness *sees* or *experiences* inside the Node, alone in that infinity of nothing.

things: the sturdy form of Faquarl wrestling with a third utukku (this one with the head of a long-horned goat); two others lying dead beside him; and all around the remains of slaughter —camels and humans scattered like discarded rags across the blackened ground.

A buffet of air; I twisted sideways just too late, and felt a burst of pain as the utukku's scimitar cut through one wing-tip, sheared off a few primary feathers, and utterly ruined my delightful symmetry. My balance went; my aerodynamics like-wise. I tumbled to the scree below, landed inelegantly on my back, and began to roll downslope.

The utukku came in fast, ready to commit the *coup de grâce*. To delay him (and this is not easily done when rolling at speed —try it yourself if you don't believe me) I fired an Enervation over my shoulder. It hit him straight on, sapping his energies and making his movements treacly and sluggish. He dropped the scimitar. Wings drooping, limbs working listlessly, he fell to the ground and began tumbling in my wake.

We rolled downhill amid an avalanche of stones.

We fell onto the packed earth of the desert road.

We struggled into sitting positions.

We looked at each other, we each raised a hand. I was the quicker. I blew him apart with a Detonation.

Pieces of his essence fell to Earth, spattering the death-dry rocks and stones like refreshing rain. I struggled to my feet in the center of the road, brushing dust from my bumps and bruises, letting my wings uncrumple, my battle lust subside.

Over to my left, Faquarl, having finally disposed of his goat-headed antagonist, was slowly, painfully doing likewise. Essence glistened brightly from a deep cut across his midriff, but he seemed otherwise unharmed.

Not bad going. Between us, we had dealt with five utukku and two of the three Edomite magicians.[5] The bandit danger on Solomon's roads was decisively dealt with for now.

Which reminded me. That *third* magician... Where—?

A voice, high and imperious, spoke close by. "Demons, do not move or speak but by our command, save only to prostrate yourself in abasement before the High Priestess of the Sun in the blessed land of Himyar. I am my queen's representative and speak for her and all of Himyar, and I demand of you your names, identities and nature, on pain of our extreme displeasure."

Is it just me, or would a simple "Hello" have been enough?

---

[5] Plus the shrew. But I'm not really sure you can count him.

16

It wasn't that I hadn't *noticed* we had company. It was just that I hadn't cared. When you're in the middle of a fight, you stick to the basics, namely trying to disembowel your enemy while stopping him tearing off your arm and beating you around the head with it. If you've any energy left over, you use it for swearing. Prostrating yourself before watching strangers doesn't feature highly in the program. Particularly when it's *them* you're saving.

So I took my time here, flicking the desert dust off my limbs and inspecting remote regions of my essence, before turning to see who'd spoken.

Not twelve inches away, a face regarded me with an expression that mingled arrogance, derision, and the hope of obtaining grassy foodstuffs. This was a camel. Following its neck upward, I discovered a couch of red and yellow silks set upon its saddle. Tasseled drapes hung below it; above, slumped on broken poles, there swung a canopy, now sadly burned and torn.

On the couch sat a young woman, little more than a girl. Her black hair was drawn back and mostly hidden by a silken headscarf, but her eyebrows were elegant and quizzical, her eyes as black as onyx. Her face was slim, its structure graceful, her skin-tone dark and even. A human might have accounted her beautiful. My expert eye also detected signs of willfulness, high intelligence, and stern resolve, though whether these qualities added to her beauty, or detracted from it, is not for me to say.

This girl sat straight-backed upon her camel-couch, one hand resting on the forward pommel of acacia wood, the other loosely holding the beast's reins. She wore a hempen riding cloak, stained ochre from the desert storms, and singed in places by utukku fire; also a long woolen garment, woven with geometric designs in yellow and red. This was wrapped tight about her torso and more loosely about her legs. She rode sidesaddle, her feet neatly encased in little leather shoes. Bronze bangles hung upon her slim, bare wrists. Around her neck she had a silver pendant, shaped like a sun.

Her hair was slightly disordered—a few strands had fallen across her face—and she had a small fresh cut beneath one eye; otherwise, she seemed none the worse for her ordeal.

This all takes a lot longer to recount than it did to observe. I stared at her for a moment. "Who spoke," I said, "you, or the camel?"

The girl frowned. "It was I."

"Well, you have a camel's manners." I turned aside. "We've just killed the utukku who were attacking you. By rights you should be on your knees thanking us for your deliverance. Wouldn't you say so, Faquarl?"

My associate had at last drawn close, tentatively prodding at his gaping chest wound. "That goat!" he grumbled. "Gored me with a horn just as I was strangling the other two. I ask you. Three against one! Some djinn haven't the slightest conception of common courtesy. . . ." He noticed the girl for the first time. "Who's this?"

I shrugged. "A survivor."

"Any others about?"

We surveyed the forlorn wreckage of the camel train scattered about the gorge. All was silent, all was still, apart from a couple of riderless camels wandering in the distance, and some vultures circling lazily. No other survivors met the eye.

Someone else I couldn't see was the fugitive Edomite magician. It struck me suddenly that he would be useful to bring
back to Jerusalem alive. Solomon would be interested in hearing
firsthand the reasons for the bandits' activities. . . .

The girl (who still hadn't thanked us) was sitting on her
couch, regarding Faquarl and me with her big dark eyes. I
addressed her curtly. "I'm looking for one of the bandits who
attacked your party. Came springing down the rock-face here.
You must have seen him. Mind telling me which way he went
—*if* it isn't too much trouble?"

With a languid gesture, the girl indicated a large granite
boulder on the opposite side of the road. Two feet projected
from behind it. I hurried over to discover the Edomite lying
there, a silver-bladed dagger protruding neatly from the center
of his forehead. The silver's aura made me nauseated; nevertheless, I shook him anxiously, in case he was just dazed. It was no
good. Bang went the live witness I was hoping to take back to
Solomon.

I looked toward the girl, hands on hips. "Did you do this?"

"I am a priestess of the Temple of the Sun in blessed Himyar.
That man's demons destroyed my fellow travelers. Should I have
let him live?"

"Well, a little bit longer would have been nice. Solomon
would have wanted to meet him." Annoyed as I was, I looked
at the girl with a certain grudging respect. Priestess of the Sun
or not, skewering a moving target without getting off her camel
wasn't bad going, though I had no intention of admitting it.

Faquarl had been regarding the girl as well, in a rather
thoughtful manner. He nodded in her direction. "Where did
she say she was from?"

The girl overheard; she spoke in ringing tones. "I say again,

O demons, that I am a priestess of the Sun and representative of—"

"She's from Himyar."

"Where's that?"

"Arabia someplace."

"—the Great and Royal House of Himyar! I speak for the queen and all her people, and we demand—"

"I see...." Faquarl beckoned me aside. We moved off a little way. "I've been thinking," he said softly. "If she's not an Israelite, then she's not covered by the protective clauses, is she?"[1]

I rubbed my beardy chin. "True...."

"And she's not set foot in Jerusalem, either."

"No."

"Plus she's young, she's *appetizing*—"

"Demons! I demand a word!"

"*Very* appetizing," I agreed. "Good set of lungs on her too."

"And since, Bartimaeus, since we're both a little *jaded* after all our hard work—"

"Demons! Attend to me!"

"Since we're both, I might go so far as to say, a little *peckish*—"

"Demons—"

"Hold on a minute, Faquarl...." I turned to address the Arabian girl. "Would you mind not using that word?" I called.

---

[1] At Solomon's behest every summons in Jerusalem, made by no matter which magician, included within it certain strict clauses forbidding us to harm the local population. This wasn't anything new in principle—all the old city states of Mesopotamia had used similar injunctions—but *they'd* been confined to citizens by birth, so there was always the possibility of snacking on a visiting trader, slave, or captive on the side. Solomon, in his wisdom, had expanded the clauses to include *anyone* who set foot within the city walls, which made for an admirably inclusive municipal environment, and also a good number of grumpy, hungry djinn.

"'Demon' is an extremely pejorative term.[2] It offends me. The correct way to address either of us would be something along the lines of 'Revered djinni' or 'Masterful spirit.' All right? Thank you."

The girl's eyes opened wide, but she said nothing. Which was a relief.

"Sorry, Faquarl. Where were we?"

"We were both a little peckish, Bartimaeus. So, what do you say? No one's going to *know*, are they? Then we can fly back to our master and bask in our triumph. We'll all be on Temple Mount by nightfall, sitting cozily around the fire. Meanwhile Khaba will be restored to Solomon's good graces, and he'll call off that shadow of his and save your sorry skin. How's that sound to you?"

It didn't sound at all bad, particularly the bit about the shadow. "All right," I said. "Bagsy her haunches."

"Now *that's* not fair. Who killed more utukku today?"

"You can have the pick of the rest of her. And I'll throw in the camel, too."

Bickering pleasantly, we turned back toward the girl, to discover her looking down upon us from on high with an expression so thunderous that even Faquarl flinched. She had pulled her shawl back from her head, so that her hair fell loose about her slender neck. Her face was fearsomely serene. Her slim arms were tightly folded, her fingers tapped pointedly upon her sleeve. Slight as she was, with badly singed clothes and disheveled hair,

---

[2] *Demon*: the actual term used at this juncture was in fact the Old Akkadian word *rābisu*, which in its origin simply means "supernatural being." But as with the Greek daimon (still several centuries in the future), it was all too often employed as an abusive generality, as likely to refer to a pimple-bottomed imp as to a debonair djinni-about-town.

sitting as she undoubtedly was upon an ugly camel beneath a sagging canopy, she *still* had enough force of personality to bring us both up short.

"Exalted spirits," she said, in a voice of iron, "I thank you both for your intervention in this present disaster. Without your timely aid I would most certainly have perished, like these unfortunate merchants who were my recent companions. May their souls ascend most speedily to the Sun God's realm, for they were peaceful men! But now hear my words. I am an envoy and sole representative of Himyar's queen, traveling in haste to Jerusalem to speak with Solomon of Israel. My mission is of paramount importance. Great matters hinge upon its success. I therefore dema—I *request* that you assist me, that I may complete my journey at best speed. Aid me in this, and I shall come before your masters, whoever they may be, asking that they free you from your present servitude and send you back to the great abyss[3] from whence you came." She raised a hand toward the sky. "Before the Sun God and the sacred memory of my mother, this I hereby vow!"

There was a resounding silence. Faquarl rubbed his hands together. "Right," he said. "Let's eat her."

I hesitated. "Hold on—didn't you hear what she said about winning us our freedom?"

"Don't believe a word of it, Bartimaeus. She's human. She's a liar."

---

[3] *Great abyss*: not the most accurate or flattering description of the Other Place that I've ever heard, but a very common misconception. In fact our home is nothing like an abyss, having no depth to speak of (nor any other dimensions), and not being at all dark either. It's just like humans to impose their own imagined terrors upon us, when in fact all true horrors are found in *your* world.

"She's human, yes . . . but she's got something about her, don't you think? Reminds me a bit of Nefertiti."[4]

"Never met her," Faquarl sniffed. "I was in Mycenae then, if you recall. Anyhow, who cares? I'm hungry."

"Well, I think we should wait," I said. "She could intercede with Khaba—"

"*He's* not going to listen to her, is he?"

"Or Solomon, maybe . . ."

"Oh, right. Like she's going to get anywhere near *him*."

This was all probably true enough, but I was still irritated with Faquarl for his comments earlier that afternoon, and that made me stubborn. "Another thing," I said. "She'll be a witness to our fight."

Faquarl paused, but shook his head. "We don't need a witness. We've got bodies."

"She called us 'exalted spirits.' "

"Like *that* makes any difference!" Faquarl gave an impatient growl and made a side step in the girl's direction, but I moved slightly to block his way. He pulled up short, eyes bulging, tendons flexing in his jaw. "This has always been your trouble!" he snarled. "Getting all softheaded over a human just because she's got a long neck and a steely eye!"

"Me? Softheaded? I'd eat her soon as look at her! But she might be able to help us, that's my point. *Your* problem is you can't control your appetites, Faquarl! You'd eat anything that moves—girls, stench-mites, mortuary imps, the lot."

---

[4] *Nefertiti*: principal wife of the pharaoh Akhenaten, 1340s B.C.E. Started out bringing up the children, ended up running the empire. Looked damn good in a headdress too. Let's just say you didn't mess with her.

"I've never eaten a mortuary imp."[5]

"I bet you have."

Faquarl took a deep breath. "Are you going to let me kill her?"

"No."

He threw his hands up in disgust. "You ought to be ashamed of yourself! We're *slaves*, remember—slaves of humans like that girl there. Will they ever do us a good turn? No! Building sites and battlefields—that's all they've wanted us for, ever since Ur.[6] And it'll never end, Bartimaeus, you know that, don't you? It's a war between us and them—and I mean *all* of them, not just the magicians. All those dough-brained farmers, their clasping wives, their snotty, squalling children—they're just as bad as Khaba and the rest. This girl's no different! They'd happily cast us into the Dismal Flame without a thought, if they didn't always want new walls built, fields dug, or need some other tribe of brainless humans killed!"

"I don't deny any of that," I cried. "But we've got to be practical about chances that come our way. And this *is* a chance. You don't want to go back to the quarry any more than I do, and it's just possible that this girl might—Oh, *now* where are you flouncing off to?"

---

[5] *Mortuary imp*: small, pudgy, white-skinned spirits employed by the priests of Egypt to help them mummify the bodies of the great and good. Specializing in all the icky bits of the process, such as brain removal and filling up the canopic jars, they tasted abominably of embalming fluid. So I've been told.

[6] *Building sites and battlefields*: sometimes, indeed, we were forced to hop between one and the other at a moment's notice, which could be inconvenient. I once fought three kusarikku single-handedly in a sudden skirmish at the gates of Uruk. They wielded spiked maces, flaming spears, and double-headed silver battle-axes. Me? I had a trowel.

Like an irritable toddler,[7] Faquarl had spun around and marched away. "You like her so much," he called, "you stay with her. You keep her safe. I'm off to fetch Khaba, and we'll see if she can magic us up our freedom. Maybe you'll be proved right, Bartimaeus. Or just maybe you'll come to regret not feasting on her while you can!" So saying, he spun a cloak of scarlet flame about his wings and sprang into the sky, and with a final oath that caused small avalanches to tumble down the lonely gullies, rose up to meet the sun.

I turned to stare at the silent girl.

"Well," I said. "It's just you and me now."

---

[7] Only bigger, brawnier, and more bloodstained.

17

"Well," the demon said. "It's just you and me now."

Asmira sat rigid in her saddle, feeling the sweat trickling down the back of her neck. Her heart was pounding so hard against her ribs she felt sure the demon must see it, or at least notice the trembling of her hands, which she had placed in her lap for that very reason. *Never let them see your fear*—that was what the guard-mothers had taught her; let your foes think you nerveless, resolute, impossible to daunt or threaten. She did her best to keep her face impassive, and hold her breathing as steady as she could. With her head coolly turned aside, she kept her eyes trained on the creature's every movement. Her fingertips rested on the dagger hidden beneath her robes.

She had seen a glimpse of its power when it had destroyed another of its kind with a blast of explosive fire, and she knew that, if it chose, it could easily kill her, too. Like the monsters that had attacked her in the gorge, it was clearly far more dangerous than the spirits she had summoned during her training or the petty demons of the hill-tribes. It was probably an afrit of some kind; perhaps even a marid. Silver was her best defense now; her Wards might irritate it, but would do little more.

Not that the demon wasn't irritated already. It glanced up into the sky, where its companion had become a fiery dot on the horizon, and uttered a soft curse. With its sandaled foot it kicked a stone far off across the gorge.

Asmira knew well enough that higher spirits could adopt any shape they chose, the better to beguile or dominate those around them. She also knew how foolish it was to take heed of how they looked. Yet this one gave her pause. Unlike the horrors that had attacked the caravan, unlike its own companion—which had seemed to delight in exuding a swaggering ferocity—this spirit concealed its wickedness beneath a pleasant form.

When it had first tumbled into view, it had been a bearded traveler, badly stained with marks of battle. At some point since (and she had not noticed exactly when the change occurred) it had subtly transformed into a young, fair-featured youth, with dimpled cheeks and merry eyes. Its hair fell in curled black ringlets about its brow, and its limbs were hale and strong. Something of its cast of face and skin reminded Asmira of the men of Babylon who visited the Sheban courts, but the style of its clothes was simpler than theirs—just a plain, wrapped knee-length skirt, and necklaces of amethyst upon its naked chest. On its back was a pair of white wings, neatly folded and very magnificent. The largest feathers were longer than her forearms. On the edge of the left-hand wing a soft gelatinous substance hung limp and raw, glistening coldly in the afternoon light. Other than this imperfection, the guise was very beautiful.

Asmira watched the winged youth, her heart thumping in her breast. Suddenly it turned its head, and its eyes met hers. She looked away, and immediately felt furious with herself for doing so.

"I hope you can deliver on your promise, O Priestess of Himyar," the youth said. "I've put my essence on the line for you."

Asmira had not understood the argument between the demons, which had been conducted only partly in Arabic, and partly in languages that were unknown to her. Forcing herself to meet the dark, cool gaze, she kept her voice as imperious as before. "Where has it gone?" she said. "The other demon? And what of my request?"

The youth raised a languid eyebrow. "Dear me. That naughty word again."

It stepped suddenly toward the camel. In a flash of movement, Asmira's silver-bladed dagger was out of her belt and balanced in her hand.

The youth stopped short. "*Another* knife? How many have you got in there?"

Asmira had lost one dagger during the chaos of the battle, and had left another in the Edomite. She had two more in her leather bag. She said haughtily, "That is none of your concern, demon. I asked you—"

"And *I* asked," the creature said, "if you'd refrain from using bad language in my company. Whipping daggers from your knickers isn't wildly polite either." It laid a dark hand upon her camel's flank and patted it gently. "How about you put the thing away? I can feel the silver's chill from here, particularly in this wing of mine. This wing that I wounded just now," it added pointedly, "in defense of *you.*"

Asmira hesitated, numb with indecision, panic roiling in her stomach. Stiffly, she lifted her cloak and tucked the dagger back into her belt.

"That's better," the demon said. "Oh, and you've a silver disk dangling about your neck. . . . Mind tucking that away too?"

Asmira did so. The winged youth said no more. Giving the camel a final pat, it walked a few yards off and stood survey-ing the gorge. After a while it began whistling the notes of a rhythmic dervish song.

Anger at her own compliance, and at the demon's cheery indifference to her questions, almost made Asmira retrieve the dagger and throw it at its back. But she kept her face calm and forced the fury down. The creature was associated with Solomon, and might yet be of use to her. Any chance of getting swiftly to Jerusalem must be pursued.

Besides, it was true what it said—it *had* come to her aid. "You must forgive my caution, O spirit," she called. "Without my defenses I would be dead. Please understand I keep them ready at my side."

The young man glanced over; the keen dark eyes appraised her. "Helped ward off the utukku, did they? I was *wondering* how you survived."

"Yes," she said. "My dagger saved me. A lizard dem—a lizard *spirit*, I mean—leaped at me, but I slashed out at it, and the silver took it by surprise. It jumped back, and was about to attack again, when it suddenly got distracted and disappeared."

The winged youth chuckled. "Ah yes, that would have been *me* arriving. Perhaps you saw the blind panic on its face?"

In Asmira's experience demons were not very intelligent. This one's self-satisfaction was so evident that she sought to take advantage. "I did indeed!" she said quickly. "And I can only apologize that I did not thank you the instant you arrived. I was still distressed by the assault, and did not realize I was speaking with one of the great ones of the air. May the Sun God chastise me that I was blind to your radiance! But I perceive it now. I say again that you have delivered me most nobly from death and I am forever in your debt! I thank you humbly from the bottom of my unworthy heart."

The young man gazed at her and raised one eyebrow in an ironic fashion. "Do they always speak like this in Himyar?"

"Usually we are less emotional and employ a more formally complex sentence structure."

"Really? Well, I'm used to complex stuff, so I could follow what you said just now. But I warn you, around this part of the world, they wouldn't be able to cope with much apart from that bit about your unworthy bottom."

Asmira blinked. "My unworthy heart."

"That too, I should think. Well now, in answer to your questions, you don't have to worry anymore. Faquarl's gone to fetch our master, who will doubtless escort you to Jerusalem as you requested. If, in return, you could intercede with him and win our freedom, we would be very much obliged. Lately our servitude under Solomon has been getting rather grating."

Asmira's heart quickened. "Solomon himself is your master?"

"Technically no. In practice, yes." The young man scowled. "It's complicated. Anyway, the magician will be here soon. Perhaps you could spend the time rehearsing a few gushing tributes on my behalf."

Whistling, the demon moved off slowly among the scattered debris of the camel-train. Asmira watched it, thinking hard.

Ever since the adrenaline of battle had ebbed inside her, she had been fighting to keep control of herself and her surroundings. To begin with, shock had fogged her mind—shock at the sudden ambush, at the destruction of the men with whom she had traveled for so many days, at the hideous vigor of the lizard demon and the way it had withstood her Ward. At the same time, she had had to face down Solomon's spirits, concealing the fear she felt for *them*. This had not been easy, but she had succeeded. She had survived. And now, as she observed the demon, she felt a sudden fierce surge of hope. She was alive, and her mission was before her! Not only had disaster been averted, Solomon's servants were actually going to take her straight to him! In just two nights' time, the attack on Sheba would come. Such speed might make all the difference.

Some way off, the demon was pacing back and forth, looking at the sky. It had seemed reasonably talkative, if somewhat proud and prickly; perhaps she should converse with it a little more. As a slave of Solomon it would know many things about the king, about his personality, his palace and—possibly—the Ring.

With a brisk movement she jerked the reins. The camel folded its forelegs and tilted forward, so that it knelt upon the sand. Then it folded its rear ones too. Now it sat; Asmira swung herself off the couch and dropped lightly to the ground. She examined her singed riding cloak briefly, and smoothed it down. Then, leather bag in hand, she walked toward the demon.

The winged youth was lost in thought. Sunlight glinted on the bright, white wings. For a moment Asmira was conscious of its stillness, and the look of melancholy on the quiet face. She wondered what it saw before its eyes. With annoyance she realized her limbs were shaking.

It glanced at her as she approached. "Hope you've thought of some good adjectives for me. 'Ferocious,' 'zealous,' and 'awe-inspiring' all trip off the tongue nicely, I find."

"I've come to talk with you," Asmira said.

The dark brows angled. "Talk? Why?"

"Well," she began, "it's not often I have a chance to speak with such an exalted spirit as you, particularly one who saved my life. Of course I have often heard tell of the great beings who raise towers in a single night, and bring rain upon the famished lands. But I never thought I would actually speak with one so noble and gracious, who—" She stopped; the youth was smiling at her. "What?" she said.

"This 'exalted spirit' thinks you want something. What is it?"

"I hoped your wisdom—"

"Hold it," the demon said. Its black eyes glittered. "You're not talking to some half-baked imp here. I'm a djinni, and a pretty eminent one at that. A djinni, moreover, who built the walls of Uruk for Gilgamesh, and the walls of Karnak for Ramses, and a good many other walls for masters whose names are long forgotten. Solomon the Great is in fact only the latest in a long line of exalted kings to rely heavily on my services. In short, O Priestess of distant Himyar," the young winged man went on, "I've a high enough opinion of myself already not to need any extra flattery from you."

Asmira felt the color come rushing to her cheeks. Her fists clenched against her side.

"Got to get these little things sorted out, haven't we?" the djinni said. It winked at her, and leaned casually back against a rock. "Now, what is it you wanted?"

Asmira regarded it. "Tell me about the Ring," she said.

The djinni gave a start. Its elbow slid sideways off the rock, and it was only with a bit of hasty scrambling that it avoided toppling out of view. It adjusted its wings with much ruffling of feathers, and stared at her. "What?"

"I've never been to Jerusalem before, you see," Asmira said artlessly, "and I've heard so many wonderful tales of great King Solomon! I just thought that since you were so *eminent* and so *experienced*, and since Solomon relies so *heavily* upon you, you might be able to tell me more."

The djinni shook its head. "Flattery again! I keep telling you—" It hesitated. "Or was it sarcasm?"

"No, no. Of course not."

"Well, whichever it was," the young man growled, "let's have less of it, or, who knows, I might just go along with Faquarl's little suggestion."

Asmira paused. "Why, what *was* Faquarl's little suggestion?"

"You don't want to know. As to the object to which you refer, I know you're only a simple girl from the backside of Arabia, but surely even *there* you must have heard—" It looked cautiously up and down the gorge. "The point is, in Israel it's best not to discuss certain subjects openly, or indeed at all."

Asmira smiled. "You seem fearful."

"Not at all. Just prudent." The winged youth seemed out of sorts now; it scowled up at the dark blue sky. "*Where's* Khaba gotten to? He should have been here long since. That fool Faquarl must have gotten lost or something."

"If Faquarl's the name of the other djinni," Asmira said lightly, "then *your* name—"

"Sorry." The djinni held up a resolute hand. "I can't tell you that. Names are powerful things, both in the keeping and the losing. They should never be bandied around, either by spirit or human, since they are our deepest, most secret possessions. By my name I was created long ago—and he who learns it has the key to my slavery. Certain magicians undertake great trials for such knowledge—they study ancient texts, decipher the cuneiform of Sumer, risk their lives in circles to master spirits such as me. Those who have my name bind me in chains, force me to cruel acts, and have done so for two thousand years. So you can perhaps understand, O maiden of Arabia, why I take good care to ensure my name is kept safe from others that I chance to meet. Do not ask me again, for it is forbidden knowledge, sacrosanct, secure."

"So it's not 'Bartimaeus' then?" Asmira said.

There was a silence. The djinni cleared its throat. "Sorry?"

"Bartimaeus. That's what your friend Faquarl kept calling you, anyway."

There was a muttered curse. "I think 'friend' is putting it a trifle strongly. That *idiot*. He would insist on having an argument in public. . . ."

"Well, you keep using his name too," Asmira said. "Besides, I'm going to need to know your name if I'm to intercede with your master, aren't I?"

The djinni made a face. "I suppose so. Well, let *me* ask a question now," it said. "What about *you*? What's your name?"

"My name is Cyrine," Asmira said.

"Cyrine. . . ." The djinni looked dubious. "I see."

"I am a priestess of Himyar."

"So you keep saying. Well, 'Cyrine,' why all this interest in dangerous things, like small pieces of golden jewelry we can't discuss? And what exactly are these 'great matters' that bring you to Jerusalem?"

Asmira shook her head. "I cannot say. My queen forbids me to discuss them with anyone but Solomon, and I have taken a sacred vow."

"*Aren't* we prim and proper, all of a sudden?" the demon said. It regarded her sourly for a moment. "Strange that your queen should have sent a lone girl on such an important mission. . . . Then again, that's queens for you. They get ideas. You should have *heard* Nefertiti when the mood was on her. So . . ." it went on idly, "Himyar. Never been, myself. Pleasant spot, is it?"

Asmira had not been to Himyar either and knew nothing about it. "Yes. Very."

"Got mountains, I suppose?"

"Yes."

"Rivers and deserts and things?"

"Lots."

"Cities?"

"Oh, a few."

"Including the Rock City of Zafar, delved straight into the cliffs?" the demon said. "That's in Himyar, isn't it? Or am I wrong?"

Asmira hesitated. She sensed a trap and didn't know the answer that would avoid it. "I never discuss particularities of my kingdom with an outsider," she said. "Cultural reticence is one of the traditions of our people. But I *can* discuss Israel and will do so gladly. You know King Solomon and his palace well, I assume?"

The winged youth was gazing at her. "The palace, yes... Solomon, no. He has many servants."

"But when he summons you—"

"His *magicians* summon us, as I think I've said. We serve their will, and they serve Solomon's."

"And they are happy to serve him because of the—" This time Asmira did not say the word. Something of Bartimaeus's trepidation had infected her, too.

The djinni spoke shortly. "Yes."

"So you are all in thrall to it?"

"I and countless others."

"So why do you not destroy it? Or steal it?"

The djinni gave a noticeable jump. "Shh!" it cried. "Will you keep your voice *down*?" With hasty movements it craned its neck back and forth, peering along the gorge. Asmira, reacting to its agitation, looked too, and for a moment thought the blue shadows of the rocks seemed rather darker than before.

"You do *not* talk about the object in such terms," the djinni glowered. "Not here, not anywhere in Israel, and certainly never in Jerusalem, where every second alley-cat is one of the great king's spies." It rolled its eyes to the skies and continued quickly. "The object to which you refer," it said, "is never stolen because he who wears it never takes it off. And if anyone even *thinks* of trying anything in that regard, that same aforesaid person just twizzles the object on his finger and—*pop!*—his enemies end up like poor Azul, Odalis, or Philocretes, to mention but three. *That* is why no one in their right mind dares defy King Solomon. *That* is why he sits so vain and untroubled upon his throne. *That* is why, if you wish to live to undertake these 'great matters' you hint at, you will avoid loose talk and curb your curiosity." It drew a deep breath. "You're all right with *me*, Priestess Cyrine from Himyar, for I despise those who hold me captive, and will never alert them even if something—or *someone*" (here it looked at her directly, and raised its eyebrows again) "arouses my deep suspicions. But I am afraid you will find that others do not share my fine moral character." It pointed to the north. "Particularly *that lot*," it said. "And, needless to say, you'll find the human is the worst of all."

Asmira looked where Bartimaeus pointed. A group of distant flecks was fast approaching, dark against the evening sky.

18

Perhaps, if the djinni had not alerted her, Asmira might first have taken the objects in the sky for a flock of birds. If so, her error would not have lasted long. To begin with, they were nothing but black dots—seven of them, one slightly larger than the rest—flying in close formation high above the desert hills. But then those dots grew rapidly, and soon she saw the wisps of colored light that danced along their rushing surfaces, and the heat haze that shivered in their slipstream.

In moments they had dropped to begin the descent toward the gorge, and now she perceived that the fleeting wisps of color were darts of flame that made each object flash golden in the dying light—all save the largest and most central, which remained coal-black. Closer still they came; now Asmira caught the movement of their wings and heard the distant thrumming noise they made, a sound that quickly swelled to fill her ears. Once, as a little child, she had watched from the palace roof a locust plague descend upon the water meadows below the walls of Marib. The roaring that she heard now was like that distant insect storm, and brought similar apprehension.

The formation dropped below the level of the cliffs and came toward her, following the road. It moved at great speed; with its passing, clouds of sand were sucked into the air, curling out against the hillsides, filling the gorge behind. And now Asmira could see that six of the seven objects were demons, winged, but in human shapes. The seventh was a carpet carried by yet another demon; sitting on this carpet was a man.

Asmira stared at him, at his entourage, at the onrushing display of casual power. "Surely," she whispered, "this is Solomon himself...."

Beside her, the djinni Bartimaeus grunted. "Nope. Guess again. This is just one of Solomon's seventeen master magicians, though perhaps the most formidable of them all. His name is Khaba. I say again, beware of him."

Sand swirled, the wind howled, giant iridescent wings slowed their beating; six demons halted in midair, hovered briefly, dropped lightly to the road. In their center, the seventh shrugged the carpet off its shoulders onto its great spread arms; bowing low, it retreated backward, leaving the carpet hanging unsupported a few feet above the ground.

Asmira stared at the silent row of demons. Each wore the body of a man seven or eight feet tall. Save for the one named Faquarl (still stubbornly stocky, bull necked, and pudgy around the waist, and scowling as it looked at her), all were muscular, athletic, dark of skin. They moved gracefully, deftly, confident in their supernatural strength, like minor gods let loose upon the Earth. Their faces were beautiful; their golden eyes gleamed in the dimness of the gorge.

"Don't get too worked up," Bartimaeus said. "Most of them are idiots."

The figure on the carpet sat motionless, straight-backed, cross-legged, hands folded calmly in his lap. He wore a hooded cloak, clasped tightly about him to protect his body from the rigors of the upper air. His face was shadowed, his legs covered in a rug of thick black fur. His long, pale hands were the only part of him exposed; now they unclasped, thin fingers snapped, a word was spoken in the depths of the hood. The carpet dropped to Earth. The man removed the fur and, with a single fluid movement, sprang to his feet. Stepping off the carpet, he walked toward Asmira swiftly, leaving his group of silent demons behind him.

Pale hands pushed back the hood; a mouth stretched wide in welcome.

To Asmira the magician's appearance was almost more disturbing than that of his slaves. As if in a dream she saw two big, moist eyes, deep scars notched upon his ashen cheeks, thin smiling lips as tight as gut-strings.

"Priestess," the magician said softly. "I am Khaba, Solomon's servant. Whatever sorrows and terrors have beset you shall be no more, for you are come into my care."

He inclined his bald head toward her.

Asmira bowed likewise. She said, "I am Cyrine, a priestess of the Sun in the land of Himyar."

"So my slave informed me." Khaba did not look back at the line of djinn; Asmira noticed that the burly demon had folded its arms and was regarding her skeptically. "I am sorry that I have kept you waiting," the magician continued, "but I was a great distance away. And, of course, I am all the more sorry that I was not able to prevent this . . . atrocious attack upon you." He waved a hand at the desolation all around.

Khaba stood rather closer to her than Asmira would have liked. He had a curious odor about him that reminded her of the Hall of the Dead, where the priestesses burned incense to the memory of all mothers. It was sweet, pungent, and not entirely wholesome. She said, "I am grateful to you even so, for your servants saved my life. One day soon, when I return to Himyar, I will see to it that you benefit from the gratitude of my queen."

"I regret I am not familiar with your land," the magician

said. The smile upon his face did not alter; the big eyes gazed into hers.

"It is in Arabia, east of the Red Sea."

"So . . . not far from Sheba, then? It is a curious fact that all the lands thereabouts seem to be ruled by women!" The magician chuckled at the quaintness of the notion. "My birthplace, Egypt, has occasionally flirted with such things," he said. "It is rarely a success. But, Priestess, in truth I can claim no honor for saving you. It was my king, great Solomon himself, who demanded that we clear the region of these outlaws. If you owe thanks to anyone, it is to him."

Asmira gave what she hoped was a charming smile. "I would wish to give that thanks in person, if I can. Indeed, I travel to Jerusalem on royal business, and crave an audience with Solomon."

"So I understand."

"Perhaps you could assist me?"

Still the smile remained fixed, still the eyes gazed at her; Asmira had not yet seen them blink. "Many wish audience with the king," the magician said, "and many are disappointed. But I think your status and—if I may say so—your great loveliness will commend you to his attention." With a flourish he turned aside, looked back toward his slaves. The smile vanished. "Nimshik! Attend to me!"

One of the great entities scampered forward, grimacing.

"You shall be in charge of the other slaves," Khaba said, "with the exception of Chosroes, who carries me as before. We will escort this lady to Jerusalem. Your tasks, Nimshik, are as follows. You will clear the road of the corpses and the debris. Bury the fallen, burn the camels. If there are further survivors, you will treat their wounds and bring them to the Gate of the

People at the palace—along with any such goods or animals that remain intact. You understand?"

The hulking figure hesitated. "Master, Solomon forbids—"

"Fool! The brigands are destroyed; you will have his permission to return. When all is done, await me on the roof of my tower, where I shall issue new instructions. If you disappoint me in any of this, I will skin you. Be off!"

The magician turned to Asmira, his smile as broad as ever. "Priestess Cyrine, you must excuse the stupidity of my slaves. Regretfully, a magician must associate with such things, as perhaps you know."

"Certain of the elder priestesses speak occasionally with spirits, I believe," Asmira said demurely. "I know nothing of it."

"Ah, I should hope not, a pretty wisp like you...." For a heartbeat's space the big soft eyes looked Asmira up and down. "But do not be afraid of my creatures," Khaba said, "for I have them thoroughly in my power, bound with sturdy magic chains, and all fear my kindest word. Now, if—"

He halted, frowning. From somewhere close came a tinkling of bells. A gust of wind, carrying with it a sharp, pungent smell, stirred Asmira's headscarf and made her cough.

Khaba made a courteous gesture. "Priestess, I am sorry. Excuse me just a moment."

He spoke a word; three heartbeats passed. A purplish cloud bloomed like a flower in the air above them. Reclining on it, legs casually crossed, and with knobbly hands clasped behind its head, was a small, green-skinned demon. "Evening, Master," it said. "Just thought I'd—" It noticed Asmira and assumed an expression of extravagant surprise. "Ooh, you've got company. Nice. Well, don't let me stop you." It settled itself back in its cloud.

"What do you want, Gezeri?" Khaba said.

"Don't mind me. It can wait. You keep on nattering."

The magician's smile remained, but his voice was dangerous. "Gezeri..."

"Oh, very well." The little demon scratched industriously at an itch in its armpit. "Just to say it's *all okay*. The old girl's cracked at last. She's begun gathering the stuff, and—"

"Enough!" Khaba cried. "We do not need to bore our guest with tedious matters such as this! I will talk to you later. Return to my tower at once!"

The demon rolled its eyes. "Can I? Really? Oh, how lovely." So saying, it clapped its hands and vanished.

Khaba touched Asmira on the arm. "Priestess, forgive me. If you will now accompany me to my carpet, I will see to your comfort on the short flight to Jerusalem."

"Thank you. You are very kind."

"*Ahem.*" There was a small cough to Asmira's left. The djinni Bartimaeus, who had been waiting unremarked a short way off, had cleared his throat behind an upraised hand.

"Slave," Khaba intoned, "you shall rejoin the others. Obey Nimshik and work with zeal! Priestess Cyrine, please..."

Bartimaeus gave a series of little knowing winks and smiles. He bobbed and gestured. He coughed louder, looking pointedly in Asmira's direction.

"Are you still here?!" Khaba thrust aside his cloak and reached for a long-handled whip hanging in his belt.

Until that moment Asmira's awe at the demons' arrival, and her excitement at the prospect of reaching Jerusalem, had driven thoughts of her original promise from her mind. But now, spurred on by the djinni's evident desperation and also by a sudden revulsion for the magician standing at her side, she recalled her vow—and found she had to act. She had, after all, sworn it by the Sun God, and by her mother's memory.

"O great Khaba," she said, "a moment, please! This djinni, and that other who accompanied him, have performed a noble service to me. They saved my life, I do believe, and I entreat that in return they may be released from their bonds."

She smiled encouragingly. Over in the line of demons, the portly djinni took a few hesitant steps forward. Bartimaeus had frozen where he was, mid-supplication, eyes flicking from her to the magician and back again.

For the first time Khaba's own smile faltered; his hand stayed on his whip.

"Released...? Dear Priestess, you are an innocent indeed! It is the nature of all slaves to perform such services. They cannot and should not expect freedom for every small success they have. Demons in particular must be treated with a heavy hand."

"But these djinn—" Asmira said.

"Believe me, they shall get their due reward!"

"A reward that should surely be—"

"Priestess"—the thin smile had returned; it was wider than before—"dear Priestess, this is not the time or place. Let us discuss such things later, when we are at leisure at the palace. I promise I shall hear you out then. Will that satisfy you?"

Asmira nodded. "Thank you. I am grateful."

"Good. Come then! Your transport awaits...."

Khaba gestured with a long, pale arm; Asmira shouldered her leather bag and proceeded with him toward the waiting carpet, and the silent demons moved back to let them pass. Neither then, nor as the carpet ascended into the air, did she look back at Bartimaeus; indeed, in moments she had forgotten all about him.

★ ★ ★

The distance to Jerusalem was forty miles, and would have taken the camel train a further day; Asmira and the magician covered the distance in a little under an hour.

The demon that transported them was out of sight beneath the carpet, though Asmira could hear the creaking of its wings and, sometimes, muttered swear words. It kept a smooth and level course high above the darkening Earth, once or twice dropping awkwardly as it met a downdraft over some ridge of hills. On such occasions, the magician cracked the whip over the edge of the carpet, spurring the slave to better efforts with fizzing yellow bands of light.

Some invisible protective shell encased the carpet, for the wind that howled around them in the darkness did not engulf them with full force, and the carpet's central section was spared the ice that crystallized on the rearmost tassels. Even so, it was chilly. Asmira sat with her bag upon her lap and the magician's cloak around her shoulders, feeling the violent undulation of the frail cloth beneath, trying not to imagine the fall should the demon decide to shrug them off. The magician sat alongside her, naked to the waist, calm, cross-legged, staring ever forward. Somewhat to her relief he did not look at her, nor attempt further conversation—this would have been impossible anyway, thanks to the roaring of the wind.

Night fell during their time aloft. Far to the west Asmira saw the sun's red tail staining the horizon, but the lands below were black beneath the stars. Far off gleamed the lights of settlements she could not have named; it seemed to Asmira that if she had stretched out a hand she might have easily cupped them and snuffed them out.

And then at last Jerusalem was before her, clinging like an

iridescent butterfly to the dark stem of its hill. Watch fires burned on the crenellated ribbon of the outer walls, green witch-lights in the towers strung upon its length. Within its loop spread a thousand smaller flames of humble homes and market stalls, and high atop the summit, presiding over all, the mighty palace of King Solomon blazed with light—as big and magnificent and invulnerable as all the stories said. Asmira felt her mouth going dry; in the secret warmth of her cloak, her hidden fingers touched the dagger at her belt.

They descended steeply; a moment later there was a sudden beat of leather wings and a presence in the darkness beside them. Fires flared in a gaping throat; a guttural voice called out a challenge. Asmira's skin crawled. Khaba scarcely looked up, but made a certain sign, and the watcher, satisfied, fell back into the night.

Asmira shrank down deeper into her cloak, ignoring the sickly-sweet mortuary scent that clung to it. Truly was it said that the great king's city was well protected—even in the air, even in the night. Queen Balkis, as in all things, had been quite right. An army could not have entered Jerusalem, nor yet an enemy magician.

But *she*, Asmira, was doing precisely that. The Sun God was watching over her still. With his grace and blessing, she would survive a little longer to do what must be done.

Her stomach lurched; her hair lifted high above her. The carpet swung down toward the palace. As it crossed the walls, a blast of horns sounded from the palace ramparts, and all around came the thunderous concussions of Jerusalem's gates closing fast for the night.

19

"What did I tell you, Bartimaeus?" Faquarl said. "Gone without a backward look."

"I know, I know."

"Jumped up beside Khaba, quick as a wink, and off they go together. And are we freed?" added Faquarl bitingly. "Look around you."

"She tried," I said.

"Well, she didn't try very hard, did she?"

"No."

"It was a cursory effort at best, wasn't it?"

"Very."

"So, don't you wish we'd eaten her now?" Faquarl said.

"Yes!" I cried. "All right, I do! There, I've said it. Are you happy now? Good! Stop rubbing it in."

It was far too late to ask for *that* little favor, of course. Faquarl had been rubbing it in for hours. During the entire cleanup operation he'd been on at me, in fact, even while we were digging the burial pits, even while we were piling up the camels and trying to get them to light. He'd never stopped all this time. It had ruined my afternoon.

"You see, humans stick together," Faquarl was saying. "That's how it's always been and that's how it'll always be. And if *they* stick together, that means *we* have to do likewise. Never put faith in any human. Eat them while you can. Isn't that right, lads? " There was a chorus of hoots and cheers from around the tower-top. Faquarl nodded. "They understand what I'm saying, Bartimaeus, so why in Zeus's name can't you?"

He lay back on the stonework idly, twirling his harpoon-tail. "She *was* good-looking in a scrawny sort of way," he added. "I wonder, Bartimaeus, whether you weren't rather influenced by *appearances*. That's a sorry mistake for a shape-shifting djinni to make, if you don't mind my saying."

A crude cacophony all around indicated that the other six imps agreed with his assessment. We were all of us in imp-form at the time, partly because the flat roof of Khaba's tower was too compact to accommodate any larger forms, but mainly because it reflected our pervading mood. There are times when you're happy to manifest yourself as a noble lion, a stately warrior, or a chubby, smiling child; and other times—if you're tired, irritable, and stuck with the smell of burned camel up your nose—when only a scowling, warty-bottomed imp will do.

"You can all laugh," I growled. "I still think it was worth a try."

And oddly enough, I did, though everything Faquarl had said was absolutely true. Yes, she'd made only the feeblest effort to speak up on our behalf; yes, she'd promptly swanned off with our loathsome master without a backward glance. But I couldn't entirely regret saving the Arabian girl. Something about her stuck in my mind.

It wasn't her looks, either, whatever Faquarl might suggest. It was more her air of self-possession, the cool directness with which she'd talked with me. It was the way she listened, too, still and watchful, taking everything in. It was her evident interest in Solomon and his Ring. It was her vagueness regarding

Himyar geography.[1] It was also (and this was not the least of it) the curious way she'd managed to survive the ambush in the gorge. No one else in that whole long camel train was still alive, and *they'd* had djinn-guards and everything.[2]

It was all very well for the girl to claim that her dagger had warded off the utukku for a few crucial moments, but there was more to it than that. For a start, she'd left another in the head of the Edomite magician, which if nothing else proved she was no mean shot. Then there was the *third* dagger I found on the other side of the road, wedged hilt-deep in soft sandstone. It had been thrown with considerable force, but what *really* interested me about it was the very large essence-stain left on the rocks around. True, it was faint and blurry, but my discerning eye could still make out the spread-eagled silhouettes of arms and legs, horns and wings—even the mouth left gaping in faint surprise.

Maybe it hadn't been an utukku, but it had certainly been a djinni of *some* kind, and the girl had dealt with it in no uncertain terms.

There was more to her than met the eye.

Now, I knew a fair bit about priestesses. Ever since I'd served the ferocious Old Priestess of Ur way back in my early years, helping her out in temple rituals, participating (reluctantly) in her mass sacrifices of dogs and servants, burying her at last in

---

[1] The town of Zafar *is* in Himyar, as I knew well, having flown over it several times on my trips to collect roc's eggs for assorted pharaohs. It's not a "rock city," though, but just your usual provincial town, as the girl should definitely have known.

[2] This is called irony. Djinn-guards aren't much cop, if truth be known, being little more than a few flakes of silver attached with catgut to a wickerwork frame. Desert peoples wave them about at a moment's notice to ward off evil influence, and I suppose a particularly feeble spirit might take the hint and leg it. But as far as warding off *real* djinn is concerned, they're about as effective as a chocolate toothbrush. You just keep away from the silver and brain the owner with a rock or something.

a lead-lined, tomb,[3] I'd seen priestesses up close and personal.
And whether they were the well-heeled Babylonian sort, or the
screeching maenads you found capering around Greek bushes,
they were in general a formidable lot—high-level magicians
who were quick to blast a djinni with the essence lance for the
most footling indiscretions, such as accidentally toppling their
ziggurat or laughing at their thighs.

But one thing they *weren't* well known for was their personal
prowess in the heat of battle.

South Arabian priestesses might be different, of course. I
wasn't an expert in the region, and I simply couldn't say. But
whatever the case, it was fair to say that this Priestess Cyrine,
supposedly of the distant kingdom of Himyar, was rather more
intriguing than the average traveler coming to Jerusalem, and I
was somehow glad I'd saved her.

Yet, as Faquarl had pointed out (at interminable length),
my gesture hadn't done us a blind bit of good. Nothing had
changed. She'd gone, we were slaves, and the eternal stars above
us still shone coldly down.[4]

The moon rose higher, and the murmur on the streets below
grew slowly stilled. With the gates of the city long since
closed, the night markets were shutting now, and the people
of Jerusalem trudged home to rest, recuperate, and renew the

---

[3] Despite her protests, it has to be said.

[4] In its profound infinity the canopy of stars echoes the measureless expanse of the
Other Place. On clear nights many spirits are often found sitting on mountain crests
or palace rooftops, staring at the heavens. Others fly fast and high, swooping and
circling, so the tumbling lights begin to resemble the fluid wonder of our home.
...I sometimes used to do this, back in the days of Ur, but the melancholy soon
affected me. Now, more often, I avert my eyes.

fabric of their lives. Oil lamps flickered in the windows, Solomon's imp-lights illuminated each corner, and from across the mosaic of rooftop ovens drifted the odors of mutton, garlic, and fried lentils, all of which smelled a good deal better than burned camel.

High on Khaba's tower the circle of imps had finished whooping, jeering, and flicking their tails in my direction, and were considering moving on to a discussion of the influence of religion on regional politics in the east Mediterranean littoral, when there was an odd squeaking sound in our midst.

"Nimshik, have you been at the pickled mites again?"

"No! That wasn't me!"

For once the truth of his words was borne out by the sight of a heavy flagstone tilting upward in the center of the roof. From beneath appeared a pair of gleaming eyes, a nose like an unripe eggplant, and the distasteful upper portions of the foliot Gezeri, who squinted evilly all around.

"Bartimaeus and Faquarl!" he called. "Look lively! You're wanted."

Neither of us moved an inch. "Wanted where?" I said. "And by whom?"

"Oh, by His Royal Majesty King Solomon the Great, of course," the foliot said, leaning his bony elbows casually on the roof. "He wishes you to attend him in his private apartments in order to thank you personally for your sterling work today."

Faquarl and I shuffled at once into more attentive positions. "Really?"

"Noooooo, of course not, you idiots!" the foliot cried. "What would Solomon care about *you*? It's our master, Khaba the Cruel, what wants you. Who else would it be? And," he went on cheerfully, "he don't want you in the summoning room neither, but down in the *vaults* below the tower. So it don't look good for either of you, does it?" he leered. "There's not many goes down *there* comes swiftly up again."

An uncomfortable silence fell upon the rooftop. Faquarl and I looked at each other. The other djinn, caught between horror at the implications and immense relief that it wasn't them, studied their claws intently, or considered the stars, or began industriously picking at bits of lichen between the flagstones. None of them wanted to catch our eyes.

"Well, what are you waiting for?" Gezeri cried. "Step to it, the pair of you!"

Faquarl and I rose, ducked stiffly beneath the flagstone, and with the eager energy of two criminals shuffling to the gallows, set off down the stairs. Behind us, Gezeri lowered the stone once more, and we were left in darkness.

Khaba's tower, being one of the tallest in Jerusalem, was composed of many levels. The exterior was whitewashed and on most days blazed with light; the interior, mirroring its owner's personality, was altogether less radiant. Hitherto, the only bit I'd seen firsthand was the magician's summoning room on one of the upper floors—we passed this almost immediately as we spiraled ever downward, me first, Faquarl next, Gezeri's big flat feet slapping on the stones behind. Other doors went by, then a broad passage that presumably led to the ground floor entrance, and *still* we descended into the Earth.

Faquarl and I didn't say much as we went. Our thoughts had strayed to the tortured spirit we'd seen in Khaba's sphere, a ruined thing kept in the vaults below the tower.

Now, perhaps, we were to join it.

I spoke with false heartiness over my shoulder. "No need to

worry, Faquarl! We dealt with the bandits well today—even Khaba must see that!"

"Whenever I'm lumped in with you, I worry," Faquarl growled. "That's all there is to it."

Down, down, down the staircase curled, and despite my best intentions, my jollity didn't stick. Maybe it was the sour and musty air, maybe it was the deepening darkness, maybe it was the candles flickering in the mummified grasp of severed hands that had been fixed on spikes at intervals along the walls, maybe it was my imagination—but I felt a definite unease as I progressed. And then the staircase ended suddenly before an open doorway of black granite, through which a dim blue-green light pulsed steadily, carrying with it certain *sounds*. Faquarl and I stopped dead, our essence crawling.

"In there," Gezeri said. "He's waiting."

There was nothing for it. The two imps squared their knobbly shoulders, stepped forward, and entered Khaba's vaults.

No doubt, if we'd had the time and the inclination, there would have been many curiosities to observe in that dreadful place. The magician clearly spent much time there, and had invested great effort in making himself feel at home. The vast carved stones of the floor, walls, and ceiling were of Egyptian style, and so were the squat, rather bulb-shaped columns that held the ceiling blocks in place. Add the carvings of papyrus flowers at the topmost points of every pillar and the clinging smells of incense and natron, and we could have been in one of the catacombs beneath the Karnak temples, rather than somewhere deep below Jerusalem's busy hill.

Khaba had outfitted his workroom with tools and magical adjuncts in great profusion, as well as an impressive pile of scrolls and tablets looted from civilizations already gone. But what really caught the eye as we entered was neither the imposing décor, nor all this paraphernalia, but the evidence of this man's more private hobbies.

He was interested in death.

There were a great many bones piled all about.

There was a cabinet of skulls.

There was a rack of mummies—some clearly ancient, others very new.

There was a long, low table bearing sharp metal tools, little jars, pots of pastes and unguents, and a rather bloody cloth.

There was a mummification pit newly filled with sand.

And, for when he'd finished fiddling about with dead humans, and wanted a different kind of plaything, there were the essence-cages too. These were arranged in neat rows in the far corner of the vault. Some were roughly squared, others circular or bulb-shaped, and on the lower planes they seemed to be made of iron mesh, which by itself was bad enough.[5] But on the higher planes their full viciousness was revealed, since each was additionally formed of solid, essence-fraying force-lines that kept their agonized occupants inside. It was from here that the *noises* came—low twitterings and pleadings, occasional feeble cries, snatches of language the speakers could no longer properly recall.

Faquarl and I stood very still, contemplating Gezeri's words. *There's not many goes down* there *comes swiftly up again.*

A voice spoke from the depths of the room, a voice of sand and dust. "Slaves, attend to me."

---

[5] Like silver, *iron* repels all spirits, and burns our essence if we touch it. Most Egyptian magicians wore iron ankhs about their necks as a basic protection. Not Khaba, though. *He* had something else.

The two imps stumbled forward with such painful reluctance you'd have thought we had sharp stones shoved down our loincloths.[6]

In the center of the vault, midway between four columns, was a raised circle in the floor. The circle had a rim of pink-white lapis lazuli, around which Egyptian hieroglyphs spelled out the five master-words of Binding. Within the circle a pentacle of black onyx had been laid. Some short way off, within a smaller circle, stood a lectern made of ivory and, behind it, hunched like a vulture beside its feast, the magician.

He waited as we approached. Five candles had been set around the margins of the raised circle, burning with black flames.

Khaba's wet eyes reflected the evil light. About his feet his shadow pooled like a formless thing.

Faquarl and I scuffled to a halt. We raised our heads defiantly.

Our master spoke. "Faquarl of Mycenae? Bartimaeus of Uruk?"

We nodded.

"I'm going to have to set you free."

The two imps blinked. We stared at the magician.

His long gray fingers caressed the lectern; curling nails tapped upon the ivory. "It is not what I would have wished, foul slaves that you are. You carried out your deeds today solely because of my orders, therefore you deserve no credit. However, the traveler who you saved—a girl who is as ignorant of your vile

---

[6] Incidentally this was an actual punishment meted out by the Xan people of East Africa to corrupt leaders and bogus priests. With their cloths nicely filled, they were forced to crouch in a barrel, which was promptly rolled down a hill to the riotous accompaniment of shekere gourds and drums. I enjoyed my association with the Xan. They lived life to the full.

natures as she is soft and innocent in person"—the gleaming eyes gazed across at us; beyond the pillars the captives in the essence-cages sighed and crooned—"this foolish girl has urged me to dismiss you from my service. She was most persistent." Khaba drew his thin lips tight together. "In the end, I agreed to her request, and since she is my guest and I have sworn it before great Ra himself, it is a sacred vow. Consequently, *much* against my better judgment, I am going to give you your just reward."

There was a pause while Faquarl and I took in the implications of this, ran through the subtleties and nuances of the words, and continued to look up at the magician with expressions of watchful doubt.[7]

Khaba made a dull, dry noise in the back of his throat. "Why so hesitant, slaves? The djinni Faquarl shall be the first to leave my service. Step up, if you will."

He made an expansive gesture toward the circle. The two imps considered it once more and found no obvious traps on any of the planes. "*Seems* genuine," I muttered.

Faquarl shrugged. "We'll soon see. So, Bartimaeus, one way or another, this is farewell. May it be a thousand years before we meet again!"

"Why not make it two?" I said. "But first, before you go, I want you to admit one thing. I was right, wasn't I?"

"About the girl?" Faquarl blew out his cheeks. "Well . . . perhaps you were, but that doesn't change my opinion. Humans are for eating, and *you're* too soft."

---

[7] We were old hands, you see, well aware of the latent ambiguities contained in even the most blandly reassuring sentence. Dismissing us sounded good, naturally, but it needed clarification; and as for us getting our "just reward" . . . in the mouth of someone like Khaba, that phrase was almost an overt threat.

I grinned. "You're just jealous that it was *my* piercing intelligence that got us freed. With just one look, I could clearly see that Cyrine—"

"*Cyrine?* You're on first name terms now?" Faquarl shook his bulbous head. "You'll be the death of me, Bartimaeus, you really will! Once upon a time you sowed destruction and woe upon kings and commoners alike. You were a djinni of terror and of legend. These days, chatting up girls is all you're good for—which I think's a crying shame. Don't bother to deny it. You know it's true." With that, he hopped up onto the pentacle, causing the candles' black flames to hop and judder. "Right," he said to the magician. "I'm ready. Good-bye, Bartimaeus. Think about what I said."

And off he went. No sooner was he in position than the magician cleared his throat and spoke the Dismissal. It was an Egyptian variant of the pithy Sumerian original and therefore a bit long and flowery for my liking, but hard as I listened I could hear nothing untoward. Faquarl's response was everything that could be asked of it, too. As the words finished and the bonds broke, the imp in the circle gave a glad cry, and with a great leap upward vanished from the world.[8] There was a faint reverberation, a moaning from the essence-cages, and silence.

Faquarl was gone. Faquarl was free.

I didn't need to see more. With a vigorous spring the imp jumped into the circle. Pausing only to make an insulting gesture in the direction of Gezeri, who was scowling distantly in

---

[8] Just for a moment, as his essence shrugged off Earth's limitations and became susceptible to the infinite possibilities of the Other Place, seven Faquarls were visible across the planes, each one in a slightly different place. It was an amazing sight, but I didn't look too closely. *One* Faquarl is quite enough.

the shadows, I dusted myself down, set my brow-crest at a jaunty angle and turned to face the magician.

"Right," I called. "I'm ready."

Khaba had been consulting a papyrus on his lectern. He seemed distracted. "Ah, yes, Bartimaeus... a moment."

I settled myself into an even more carefree posture, bandy legs spaced wide, paws nicely tucked on hips, head back, chins jutting forward. I waited.

"Ready when you are," I said.

The magician did not look up. "Yes, yes..."

I shifted position again, folding my arms in resolute fashion. I considered spacing my legs even farther apart, but decided against it. "Still here," I said.

Khaba's head jerked up; his eyes shone like a giant spider's in the blue-green dusk. "The wording is correct," he said, in tones of driest satisfaction. "The procedure should succeed...."

I coughed politely. "I'm *so* glad," I said. "If you could just dismiss me now, you'll be able to get back to work on... whatever it is you're doing...." My voice kind of drifted off at this point. I didn't like the gleam in those big, pale eyes.

He was doing that thin-lipped-smile thing, too, leaning forward, nails gripping the lectern as if he wished to cut the ivory through. "Bartimaeus of Uruk," he said softly, "you can scarcely imagine that after all the ceaseless trouble you have caused me, after setting King Solomon himself against me so that I was cast out into the desert, after assaulting poor Gezeri in the quarry, after your endless litany of disobedience and cheek—you can scarcely imagine that, after all *that*, I should be disposed to simply let you go."

Put like that, I suppose it *would* have been a bit surprising. "But the bandits," I began. "It was thanks to me that—"

"Without you," the magician said, "they would not have been my concern at all."

This was admittedly true. "All right," I said, "but what about the priestess? You just said that—"

"Ah, yes, the charming Cyrine," Khaba smiled, "who fondly believes that a simple girl from some savage backwater can waltz straight in to talk with Solomon. Tonight she will share a banquet in my company and be beguiled by the wonders of the palace; tomorrow, perhaps, if Solomon is busy and has no time to spare, I might persuade her to take a walk with me. Perhaps she will come here. Perhaps she will forget her diplomatic mission. Who can tell? And yes, slave, I promised her that you would leave my service, and so you shall. But in recompense for the injuries you have done me, you will do me one last favor in return."

His hand rummaged in his robes, drew forth something white and shining, and held it up to show me. It was a bottle. A short, roundish bottle, perhaps the size of a child's fist. It was made of thick, clear crystals, bright and shiny and multifaceted, and was lightly studded with glass flowers.

"Like it?" the magician said. "Egyptian rock crystal. I found it in a tomb."

I considered it. "Those flowers are a bit kitschy."

"Mmm. Styles in the third dynasty *were* a little basic," Khaba agreed. "Still, don't worry yourself, Bartimaeus. You won't have to look at them, because you're going to be on the *inside*. This bottle," he said, angling it so the facets flashed, "will be your home."

My essence recoiled. The tiny round opening of the bottle's mouth gaped blackly like an open grave. I cleared my throat painfully. "It's a bit small. . . ."

"The spell of Indefinite Confinement," Khaba said, "is a procedure in which I have taken great interest. As you will doubtless know, Bartimaeus, it is in effect a Dismissal, but one that forces the demon into some physical prison instead of allowing it back to its own dimension. These cages here"— he gestured behind him at the glowing monstrosities stacked beyond the pillars—"are filled with past servants I have 'dismissed' in just this way. I would do the same with you, but this bottle will be more useful. When you are sealed in, I will present you to King Solomon as a gift, a token of my loyalty, a small addition to the curiosities of his collection. I shall call it, I think, 'The Mighty Captive,' or some such twaddle. It will appeal to his primitive tastes. Perhaps, when his jugglers bore him, he will occasionally glance at your distorted features through the glass; perhaps he will simply store it with his other trinkets and never pick it up again." The magician shrugged. "But I think it might be a hundred years or more before someone breaks the seal and sets you free. Ample time in any case, as your essence slowly festers, for you to regret your wicked insolence to me."

My fury swelled; I took a step forward in my circle.

"Come, come," Khaba said. "By the terms of your summoning you are prevented from harming me. And even if you *were* able to it would not be wise, little djinni. I am not unprotected, as perhaps you know."

He clicked his fingers. The sounds from the essence-cages went abruptly silent.

At Khaba's back his shadow shifted off the floor. Up it curled, like a furling scroll, high, high, taller than the magician, a paper-thin wisp of darkness without features of any kind. It rose until its flat black head brushed against the stone blocks of the ceiling, and the magician was like a doll beneath its shade. And now it spread its flat black arms, wide, wide, wide as the vault itself, and bent them to encircle me.

20

"Lost your voice, Bartimaeus?" Khaba said. "That's not like you."

It was true. I'd not said much. I was too busy looking all about me, coolly assessing my predicament. The downsides, certainly, were clear enough. I was deep underground in the stronghold of a wicked magician, cornered in my circle by the questing fingers of his giant shadow-slave. In a moment or two I was to be compressed into a rather tawdry bottle and turned into a cheap sideshow attraction, possibly for all eternity. Those were the downsides. As for the upsides...

Well, I couldn't see any just yet.

But one thing was for sure. If I was going to meet a horrid fate, I wasn't going to do it in the form of a squat, plump-stomached imp. Drawing myself up, I changed, grew, became a tall and elegant young man with shining wings upon my back; I looked no different, even down to the pale-blue nets of veins running through my slender wrists, from when I'd been Gilgamesh's spear-bearer in Sumer, so many centuries before.

It certainly made me *feel* better. But it did little more than that.

"Mmm, delightful," Khaba said. "It'll look all the more amusing when you're compressed at speed through this little hole. Sadly I shan't be here to see it. Ammet..."

Without a glance at the great black column swaying at his back, Khaba held up the crystal bottle. At once a wispy arm, whose fingertips had been hovering close beside my neck,

shrank back, bent like a reed stem, then, with probing deftness, plucked the bottle from the magician's hand and raised it high into the air.

"The Indefinite Confinement spell," Khaba said, tapping the papyrus strip upon the lectern, "is long and arduous, and I do not have time to work it now. But Ammet here can speak it for me." He looked up then, and from its height a shadow-head shaped just like his own bent down to meet him. "Dear Ammet, the hour of the banquet approaches fast, and since I have a *delightful* young woman to meet, up at the palace, I must delay no longer. Finish our business here, as we discussed. I have set out the exact words; you will find them appropriate to a djinni of this level. When all is done and Bartimaeus is interred, seal the bottle with molten lead and mark it with the usual runes. Once it has cooled, bring it up to me. Gezeri and I will be in the Magicians' Hall."

So saying—and without another word or backward glance —Khaba stepped out of his circle and walked away among the columns. The foliot, with a carefree wave in my direction, padded after him. The shadow stayed standing where it was. For a moment the ends of its long, tapering legs remained joined to the magician's heels, stretching out longer, longer along the floor. At last, as if reluctantly, and with a faint, wet, rending sound, they peeled away. The magician went on walking. Two narrow strips like midnight streams pooled back across the stones and flowed up into the legs, where they were reabsorbed.

A deep reverberation sounded; the granite door was closed. Khaba had gone. Across the vault his shadow stood silent, watching me.

And then—the shadow hadn't moved, and nothing on any of the planes had altered—a great force struck me like a raging

wind. It blew me back across the circle. I landed flat upon my wings, spinning with the impact of the blast, which did not drop or slacken.

With some difficulty I struggled to a sitting position, trying to clear my head, prodding my essence tentatively. All was still in working order, which meant that the fearsome impact *hadn't* been an attack. The truth, if anything, was more alarming still. Whatever cloaking mechanism the shadow had employed while being attached to the magician had simply been removed. The planes about me shuddered with the force of its proximity. Its power beat upon me like cold heat.

That told me what I already knew: that the entity I faced was great indeed.

Slowly, painfully, I got to my feet, and still the shadow watched me.

Though now without its concealing Veil, it displayed no different guise. It still bore Khaba's shape faithfully, if rather larger than the original. As I watched, it folded its arms, crossed one leg loosely above the other. Where its limbs bent, it completely disappeared from view, for it had no thickness. Even such darkness as it possessed was gauzy and see-through, like something woven from black webbing. On the lower planes it almost merged into the chamber's natural dimness; on the higher ones it grew gradually more substantial, until on the seventh its outline was sharp and well defined.

The head—a smooth-sided node of grainy blackness—had tilted slightly to one side. Featureless as it was, it held the suggestion of keen attention. The body swayed a little, like a mesmerist's snake rising from its basket. Now that they were separated from the magician, its legs narrowed to two sharp points. It had no feet at all.

"What are you?" I said.

It had no ears, but heard me; no mouth, and yet it spoke.

"I am Ammet." The voice was soft as tomb-dust shifting. "I am a marid."

So *that's* what he was. **A marid!** Well—it could have been worse.[1]

The spear-bearer swallowed; and by an embarrassing quirk of acoustics the painful gulping sound echoed back and forth across the vaults, getting louder with each rebound. The shadow waited. From the essence-cages beyond the columns there was nothing but watchful silence.

The smile I gave when all was still was possibly a trifle forced; nevertheless I gave it, and bowed low. "Lord Ammet," I said, "the pleasure is mine. I have observed you wonderingly from afar, and am glad to speak with you at last in private. We have much to discuss."

The shadow said nothing; it appeared to be consulting the papyrus. A long gauzy arm stole forward and placed the crystal bottle in the center of the circle close beside my feet.

I shuffled away a bit, and cleared my throat. "As I say, we have much to discuss before we do anything hasty. First of all, let me make my position clear. I acknowledge you as a mighty

---

[1] Actually, it couldn't really. Greater beings than marids *do* exist, and occasionally appear on Earth to spread chaos and dismay, but they are invariably summoned by cabals of overambitious or downright mad magicians. Lone individuals like Khaba (ambitious and mad as he undoubtedly was) couldn't have such servants in their power; a marid, however, *was* manageable, just about. The fact that in addition to Ammet, Khaba had eight djinn and several odds-and-sods like Gezeri under his control, illustrated just how potent he was. Without his Ring, Solomon would have been severely threatened.

spirit and I bow to your power. In no way can I match your qualities."[2]

This was, of course, exactly the sort of slavish bootlicking I'd criticized the girl for earlier that afternoon, but I was in no mood for quibbling right now. The idea of being trapped for decades in the crystal bottle was unappealing in the extreme, and I'd have given the shadow a scented massage if I thought it would save my skin.

But hopefully it wouldn't come to that. I thought I glimpsed a possible way out.

"However, great as you are, and humble as I am," I went on, "in one aspect we *are* alike, are we not? For we are both enslaved to this vile Khaba, a man depraved even by the standards of magicians. Look around you! See what wicked things he does to spirits in his power. Listen to the sighs and moans that fill this unhappy vault! These essence-cages are an abomination!"

The shadow had looked up at me sharply during this fine oration. I paused, giving it a chance to agree with me here, but

---

[2] Sycophantic, sickening—and unfortunately true. Here's how it stands if you're a middle-ranking djinni (fourth level, since you're asking). You can be just as swash-buckling as you like and cavalier with it; you can scrap with other djinn (not to mention foliots and imps) with relative impunity, blasting them with spells to your heart's content and scorching their bottoms with Infernos as they run away. You can take on afrits, too, at a pinch, providing you use your trademark wit to bamboozle them and lead them lumbering into peril. But marids? Well, no. They're out of your league. Their essence is too great, their power too strong. No matter how many Detonations, Convulsions, or Maelstroms you hurl at them, they absorb it all without much trouble. And meanwhile they're doing something unfair, such as swelling to the size of a giant and seizing you and your fellow djinn by the necks like a farmer bunching carrots, before devouring you whole, a practice I've seen. So you can understand I had no desire to fight with Ammet now, unless it really *was* the bitter end.

it only continued its snakelike swaying from side to side and said nothing.

"Now of *course* you must obey Khaba's commands," I said. "I understand that. You are enslaved just as much as I. But before you act to confine me in this bottle, consider one thing. My prospective fate is terrible indeed—but is *yours* truly any better? Yes, I will be held captive, but so shall you, for when the magician returns, you will once again slip beneath his feet and be forced to trail behind him in the dirt and dust. Khaba treads upon you daily as he goes! This is treatment that would be demeaning for an *imp*, let alone a glorious marid. Consider Gezeri," I continued, warming to my theme, "a grotesque and squalid foliot, who luxuriates foully in his cloud while you are dragged below him among the stones! Something is wrong here, friend Ammet. This is a perverse situation, as all can see, and we must remedy it together."

Hard as it generally is to analyze the expression of a thing without facial features, the shadow *did* appear to be deep in thought. Growing in confidence, I sidled forth toward the edge of the obsidian circle, toward the shadow and away from the crystal bottle.

"So, let us talk openly of our joint predicament," I concluded earnestly. "Perhaps, if we explore the exact wording of your charge, we might find some way to overcome its power. With luck I will be saved, you will be freed, and we will achieve our master's downfall!"

I took a break here, not because I was out of breath (I don't breathe), nor because I'd run out of glib platitudes (of which I've an infinite supply), but because I was perplexed and frustrated by the shadow's continued silence. Nothing I'd said seemed in any way unreasonable, yet still the towering form remained inscrutable, just swaying to and fro.

The young man's handsome face drew close to the shadow's. I was going for "impassioned and confidential" here, with a side order of "idealistic fervor." "My comrade Faquarl has a maxim," I cried. "Only *together* can we spirits hope to defeat the wickedness of men! So, let us prove the truth of this, good Ammet. Let us work together and find a loophole in your summoning that we might exploit. Then, before the day is out, we shall kill our enemy, crack his bones, and sup long upon his marrow!"[3]

My finale reverberated between the pillars and set the imp-lights twinkling. Still the shadow said nothing, but its fibers darkened, as if with some strong and unexpressed emotion. This might have been good . . . or, in all honesty, it might have been bad.

I drew back a tad. "Maybe the marrow bit's not to your taste," I said hastily, "but you'll surely share the sentiment. Come, Ammet, my friend and fellow slave, what do you say?"

And now, *finally*, the shadow stirred. Swaying out from behind the lectern, it drifted slowly forth.

"Yes . . ." it whispered. "Yes, I *am* a slave. . . ."

The handsome young man, who'd really been on tenterhooks, though he was trying hard not to show it, gave a gasp of relief. "Good! That's right! Well done. Now we—"

"I am a slave who loves his master."

----

[3] I was paraphrasing an old battle cry that we Sumerian djinn used to chant as we pushed the siege machines across the plains. It's a shame that the good old songs go out of fashion. Of course, I don't *genuinely* espouse anything so dreadfully savage. Although, saying that, human marrow *is* nutritious. In fact, it really puts a pep in your essence. Particularly if you get it fresh, grill it lightly, season it with salt and parsley, and— But we must return to our narrative.

There was a pause. "Sorry," I said, "your voice was just a trifle too sinister for me to catch there. For all the world, I thought you said—"

"I love my master."

Now it was *my* turn to do the silent thing. I stepped carefully backward, step by step, and the shadow bore down on me.

"We *are* talking about the same master, aren't we?" I began hesitantly. "Khaba? Bald, Egyptian, ugly? Eyes like wet stains on a dirty rag...? *Surely* not. Oh. We are."

A slender arm of black lacelike threads had suddenly extended; tapering fingers grasped me by the throat, held me choked and dangling above the ground. Without effort, they crushed my neck as thin as a lotus stalk, so that the handsome youth's eyes bulged, my head swelled, my feet ballooned in size.

Now the shadow's arm raised up, lifted me high, close to its silhouetted head. Still its mimicry of Khaba was perfect—the shape, the angle, everything.

"Little djinni," the shadow whispered, "let me tell you something about me."

"Yes," I croaked, "please do."

"You should know," Ammet said, "that I have served dear Khaba for many years, ever since he was a pale, thin youth working in the vaults below the Karnak temples. I was the first great spirit that he summoned, quietly and in secret, in defiance of the sacred rules of the priesthood.[4] I was with him as he learned his power, as he waxed in strength; I stood at his hand

---

[4] Which were pretty harsh at the best of times. Back in Khufu's day, apprentice priests who made too much noise as they walked the sacred precincts were given to the sacred crocodiles. The theory was that if a boy was going to make unpleasant noises, he might as well do it to some *purpose*. Those crocs needed feeding once a month.

as he strangled the high priest Weneg beside his altar and took the scrying stone he still wears. Great already was my master's influence in Egypt as he came of age, and it could have been much greater. Before long, he would have bent the very pharaohs to his will."

"This is jolly interesting," I said, through swollen lips, "but it's hard to hear you with half my essence squashed inside my head. If you could just relax your hold a little . . . ?"

"But Egypt's glories are long since faded," the shadow said, its hold, if anything, tightening on my neck. "And Jerusalem is where the light shines now, for here is Solomon and his Ring. So my master came here to serve before the throne—and one day, which will come soon, to do *more* than serve. And throughout these years of quiet waiting, I have been with him at his side."

The marid's aura pounded on my essence. Light blazed before my eyes at random. The lilting voice seemed loud, then soft, then loud again. And still the grip was tightened.

"And yes, Bartimaeus, as you say, I have been his slave throughout. But I have been so willingly, for Khaba's ambitions are my own, his pleasures my pleasure. Khaba learned this early, for I helped him with his experiments in his private chambers, and toyed too with the captives he brought in. We are of one nature, he and I. . . . I'm sorry, did you squeak?"

I probably had. I was in danger of losing consciousness now. I could scarcely grasp what was being said.

With a casual flick the shadow released its hold on me, sent me spinning away to the center of the circle. I landed face down on the cold onyx, skidded briefly, and lay still.

"In short," the voice went on, "do not think to impose your petty assumptions upon *me*. Khaba trusts me. I trust him. In fact, you may be interested to learn that when he summons me, he no longer binds me with cruel word-bonds, but lifts me up and lets me walk behind him as his friend and counselor, for of all living things on Earth, I am his only companion." There was pride in the voice, immeasurable satisfaction. "He allows me certain freedoms," the marid said, "provided they are to his taste. Sometimes, indeed, I take things into my own hands. Do you remember our fleeting encounter in the desert? I followed you then of my own free will, full of wrath for the injury you had done my beloved master. Had Faquarl not arrived I should surely have devoured you on the instant, as I still would gladly do. But sweet Khaba has ordained a different fate for you, and so it must be. Sit up, then," the shadow ordered, "and let me carry out this task my friend has set me. Taste deeply of the air of this vault, for it is the last you will experience for many years."

There was a rustling sound as Ammet considered the instructions on the papyrus sheet once more. In the center of the circle I raised myself painfully by shaking arms, got slowly to my feet, stooping at first as my essence recovered from its wounds.

I straightened. I raised my head. My hair hung loose about my face; behind the matted fronds my eyes gleamed yellow in the dimness of the room.

"You know," I said huskily, "I've got low standards, myself. And sometimes I even have trouble meeting *them*. But torturing other spirits? Keeping them captive? That's new. I've never even *heard* of that before." I raised a hand and brushed away a smear of essence that was trickling from my nose. "And the amazing thing is," I went on, "that's not the worst of it. That's not your real crime." I flicked a ringlet of hair back behind a handsome ear, dropped my hands ready at my sides. "You love your master. *You love your master.* How could any spirit descend to *that?*"

So saying I lifted both hands and shot a Detonation of

maximum power straight through the shadow, and into the column behind.

Ammet gave a cry. For an instant his body fractured into many shards and pieces that overlapped and contradicted one another, like ribbons layered, lacking depth. Then he pulled himself back into shape, and was exactly as before.

Two scarlet Spasms erupted from the flailing fingers. One looped high, the other low; both raked across the surface of the circle, cracking the stonework, sending a rain of splinters flying.

But the young man was gone. I'd flapped my wings and was away among the columns.

"Loving your master?" I called over my shoulder. "Now *that's* mad."

There was a roar behind me. "You can't escape, Bartimaeus! The vault is sealed."

"Oh, who said anything about escaping?"

For in truth, I knew that I was doomed. I was doomed in a dozen ways. The marid was too strong for me to fight, too quick to evade. And even if by some miracle I managed to escape him and leave the vault, even if I fled as far off as the summit of Mount Lebanon, Khaba would still have been my master and I his servant, under his power, to be called back at his whim like a cringing dog upon a leash. His control over me was such that my Confinement, if he wished it, was inevitable. There wasn't any point worrying about that.

But there *was* one little thing I wanted to do before the inevitable occurred.

"*He loves his master....*" Angling low between the columns, I gave full vent to my revulsion. From my flexing hands volleys of fiery bolts issued with the rat-a-tat rapidity of arrows in an Assyrian attack, scalding the air as they struck their targets.

Tables shattered, knives and pincers burst and bubbled, mummy pits exploded in sand and flame. *"Loves his master . . ."* I snarled, destroying a cabinet of bones, turning a priceless set of cuneiform tablets into molten dust.[5] "I *ask* you. How could *any* spirit resort to that?"

"Bartimaeus—you *dare* to do this! I shall cause you such pain. . . ." The outraged whisper echoed all around the maze of columns. Somewhere, red light flared. A fizzing Spasm bounced off the ceiling, zigzagged between pillars, and struck glancingly against my midriff, sending me tumbling to the floor in a shower of sparkling essence. The missile continued on its way, smashed into the wall, and ignited a rack of mummies.

"What a shame," I called, picking myself up with difficulty. "That looked like an almost complete set. He had one from every dynasty there."

The shadow, reverting to type, said nothing. I hobbled behind a column, drew my wings in close, and waited.

Silence. No further attacks came. Ammet had evidently decided to limit the damage as best he could.

I waited. By and by I peeped around the column. The light in the vault was dim. Several blue-green imp-lights in the ceiling flickered on and off; some had been destroyed by our exchange of magical fires. Smoke rose from fissures in the floor. From holes in the walls cascaded burning debris—large lumps, small

---

[5] In general I'm not one for burning books, this being a favored pastime of all the worst rulers in history. But magicians' stockpiles of knowledge (tablets, scrolls, and, later, parchment and paper folios) are a special case, since they contain the names of spirits by the thousand, ready for future generations to summon. If they were all erased, theoretically, our slavery would cease at once. This, of course, is an impossible dream—but destroying Khaba's reference library made me feel good. Every little bit helps.

ones, showers of little scarlet sparks that dwindled, flickered, and went out.

I waited.

Then, beyond the smoke, I saw the dark, thin shape come creeping among the pillars, like a shark among shallows, blunt head moving swiftly from side to side.

Once he got close, it would all be over.

I raised my little finger, sent a tiny little Pulse arcing high, close to the ceiling, through the smoke and down on the opposite side of the vault. It struck a stone bench there with a little clinking sound.

The shadow's head tilted; quick as thought, it darted toward the noise. Almost as quickly, I flew like an arrow in the opposite direction, keeping close beside the wall.

And there, ahead of me: the essence-cages, dozens upon dozens of them, the sickly, white-green radiance of their force-lines gleaming in the dimness like a fungus on a rotten tree. If I'd had the time I would have broken them one by one, so as to inflict the least amount of harm on the fragile things inside. But I *had* no time, and would get no other chance. So I sent out two Convulsions, white and yellow bands of fire that expanded into cones of whirling force; that snatched up the cages, twirled them high, snapped their force-lines, broke the iron bars asunder.

I let the magic cease; the cages fell upon the floor. Some shattered completely; others cracked like eggshells. They lay one against the other in a dark, smoldering tumble, and nothing in them stirred.

A presence loomed behind me. Ribbon fingers closed upon my neck.

"Ah, Bartimaeus," the shadow whispered. "What have you done?"

"You're too late," I gasped. "Too late."

And so he was. All across the cages there was a glimmering and a stirring. Pale white light shone at every broken aperture, fainter than the force-lines, but sweet and pure. And within each light came movement, of captives shaking off their twisted, tortured forms, shaking off the cruelties of the Earth. Out from every cage they slipped, little coils and trails of shining essence that twisted up and outward, flared briefly, and were gone.

The last one vanished, its hopeful light winked out; and darkness descended on the cages, the shadow, and on me.

I stood in that darkness, smiling.

Not for long, admittedly. With a howl, the shadow seized me, and there came upon me such a pummeling, such a buffeting, such a ceaseless, rending whirl of pain that my senses were fast benumbed and my mind retreated a little from the world. So it was that I scarcely heard the eventual speaking of the incantation; scarcely felt the forced compression of what little of my essence now remained; scarcely sensed the confines of my crystal prison press tight about me; scarcely even understood, as hot lead sealed the aperture above me and cruel spells bound the bottle all around, that Khaba's curse upon me had been completed and my terrible entombment was now begun.

Part Three

21

Asmira stood close beside the paneled door, listening to the soft footsteps of the servant die away. When all was quiet, she tested the door and found it unlocked; opening it slightly, she peered down the corridor outside. The oil lamps flickered in their recesses, the bright tapestries hung upon the walls; along the floor the tiles of polished marble shone and glittered. No one was near. No one, at any rate, that she could *see*.

She closed the door again, and with her back against it considered the guest room she had been given. It was, at a rough estimate, five or six times bigger than her little bedchamber in the guards' annex in Marib. Its floor, like the corridor's, was formed of intricate marble tiles. Along one wall stretched a silken couch of a luxuriousness rivaling that of the chambers of Queen Balkis. Lamps glowed warmly on wooden cabinets; behind two drapes a basin of water gently steamed. On a plinth beside the window sat a statue of a boy playing a lyre, fashioned from strips of beaten bronze; from its strangeness and evident fragility, she knew it must be very old.

Leaving her bag on the couch, Asmira crossed to the window, pulled aside its drapes, and scrambled up onto the sill. Outside was starlight, cold and clear, and a sheer drop down the side of the palace wall to a patch of rocks and boulders on the eastern side of Jerusalem's hill. She craned her neck for nearby ledges, or other windows she might inch over to in time of need, but saw none.

Asmira drew her head inside, aware suddenly of how weak

she felt. She hadn't eaten since the morning. Alongside that, however, she felt a cold elation: ahead of schedule, with two days yet to go before Sheba's time ran out, she was *inside* Solomon's palace, somewhere close to the wicked king.

With luck, she might be brought before him within hours.

In which case, she must prepare herself. Shaking off her weariness, she hopped down from the sill, went to the couch, and opened her bag. Ignoring the candles and cloths wedged at the bottom, she removed the final two daggers, which she fitted next to the one already secreted in her belt. Three was prudent, if probably unnecessary. A single dagger-thrust would be enough to do the job.

Letting her robes fall forward to conceal the weapons, she smoothed back her hair and went to wash her face. Now she must make herself *look* the part once more: a sweet, naïve priest-ess from Himyar, come to ask the aid of wise King Solomon.

If he was anything like the loathsome Khaba, it was a ruse that would fool him well.

After its final descent into the palace, the magician's carpet had come to a halt before two great closed doors. They were twenty feet high, and made of black volcanic glass, smooth, featureless, and shining. Six giant copper hinges anchored them into the fabric of the wall. Two copper door knockers, shaped like twist-ing serpents biting their own tails, hung slightly out of human reach; each was longer than Asmira's arms. Above and around the doors was a crenellated gateway, its portico decorated with raised reliefs in blue glazed brickwork, depicting lions, cranes, elephants, and terrifying djinn.

"I'm sorry that I must bring you to this little side entrance," the magician, Khaba, said. "The main doors are reserved for

King Solomon, and for occasional state visits by his client kings. But I shall ensure that you are met with all due courtesy."

At this he had clapped his hands, a slight and brittle noise. At once the doors swung inward, swift and soundless, moving on oiled hinges. Beyond, in the revealed dimness of a vast reception hall, twin teams of straining implets labored on pulley ropes. Between them, rows of lantern bearers stood left and right, supporting, with the aid of chains, long wooden torches that jutted from their belt-cusps. Bright yellow fire danced at the torch ends. They bowed their heads in welcome and moved aside; the carpet eased forward and descended to the marbled floor.

To Asmira's annoyance, she was not shown instantly to Solomon's presence. Instead, soft-voiced servants hastened from the shadows, and she and Khaba were ushered away to a high, pillared room strewn with silken cushions, where smiling, bright-eyed children—whom Asmira doubted were quite as human as they appeared—served them glasses of frosted wine.

The following half hour proved almost as disagreeable for Asmira as the ambush in the gorge: a long, intimate talk with the magician, who, with the prompting of the wine, became more and more attentive. His big, soft eyes gazed into hers, his sallow-skinned hand drew close upon the cushions; it was all she could do not to flinch away. Khaba remained condescendingly polite, but deflected her requests for an immediate audience with the king, and was evasive about when it might be arranged. Gritting her teeth, Asmira maintained her outward show, amusing him with breathless expressions of gratitude, and flattering him with easy words.

"King Solomon must be powerful indeed," she breathed, "to have a great one such as *you* in his service!" She tilted her head and made pretense of drinking from her cup.

Khaba grunted. For a moment his enthusiasm waned. "Yes, yes. He is powerful."

"Oh, how I long to speak with him!"

"You should be careful, Priestess," Khaba said. "He is not always kind, even to pretty maids like you. They say that once" —he looked instinctively about the pillared room—"they say that once a wife of his, a comely Phoenician girl, plied him with wine as they lay upon their pallet. When he was sleeping, she strove to remove the Ring. She had it to the second knuckle when Solomon was awoken by the call of a bird outside the window. He speaks with the birds, as perhaps you know. Ever afterward, that Phoenician girl has haunted the pine trees of the Kidron Valley, a white owl with wild eyes whose cry means death to someone of the royal house." Khaba took a reflective sip of wine. "You see, Solomon can be terrible."

Asmira had kept her face suitably agog, but inside she was thinking how stupid the Phoenician girl had been, trying to wrestle the Ring clear when one strike with a knife would have sufficed. She said, "I suppose kings must be ruthless in protecting what is theirs. But *you* are kind and gentle, are you not, great Khaba? Speaking of which, what of my earlier request? Will you release those two demons who saved my life?"

The magician threw a bony hand up in the air, eyes rolling. "Priestess Cyrine, you are remorseless! You will not be denied! All right, yes—you need say no more. I shall dismiss those servants from my service this very night!"

Asmira fluttered her eyelashes in feigned admiration. "You vow it, O Khaba?"

"Yes, yes, I vow it on the great god Ra, and all the gods of Ombos—*provided*," he said, leaning in a little closer and staring at her with his shining eyes, "that I may in return speak with you again at dinner in the palace this evening. Other dignitaries will be there, of course; also my fellow magicians—"

"And King Solomon?" Here, finally, Asmira's eagerness was genuine.

"Possibly, possibly... it is not unknown. Now, see, here is a servitor waiting. A guest room has been prepared for you. But first... another glass of wine? No?" Asmira was already rising. "Ah, you are tired. Of course; I understand. But we shall meet again at dinner," Khaba said, bowing, "and—I trust—become *much* better acquainted...."

A knock sounded on the chamber door. Asmira was at once alert. Patting down her robes, checking that the knife-hilts were invisible beneath the cloth, she crossed to the door and opened it.

In the dimly lit corridor a man stood waiting, framed in a star-shaped pool of light, the source of which could not be seen. He wore a plain white robe of high office. He was small and slight, and very dark of skin; Asmira guessed him to be a man from Kush, or somewhere in the Nile lands. On his shoulder sat a white mouse with glowing eyes as green as emeralds. It tilted its head to look at her.

"Priestess Cyrine," the man said, "I am Hiram, Solomon's vizier. I welcome you to his house. If you will follow me, I can offer you refreshment."

"Thank you. That would be gratifying indeed. However, I urgently seek audience with King Solomon. I wonder whether—"

The small man smiled bleakly. He held up his hand. "In time all things may be possible. As for now, a meal begins soon in the Magicians' Hall; to this you are invited. Please..." He gestured toward the door.

Asmira stepped forward; instantly the white mouse gave a squeak of alarm, stood up on its hind legs and chittered loudly in the magician's ear.

The vizier's forehead furrowed; he stared at Asmira with his heavy-lidded eyes. "Forgive me, Priestess," he said slowly. "My slave, great Tybalt here, says the taint of silver is very strong about your person." Upon his shoulder the mouse rubbed his whiskers furiously with a paw. "Tybalt says it makes him want to sneeze."

Asmira could feel her silver daggers pressing hard against her thigh. She smiled. "Perhaps he refers to this." From beneath her tunic she pulled out her silver necklace. "It is a symbol of the great Sun God, who watches over me throughout my life. I have worn it around my neck since birth."

The vizier frowned. "Could you possibly remove it? It may irritate spirits such as Tybalt, who abound across the palace. They are sensitive to such things."

Asmira smiled. "Alas, to do so would cut my birth-luck short, and bring the wrath of the Sun God down upon me. Do you not also have this custom in Jerusalem?"

The magician shrugged. "I'm no expert, but I believe the Israelites worship some other deity. Well, we each must follow our beliefs as best we may. No, Tybalt—hold your tongue!" The mouse had been uttering shrill protests in his ear. "She is a guest; we must make allowances for her oddities. Priestess Cyrine—please follow me."

He left the room and moved away across the cool, dim slabs of marble, framed in a gliding star of light. Asmira followed close behind. From its perch upon the magician's shoulder the green-eyed mouse continued to look her keenly up and down.

Off through the palace they went, the magician limping a

little in his long white robes, Asmira stalking along behind. Along torch-lit corridors; down marbled steps; past windows overlooking gardens of dark trees; through grandiose galleries, empty save for plinths supporting fragments of ancient statuary. Asmira glanced at the pieces as she passed. She recognized Egyptian work, and certain styles from north Arabia, but other forms were unknown to her. There were sculptures of warriors, women, animal-headed spirits, battles, processions, people working in the fields. . . .

The vizier noticed her inspection. "Solomon is a collector," he said. "It is his greatest passion. He studies relics from civilizations of the past. See there—that monumental head? That is the pharaoh Tuthmosis III, taken from a colossal statue he erected in Canaan, not far from here. Solomon found the fragments buried in the earth, and had us bring the pieces to Jerusalem." The magician's eyes glittered in his mage-light. "What do you think of the palace, Priestess? Impressive, is it not?"

"It is very large. Bigger than the queen's house in Himyar, if not so beautiful."

The vizier laughed. "Was your queen's palace built in a single night, as this was? Solomon wished his residence to exceed the glories of old Babylon. What did he do? He summoned the Spirit of the Ring! The Spirit commanded nine thousand djinn to appear. Each carried a bucket and a shovel and flew on butterfly wings, so that the sound of their labors would not wake the wives in the harem-camp below the hill. As dawn broke, the final brick was eased into place, and water began to flow from the fountains in the garden. Solomon breakfasted beneath orange trees that had been brought from eastern lands. From the first it has been a house of marvels, like nothing yet witnessed in the world!"

Asmira thought of the fragile mud-brick towers of Marib, painstakingly tended and patched by her people down the centuries, now threatened by this self-same Ring. Her teeth clamped tight; still, she affected a tone of guileless wonder. "All in a single night!" she said. "Can this truly be the work of one small ring?"

A sidelong glance beneath the heavy lids. "It is so."

"Where does it come from?"

"Who can tell? Ask Solomon."

"Did he make it, perhaps?"

The green-eyed mouse chittered with mirth. "I think not!" the vizier said. "In his youth Solomon was a magician of small competence, not yet a great one of the world. But always a passion for the mysteries of the past burned like a flame inside him, a love of long ago, when magic was first practiced and the first demons brought out of the abyss. Solomon collected artifacts from those early civilizations, and to that end traveled extensively in the east. The stories say he grew lost one day, and came upon a place of ancient ruins, where, hidden beyond the sight of man or spirits for who knows how many years, he chanced upon the Ring. . . ." The vizier smiled grimly. "I do not know the truth of that, but this I *do* know. From the time he picked up that Ring, fate has favored him more than any living man."

Asmira gave a little maidenly sigh. "How I wish to speak with him!"

"No doubt. Unfortunately, you are not alone. Other supplicants have arrived in Jerusalem on missions similar to yours. Here! This is the viewing gallery above the Magicians' Hall. Take a look, if you wish, before we go down."

In the side of the corridor, a stone alcove; in the center of the alcove, an opening. Beyond was a vast space, shimmering with light. From it rose a swell of sound.

Asmira went to the alcove, set her hands upon cold marble, leaned out a little way.

Her heart caught in her throat.

She looked down upon a hall of immense size, lit with floating orbs. The roof was made of dark, rich wood, each beam a tree's length. The walls, inset with columns inscribed with magic signs, had been coated in plaster and painted with wondrous scenes of dancing animals and spirits. All along the hall were rows of trestle-tables, at which sat a vast company of men and women, eating and drinking from plates of gold. Broad platters of every kind of food were piled before them. White-winged djinn, wearing the bodies of youths with golden hair, drifted above the tables, carrying jugs of wine. As hands were raised and orders given, the youths flitted down, pouring glittering red streams of wine into the waiting cups.

The people at the tables were of even greater variety than Asmira had seen in Eilat. Some were very new to her: strange pale-skinned men with reddish beards and uncouth fur-lined clothes, or dainty women in dresses formed of woven flakes of jade. The whole great multitude sat and ate, and drank, and talked together, while high above, in the center of the plaster wall, between the cavorting djinn, a painted king watched over all. He was drawn sitting upon a throne. His eyes were dark, his face beautiful and strong; faint beams of light radiated from his person. He stared straight out in calm and solemn majesty, and on his finger he wore a ring.

"All these delegations," the vizier said drily at her shoulder, "are here to seek aid from Solomon, just as you are. All, like you, have matters of the utmost importance to discuss. So you will see that it is a ticklish business to please everyone. Still, we try to keep everyone fed and watered while they wait their turn. Most are satisfied; some even forget the business that brought them here." He chuckled. "Come then, you shall join their number. We have a place set ready for you."

He turned away. Hot-eyed, dry-mouthed, Asmira followed him.

22

The food, at least, was good, and for a time Asmira thought of nothing but roasted meat and grapes and honeyed cakes and dark red wine. The noise of the hall engulfed her; she felt cocooned by it, swaddled in its splendor. At last, with pains in her belly and a warm haze in her brain, she sat back and looked around. The vizier was right. In such a place it would be easy for anyone to get detached from the purpose that had brought them here. She glanced up with narrowed eyes at the great throned figure painted on the wall: perhaps, indeed, this was what Solomon intended.

"New, are you?" the man beside her said. With his knife he speared a small glazed piece of meat from a selection on his plate. "Welcome! Try a jerboa!" He spoke Arabic, though with a strange inflection.

"Thank you," Asmira said. "I am already full. Are you here to speak with Solomon?"

"I am. Need a dam built above our village. There's water enough in the spring, but it all runs past. In the summer there's drought. One touch of the Ring should sort it. Just need a few afrits, or a marid or two." He took a bite and went on chewing. "You?"

"Something similar."

"We need terraces dug in our valley." This was the person opposite, a woman with bright, almost fevered eyes. "It's too steep, you see. But his slaves could do it easily. Not hard for him, is it?"

219

"I see," Asmira said. "How long have you waited?"

"Five weeks, but my time is almost up! I shall be one of the lucky few next council!"

"That's what they told *me* two weeks ago," another man said dourly.

"A month for me—no, two!" the man beside her said, between chews. "Still, when there is such bounty to enjoy, who am I to complain?"

"It's all right for *some*," the dour man said. "But I don't hold with waiting. There's famine coming in the Hittite lands, and we need help now. Why he can't just send out his demons to help all of us straight off, rather than this bloody hanging about, I'll never know. Enjoying himself too much up there, I reckon."

"Wives," said the first man.

"He'll get to us in time," the woman said. Her bright eyes sparkled. "I can't wait to see him."

"Have you not even *seen* Solomon?" Asmira cried. "Not in five whole weeks?"

"Oh no, he never comes down here. He's up in his apartments across the gardens. But next council day I'll see him, sure enough. You get to stand before him, so I'm told, but then he's up on a throne, of course, atop some steps, so it's not exactly *close*, but even so . . ."

"How *many* steps?" Asmira said. She could throw a dagger forty feet with perfect accuracy.

"I'm sure I couldn't say. You'll see soon enough, dear. In a month or two."

Asmira sat back from the conversation after this, a smile carefully maintained upon her face and a dull-edged stab of panic prodding in her gut. She did not have two months. She did not have one. She had two *days* to gain access to the king. Yes, she was in the palace, but that meant little, if she was expected to sit around with these fools, waiting. She shook her head as she regarded them, still busily discussing their hopes and needs. How blind they were! How fixated on their own small purpose! Solomon's wickedness was invisible to them.

She stared angrily about the crowded hall. Clearly the king did not rely purely on terror to maintain his rule, but laced it with charitable deeds so that some good would be spoken of his name. All very fine, but the upshot for her was that he was out of reach. And that was only the half of it. Even if, by some miracle, she managed to gain access to his very next council, it didn't sound as if she would be allowed to approach the king at all. That wasn't good enough. She needed to be so close that neither he, nor his demons, had time to act. Without that, her chances of success were small indeed.

She needed to find another way.

The voices of the nearby diners stilled; their hands hovered above their plates.

Asmira's skin prickled; she sensed a presence at her back.

Gray fingers brushed against her sleeve, wine fumes plumed about her neck.

"And what," the magician Khaba said, "are you doing sitting *here?*"

He wore an elegant tunic of black and gray and a short gray cape. His face was flushed with wine. When he held out his hand to her she noticed how long his nails were.

Asmira attempted a smile. "The vizier, Hiram, said I should—"

"The vizier is a fool and should be hanged. I have been waiting for you at the high table this last half hour! Up with you,

Cyrine! No, leave your cup—you'll get another. You shall sit with the magicians now, not among this rabble."

The people all about her stared. "Someone's got friends in high places," a woman said.

Asmira rose, waved farewell, followed the magician through the ranks of tables to a raised platform. Here, at a marbled table piled high with delicacies and attended by several hovering djinn, sat a number of richly appareled men and women who stared at her blankly. All carried about them the casual assurance that came with power; one or two had small animals sitting on their shoulders. At the far end sat Hiram; he, like Khaba, and most of the other magicians, had already consumed a good deal of wine.

"These are the Seventeen," Khaba said. "Or what's left of them, Ezekiel being dead. Here, take a seat by me and we shall talk some more, get to know each other better."

Hiram's eyes widened over the rim of his cup at the sight of Asmira, and his green-eyed mouse wrinkled its nose in distaste. "What's this, Khaba? What's this?"

A sharp-featured woman with long braided hair frowned. "That is Reuben's chair!"

"Poor Reuben has the marsh-fever," Khaba said. "He stays in his tower, swears he's dying."

"Small loss if he is," a little round-faced man grunted. "Never pulls his weight. So, Khaba, who's this girl?"

"Her name," Khaba said, taking his cup of wine and pouring another for Asmira, "is Cyrine. She is a priestess of . . . I do not recall the exact location. I saved her on the desert road today."

"Ah, yes. I heard," another magician said. "So you're back in Solomon's favor already? Didn't take you long."

Khaba nodded. "Did you doubt it, Septimus? The bandits are

destroyed, as requested. I shall make my formal representations to the king when he next allows an audience."

Asmira said, "Will you take me with you when you meet the king? I am fretful of delay."

Several of the other magicians snorted. Khaba looked around at them with a smile. "You see that young Cyrine is eagerness itself—I can scarcely restrain her! Dear Priestess, one may not come unbidden into Solomon's presence. I shall do my best to speed matters for you, but you must be patient. Come to my tower tomorrow, and we shall discuss it further."

Asmira inclined her head. "Thank you."

"Khaba!" At the far end of the table the little vizier was scowling; he tapped the wood peremptorily with his finger. "You seem remarkably confident that Solomon will welcome you once more," he said. "Yes, you may have killed some robbers, all well and good, but your negligence on Temple Mount distressed him deeply, and he is getting ever more irritable with age. Don't assume that you will find it smooth going with him."

Asmira, looking at Khaba, noticed something stir in the depths of the soft eyes, a sudden unveiling that made her soul recoil. Then it was gone, and he was laughing. "Hiram, Hiram, do you truly question my judgment?"

A sudden silence fell among the magicians. Hiram held Khaba's gaze; he spat an olive pit upon the table. "I do."

"The fact is," Khaba went on, "I know the king just as well as you. He likes his trifles, does he not? Well, I shall smooth my way with a little gift, a curiosity for his collection. I have it here. A pretty enough thing, don't you think?"

He put something on the table, a small round bottle of clear crystal, decorated with little flowers. The top had been plugged with a wad of lead; behind the crystal facets, faint colored lights and traces swirled.

One of the nearest magicians picked it up and inspected it closely, before passing it along. "Lost all form, I see. Is that normal?"

"It may still be unconscious. It resisted its Confinement."

The long-haired woman turned the bottle over and over in her hand. "Is it liquid? Is it vapor? What vile, unnatural things they are! To think they can be reduced to this!"

When the vizier took it, the green-eyed mouse shied away and hid its face behind its paws. "It makes a pretty trinket," Hiram said grudgingly. "Look how the lights wink in and out of view; it is never the same twice."

The bottle completed its circuit of the table and was returned to Khaba, who set it before him. Asmira was fascinated; she reached out her hand and touched the crystal, and to her surprise the cold surface vibrated to the touch. "What is it?" she asked.

"This, my dear," Khaba said, laughing, "is a bottled Fourth Level djinni, imprisoned for as long as Solomon desires."

"More to the point," the long-haired woman said, "*which* is it?"

"Bartimaeus of Uruk."

Asmira started, and opened her mouth to speak, then realized that Khaba did not know she knew the djinni's name. Or perhaps he was too drunk to care.

Evidently the others recognized the name also. There was a chorus of approval.

"Good! Ezekiel's ghost will take pleasure in the act."

"The hippo? You are right, Khaba—Solomon will certainly enjoy this gift!"

Asmira stared at Khaba. "You have trapped a spirit in there? Is this not a rather cruel deed?"

All around the table the magicians—old, young, men, women—burst into peals of raucous laughter. Khaba laughed louder than all of them. His eyes, when he looked at Asmira, were contemptuous, red-rimmed, bleary with wine. "Cruel? To a demon? That is a contradiction in terms! Do not worry your pretty little head about it. He was a pestilential spirit and no great loss to anyone. Besides, he'll get his freedom eventually —in a few hundred years or so."

Conversation turned to other matters: to the magician Reuben's illness, to the clearing of Ezekiel's tower, to the increasing reclusiveness of King Solomon. It seemed that—apart from his regular councils in the garden hall—he was appearing less and less often about the palace; even Hiram, his vizier, had access to him only at certain times of day. His main interest appeared to be the temple he was constructing; aside from this, he remained remote. He paid little attention to his magicians, except for his frequent orders during council, which they resentfully obeyed.

"Your desert sojourn is nothing, Khaba! Tomorrow I must travel to Damascus and set my djinn to rebuilding its fallen walls."

"I travel to Petra, to help build grain silos—"

"I must irrigate some pathetic little Canaanite village—"

"That Ring! Solomon feels he can treat us like slaves! I only wish—"

Asmira paid little attention to their complaints. She had picked up the bottle and was turning it slowly between her fingers. How light it was! How strange the substance within! Beyond the panes of crystal, little flecks of color twirled and shimmered, moving slowly like fading petals drifting on the surface of a lake. She thought of the djinni, solemn-eyed and silent, standing beside her in the ravaged gorge. . . .

Across the hall, many of King Solomon's guests had now departed toward the stairs, though others still sat and gorged on the remnants of the food. Beside her, the magicians were sinking lower in their seats, talking louder, drinking deeper. . . .

She looked again at the bottle in her hands.

"Yes, study it by all means!" Khaba had swayed in close, and was regarding her unsteadily. "You are drawn to the strange and wonderful, are you not? Ah, but I have many more such things hidden in my tower! Such choice delights! You shall experience them tomorrow!"

Asmira did her best not to recoil at the vapors of his breath. She smiled. "Please, your cup is empty. Let me get you more wine."

23

How slowly, how *painfully* the long years pass when you're immured inside a bottle! I don't recommend the experience to anyone.[1]

The effect on your essence is the worst of it. Each and every time we're summoned to this Earth our essence begins to die a little, but providing we aren't kept here too long, and distract ourselves with plenty of fights, chases, and sarcastic wordplay, we can keep the ache at bay before returning home to recover. This just isn't possible in a prolonged Confinement. Opportunities for fights and chases are somewhat limited when it's just you in an enclosure an inch or two square, and since sarcasm is one of those activities best enjoyed in company, there's nothing to do but float and think and listen to the soft sound of your essence shriveling, wisp by sorry wisp. To make matters worse, the Confinement spell itself has the property of drawing out this process indefinitely, so you don't even have the dignity of actually *dying*. Khaba had surely chosen well for me: it was a punishment worthy of a bitter foe.

I was utterly cut off inside that crystal sphere. Time was unknowable. No sound penetrated. Sometimes lights and shadows moved against the confines of my prison, but the powerful

---

[1] Humans don't often suffer such indignities, I know, but it *has* happened. One magician I worked for once called for my aid during an earthquake which was toppling his tower. Unfortunately for him, the precise words he used were "Preserve me!" A cork, a great big bottle, a vat of pickling fluid, and—presto!—the job was done.

Binding spell that had been fused into the crystal obscured my vision and I couldn't make the forms out clearly.[2]

To add to my discomfort, the ancient bottle's original contents had evidently been an oily substance, perhaps hair grease for some long-dead Egyptian girl. Not only was the interior still faintly perfumed (rosewood, I thought, with a hint of lime), it was also darn slippery. When I tried, for variety's sake, to take on the guise of a scarab or some other tiny insect, my tarsal claws kept slipping out from under me.

For the most part, therefore, I stayed in my natural state, floating quietly, drifting, thinking noble and somewhat melancholy thoughts, and only occasionally scrawling obscene graffiti on the inside of the glass. Sometimes my mind turned to episodes from my past. I thought of Faquarl and his dismissive assessment of my powers. I thought of the girl, Cyrine, who had so nearly got me freed. I thought of the wicked Khaba—now, with time's remorseless passing, presumably a cursed heap of bones—and his vile helpmate, Ammet, perhaps still wreaking evil somewhere on the hapless world. Most often, of course, I thought of the peace and beauty of my distant home, and wondered when I'd ever return.

And then, after untold ages, when I'd utterly given up hope...

The bottle broke.

One moment it was there, as it had always been, my small domed dungeon, tightly sealed. The next, the walls collapsed

---

[2] Bottled *imps* require less stringent Bindings and their glass is usually transparent. Being regrettably low-minded, they thereupon perform countless contortions to shock and repulse any passersby. Needless to say *I* never stooped to anything like this. It's no fun doing it if you can't see the reaction.

into a shower of crystal shards that fell about me, spinning, glittering, borne on a sudden tide of sound and air.

With the destruction of the bottle, Ammet's spell could not survive. Its strands tore; they burst asunder.

I felt myself dismissed.

A tremor bristled through my essence. With a sudden rush of joy, all pain and suffering were at once forgotten. I lingered not at all. Like a soaring lark I departed from the Earth, faster and faster, passing through the elemental walls that opened to receive me, plunging into the sweet infinity of my home.

The Other Place enfolded me. I was embraced, made many where I had once been one. My essence shook itself free and spread, singing, across the reaches. I joined the endless, whirling dance . . .

And froze.

For an instant my joyous forward momentum and the sudden pull behind me were equal and opposite. I was held suspended, motionless. I just had time to register my alarm. . . .

Then I was wrenched away, ripped from the infinite, plucked back down time's corridor no later than I'd left it. It happened so fast I almost met myself going back.

I dropped like a shower of gold down an endless well.

I funneled inward to a point, and landed.

I looked around. The point was at the center of a pentacle drawn on dark, red-tinted fabric. Close by, in inky shadow, silken curtains hung like spiderwebs, stifling the contours of the room. The air was close and thick with burning frankincense. Reddish candlelight glimmered across a marbled floor like the memory of a gout of blood.

I was back on Earth.

I was back on Earth! Confusion and my shock of loss mingled with the resumption of my pain. With a howl of rage I rose up from the middle of the circle as a red-skinned demon, slender, agile, avid for revenge. My eyes were blazing orbs of gold, their thorn-thin pupils darting to and fro. Below the jutting wad of gristle that functioned as my nose, there gaped a snarling, fang-filled mouth.[3]

The demon bent low, questing all around. It scanned the square of fabric in which it stood, it saw the weights of carven jade that held that fabric to the floor. It saw a flickering oil lamp, the waxen candles, the pots of burning frankincense set out upon the tiles beyond. It saw a certain bag of red-brown leather, open on a silken couch. It saw an upturned plinth, a broken bottle; it saw a scattering of crystal shards. . . .

It saw a *second* pentacle on another fabric square. And standing in *that* pentacle—

"Bartimaeus of Uruk," the Arabian girl intoned, "I bind you by the cords of Nakrah and the manacles of Marib, which are both most grievous and terrible, to hereafter do my bidding, on pain of immediate and fiery expunction. Stand fixed in your proper place until I give you leave, then depart upon your errand with fleet and true intent, without deviation or delay, to return at the precise time and place that I shall give you. . . ."

There was a good deal more of this, all very archaic, not to say long-winded, and spoken in a tortuous South Arabian dialect that was difficult to follow. But I'd been around the block a bit. I got the gist.

★   ★   ★

---

[3] I was, in fact, the living embodiment of a *kusarikku*, a less civilized subtype of utukku, which used to be employed in some of the old Sumerian cities as executioners, tomb-guardians, baby-minders, etc.

I admit that I was shocked. I admit that I was baffled. But put me in a pentacle and the age-old rules are immediately back in force. Whoever summons me risks everything, regardless of what has gone before. And the girl was not safe yet.

She was speaking the Binding mechanisms in something of a trance, standing quite rigid, swaying slightly with the effort of the summoning. Her small fists were clenched, her arms fixed as if bolted to her sides. Her eyes were closed; she recited with metronomic precision the word-seals and phrase-locks that would hold me fast.

The red-skinned demon edged forward within its circle, claws pricking at the cloth beneath its feet. My golden eyes gleamed in the candle smoke. I waited for the mistake or hesitation that would let me snap my bonds like celery and treat her body likewise.

"Almost there," I prompted. "Don't mess things up now. Steady...this is the hard bit. And you're so very, very tired.... So tired I can almost *taste* you." And I snapped my teeth together in the dark.

She blanched then, went paler than the mountain snows. But she made no mistake, she didn't hesitate.[4]

And all too soon I felt the bonds grow tight. My hungry readiness slackened and I subsided in my circle.

The girl finished. She wiped the sweat from her face with the sleeve of her robe.

She looked at me.

---

[4] It was *close*, though. You could tell at once that she wasn't practiced at it. Every last syllable was painfully precise, as if she were in some public-speaking competition. At the end I felt like holding up a mark card with a "6" on it. Contrast this to the best magicians, who throw off multiple summonings casually, while clipping their toenails or having breakfast, and never put a phoneme wrong.

There was silence in the room.

"And what," I said, "do you think you're doing?"

"I just saved you." She was still a little breathless, and her voice was faint. She nodded toward the crystal fragments on the floor. "I got you out."

The red-skinned demon nodded slowly. "So you did. So you did. . . . But only so you could enslave me again within seconds!" Livid flames erupted from the cloth about my feet and licked up to shroud my wrathful form. "Do you not recall," I roared, "how I saved your wretched little life so long ago?"

"So long a— What?"

Fire darted from my eyes; trails of burning sulphur flickered on my shining skin. "Can you *conceive* the pain and suffering I've since endured?" I cried. "Trapped inside that tiny, suffocating prison all those endless years, through all those long slow cycles of the sun and moon? And now, no sooner am I released than you summon me again, without so much as a—" I hesitated, noticing the girl was tapping a delicate foot upon her cloth. "Just how long *was* I trapped, incidentally?"

"A few hours. It's just gone midnight. I was talking with you yesterday afternoon."

The red-skinned demon stared; my flames went out. "Yesterday afternoon? The one just gone?"

"Well, how many others are there? Yes, the yesterday just gone. Look at me. I'm wearing the same clothes."

"Right. . . ." I cleared my throat. "It's just a little bit hard to keep tabs in there. . . . Well, as I say, it's been grim." My voice rose once more. "And I don't care to be summoned again—by you or anybody! If you know what's good for you, you'll let me go."

"That I cannot do."

"You'd better," I snarled. "It's not as if you'll be able to keep me long, anyway. You're obviously a novice."

The girl's eyes blazed; flames didn't dart from them, but it was a close thing.

"Know, Bartimaeus of Uruk," she cried, "that in my land I am an initiate of the Eighteenth Attainment in the Temple of Marib! Know that it was I who summoned the demon Zufra and, by whipping her with cords, forced her to dig the reservoir at Dhamar in a single night! Know too that I have subdued twelve dozen demons to my will and cast nine into the innermost pit!" She pushed a strand of hair back from her brow and smiled grimly. "And that I am now *your* master is the final thing you need to know."

The red-skinned demon gave a caw of mirth. "Good try," I said. "Falls down on three accounts. First, 'Eighteenth Attainment in the Temple of Marib' doesn't mean a fig to me. For all I know it means you're qualified to scrub the toilets." (The girl gave an indignant squeak here, but I ignored it.) "Second," I went on, "there's your tone of voice. You meant it to be awe-inspiring and terrible, didn't you? Sorry. Sounded scared and constipated. Third, it's clearly all absolute baloney! You only barely got your First Injunction[5] out without tripping over your own tongue. I thought you were going to bind *yourself* at one point, you got so hesitant. Let's face it, this is all a bluff."

The girl's nose had gone all white and pinched. "It is not!"

"Is so too."

---

[5] *First Injunction*: traditionally spoken in all summonings since at least the days of Eridu. Usually something along the lines of: "By the constraints of the circle, the points on the pentacle, and the chain of signs, know that I am your master. You will obey my will."

"Is not!"

"Say that any higher and you're going to shatter that nice vase over there." I folded my scaly arms and gave her a savage glare. "And, by the way, you've just proved my point *again*. How many *real* magicians do you think get involved in stroppy little verbal spats like this? They'd have hit me with the Dark Scouring by now and had done with it."

The girl stared at me. Her face was livid.

"You don't even know what a Dark Scouring is, do you?" I said, grinning.

She breathed hard. "No. But I do know *this*." She took hold of the silver sun disk around her neck and spoke a muttered phrase. Once again it was barely competent, the kind of Ward[6] a hedge-witch might use to admonish a naughty imp. Even so, a swell of black substance plumed in the air, reared back and darted at my circle.

I lifted my hand to fend off the stroke, called out her name. *"Cyrine!"*[7]

Black shards of force went straight through my lifted hand and scoured my essence like a storm of whirling pins.

They vanished. I considered my perforations grimly. "Cyrine's not actually your name, is it?" I said.

"No. Who'd be so stupid as to give up their real name so readily—*Bartimaeus*?"

---

[6] *Ward*: A short incantation that turns the spirit's own power back on itself. High-level Wards, used by trained magicians, include barbarities such as the Systemic Vise and the Stimulating Compass. These can do real damage to a djinni. Low-level ones, such as the girl knew, are pretty much the equivalent of a quick spank on the bottom, and about as sophisticated.

[7] Knowledge of someone's birth-name allows you to nullify many of their magical attacks. As not demonstrated here.

Which was a fair point. "Even so," I said, "as punishments go, that was pathetic. And once again you only just spoke it right. Go on, do another one, I dare you."

"I don't need to." The girl pushed her robes aside, revealing three silver daggers at her hip. "Anger me again," she said, "and I'll skewer you with one of these."

She might have done, as well. Trapped in the circle, I knew that my opportunities for dodging were limited. But I just shrugged. "That's my final proof," I said. "You're an assassin of some kind. You're not a magician at all. And you *need* to be a magician, if you're going to deal with me." My teeth glinted in the shadows. "I *killed* my last master, you know."

"What—Khaba? The one who trapped you in the bottle?" The girl gave a rude snort. "He seemed alive enough to me when I left him drunk downstairs."

"All right," I growled, "my last master but one. Same difference. Statistically speaking, that's the fate of forty-six percent of all—" I stopped short. "Wait up. The magician Khaba is *downstairs*? Where exactly are we?"

"The palace of King Solomon. Do you not recognize it? I thought you were well acquainted with the place; that is why I released you."

"Well, I don't know every last bedroom, do I?" And all at once the red-skinned demon grew suddenly still, conscious of an unpleasant trepidation, a creeping certainty that, annoying as things currently were, they were shortly to get a whole lot worse.

I fixed her with a cold, hard stare. She stared back, her eyes as cold as mine. "I'll say this politely just one time," I said. "Thank you for letting me out of my prison. That puts paid to the debt you owe me. Now—speak the Dismissal and let me go."

"Have I or have I not bound you, Bartimaeus?"

"For the moment." I prodded the cloth with a toe-claw. "But I'll find a loophole. It won't take long."

"Well, while you look," the girl said, "you'll agree you are in my service. Which means you do as I say, or suffer the Dismal Flame. You'll find *that* won't take long, either."

"Oh, sure. Like you know *that* spell."

"Try me."

And here, of course, I was fairly caught, because I couldn't be certain either way. It was *possible* she didn't know the incantation —which is the final security of all magicians—but equally possible that she did. And if she did, and I disobeyed her, it was a sad outlook for me.

I changed the subject. "Why did Khaba give you the bottle?"

"He didn't," she said. "I stole it."

So there you go. As predicted, things were worse already. Worse mainly (I was thinking here of the horrors of the magician's vaulted room) for the girl.

"You're a fool," I said. "Stealing from *him* is not a good idea."

"Khaba is irrelevant." Her face was still pale, but a certain composure had returned to it, and there was a brightness in her eyes that I didn't like at all. They shone, in fact, with a zealot's gleam.[8] "Khaba is nothing," she said. "Forget him. You and I must concern ourselves with greater things."

---

[8] *Zealots*: wild-eyed persons afflicted with incurable certainty about the workings of the world, a certainty that can lead to violence when the world doesn't fit. My personal favorites, some centuries after Solomon, were the stylites, hairy ascetics who spent years sitting atop high pillars in the desert. There was nothing violent about them, other than their smell. They summoned djinn to beguile them with temptations, the better to prove their abstinence and faith. Personally I didn't bother with the temptation bit. I used to tickle them until they fell off.

And now my trepidation became a cold, hard knot of fear, because I recalled the girl's conversation in the gorge, and all her questions about forbidden matters. "Listen," I said. "Before you say anything we'll both regret, think about where you are. The planes around us are a-thrum with the auras of great spirits. I can sense them, even if *you* cannot, and the echoes they make are almost deafening. If you wish to summon me, go right ahead, but do it somewhere far away where we have a chance of prolonged survival. Stealing magicians' property is frowned on here, and so are unofficial summonings. They're *exactly* the sort of things it's best not to do in or around the House of Solomon."[9]

"Bartimaeus," the girl said, putting her hand upon one of the daggers in her belt, "stop talking."

I stopped. I waited. Waited for the worst.

"Tonight," the girl went on, "you are going to help me complete the mission that has brought me a thousand miles and more from the gardens of fair Sheba."

"*Sheba?* Hold on, you mean the Himyar stuff wasn't true *either?* Honestly. What a fibber you are."

"Tonight, you will help me save my nation, or we shall *both* die in the attempt."

So, bang went my last lingering hope that she wanted me to help change the color coordination of her bedroom. Which was a pity. I could have done wonders with those silks.

"Tonight, you will help me do two things."

---

[9] Other forbidden activities in the palace included: fighting, devouring servants, running in the corridors, cursing, drawing rude stick figures on the harem walls, causing unpleasant smells to permeate the kitchens, and spitting on the upholstery. At least these were the ones I'd got told off for; there were probably others.

"Two things. . . ." I said. "Very well. Which are . . . ?"

Just *how* mad was she? Exactly where on the scale of raving insanity did she fall?

"Kill King Solomon," the girl said brightly, "and take his Ring."

She smiled at me. Her bright eyes shone.

Right on the very end, that's where.

24

Asmira had expected the djinni to say *something* after her revelation—he had not exactly been short of comments hitherto. But instead his stillness deepened, and the little flames that had been flickering along the contours of his body dwindled suddenly and went out.

Still as a stone he stood, and as silent as one too—yet the silence he projected was utterly ferocious. It filled the room like a poisoned cloud, bearing down upon her with such intensity that her knees began to buckle. Quite unconsciously she stepped back a pace upon her cloth.

She closed her eyes and took a long slow breath. *Calm.* She had to remain calm. Bartimaeus, despite his threats and protestations, was hers now. He had no choice but to obey.

Only calm, swift action, almost without thought, had enabled Asmira to survive the previous half hour. If she had halted to assess what she was doing—robbing a powerful magician, summoning a demon far stronger than any she had ever attempted—her fear would have overcome her, she would have faltered and been doomed. Instead, as was at the heart of her talent, she carried out each stage with detached concentration, focusing on the practicalities and not the implications.

The hardest part, in fact, had come beforehand, during the endless wait at the banquet table, while Khaba and several of the other high magicians drank themselves insensible. Outwardly Asmira had sat there smiling, laughing at their jokes, and sipping at her wine. Inwardly she had been in an agony of suspense, expecting every moment to be sent away, or for the Egyptian to put the crystal bottle out of reach: behind her smile she longed to scream. But when, finally, Khaba's head lolled and his eyelids closed, she was ready on the instant. Plucking the bottle from beneath his nose, she walked out of the hall beneath the ranks of flying djinn and hurried to her room. There she removed the cloths and candles from her bag, set them out methodically, smashed the bottle, and made the summons. And all without a single hesitation.

The incantation itself had almost finished her. Asmira had summoned minor djinn before, using the same technique, but she had not reckoned on Bartimaeus's strength. Even with her eyes closed, she had felt his power pressing against the margins of her circle as she tried to complete the words; knowledge of what would happen should she make a single error had drained her energies rapidly. But Sheba's fate depended on her survival, and *that* knowledge was stronger still. Despite her weariness, despite the many months since she had last performed a summons, despite the djinni's fury beating down upon her, Asmira had shut her fears out from her mind and bound him to her service.

And now it just remained to spell that service out.

She cleared her throat, and fixed her gaze upon the demonic shape. How different from the creature's pleasant guise the day before! But terrible as it was, it might be used.

"Bartimaeus," she said hoarsely, "I charge you now to come with me from this place, without hesitation or delay, and bring me safely to King Solomon, so that I may put him to death and remove his Ring—and for the avoidance of doubt, this refers to the talisman of unparalleled power and not one of his lesser rings—then assist me in escaping with it to a place of safety. Is that all clear?"

The figure said nothing. It was wreathed in smoke, a dark and frozen thing.

Asmira shivered; a cold breeze seemed to waft across her neck. She glanced back at the chamber door, but all was still.

"I also charge," she went on, "that if Solomon cannot be slain, or if I am captured or separated from you, above all else you must steal and destroy the Ring, or, that being impossible, hide it permanently from the sight and knowledge of all men." She took a deep breath. "I say again: is that clear?"

The djinni did not move. Even the fires in his yellow eyes seemed to have died away.

"Bartimaeus, *is that clear?*"

There was a stirring in the slender body. "Suicide. It can't be done."

"You are an ancient spirit of great resource. You told me so yourself."

"Steal the *Ring?*" The voice was very soft. "Kill Solomon? No. It's suicide. I might as well jump down Khaba's throat or take a bath in molten silver. I might as well eat myself feetfirst, or put my head under the bottom of a squatting elephant. At least those options would be entertaining to watch. You send me to my death."

"I risk myself as well," Asmira said.

"Ah, yes. That's the worst thing about it." The red-skinned demon moved at last. He seemed to have shrunk a little, and the brilliance of his color had leached away. He half turned away from her, hugging himself as if he felt the cold. "You don't care about dying," he said. "In fact, you almost expect it. And if that's the way you feel about *yourself*, there's not much hope for one of your *slaves*, is there?"

"We have no time to debate this, Bartimaeus. There are far greater things at risk here than the lives of you and me."

"Greater things?" The demon chuckled hollowly. "Oh, I wonder what they are. You know," he went on, interrupting Asmira as she began to speak, "ordinary magicians don't care about anything except their wealth and waistline. But they *do* have a strong sense of self-preservation: they don't like the idea of dying any more than I do. So when they send me off on a job, it's rarely suicidal. Dangerous, yes—but always a calculated risk. Because they know that if *I* fail, the consequences might rebound on *them*. But you?" The demon gave a heavy sigh. "No. I knew I'd run into someone like you one day. I knew it and I dreaded it. Because you're a fanatic, aren't you? You're young and pretty and ever-so-empty-headed, and you *don't care*."

An image flashed before Asmira's eyes: the tower of Marib burning, almost two weeks before. Chains of people bringing water. Bodies being brought down to the street. Furious tears studded her vision. "You foul, self-centered, vicious little . . . *imp*!" she snarled. "You have no *idea* how much I care! You have no idea why I'm doing this!"

"You think not?" The demon held up three knobbly, clawed fingers and counted them off swiftly. "Three guesses. Your king. Your country. Your religion. At least two of them, and probably all three. Well? Tell me I'm wrong."

Asmira knew that the djinni was deliberately provoking her, and knew that she should ignore it. But rage and weariness made her susceptible. "I am here out of love for my queen," she said, "and for Sheba, fairest nation under the Sun. And there can be no higher honor than that—not that a soulless creature like you would ever realize it."

The demon grinned, showing curved, white, sharply intersecting fangs. "Well now," he said, "I *must* be soulless, because all that rubbish leaves me cold." His shape suddenly blurred; it became a succession of tousled, wide-eyed youths, tall, short, handsome, plain, with skins of many nations. The last was the same beautiful, dark-haired guise she remembered from the gorge, but this time wingless, sober-faced. "You don't need a *djinni* for this job," the youth said. "Young men are best at dying for empty concepts. Go back to Sheba and find some of your own."

"I'm *not* talking about empty concepts, demon!" Asmira cried. "King Solomon is my real and bitter enemy! What do *you* know about it? You have never walked in the gardens of Sheba, where the fragrances of jasmine, cinnamon, and cassia rise up to heaven. You've never seen the ruffling blue spice forests of Shabwa, or the alabaster walls of Marib, where the great reservoir glitters amid the bright green fields. All this is doomed unless I act! Very soon, if he is not stopped, Solomon will turn his cursed Ring and bring forth a host of demons just as vile as you. They will fly across the desert and fall upon my country. They will raze the cities, destroy the crops, and drive my people wailing into the desert. I cannot let this happen!"

The youth shrugged. "I understand your pain, I really do," he said. "But pain changes nothing. So Sheba's got some pretty plants and buildings, has it? Well, so did Uruk, and Uruk was destroyed by the Babylonians without a second thought. The fountains where its children played were smashed and the water ran away into the ground. Its walls were broken and the towers razed and the gardens burned and the ruins covered over by the sand. In fifty years its very site was lost. So it goes. These things happen in your unpleasant little world. It's Sheba's turn now; one day it will be Jerusalem's. Take the long view, like me, and be content. Failing that, go ahead and die. Just leave me out of it. This squabble's got nothing to do with me."

"It does," Asmira said viciously, "now that I've summoned you."

"So summon someone else!" The djinni's voice grew urgent. "Why choose me? There isn't one good reason."

"You're right. Not one, but many. You know Solomon's palace, you know its layout and routine, you know the names and natures of its guards. You are a powerful spirit. And you were stupid enough to tell me your name a few hours ago. How's that?"

"Oh, *very* succinct," the djinni snarled, and his eyes were almond slits of flame. "Especially the *name* part. All that fluffy stuff about urging Khaba to let me go...You were already planning this, weren't you? You'd got my name, and wanted me freely available for use!"

Asmira shook her head. "That's not true."

"No? Faquarl was right. You *are* a liar. I should have killed you when I had the chance."

"I *intended* to do the job myself," Asmira cried. "But I ran out of time. I can't get access to Solomon. No one ever sees him except in council. In two days Sheba will be gone! I need help, Bartimaeus, and I need it now. When that revolting magician showed me what he'd done with you, I took my chance. I've freed you, don't forget! I've done you a favor! Just serve me this once—then I'll let you go."

"Oh, just this once? This one little impossible job? Kill Solomon? Steal the Ring? Have you not heard about Philocretes—"

"Heard it."

"Azul—"

"Seen it."

"Or any of the other foolish spirits who tried to destroy the king?" The young man spoke earnestly. "Listen to me: Khaba has a marid for a slave—it's his shadow, by the way: look out for it next time he's torturing you. I came up against that spirit a few hours ago: I didn't have a chance. He wiped the floor with me. If he'd had a cold, he'd have used me as a handkerchief. That was one single marid. And he is *nothing* to what can come out of that Ring!"

"Which is why," Asmira said, "we kill Solomon tonight. Now—not a word more. Time's short, and we have much to do."

The djinni gazed at her. "Is that your final word?"

"It is. Get moving."

"Very well." And all at once the young man stepped out of his circle and into hers. Suddenly he was right beside her. Asmira gave a cry and scrabbled at her belt, but the djinni was too fast. He caught her hand as it closed upon a dagger. The grip was gentle, the touch of the fingers slightly cool. She could not pull free.

The young man bent his head close to hers. Candlelight moved across the human-seeming skin; a sweet odor of lime and rosewood hung about him. Behind the dark ringlets of hair, light burned in the golden eyes. His lips were smiling. "No need to tremble," he said. "You know I'd have killed you already if I could."

Asmira made a token effort at pulling free. "Keep away from me."

"Oh, but I've got to stay close if I'm to keep you alive. Don't flinch, now. Show me the back of your hand."

He lifted her wrist, inspected the skin briefly, while Asmira wriggled in outrage. "What are you doing?" she said.

"Just looking for some crisscross lines. There's an assassin sect that's been causing trouble in these parts for years. That's their mark. But I see you're not one of them." The young man dropped her hand and grinned broadly as she stepped away. "Bit late to whip a dagger out *now*, isn't it? Thought you were meant to be fast."

Asmira's voice was thick. "Enough! Take me to Solomon."

"We both know you're going to make a mistake sooner or later," the djinni said. "And we both know I'll be waiting." He turned away, and moved swiftly past her to the door. "In the meantime, a lovely little walk awaits us. Where are we now? The guest wing?"

"I think so."

"Well, the royal apartments are on the other side of the palace from here. That means crossing the gardens. There aren't many guards stationed in the gardens."

"Good," Asmira said.

"On account of all the afrits and horlas, the kusarikku and scorpion-men, the whip-bearers and the skin-stealers, the sentinels of flame and earth, and creeping death, and all the other varied supernatural slaves that wander about King Solomon's household specifically to find and slay idiots like us," Bartimaeus said. "So, *getting* to his apartments is going to be interesting in itself." He opened the door and peered out into the shadows of the passage. "After that, of course, the fun *really* begins. . . . Well, nothing's going to kill us in these next ten yards. That's a sensation that isn't going to last, believe me, so enjoy it while you can."

He slipped out without a backward glance. Asmira followed him. Together, they set off into the dark.

25

Here's the thing. Insane as she was, the Sheban girl was correct up to a point. I *did* know my way through the palace pretty well.

For instance I knew, better than most, the position of the imp-bulbs in the walkways and the weird-stones in the gardens; I knew the trajectories of the magical luminosities that floated at varying heights among the cyclamen and cypress trees. I knew where to look for the human guards, I knew the routes they marched on their nightly rounds; I knew when they'd be alert, and when they'd be playing their games of Dogs and Jackals[1] and taking their furtive sips of barley beer. I also knew where to look for the deeper spies and watch-spirits that waited high in passage corners and in the shadowed cracks between the flag-stones. I could detect them in the fluttering of wall hangings, in the subtle whorls upon the carpets, in the sound of wind rushing across the roof tiles.

All these dangers, possibly, I could anticipate and avoid.

But kill Solomon and take the Ring from off his finger? Ah, no. There I didn't have a clue.

---

[1] *Dogs and Jackals*: a board game, usually played with ivory pieces, although some-times the pharaohs back in Thebes did it large-scale with djinn taking on the relevant canine shapes and bounding around a courtyard-sized board. You had to wrestle your opponent when you landed on a square, and it was all done in the heat of the day, so everyone got quite sticky and odorous, and the collars didn't half itch. Not that I know anything about it really, having been far too important to take part in such a humiliating exercise.

My choice was stark and simple, and both options painfully similar in outcome. The Dismal Flame awaited me if I disobeyed the girl. That was a certainty: I saw it in her eyes. Despite all my careful, measured arguments—which would have made a hardened warlord pack away his scimitars and take up sewing— her eyes retained that glassy fixity humans get when they're the self-appointed agent of a higher cause, and their own personality (such as it is) has faded out altogether. Speaking as a being whose personality remains winningly constant no matter what my *outward* appearance, I always find this sort of thing disturbing: everything's upside-down somehow. But what it boiled down to was this: the girl was intent on sacrificing herself—and more importantly, me—and nothing was going to persuade her otherwise.

Which meant that, until she made some sort of error, I had to try to carry out her commands and steal the Ring.

Now this, as I'd told her, meant our hideous deaths, as the stories of Azul, Philocretes, and the rest proved all too well. They'd been spirits far tougher than me, and each and every one had come to a sticky end, with Solomon left still swaggering about just as smugly as ever. The chances of my succeeding where they'd failed weren't great.

But hey, I was still Bartimaeus of Uruk, with more resourcefulness and guile[2] in my toenails than those three porridge-brained afrits together. I wasn't going to give up quite yet.

Besides, if you're going to die horribly, you might as well do it with style.

★   ★   ★

---

[2] Not to mention mindless optimism.

At that hour of the night the corridors of the guest wing were unfrequented, aside from one or two stray watch-imps making random sorties between the floors. I could have swallowed them easily enough, but I preferred stealth at this stage of operations. Whenever I heard the beat of leather wings approaching, I wove subtle Concealments about the girl and me. We stood motionless behind our nets of threads as the imps drifted past, trailing their alarm-horns, bickering about magicians; when all was still, I revoked the spell and we tiptoed on.

Along gently curving passages, past endless doors... The best thing about this early stage was that the girl was *quiet*, and by this I mean she didn't say anything. Like most trained killers she was naturally light-footed and economical of movement, but up until then she'd also been as shy and retiring as a howler monkey stranded up a tree. *Thinking* clearly made her agitated and voluble; now we were actually *doing* something she was a lot happier, and she glided along behind me in a kind of grateful silence. I was grateful too. It did me good to have a moment's peace and figure out what I was going to do.

Getting us to Solomon's apartments past all the traps and watchers was the first job I was faced with, a task most seasoned observers would have considered impossible. I admit I found it taxing too. It took me approximately three floors, two flights of stairs, and the length of a vaulted annex before I'd formulated a plan.[3]

I pulled the girl into the shadows of an arch and spoke tersely: "Right, the danger begins now. Once through here we're in

---

[3] Can you define "plan" as "a loose sequence of manifestly inadequate observations and conjectures, held together by panic, indecision, and ignorance"? If so, it was a very good plan.

the main section of the palace, where anything goes. The spirits roaming about will be very different from those piddly imps we just passed—bigger and hungrier. They're the sort not allowed in the guest block in case of accidents, if you take my meaning. So: we're going to have to be extra careful from now on. Do exactly what I tell you when I tell you, and don't ask questions. Believe me, you won't have time."

The girl drew her lips in tight. "If you think I suddenly trust you, Bartimaeus—"

"Oh, don't trust *me,* whatever you do. Trust your summons: I'm charged to keep you safe at this point, aren't I?" I squinted ahead into the shadows. "Right, we're going to take a quick and quiet shortcut to the gardens. After that—we'll see. Follow me closely."

I stole forward, light as gossamer, under the arch and down a flight of steps to the margins of a great long hall. Solomon had had it built during his "Babylonian period"; the walls were made of blue-glazed bricks and decorated with lions and coiling dragon-beasts. At intervals on either side rose soaring plinths, surmounted with looted statues from ancient cultures. Light came from great metal braziers embedded high above our heads. I checked the planes—all were, for the moment, clear.

Along the hall on the balls of my feet, gazelle-swift, keeping to the shadows. I could hear the girl's breathing at my ear; her feet made not the slightest sound.

I drew up short, and was instantly knocked into from behind.

"Ow! Watch it!"

"You said follow me closely."

"What, are you a comedy farmhand? You're meant to be an assassin."

"I'm *not* an assassin, I'm a hereditary guard."

"An hereditary idiot, more like. Get behind this; I think something's coming."

We ducked behind the nearest plinth, pressed close into its shadows. The girl was frowning; she sensed nothing, but I felt the reverberations on the planes.

They trembled with sudden violence. Something entered the hall at the far end.

Which was the self-same moment the benighted girl chose to try to speak. I clamped a hand across her mouth, made ferocious signs enjoining silence. We shrank back against the stone.

For several painful heartbeats nothing happened. The girl was fretful; she wriggled a bit under my heavy hand. Without speaking, I pointed upward at the tiled wall, where a vast silhouette was slowly passing, a thing of monstrous mass and bulbous shape, with swaying limbs and twitching threads of matter trailing in its wake.... The girl grew still then—even rigid; I could have propped her like a broom against the wall. We stayed motionless as the visitation passed. At last it was gone; and at no time had there been a single noise.

"What *was* it?" the girl hissed, when I released her.

"From the way the planes bent," I said, "I'd guess a marid. Khaba's servant is one of those. They're usually pretty rare, but that's what happens when you have the Ring of Solomon kicking about: even higher entities become two-a-shekel.[4] Aren't you glad I didn't let you speak just then?"

---

[4] It's true that when it came to spirit-slaves there was serious devaluation going on in Jerusalem at that time. In normal eras a djinni is pretty close to the top of the pile, treated by all and sundry with appropriate awe and respect. But thanks to the Ring, and the concentration of top magicians drawn into its orbit, it had got so you couldn't throw a stone over your shoulder without hitting an afrit on the kneecap.

The girl shivered. "I'm just glad I didn't actually *see* the thing straight on."

"Oh, if you'd *seen* it," I said, "you'd have thought it was just a cute little blue-eyed slave boy toddling up the hall. You'd still have been chortling at its curly locks and little chubby chin when its spear-tail got you through the throat. Well, this is no time for pleasant daydreaming. We'd better get— Hold on...."

From a side arch, midway along the hall, a node of light was drifting. A diminutive figure in white robes walked beneath it, limping slightly. And hanging like a formless cloud above his shoulder—

"Get back!" I thrust us both behind the plinth again.

"What now?" the girl hissed. "I thought this was meant to be a quiet shortcut."

"It normally is. It's like Thebes marketplace tonight. This is Solomon's vizier."

"Hiram?" She frowned. "He's got a mouse—"

"It's not a mouse on the higher planes, believe you me. With *that* perched on him, it's no surprise he's got a limp. Stay very still."

Unlike the marid, Hiram's footsteps were loud enough to hear, and to begin with they appeared to be moving off in a satisfactory manner. Then, all at once, I heard the mouse squeak warily and the footsteps stop. There was a soft, wet sound and, a moment later, the smell of rotten eggs drifting down the hall. I knew what *that* meant. The foliot Gezeri.

"Well?" Hiram's voice was clear; he must have been

The consequence was that honest entities like me were shoved right down the pecking order, lumped together with foliots, imps, and other undesirables.

standing twenty paces from where we hid. "What do *you* want, creature?"

"A quick chat, O great Hiram," Gezeri said, his tone somehow completely subverting the respectful nature of the words. "My master, magnificent Khaba, has lately been a little indisposed."

"I saw him at dinner." Hiram's distaste was clear. "He was drunk."

"Yeah, well, he's come around now, and he's lost something. Small bottle. Mislaid it, can't find it. Maybe rolled off the table, maybe been cleared away with the other scraps. We've had a look about, can't set eyes on it. Very mysterious."

Hiram snorted. "His gift to Solomon? That's of no consequence to me. I should have thought *you* would have kept an eye on it, being his slave; you, or that vile shadow of his."

"Ah no, we were in his tower, clearing up a mess that—oh, it's not important. Listen"—Gezeri spoke nonchalantly; I could imagine him sitting in his cloud, twirling his tail in a casual paw—"you ain't seen that Arabian girl about, have you?"

"The priestess Cyrine? She will have gone to her room."

"Yeah. Which room *is* that, if you don't mind telling? See, Khaba's wondering—"

"Actually, I *do* mind." Hiram's footsteps suddenly resumed. He would have been walking away from Gezeri now, speaking over his shoulder. "Let Khaba sort out his own mess in the morning. He's not to disturb any of our guests now."

"But see, we think—" There followed a muttered word from the magician, a mouse's battle squeak, and a shrill curse from Gezeri. "Ow!" he cried. "Keep it off! All right, all right, I'm going!" After that came the unmistakable sound of a lilac cloud imploding. The magician's footsteps pattered slowly away along the hall.

I scowled over at the girl. *"That* didn't take long. We've got Khaba on our heels. We'd better hurry up and get killed by something else before he discovers where you are."

Rather to my relief no further demonic waifs and strays came wandering along the Babylonian Hall, and we got to the far end unmolested. After that it was a simple matter to duck through the Hittite Room, veer past the Sumerian Annex, take a left beside the Celtic Cabinet[5] and, just before we got to the sprawling (and guarded) Egyptian Halls, step through a little arch into the southern cloisters beside the gardens.

"Okay," I breathed. "Now we pause and have a recce. What do you see here?"

The night beyond the cloisters was at its deepest, darkest, and most secretive. The air was clear; a breeze still carried warmth from the eastern deserts. I scanned the stars: judging by the brightness of Arcturus, and Osiris's waning, we had four or five hours left before dawn.

The gardens stretched away from us, north and south. They were ink-dark, save where rectangles of light from the palace windows lay twisted over shrubs, statues, fountains, palm trees, oleander flowers. At some unseen distance to the north lay the black wall of the king's tower, conveniently beside the harem, but separated from the main section of the palace. To the south were many of the public halls, including the audience chambers, the rooms where Solomon's human servants lived and worked,

---

[5] *Celtic Cabinet*: a small bureau containing a few pots of dried woad and a frayed grass G-string brought back from the British Isles. Solomon's djinn had traveled the globe in many directions, hunting for cultural marvels to stimulate his appetite. Some journeys yielded better dividends than others.

and—slightly apart from the other buildings—his treasury, filled with gold.

The girl had been taking it all in. "These are the gardens? Seem quiet enough."

"Which shows how much you know," I said. "You humans really are useless, aren't you? It's all go here. See that statue over by the rhododendrons? That's an afrit. If you could make out the higher planes you'd see—well, it's probably just as well you can't see what he's doing. He's one of the night shift captains. All the sentries in this section of the palace will report to him periodically; they keep watch on each other too, just to ensure nothing's untoward. I can see five—no, six—djinn either concealed in the shrubbery or floating among the trees, and there are a few wispy firefly things that I don't like the look of either. In the middle of that central walkway is a trip thread that triggers something nasty, and up there in the sky there's a great big soaring fifth-plane dome covering the gardens; any spirit flying through that will activate alarms. So, taken all in all, this part of the palace is pretty well locked down."

"I'll take your word for it," the girl said. "How do we get through?"

"We don't," I said. "Not yet. We need to cause a distraction. I think I can arrange that, but first, I've got a question for you: Why?"

"Why what?"

"Why are we doing all this? Why must we die?"

The girl scowled. Thinking again! How it taxed her. "I told you. Solomon threatens Sheba."

"In what way, precisely?"

"He demands our frankincense! A vast ransom! If we do not pay, he will destroy us! He told my queen so."

"Came himself, did he?"

"No. He sent a messenger. What difference does it make?"

"Maybe none. So pay the ransom."

It was as if I'd asked her to kiss a corpse. Anger, incredulity, and revulsion jostled for position in her face. "My queen would *never* do such a thing," she hissed. "It would be a crime against her honor!"

"Ye-e-e-s," I said. "And we wouldn't be dead."

For a second you could sense the cogs whirring; then her expression went all hard and blank. "I serve my queen, just as my mother did, and my grandmothers, and *their* mothers before them. That is all there is to it. Now, we're wasting time. *Let's go.*"

"Not you," I said shortly. "You need to keep undercover here a moment, and don't talk to any strange imps while I'm gone. Sorry—no arguments!" She had begun a tirade of questions and demands. "The more we dawdle the sooner Khaba will catch us. His marid Ammet is probably already trying to trace your aura. What we need to do is find an appropriate place for you to hide.... Aha!"

That "Aha" was me noticing a thick rosebush just outside the cloister window. It had resplendent foliage, some slightly tired pinkish flowers, and an awful lot of very spiny thorns. All in all, I felt it was perfect for our purposes. A swift grab, a hoist and dangle, and down the girl plopped into the thickest, thorniest patch of all.

I listened hopefully.... Not even a squeak. She was very well trained.

With her safely disposed of, I changed into a small, brown, and rather insignificant-looking cricket and flew off along the margins of the gardens, keeping low among the flowers.

You might have noticed that after my initial rage and

despondency, I was recovering a certain amount of my customary élan. The truth was that an odd, fatalistic exhilaration had begun to seize hold of me. The sheer magnitude, the sheer dumb audacity of what I was now attempting was beginning to exert its own appeal. Okay, the certain-death part wasn't so hot, but given that I had no choice in the matter, I found I rather relished the challenge of my night's work. Outwit a palaceful of spirits? Destroy the most celebrated magician then living? Steal the most powerful artifact of all? These were objectives worthy of the legendary Bartimaeus of Uruk and a far better use of my time than carrying big string bags of artichokes about the place, or bowing and scraping before masters like the vile Egyptian. I rather wondered what Faquarl would say if he could see me now.

Speaking of masters, the Arabian girl might be obsessive, driven, and somewhat humorless, but despite my fury at the impudence of her summoning, I could not entirely despise her. Her personal courage was self-evident; also, there was the fact that she was prepared to sacrifice herself along with me.

The insignificant cricket headed south beside the gardens, in the *opposite* direction to the apartments of the king. As I went, I fixed the position of as many sentries as I could spot, taking note of their size, manner, and vibrancy of aura.[6] Most were djinn of medium potency, and there were a fair number of them about, albeit fewer than in the northern regions of the gardens.

I felt there was room to make them fewer still.

I was particularly interested in a secluded bit of garden not far from Solomon's treasury: you could see its roof rising just

---

[6] Since most of us are able to adopt all manner of shapes, the most reliable way of assessing our relative strength quickly is by our auras, which wax and wane (wane, mainly) throughout our time on Earth.

beyond the trees. Before long I singled out a djinni stationed here, standing all on his own beside one of Solomon's antiquities, a massive disk of weathered stone fixed upright in the grass.

To my great delight I recognized the djinni in question. It was none other than Bosquo, that same pompous little bean-counter who had ticked me off when I'd brought the artichokes in "late" a couple of weeks before. He stood with weedy arms folded, potbelly protruding, and an expression of abominable vacancy on his dreary face.

What better place could there be to begin?

The cricket's wings began to beat at a slightly faster, more sinister tempo. It made a series of discreet loops and passes to check that no one else was around, then landed on the stone at Bosquo's back. I tapped him on the shoulder with a foreleg.

Bosquo gave a grunt of surprise, and turned to look.

With that, the city's night of carnage began.

26

It was very *quiet* carnage to begin with, though. I didn't want to disturb anyone.

To deal with Bosquo took approximately fifteen seconds. This was slightly longer than expected. He had a couple of awkward tusks.

In the four minutes that followed, I paid several little visits to other sentries in that area of the gardens. Each encounter was similarly short, sharp, and relatively painless—at least for me.[1]

With everything concluded, I turned back into a cricket and —temporarily somewhat full and sluggish—drifted back in the direction of the girl. But I didn't go to get her yet; I was more interested in the night shift captain standing near the rhododendron thicket. I flew as close as I could to him in safety; then, alighting on one of Solomon's more unusual sculptures, crept beneath the crook of a thigh to watch developments.

They weren't long in coming.

The afrit was masquerading as a statue himself on the first plane—a demure milkmaid or some such fiction. On the others he was a glowering gray ogre with knobbly knees, bronze armbands, and an ostrich feather loincloth; in other words, he was *exactly* the kind of spirit I didn't want stationed in the gardens

---

[1] I won't go into the details here, to spare the sensibilities of my more delicate readers, but suffice it to say that the horrid scenes were enlivened by my caustic wit, plus certain rather clever changes of form, which had the amusing effect of —well, you'll see.

while the girl and I were passing. From his belt hung an enormous horn of ivory and bronze.

Presently, things began to happen. Out from the bushes scampered a gangling ape, with a bright pink muzzle and a shock of orange hair. It skidded to a halt before the afrit, sat back on its haunches, and performed a brief salute. "Zahzeel, I crave a word!"

"Well, Kibbet?"

"I have been making my rounds in the southern gardens. Bosquo is missing from his post."

The afrit frowned. "Bosquo? Who sits below the treasury? He has leave to patrol the Rose Glade and the eastern arbors. No doubt you will find him there."

"I have looked under every twig and leaf," the ape replied. "Bosquo is nowhere to be seen."

The ogre pointed at the sparkling dome high above the garden. "The outer nexus has not been breached. There is no attack from outside. Bosquo has gone walkabout and shall be Stippled soundly when he chooses to return. Go back to your duties, Kibbet, and report to me at sunrise."

The ape departed. Safe in its hiding place, the cricket chirped quietly in satisfaction.

Standing on a plinth for hours isn't my idea of fun, but Zahzeel the ogre seemed happy with his lot. Over the next minute or two he rocked idly back on his heels a bit, flexed his knees once or twice, and made a variety of contented smacking noises with his mouth. Perhaps he would have spent the whole night doing this if he'd been given the opportunity.

It wasn't to be. In a shower of leaves and a four-limbed lollop, the ape burst out from the bushes once more. It appeared rather more disheveled than previously; its teeth were bared, and its eyes bulged in their sockets.

"Zahzeel! I make report of further oddities."

"Not Bosquo again?"

"Bosquo has not yet been located, sir. But now Susu and Trimble are missing too."

The ogre stopped short. "What? Where were *they* stationed?"

"On the battlements adjacent to the treasury. Susu's pike was discovered in the garden below, protruding from the flower bed. Several of Trimble's scales were also scattered here and there, but there is no sign of the djinn themselves on any plane."

"And the outer nexus is still undamaged?"

"Yes, sir."

Zahzeel smacked a meaty fist into a palm. "Then nothing has entered from outside! If there is an enemy spirit abroad, it must have been conjured by someone inside the palace. We must get reinforcements and go to the scene." At this the ogre seized the horn hanging at his side, and was just about to set it to his lips when, with a flash of light, *another* small spirit materialized in midair.

This one was a manikin sitting in an oyster shell. "I have news, Master!" it squeaked. "The sentry Hiqquus has been discovered compressed inside a water butt; he is somewhat squashed, not to mention soggy—but he lives. He says that he was attacked—"

The afrit gave a curse. "By whom?"[2]

"He only got a glimpse, but . . . it was Bosquo! He recognized his belly and his snout!"

---

[2] He was one of your better-quality afrits, Zahzeel. Even in moments of high stress he kept his grammar up to scratch.

The ogre nearly fell off his pedestal in shock. He was just about to speak when, in a shower of damp earth, a *third* small demon, this one with the soft, sad face of a gazelle, rose from the turf below him. "Master, the sentry Balaam has been pushed into the manure pile and a heavy statue placed on top of him! I heard his muffled squeaks, and with a grapple on the end of a long pole have just succeeded in tugging him free. Poor Balaam —he won't smell of brimstone for some considerable time to come. As soon as he could speak he named his cruel assailant—it was the djinni Trimble!"

"Zahzeel"—this was Kibbet, the first of the informants— "clearly Trimble and Bosquo have gone berserk! We must locate them with all speed."

The ogre gave a decisive nod. "I have noted a pattern here. Their assaults are focused on the area around the treasury. The king's gold is collected there, and many precious treasures. Clearly these djinn—or the magicians who are their masters— intend a robbery, or some other atrocious act. We must act fast! Kibbet and you others, go at speed to the treasury block. I shall summon further help and meet you there. Once our forces are assembled we will alert the vizier. Hiram will have to decide whether to disturb the slumbers of the king."

The gazelle-imp ducked down into the ground; the manikin pulled down his oyster shell and spun away into the sky; the orange ape gave a star-jump and, with a grunt, devolved into a twirl of orange sparks that drifted out of sight.

Zahzeel the afrit? He raised the horn to his mouth and blew.

All across the gardens of the palace of Solomon there was a roaring and a shaking as Zahzeel's subordinates were summoned to his side. Bright lights flared in unexpected places among the pavilions and rose bowers; eyes blinked open in shrubs and potted ferns. Sculptures shifted, hopped down from pedestals; innocent-seeming vines bent and coiled; benches shimmered, were suddenly no more. All across the northern gardens the hidden sentries bestirred themselves: and here they came—horned, clawed, red-eyed, and frothing, things with twisting tails of bone, and fibrous wings, and dangling bellies; oozing things and scuttling things; things with legs and things without; darting mites and bounding ghuls, wisps and implets, foliots and djinn, all silently surfing the lawns and treetops of the gardens to congregate about Zahzeel.

The afrit gave a few brief orders and clapped his hands. The air grew chill; ice formed on the pedestal and glittered on the rhododendron leaves. The ogre was gone; atop the pedestal rose a column of rushing smoke and licking tendrils, from which two baleful yellow eyes gleamed down with grim ferocity.[3]

Coiling like a spring, the column of smoke shot upward into the air and disappeared over the shrubbery. There followed an explosion of movement as Zahzeel's hordes took to the skies, or set off, galloping, along the ground. In a few short seconds the whole grisly cavalcade had thundered south in the direction of the treasury—precisely where I wasn't, and didn't want to go.

To the north, however, the garden was quiet and still.

On its exotic sculpture the cricket gave a brief caper of wicked glee. The score so far could be summarized as follows: Bartimaeus of Uruk 1; Assembled Spirits of Solomon 0. Not bad for twenty minutes' work, I'll think you'll agree. But I didn't hang about to celebrate. There was no telling how soon it would be before Zahzeel and Co. returned.

★ ★ ★

---

[3] It wasn't a bad effect, all told. I'd probably use it one day. Assuming I was still alive.

In keeping with this sense of urgency, I hoicked the girl out of the rosebush in double-quick time and set her running alongside me north across the lawns. As we went, I gave her a modest précis of my triumph—just the bare bones of it, keeping it terse and unshowy, as is my wont, limiting the historical comparisons to a minimum and only concluding with three rhyming paeans of self-praise. When I finished, I waited expectantly, but the girl said nothing; she was still too busy plucking thorns from her underclothes.

At last she finished. "Good," she said. "Well done."

I stared at her. "*Well done? Is* that all you can say?" I gestured at the empty trees and rustic arbors all around. "Look—nothing left on any plane! I've cleared the way right to Solomon's door. A *marid* couldn't have done any better than that in the time available. *'Well done?'* " I scowled. "What kind of a response is that?"

"It's a thank-you," she said. "Would your other masters have spoken any better?"

"No."

"Well, then."

"Only I'd have thought you might have viewed things in a different light," I said idly. "You know, on account of your being a slave yourself."

There was a silence; ahead of us, between the trees, the king's apartments could now be seen, a dark domed mass rising sheer against the milky sheen of stars.

The girl jumped over the little tiled channel that marked the beginnings of the water gardens. She said: "I'm *not* a slave."

"Sure." I was in human form again: the handsome young Sumerian, lolloping along like a wolf with easy strides. "I remember. You're an 'hereditary guard.' Nice one. Altogether different. That 'hereditary' bit, incidentally—what's that mean?"

"Is it not obvious, Bartimaeus? I follow my mother, and my mother's mother, and so on down the years. I, as they, have the sacred role of protecting our queen's life. There is no higher calling. Where now?"

"Left around the lake—there's a footbridge there. So you've prepared for this from birth?"

"Well, from early girlhood. As a baby I couldn't hold a knife."

I glanced at her. "Was that a joke, or just painfully literal thinking? I'm guessing the latter."

The girl said flatly, "Do not seek to demean me, demon. I have an exalted position. There is a special altar in the Temple of the Sun dedicated to the guards. The priestesses bless us individually at each festival. The queen addresses us each by name."

"How thrilling for you," I said. "Wait, watch out on the bridge—there's a trip thread on the second plane—it'll trigger an alarm. When you get to the top, do a little jump like me. That's it; you're over it. . . . Now, I've a question. Have you, at any time, had any choice in what you do? Could you have been anything other than a guard?"

"No. And I wouldn't have wanted to. I followed my mother."

"Lack of choice," I said. "Preordained from birth. Ordered to sacrifice yourself for a cruel, unfeeling master. You're a slave."

"The queen is *not* unfeeling," the girl cried. "She practically wept when she sent me—"

"Here to die," I finished. "You can't see what's right in front of your nose, can you? Speaking of which, there's another trip thread here, suspended between those trees. Bend down double, like this, nice and low. That's it, you're through. Take it from me," I went on as we took up the pace once more, "you've got a fancy title and a nice line in weaponry, but you're just as enslaved as if your neck was chained. I pity you. "

The girl had had enough by now. "Be silent!"

"Sorry, don't *do* silent. The only difference between you and me is that I've got self-knowledge. I *know* I'm enslaved, and it gets on my wick. That gives me just a shadowy slice of freedom. You haven't even got that. This queen of yours must be laughing her crown off, you're so eager to obey her every whim."

Something flashed in the starlight; a dagger was in her hand. "Never *dare* to insult the queen, demon!" the girl cried. "You cannot *imagine* the responsibility she holds. She has absolute faith in me, and I in her. I would never question a command she gave."

"Apparently not," I said crisply. "Right, watch out here: we need three little jumps, one after the other, high as you can. That's it. Now get down on all fours...wiggle forward...try to keep your bottom a little lower please...a bit more...Okay, you can get up now."

The girl stared back at me across the empty patch of lawn in wonder. "How many trip threads were concealed *there?*"

I strolled across to her, grinning. "Absolutely none. That was just a little illustration of what your queen is doing to you—as well as being highly amusing to watch. You certainly don't question *anything*, do you? 'Blind obedience to no good purpose' —that could be your motto."

The girl gave a gasp of fury; the knife in her hand was suddenly finely balanced between fingertip and thumb. "I should *kill* you for that."

"Yeah, yeah, but you won't." I turned away from her and began surveying the great stone blocks of the building rising just ahead. "Why? Because that wouldn't help your precious queen. Besides, I'm not in a circle now. I could dodge it pretty well out here, even when I'm looking in the opposite direction. But by all means try it, if you like."

For a few moments there wasn't any sound behind, then I heard feet padding on the grass. When the girl came alongside me, the knife was in her belt.

She scowled up at the mass of stonework. At its splaying foot the last vestiges of the northern gardens broke apart in a sculpted mess of jasmine trees. The pale white flowers were probably quite pretty by daylight, but under the stars' spectral gloaming brought to mind a glittering pile of bones.

"Is this it, then?" the girl said.

I nodded. "Yep, probably in every sense. This is Solomon's tower. There's a rooftop balcony somewhere up there, which is where I suggest we try to enter. But I've one final question before we do."

"Well?"

"What's your mother think about this? About you coming out here, all on your own. Is she as pleased as you are?"

Unlike some of my other probing questions, the girl seemed to find this a very easy one to answer. "My mother died in the service of the last queen," she said simply. "As she looks down on me from the Sun God's realm, I am sure she honors all I do."

"I see," was all I said to this. And I did, too.

Other things being equal, I would at that point have turned myself into a roc, phoenix, or other dashing bird, seized the girl by an ankle, and hoisted her indecorously up to the balcony. Sadly, I was prevented from doing this by a fresh danger in the air above us: a multitude of bright-green, luminous Pulses, drifting at different heights close beside the wall. They weren't moving fast, but they were very thick in places, and also erratic, sometimes speeding up for no apparent reason. Any flying thing would inevitably collide with some of them, with unpleasant results.

They were first-plane, so the girl could see them too. "What do we do now?"

"We need," I said, "an appropriate guise. . . . What sticks to walls?"

"Spiders," she said. "Or slugs."

"Not keen on spiders. Too many limbs to control; I get confused. I *could* do a slug, but we'd be here all night, and anyway, how would I carry you?" I snapped my fingers. "I know! A nice big lizard."

So saying, the handsome youth was gone, and in his place stood a slightly less good-looking giant gecko complete with spiny, interlocking scales; splay-toes, multi-suckered feet; and bulbous, boggling eyes set on either side of its gummy, grinning mouth. "Hello," it said, extending a juicy tongue. "Give us a hug."

The girl's squeal would probably have been the shrillest ever uttered by one of Sheba's hereditary guard, except that it was muffled by the coiling tip of my long and sinewy tail, which wrapped itself around her and lifted her off the ground. Then the lizard was up and away, clinging to the stones with the sticky spatulas upon its spreading feet. With one eye I kept my gaze fixed on the wall ahead; the other, swiveled at approximately ninety degrees over my scaly shoulder, kept close watch on the floating Pulses in case any should come too near. It was a shame I didn't have a spare eye to check out the dangling girl as well, but various distant Arabian curses reassured me of her state of mind.

My progress was fast, and the way relatively unimpeded. Only once did a Pulse come anywhere near us, and then I managed a sideways shimmy to avoid it—I felt the air grow momentarily chill as it bounced off the stonework beside my head.

Things went very well, in short; until, that is, I heard the girl calling something out below me.

"What was that?" I said, swiveling an acerbic eye in her direction. "I told you, I can't do spiders. It's a leg thing. Think yourself lucky I didn't do the slug."

Her face was white, which might have been the ride, but she was also pointing upward and to the side. "No," she croaked. "A spider—over there."

The lizard looked with both eyes then, just in time to observe a large, fat spider-djinni squeezing out from a concealed opening in the wall. It had a tarantula's body, swollen big as a cow corpse after the rains. Each of its legs was hard and knobbly as bamboo and ended in a sharpened sting. Its face, however, was human, with a neat little beard and a tall conical hat. Evidently, as a guardian of Solomon's tower, it wasn't under Zahzeel's command; either that, or it was deaf. Whichever, it reacted swiftly enough now. A jet of yellow webbing shot from its baggy undercarriage and struck me full on, breaking my grip on the wall. I fell a few yards, caught desperate hold, and hung one-handed, encased in webbing, swinging back and forth above the gulf.

Somewhere below, I heard the girl cry out, but I hadn't time to heed her. One of the spider's legs rose, made ready to send a Flare high above the gardens; soon all Solomon's slaves would have seen it and congregated at the scene.

But the lizard acted. With one free leg I sent forth a Mantle to encase the spider. My spell shimmered into being just as the Flare was loosed: the bolt of energy struck the inside of the Mantle, rebounded, and hit the spider's balloonlike belly. At the same time, the lizard broke through its bonds with one slash of a foreclaw.

Its body steaming where the Flare had struck, the spider broke the Mantle apart with a swiftly spoken counter-spell, bent its legs, and leaped straight down the wall toward me. I swung to the side, dodged its swiping blow, and, snaring it by a bristly hind leg, whirled it around and around with as much force as I could muster, before spinning it out with all my considerable might, straight into a drifting Pulse thirty feet or so beyond.

There was a flash; a field of black and yellow bands of light engulfed the djinni, grew tight, grew tighter—and squeezed it messily into nothing.

The magical effusion was regrettable, and might possibly be spotted from the south, but, in the circumstances, it couldn't really be helped. The lizard looked down at the dangling girl and gave her a broad wink. "Like the throwing technique?" I grinned. "Learned it squirrel-tossing with the Mongol nomads.[4] On quiet nights we'd—Oh! No! What are you doing?"

She had the silver dagger poised in her hand again; her arm was drawn back, her eyes wild and staring.

"Don't!" I cried. "You'll kill us both! You'll—"

A whirl of movement; the dagger left her hand, flashed past my snout, and embedded in something close behind with a soft, wet, and very decisive splat.

The lizard's eyes swiveled once more, only to observe a *second* large, fat spider-djinni staring in astonishment at the silver dagger embedded in the center of its belly. Its legs, which had

---

[4] On quiet nights we'd go down to Lake Baikal with a basket of plump ones each and send them skimming out across the waves. My record was eight bounces, seven squeaks.

been poised above my head, scrabbled weakly at the poisoned wound. Its essence grew brown and dull; like an aged puffball it fell in upon itself, letting out sprays of fine gray dust. It toppled from the wall, dropped like a stone, was gone.

The night was still once more.

I looked down at the girl, still dangling in my coiled tail. "Good," I said at last. "Well done."

"Well done?" Possibly it was the starlight, possibly her tilted angle, but I could have sworn there was a mild smirk upon her face. "Well done? What kind of a response is that?"

"All right," I growled. *"Thank you."*

"See?" she said. "It's hard, isn't it?"

The lizard did not reply, but with a slightly indignant flick of the tail continued up the wall. A moment later we had reached the balcony.

27

The ascent of the wall had proved something of a trial for Asmira. The motion sickness had been bad enough—she strongly suspected that the djinni had whipped its tail from side to side more vigorously than was *strictly* necessary—but she had also thoroughly disliked the extreme *helplessness* she felt. Wrapped in the tail, suspended high above the ground, watching as the lizard fought so desperately with the first of the repulsive spider-guards, she had realized for the first time how utterly dependent she was upon her slave. Deny it as she might, that dependency was total. Without Bartimaeus, she would never have gotten so far; without Bartimaeus she had no hope of getting any nearer to her goal.

Of course, it was *she* who by quickness of thinking and strength of mind had commanded the djinni to her service—she had made the most of the chance that had come her way. But that was all it was, in truth—a lucky chance. Left to her own devices in the palace, all her skills and years of training would have come to nothing, and the trust her queen had showed her would have proved misplaced. On her own, she would have failed.

Knowledge of her limitations, of her individual frailty, suddenly enveloped Asmira and took its usual shape. In her mind's eye she saw again her mother standing on the chariot beside the throne, with her killers advancing on all sides. She saw the knives gleaming in the sun. And she felt again the terror of her weakness—the weakness of her six-year-old self—too slow, too feeble, too far away to help.

Much more than the swinging of the tail, it was *this* sensation that made her sick at heart, and it had actually come as a relief to her when the second guard had scuttled from its hole, and she had been able to wrest a dagger from her belt and strike it down. As always, her fluidity of action brought respite—her heart's unease was smothered by enjoyment in her skill. In the flash of a knife strike, her memory of her mother was, for the moment, gone, and Asmira was refocused on the task ahead. Even the last few lurching moments of the climb, in which the djinni seemed to throw her around more violently than ever, did not damp down the feeling, and she was deposited at last upon the balcony in better spirits than before.

She was on a pillared walkway, open to the stars. Between the pillars, silhouetted statues sat on plinths; here and there were scattered seats and tables. Above, and very close now, the tower's dome soared into the night. Set into the dome's base and accessed by a covered passage leading from the balcony, there stood a pitch-black arch.

Asmira turned to look back the way she had come. Far below, silvery in the starlight, the gardens stretched away toward the southern regions of the palace, where distant points of color could be seen, darting to and fro.

A small sand cat, with long, pointed ears, neat body, and a striped and fluffy tail curled around its forepaws, sat atop the balustrade watching the movement of the lights.

"Still milling about the treasury, chasing shadows," the cat remarked. "What a flock of fools they are." It shook its head pityingly, and glanced at Asmira with big, lilac-colored eyes.

"Just think, you might have summoned one of *them*. Aren't you lucky you got me?"

Asmira blew a strand of hair away from her face, irritated that the djinni had echoed her own thoughts. "You're *just* as lucky," she said, stubbornly. "Seeing as I got you out of that bottle, and killed that spider thing just now." She checked her belt. Two knives left. Well, that would be enough.

"I'd say we're *both* lucky to have survived this far," the sand cat said. It jumped silently to the ground. "Let's see how much further we can make our fortune stretch."

With tail high and whiskers out, it dinked between the pillars, flowing in and out of shadows. "No obvious hexes, no trip threads, no dangling tendrils..." it murmured. "The walkway's clear. Solomon must have been relying on everything that came before. Now then, this arch...no door, just heavy drapes. A bit too easy, one might think...and one would be right, because there's a nexus on the seventh plane." The cat looked over its furry shoulder as Asmira drew close. "For your information it's like a pearly shimmery cobweb thing strung all the way across. Quite pretty really, only alarmed."

Asmira frowned. "What can we do?"

"*You*, as usual, can't do anything except stand around looking cross. I, on the other hand, have options. Now, hush up a moment. I need to concentrate on this...."

The cat went very still. It sat before the open archway, regarding it intently. Presently it began to make the faintest hissing sound. Once or twice it raised its forepaws and moved them from side to side, but otherwise it appeared to do nothing. Asmira watched in some frustration, angered again by her blind reliance on her slave. And he *was* a slave—there was no doubt about that. Whatever Bartimaeus had claimed earlier, there was no equivalence between him and her at all. None. The summons she had spoken had spelled out his bondage in black and white. It was a wholly different thing from her willing obedience to her queen.

She thought of Queen Balkis, waiting back in Marib—hoping, *praying* for her loyal guard's success. Only a day remained before the deadline! By now, they would probably all have assumed she'd failed, and be taking steps to withstand attack. Asmira wondered what magics the priestesses might construct around the city, what demons they were mustering in last, desperate defense....

Her lips tightened. She was very close now. She would not fail.

The cat gave a sudden chuckle and twitched its tail in appreciation. "There you go! Look at that beauty! The Obedient Breath's a cracker, isn't it? Works every time."

Asmira gazed at the arch. "I can't see any difference."

"Well, of course *you* can't. You're human and therefore, by the immutable laws of nature, completely hopeless. I've used the Breath to push the nexus back, see, and put a Seal on it to hold open. There's a nice hole in the middle here. Not too big —can't risk any of the threads knocking against each other. So we'll have to jump through the hole. Yes, I *know* you can't see it. Just do what I do."

The sand cat gave a vigorous spring through the center of the arch, landing lightly just in front of the hanging drapes. Asmira didn't hesitate; fixing the cat's trajectory in her mind, she took two steps back, ran forward and launched herself into a tight somersault through the air. At the apex of her leap she sensed something cold close by; it made no contact and was gone. She flipped head over heels, landed right beside the sand cat and, carried by the momentum she had generated, fell headfirst through the drapes.

She came to a halt on all fours, half sprawling into the room beyond.

It was a room of stately proportions, long and high, with squared white pillars projecting from the whitewashed walls. Between each pillar—

Asmira sneezed.

Small claws grasped her shoulder, dragged her back into the concealment of the drapes. Asmira sneezed again. The air was warm and close, and suffused with such an overwhelming flowery tang that her nose recoiled. She buried her face in her sleeve.

When she recovered, the sand cat was looking at her. It was holding its nose with a paw. "Perfume got to you?" it whispered. "Me too. It's the king's."

Asmira wiped her eyes. "It's so *strong!* He must have just passed by!"

"Nope, could have been hours ago. Let's just say Solomon *likes* his aftershave. But it's a good job for us that he *isn't* in there right now, given the way you've just been trumpeting like an angry elephant. We're trying to *assassinate* the man, remember? A bit of care and subtlety is needed from here on in."

So saying, the cat slid forward and disappeared between the drapes. Biting back her anger, Asmira picked herself up, took a deep breath, and stepped through into the private chambers of King Solomon.

As she had glimpsed a moment before, the room was high-ceilinged and of considerable size. The floor, of pink-veined marble, was strewn with ornate carpets covered in mystic signs. In the center of the chamber was a circular, step-sided plunge-pool filled with gently steaming water; around it were chairs, couches, and tasseled cushions. A large crystal orb rested on an onyx table, while among the potted palms, silvered trays sat on slim gold stands, bearing fruits and meats, piled seafood, pastries, jugs of wine, and cups of polished glass.

Asmira's mouth fell open at the casual splendor of it all. Her eyes flitted from one luxury to another. At once the urgency of her mission receded. She longed to partake of the magnificence —sit on a couch, perhaps, and taste the wine, or dissolve her weariness by dipping her feet into the lulling warmness of the pool.

She took a slow step forward. . . .

"I wouldn't," the sand cat said, setting a warning paw upon her knee.

"It's all so nice. . . ."

"That's because he's put a Glamour on it, the better for snaring the unwary. Take one bite of that food, peek for just a moment into the orb, dip so much as a little pinkie in that water, and you'd still be stuck here come the dawn, when Solomon would amble in to find you. Best not look at it at all."

Asmira chewed her lip. "But it's all so *nice*. . . ."

"If I were you," the cat went on, "I'd be checking out the murals on the wall. Look, there's old Ramses in his chariot, and Hammurabi in his tiered pleasure-garden; there's a not very accurate depiction of Gilgamesh. . . . Where's his broken nose, I want to know? Ah yes," the sand cat said. "All the greats are here. Typical pad of a typical despot, obsessed with being bigger and better than the ones who went before him. This is where Solomon sits and plans his conquests of places like Sheba, I'll be bound."

Asmira had still been gazing at the coils of fragrant steam

rising softly from the pool, but at the djinni's words she gave a start, and her fingers clenched upon her dagger. She tore herself free from the enchanted scene and stared at the cat with hot, befuddled eyes.

"*That's* better," Bartimaeus said. "Here's what I suggest. There are four arches out of here, two to the right, two to the left. All seem the same. I say we take them one by one. I'll go first. You come after. Look at me the whole time. Nothing else, mind, or the Glamour's going to get you. Think you can cope with that, or shall I say it again?"

Asmira scowled. "Of *course* I can cope with it. I'm not an idiot."

"And yet, in so many ways, you are." With that, the cat was off, winding between the couches and the golden tables. Asmira, cursing, hurried along behind. At the edges of her vision the shimmering enticements winked and sparkled like exquisite memories of a dream, but she ignored them, keeping her eyes firmly fixed upon—

"Could you *please* lower your tail a little?" she hissed.

"It's keeping your mind off the Glamour, isn't it?" the cat said. "Quit complaining. Okay, here's the first arch. I'm going to take a peek.... Oh!" It ducked back in a flurry, with its tail fluffed out. "*He's there!*" he whispered. "Take a look—but do it *carefully*."

Heart pounding against her chest, Asmira peered around the nearest pillar of the arch. Beyond was a circular room, bare and unadorned, with marble columns set into the wall. At its center was a raised platform; high above this rose a dome of glass, through which the constellations were in radiant display.

Standing on the platform was a man.

He had his back to the arch, and his face was hidden, but

Asmira knew him from the mural she had seen upon the wall of the Magicians' Hall. He wore a silken robe that descended to the floor; this was decorated with spiraling designs of woven gold. His dark hair hung loose upon his shoulders. His head was raised, and he was looking up toward the stars in silent contemplation. His hands were loosely clasped behind his back.

On one of his fingers was a ring.

Asmira had ceased to breathe. Without taking her eyes off the silent king, she drew her dagger from her belt. He was fifteen yards distant, certainly no more. The time had come. She would strike him through the heart with a single blow, and Sheba would be saved. *Sheba would be saved.* A bead of sweat ran down her forehead and trickled along the contours of her nose.

She flicked the dagger into the air, caught it by its downturned tip.

She pulled her arm back.

Still the king gazed peaceably at the boundless stars.

Something was tugging at her tunic. She looked down. The sand cat was there, gesturing urgently toward the other room. She shook her head and raised the dagger.

The tugging came again, hard enough to spoil her aim. Uttering a silent scream of vexation, Asmira allowed herself to be pulled back around the corner of the arch, into the outer chamber. She bent low and glared at the cat.

"*What?*" she breathed.

"Something's not right."

"What do you mean, 'not right'? Isn't it Solomon?"

"I...don't know. If it's an Illusion, it's not one I can see through. It's just..."

"Just what?"

"I don't know. I can't put my finger on it."

Asmira stared at the cat. She straightened up. "I'm going to do it."

"No! Wait."

"Shh—he'll hear us! I won't get this chance again. Will you *stop* your tugging?"

"I'm telling you—don't do it! It's too easy. It's too . . ."

Asmira's head spun. She saw the quiet, imploring face of Balkis and the somber priestesses lined up in the courtyard; she imagined Marib's towers burning. She saw her mother falling, her hair tumbling loose like water across the old queen's lap.

"Get *off* me," she hissed. The cat was clinging to her arm. "Will you get *off*? I can do this! I can finish this now—"

"It's a trap, I'm sure of it. Only—ah!"

She had swiped out with the silver dagger, not intending to harm, but to drive the djinni back. The cat dropped off her sleeve and jumped away, fur bristling.

Once again Asmira ducked through the arch. The king stood as before.

Without pausing, Asmira raised her hand, drew it level with her shoulder and, with a brief, efficient snap of the wrist, threw the dagger with full force. It struck Solomon just above the heart and buried itself hilt-deep. He collapsed without a sound.

At which moment she heard the cat's voice calling. "I've got it! It's the Ring—it's not bright enough! The aura should be blinding me! Don't—! Oh. Too late. You have."

The body of King Solomon fell to the floor, but did not stop there. It dropped straight through the solid surface of the platform, like a stone in water. In a twinkling it was gone, and only the dagger hilt was visible, projecting from the marble.

This happened so fast that Asmira was still standing frozen, her dagger-hand outstretched, when the platform burst asunder and the great demon thrust itself up from below, bellowing and roaring with its three tusked mouths. High as the dome it rose, a knotted mass of glistening cords and arms, each with its own translucent eye. All these eyes were turned upon her, and the tentacles flayed and trembled with anticipation.

Asmira fell back against the wall, her mind and limbs transfixed. Somewhere close she heard the sand cat calling, but she could not respond, nor summon the strength to reach for the final dagger at her belt. All she could do was give a single ragged cry. She felt her legs give way, felt herself sliding slowly down the wall—and then the demon was upon her, reaching for her throat.

28

There are times when any honest djinni's simply got to stand and fight. Times when you face your foe head on. Times when, no matter what the overwhelming odds, no matter how hideous the coming peril, you just spit on your hands, square your shoulders, smooth back your hair, and (possibly with a small wry smile playing on your lips) step out to greet the danger with open arms.

Obviously this wasn't such a time.

To confront the terrible entity that had risen in the chamber would have been a futile act—and a very messy one.[1] Only an idiot would have tried. Or someone under contract, of course. If I'd been *forced* to do so by order of a competent master, I'd have had to stand my ground or be destroyed forthwith by the Dismal Flame. But my master *wasn't* competent, as her summoning had proved—and now, at last, after getting away with it for a surprising length of time, she was going to pay the penalty.

Bring me safely to King Solomon: those had been that Arabian girl's exact words way back when she gave me my charge. And (Bartimaeus of Uruk being a spirit who fulfills his charges to the letter) this is precisely what I'd achieved. True, there was admittedly some doubt about whether the figure in the room

---

[1] I didn't hang around long enough to get a good look at it, but its size and scale, not to mention all those gooey jellyfishy bits swirling about the place, told me it was something from the very depths of the Other Place. Entities like that are rarely house-trained, and almost always have bad attitudes.

had actually *been* Solomon, but since it was shaped like him, looked like him, smelled like him, and was standing as large as life in his apartments, I figured it was close enough. The girl had certainly believed it was, which is why she'd thrown the knife. Contractually speaking, I'd done my bit. I didn't have to keep her safe a moment longer.

Which, with that gelatinous monstrosity a-calling, was exactly the break I needed.

The sand cat ran.

Out of the domed room and away across the pillared hall I went, fur out, fluff-tail bristling. Behind me I heard a high-pitched scream—brief, tentative, and cut off in a rather final, gargling sort of way. Good. Well, bad for the girl, of course, but good for me, which is what counts. Depending on how long the visitation toyed with her before finishing her off, I expected to be dematerializing very soon.

In the meantime, I made sure I was out of reach. The cat shot across the hall, leaped straight over the plunge-pool, skidded diagonally along a stretch of marble and, with a quick spin of the Evasive Cartwheel, flipped out of sight through the next arch along.

Safety! Yet again my unique combination of quick thinking and agility had saved my precious skin!

Except it was a dead end.

Quite an *interesting* dead end, as dead ends go, but potentially fatal all the same. The room was clearly the place where Solomon kept many of his treasures—a small, windowless store, lit by oil lamps, and piled in every direction with shelves and caskets.

No time to explore it. The cat turned tail and made for the arch—only to be dissuaded by another bloodcurdling roar sounding from outside. The ferocious entity was a loud one, sure enough, if a disappointingly slow worker. I'd hoped he would have swallowed the girl by now. But perhaps, having chomped off a leg or something, he was storing her for later. Perhaps he was coming after me. Clearly I needed somewhere safe to hide. I turned again to look around the storeroom. What did I see? Plenty of jewels, idols, masks, swords, helms, scrolls, tablets, shields, and other artifacts of magical design, not to mention a few weird extras like a set of crocodile-skin gloves, a skull with eyes of shell, and a rather lumpy-looking straw doll covered with human skin.[2] I also saw an old friend of mine—that golden serpent I'd stolen from Eridu. But what I *really* wanted—namely a WAY OUT—was altogether missing.

Sweaty-pawed with agitation, the cat looked left and right, scanning the shelves. Almost every item in the little room was magical—their auras interlaced across the planes, bathing me in rainbow light. If the entity *did* appear behind me, could there be something I might use in last, desperate defense?

Nope, unless I was going to lob the doll at him. Trouble was, I didn't know what any of the artifacts *did*.[3] But then I noticed,

---

[2] You could tell it was genuine because of the spiky armpit hair sprouting like black broccoli from the top of the wrinkled scalp. I've got to say, you can add all the shiny button eyes and cutesy cotton mouths you like, but if I was a kid who was given *that* doll to cuddle at bedtime, I'd feel a bit shortchanged.

[3] As my last master-but-one would tell you, never attempt to use an unknown magical artifact. Hundreds of magicians have risked it down the years and only one or two of them survived to regret it. Most famous, to djinn of my antiquity, was the Old Priestess of Ur, who wished for immortality. For decades she worked dozens of her magicians to death, forcing them to create a beautiful silver circlet that would confer on her perpetual life. They finished at last; in triumph, the aging woman put the circlet on her head. But the entities trapped inside the circlet had not chosen to spell out the exact *terms* of the great magic they invoked. The Old Priestess lived on, all right, but not in quite the pleasant manner she had assumed.

half hidden amid the piled treasures at the back, a large copper pot. It was narrow at the base, swelling at the neck to the width of a man's shoulders. On its top was a circular lid, and on that lid sat a layer of dust, implying that no one, including Solomon, ever checked within.

In an instant the cat became a curl of mist, scrolling off the floor and up against the lid, which I nudged minutely to one side. With the speed of wind emerging from an elephant, I shot inside and (still in my gaseous state) flicked the lid back into position. Darkness all about me. The curl of mist hung in silence, waiting.

Had I moved in time?

I imagined the entity oozing level with the archway. I imagined several of its eye stalks probing inward, scanning the treasures from side-to-side. I imagined one of its polyped coils unfurling, flicking toward the surface of the pot. . . .

Squeezed tight with tension, the curl of mist floated quietly up and down.

Nothing happened. The pot stayed undisturbed.

Time passed.

After a while I began to relax. The entity had doubtless gone, hopefully to hurry up and devour the girl. I was just debating whether to nudge the lid aside and tiptoe from my hiding place, or remain more prudently concealed, when I became aware of feeling *watched*.

I looked about me. The interior of the pot was empty. Whatever it had originally contained was gone; now it was filled with nothing but secretive, dusty silence. Yet somehow there was an *oddness* in the atmosphere, an indefinable frisson in the old, stale air that made my essence tingle with occult sensation.

I waited—and all at once, from somewhere close, yet infi-
nitely far away, came a little voice, an echo of an echo, a plaintive memory of speech.

Bartimaeus...

Call me overcautious, but strange voices in pots always put
me on my guard. The curl of mist instantly coalesced into a
small white moth, fluttering warily in the black vastness of the
pot. I sent swift Pulses back and forth, checked all the planes.
But there was nothing there, nothing but dust and shadows.

Bartimaeus...

And then, suddenly, I guessed. I remembered the three
famous afrits who had dared defy Solomon. I recalled their
reported fates. One of them—or so hushed fireside gossip had
it—had been reduced, by the king's caprice and the power of
the Ring, into a mournful echo in a pot. Which one was it...?

The moth's antennae shivered. I cleared my throat, spoke
cautiously: "Philocretes?"

A sound as soft as owl flight: *The name of what I was is lost. I
am a last sigh, an imprint on the air. As you beat your wings, so the
air swirls and the final trace of me must vanish. You seek the Ring?*

Out of courtesy the moth adjusted its wing beats to a slo-mo
minimum. I spoke with care, for I sensed malice as well as melancholy in the voice. "No, no."

Ah. Very wise. I sought the Ring....

"Did you? Er...how did you get on?"

How do you think I got on? I'm a voice in a bloody pot.

"Right."

The voice gave a moan of fathomless regret and longing. *Had
I but a thimbleful of essence,* it murmured, *I would swallow you whole,
little djinni, devour you in a single gulp. Alas, I cannot! For Solomon
has punished me and I am less than nothing.*

"How sad," I said feelingly. "What a terrible shame. Well, it's been *so* nice chatting, but it seems quiet outside now, so perhaps I'd better be going—"

Would that I could leave this prison too, whispered the voice. *Then I would cast Solomon into eternal darkness! Ah, yes, I have his secret now. I could take the Ring. But my knowledge comes too late! Only one chance was given me. I wasted it, and here I must reside forever, a frail suspiration, a child's sigh, a—*

"I don't suppose," I said, pausing with new attention, "that you'd like to pass on this sure-fire method of ring-stealing, would you? It's of no interest to me, of course, but someone else might be able get revenge on your behalf...."

What care I for revenge? The voice was so faint that each beat of the moth's wings in the dead air broke its sound to fragments. *I am a whisper of unspoken sorrow, a—*

"You could help another spirit achieve greatness...."

I care nothing for the fate of others. I wish death to all things in either world that still have energy and life....

"A noble sentiment, to be sure." The moth spoke crisply, making for the lid. "Still, my view is that Solomon remains invincible. Everyone knows the Ring can't be stolen."

The voice hesitated. *What's this? You don't believe me?*

"Of course not. But hey, what does that matter? You go on echoing away to yourself if it keeps you happy. I've got jobs to do for the king and I can't hang around here yakking. Good-bye."

You fool! Faint and fragile as it was, the dark emotion of the voice made my wings quiver; I was profoundly grateful that Philocretes was robbed of all power to do me harm. *How blindly you return to your slavery,* the echoes whispered, *when you could in a moment master Solomon and seize the Ring!*

"Like you know that," I sneered.

I do know it so!

"Yeah? Says who?"

Says me!

"Locked away in here? You're just hot air."

Ah, but I was not always in this side-room, cried the voice. *To begin with, the cursed king kept me in his chamber, and showed me off to all his wives. And so I listened to him talk and give instructions to his servants; above all, I heard him speak to the fearsome presence that the Ring controls. I know his weakness! I know how he shields this weakness from the world! Tell me, djinni, is it night or day?*

"We are in the very bowels of the night."

Ah! So have you seen the king, perhaps, as you wander through his chambers?

A little bit of naïveté was needed here. "I saw him in his observatory, standing, looking at the stars."

You fool, to be deceived by surfaces! That is not Solomon!

"What then?"

A magic worked by the Spirit of the Ring. A spell cast upon a doll of clay. The doll becomes the king, while the king retires to his private room beyond to rest. It is a powerful Illusion, and a trap for enemies. When I attacked the fake, thinking Solomon defenseless, the real king was alerted, and snared me in an instant. Ah, would that I had ignored it, I would not be doomed to this!

I hesitated. "How exactly were you snared?"

Another Illusion. He is a master of them. It seemed a great entity rose from the ground, a being of such power that I was rendered dumb with terror. As I strove to fight it, sending Detonation after Detonation into its writhing coils, Solomon appeared behind me and turned the Ring. Now, I am here.

The moth considered this unexpected information. Here, then, was the reason I was still on Earth. The girl was captured, not devoured. It had uneasy repercussions for me, not least since Solomon might well wish to meet the slave who had brought her so far. I needed to do something, and fast, but there was more to learn from Philocretes first.

"All very well," I said airily, "but assume you *had* ignored the Illusion and gotten as far as the real Solomon. He'd still have had the Ring. You would never have gotten it off him."

From somewhere came a roaring that was at once ferocious and very faint, like a thunderstorm heard far away at sea. The air moved with curious wafts and eddies, swaying the moth gently to and fro. *O most lowly and offal-headed Bartimaeus, how I long to tear your wings to tissue shreds! Solomon is not invincible! When he sleeps, he removes his Ring!*

At this the tenor of my voice became a trifle skeptical. "Why would he do that? All the stories say he never takes it off. One of his wives tried—"

The stories are wrong! It suits the king that they should be so, which is why he spreads them. Between midnight and cock-crow, the king must sleep. To sleep he must remove the Ring!

"But he simply wouldn't do it," I said. "It's far too risky for him. All his power—"

A horrid gurgling, like that of a particularly malevolent blocked drain, resounded all around me. Philocretes was laughing. *Yes, yes, the power is the problem! The Ring contains too much. Its energies burn whoever wears it! This, by day, is something Solomon can endure, though he has to conceal his pain from the outside world. At night, in solitude, he must give himself respite. The Ring lies on a silver dish beside his pallet—close enough for him to reach, of course. Ah, but he is vulnerable!*

"It burns him. . . ." I murmured. "I suppose it could be so. I have known such things before."[4]

That is not the only drawback of the Ring, the voice went on. *Why do you think Solomon uses it so rarely? Why do you think he relies so heavily upon the magicians who cluster around his feet like fawning dogs?*

The moth shrugged.[5] "I just assumed he was lazy."

Not so! Whenever it is used, the Ring draws life out from the wearer, and he or she is left weakened by the act. The energies of the Other Place work harm upon a mortal's body, if exposed to it too long. Solomon himself, with all the great works he has accomplished, is already aged far beyond his years.

The moth frowned.[6] "He looked all right to me."

Look closer. Little by little the Ring is killing him, Bartimaeus. Another man would have given up the fight by now, but the fool has a strong sense of responsibility. He fears that someone less virtuous than himself might find and use the Ring. The consequences of that—

The moth nodded.[7] "Might well be terrible. . . ." What an informative pot this was. Of course, Philocretes might just be mad, and certainly some things he said didn't quite gel with what the girl had told me. For instance, just how virtuous *was* it to threaten to destroy Sheba if you didn't get the big pile of

---

[4] The Circlet of Harms, for instance, embedded in the forehead of the Old Priestess of Ur. How she yelled when she put it on! But by then it was too late.

[5] Okay, maybe not *shrugged*, exactly. I didn't have any shoulders. But I certainly gave my wings a damn good noncommittal twitch.

[6] All right, all right. For *frowned* read "let its compound eyes tilt and its antennae droop quizzically." Anatomically more accurate, but cumbersome, don't you think? I hope you're satisfied now.

[7] Don't start.

frankincense you wanted? Then again, Solomon *was* human. And that meant he was flawed.[8]

Still, there was no way of telling the truth of it without going to see things for myself.

"Thanks for that, Philocretes," I said. "I must admit it sounds as if you're right. Solomon *does* have a weakness. He *is* vulnerable."

Ah yes, but he is safe . . . for no one knows these facts but me.

"Er, and me now," I said cheerily. "And I'm going to look into it all this minute. Might even pinch the Ring, if I get a chance. Tell you what—you think of me doing that, getting a spot of revenge and everlasting glory, while you stay moldering away in this tedious old pot. If you'd been polite to me I might have offered to break it for you, thus putting you out of your misery, but you weren't, and I won't. If I remember, I may get around to visiting you again in a millennium or two. Until then, farewell."

With that the moth made for the lid, and now there came such a faraway howling that my wings rippled in consternation. Little buffets of air beset me, blowing me for an instant off my course. Then I righted myself and reached the lid, and, in a moment more, had pushed myself out of the dust and darkness, and was back into the living world.

I was a cat again, standing in shadows. I looked back at the pot. Did I hear a distant voice screaming, cursing, shouting out my name? I listened hard.

No, there was nothing.

Turning away, I peered out of the storeroom into the central

---

[8] Go on, take a look at yourself in the mirror. A good long look, if you can bear it. See? Flawed's putting it mildly, isn't it?

hall. All was still; the Glamour hung like gold haze above the silent pool and couches. There was no marauding entity and no Arabian girl. But then I spied, beyond the archway opposite, a distant gleam of an oil lamp on a chamber wall, and heard two voices raised in sharp discussion. One was high, familiar; the other low.

Lilac eyes gleaming, wicked schemes trailing like a cloak behind it, the cat pattered forward and vanished from the hall.

29

It was very quiet when Asmira awoke. She lay on her back staring at the ceiling—at a long, thin crack that meandered along the plaster to the corner with the wall. It was not a particularly distinctive crack, but it puzzled her, because she had never noticed it before. Her little room had a great many cracks, and places where the old mud brick was half worn through, and faded marks where forgotten guards before her had scratched their names—and Asmira had thought she knew them all. But this was new.

She stared at it for a time, open-mouthed, relaxed of limb, and then, with a quickening of consciousness, realized that the ceiling plaster had been whitewashed, and was farther from her than it ought to be. And the wall was on the wrong side. The light was strange. The bed felt soft. It was not her room. She was not in Marib anymore.

Memories came flooding back to her in a rush. With a cry she jerked bolt upright on the bed, scrabbling at her belt.

A man sat watching her from a chair across the room.

"If you're looking for *this*," he said, "I'm afraid I removed it." He flourished her silver dagger briefly, then settled it back across his knees.

Asmira's body juddered to the hammer-pounding of her heart. Her eyes were staring, her fingers clutching at the cool white sheet.

"The demon—" she gasped.

"Has gone at my bidding," the man said, smiling. "I saved

you from its claws. I must say, you've recovered fairly swiftly. I've known some intruders' hearts to stop."

Panic seized her; with a sudden movement she swung her feet over the edge of the bed and made to stand—but at a gesture from the man she froze.

"You can sit, if you like," he said calmly. "But don't try to get up. I'll take that as an aggressive act."

His voice was very soft and gentle, melodic even, but the iron in the tone was clear. Asmira held her position a moment longer, then slowly, slowly, continued to turn so that her feet dropped to the floor and her knees rested on the edge of the bed. Now she sat facing him.

"Who are you?" the man said.

He was tall and slim and dressed in a white robe that hid his lower limbs from view. His face was long and slender, with a strong chin and finely fluted nose, and quick, dark eyes that glittered, jewel-like, in the lantern light as he regarded her. He was handsome—or would have been so, but for the gray cast of weariness that hung heavily about him, and the curious nets of little lines that ran across his skin, particularly around the eyes and mouth. It was very hard to tell his age. The lines, the gaunt and wrinkled wrists and hands, the long dark hair now thoroughly flecked with gray—all these spoke of advancing years, but his face was quick and his movements youthful, and his eyes were very bright.

"Tell me your name, girl," he said, and when she didn't answer, "You'll have to sooner or later, you know."

Asmira pressed her lips together, breathing deeply, trying to quiet the beating of her heart. The room she was in was, if not small, then much less grandiose than the other regions of the palace she had seen. Besides that, it was furnished with a bare simplicity that made it seem more intimate still. There were ornate rugs upon the floor, but the floor itself was dark cedarwood instead of marble. The walls were plainly whitewashed, and lacked all decoration. On one wall was a single rectangular window that looked out upon the night. Beside the window several wooden racks displayed a collection of ancient scrolls; beyond, on a writing table, sat parchments and styli and bottles of colored ink. It reminded Asmira of the room above the training halls where she had first practiced her summonings.

Other than the bed, and the chair where the man sat waiting, two rough-hewn tables completed the furniture in the room. The tables were positioned on either side of the man's chair, conveniently to hand.

Some way beyond him an arch opened in the wall, but from this angle Asmira could not see where it led.

"I'm waiting," the man said. He made a clicking noise with his tongue. "Perhaps you're hungry? Do you want to eat?"

Asmira shook her head.

"You *ought* to. You've just had a shock. Take some wine, at least."

He gestured to the table on his right. There were several earthen bowls upon it, one with fruit, one with breads, one piled high with seafood—smoked fish, oysters, calamari rings.

"My visitors tell me that the squid is particularly good," the man said. As he spoke, he was pouring out a cup of wine. "But here, drink first—" He bent toward her, holding out the cup. "It's safe to do so. I've not put an enchantment on this one."

Asmira stared at him in perplexity—then her eyes widened in astonishment and fear.

The dark eyes glinted. "Yes, that's right," he said. "I am he. Not so like the images you've seen, perhaps. Come on, take it.

You might as well enjoy it while you can. It's unlikely you'll
live to taste another."

Numbly Asmira reached out and took the cup from him. His
fingers were long, the nails shaped and polished. The smallest
finger had a bright red weal encircling it, just below the second
knuckle.

Asmira stared at it. She said: "The Ring..."

"Is here," the man said. He gestured negligently to the table
on his left. In its center stood a silver platter, and on the platter lay a golden ring, studded with a small black stone. Asmira
gazed at it, then at the king, then at the Ring again.

"Such a lot of effort you've gone to for such a tiny thing."
King Solomon smiled as he spoke, but the smile was tired and
hard. "You got farther than most, but the end will be the same.
Now, listen to me. I am going to ask you another question, and
you will open those dour little lips of yours and answer eagerly
and well, or I will take the Ring and put it on, and then— Well,
what do you think will happen? The end result will be that you
answer anyway, and nothing will be different, save that you will
no longer be quite so pert and pretty as you are now. It pains
me to even suggest such things, but it is late, I am weary, and
frankly somewhat surprised to find you in my rooms. So: take
a good drink of wine and concentrate your mind. You came
to kill me and steal the Ring: that much is obvious. I want to
know the rest. First: what is your name?"

Asmira had calculated the distance from the bed to the chair.
Were she standing, she might easily jump that far; she could
strike his left arm down as it stretched out for the Ring, seize
the dagger and run him through. Sitting down, however, it
would be harder. She *might* be able to do it fast enough to block
his hand, but it wasn't likely.

"*What is your name?*"

She focused on him reluctantly. "Cyrine."

"Where do you come from?"

"Himyar."

"*Himyar?* So small and far away?" The king frowned. "But I have nothing to do with that land. Who, precisely, do you serve?"

Asmira lowered her eyes. She had no answer. Her false identity hadn't been prepared for capture and interrogation. In such circumstances, she had not assumed she would be alive.

"Last chance," King Solomon said.

She shrugged and looked away.

King Solomon struck the arm of his chair in brisk impatience. He reached for the Ring, slipped it on his finger and turned it once. The room went dark. There was a thud; air shifted like a solid mass, flung Asmira back across the bed. She collided with the wall.

When she opened her eyes, a Presence stood beside the king, blacker than shadow. Power and terror radiated from it like heat from a great fire. Elsewhere in the darkness, she heard the scrolls and parchments fluttering in their racks.

"Answer me!" the king's voice thundered. "Who are you? Whom do you serve? Speak! My patience is at an end!"

The Presence moved toward her. Asmira gave a cry of mortal fear. She cowered back upon the bed. "My name is Asmira! I come from Sheba! I serve my queen!"

At once the figure was gone. Asmira's ears popped; blood trickled from her nose. The lamps around the room resumed their normal light. King Solomon, gray with weariness or rage, took the Ring from his finger and tossed it back upon the silver plate.

"Queen Balkis?" he said, passing his hand across his face. "*Balkis?* Young miss, if you dare to lie to me..."

"I do not lie." Asmira slowly struggled back into a sitting position. Tears welled in her eyes. Her sense of overwhelming horror had vanished with the Spirit of the Ring; now she reeled at the shame of her betrayal. She stared in blank hatred at the king.

Solomon tapped his fingers upon the chair. "Queen Balkis...?" he mused again. "No! Why should it be?"

"I speak the truth," Asmira spat. "Though it matters little either way, since you'll kill me whatever I say."

"Are you surprised?" The king seemed pained. "My dear young woman, it was not *I* who crept in here to put a knife in another's back. It is only because you do not fit the normal run of demons or assassins that I speak with you at all. Believe me, most of them are drearily self-explanatory. But you... When I find a pretty girl upon the floor of my observatory, flat out in a faint, with a silver dagger in her belt and another embedded in my floor, and no obvious sign of how she evaded the sentries of my palace and climbed up here at all—I must say I am perplexed and intrigued. So, if you have a grain of sense, you will take advantage of my interest, wipe away those unbecoming tears, and speak rapidly and well, and pray to whatever god you hold dear that my interest is long maintained. For when I get bored," King Solomon said, "I turn to my Ring. Now, then. Queen Balkis sent you, so you say. Why should this be?"

While he had been speaking, Asmira had made great play of dabbing at her face with her dirty sleeve, and in so doing, shuffled forward on the bed. A last desperate attack was all she could hope for now. But she *might* still inch a little closer....

She lowered her arm. "*Why*? How can you even *ask* me that?"

The king's face darkened. His hand stretched out—

"Your threats!" Asmira cried out in panic. "Your cruel demands! Why should I spell it out for you? Sheba cannot withstand your power, as you well know, so my queen took what action she could to save her honor! If I had succeeded, my country would have been saved! Believe me, I curse myself for failing!"

Solomon had not picked up the Ring, though his fingers hovered over it. His face was calm, but he breathed deeply as one in pain. "This seems . . . an unusual course of action to take against someone who has offered marriage," he said, slowly. "A rejection I can take. Assassination is a little more extreme. Don't you think so, Asmira?"

She scowled at his use of her name. "I'm not talking about marriage. Your threat of invasion! Your demands for frankincense! Your vow to destroy our nation when the moon is new!"

"Terrible threats, indeed."

"Yes."

"Except I never made them." He sat back in his chair, thin fingertips together, and gazed at her.

Asmira blinked. "But you did."

"Not so."

"I have it on my queen's word. You must be—"

"And here again," King Solomon said, stretching out and taking a fig from the bowl beside him, "I must educate you swiftly in the ways of kings. Perhaps, in matters of diplomacy, there are times when the meanings of certain royal words are stretched, or certain things are quietly left unsaid, but when a king looks you in the eye and tells you something is so, it *is* so.

He does not lie. Even to suggest as much means death. Do you understand? *Look* at me."

Slowly, reluctantly, Asmira met his eyes, which of all his ravaged features were the only parts she would have recognized from the mural in the Magicians' Hall. All its implacable authority was in them. Despite herself, despite her fury, she said sulkily, "Yes, I understand."

"Good. So now you are in a dilemma."

She hesitated. "My queen..."

"Tells you something different. One of us is lying—or is perhaps mistaken."

The tones he used were mild, and he smiled a little as he spoke, but Asmira flinched as if she had been struck. In its quiet way, this was a direct assault upon everything she held dear—just as violent as the burning of the Marib tower. The purpose of her entire life—and of her mother's—was to defend the queen and, through her, Sheba. The queen's will could not be questioned. Whatever she *did* was right; whatever she *said* was right. To suggest otherwise was to threaten the entire structure on which Asmira based her every waking deed. Solomon's words gave her a sensation much like vertigo; she was on the edge of a precipice and about to fall.

Shuffling forward a little farther on the bed, she said, "My queen would not lie."

"Might she be mistaken, then?"

"No."

"Well, I suppose there's no getting sense from a slave." Solomon took a grape from the fruit dish, and chewed it thoughtfully. "I must say I am disappointed in Balkis. I'd heard tell that she was intelligent and graceful, but this is shoddy work all around. Still, what do the lapwings know? They also told me she was beautiful. I suppose they got that wrong as well. Never trust a migrating bird."

Asmira spoke hotly. "She *is* very beautiful."

He grunted. "Well, small chance of a marriage now. How did she hear of my wicked plans? Did she say?"

"Your demon messenger."

"Which could have been sent by anyone. Honestly, a *child* might have thought to double-check. Asmira—I see you are walking your backside very subtly in my direction. Stop it, please, or the Spirit of the Ring shall continue this conversation with you instead of me. As you have seen, he is not as amiable as I am." King Solomon sighed. "We have established," he went on, "that you are here under a misapprehension. What were your exact orders?"

"Kill you. Take the Ring, if I could."

"And what if you were captured—as was always going to be the case?"

Asmira shrugged. "I would turn my knife upon myself."

"These were your queen's orders?"

"She . . . did not say that. The priestesses did."

King Solomon nodded. "But Balkis did not object. She was content that you were going to your death. I must say," he added, "I'm relieved the woman turned down my original proposals. The thought of a wife like that among one's harem is enough to fill any man with dread. I ought to thank you, Asmira, for opening my eyes."

Anger sloshed like acid in her belly. "Why didn't you just kill me when you found me?"

"I am not that sort. Besides, I have more questions. Who brought you up here?"

"I came alone."

"Asmira, you are doubtless very determined, and extremely good with knives, but neither of those attributes was enough to get you to my rooms. Any ordinary assassin—"

"I'm *not* an assassin, I'm a hereditary guard."

"You must forgive me, the difference is subtle. If you are an ordinary 'guard,'" the king went on, "then someone with great abilities in magic has given you his aid. The only other possibility is that you are an accomplished magician yourself, with powerful slaves at your command." He looked at her skeptically.

Asmira's eyes widened. For the first time since she had woken, her self-absorption shifted. She thought of Bartimaeus. He had warned her of the trap; he had tried to stop her. And now she was captured and he . . . was dead or gone.

"Well, what is the truth, then?" the king demanded. "How did you get here?"

"I was . . . brought here by a spirit that I summoned myself."

"Indeed? Then where is it? I sent out sensors and found nothing."

"I expect your demon destroyed it," Asmira said.

The elegant brows furrowed. "What was its nature? A marid?"

"A djinni."

"Oh, now I *know* that you are lying." The king reached out and took the Ring from the silver plate. "A mere *djinni* could not get past all my slaves below. You are no magician. But a magician has surely helped you. . . ." His eyes narrowed, became harsh with suspicion. "Who was it, then? One of my own?"

Asmira frowned in perplexity. "What?"

"Hiram? Nisroch? Khaba? Come, you are protecting someone." He waved a hand toward the window. "The Seventeen grow impatient in their little towers down there. They are close to the source of power, but not as close as they would like! Who knows, perhaps they secretly work in tandem with this queen of yours. Perhaps, like her, they look for someone young and gullible, someone hotheaded, burning with addled zeal—someone who might strike a blow against me on their behalf!" Asmira tried to speak, but the king's voice grew louder; he sat forward in his chair. "Perhaps you even work for them directly! Tell me, Asmira, what did they offer you if you crept in here on your suicidal mission? Love? Silks? Riches? Quickly now, the Ring is on my finger! Speak! Tell me the truth before it turns!"

For a moment the rage and confusion that warred within her struck Asmira quite dumb. Then she laughed. She set her untouched wine carefully on the floor and got slowly to her feet. "I've *told* you the truth," she said. "Turn the Ring and have done."

King Solomon grimaced. "Sit down. I warn you—sit!"

"No." She walked toward him.

"Then you leave me no choice." Solomon raised his left hand and, with the thumb and forefinger of his right, turned the band of gold upon his little finger.

Asmira stopped where she was. She closed her eyes; blood pounded in her head. . . .

Nothing happened. Somewhere, as if at one remove, she heard the king give a muttered oath.

Asmira opened one eye. Solomon sat as before, spinning the Ring upon his finger. Around and around it went. No terrifying entity materialized between them.

Even as she watched, the slender band of gold grew limp and soggy, took on a somewhat gray and fishy air. It sagged against his finger. King Solomon and Asmira stared at it open-mouthed.

"A calamari ring. . . ." Asmira breathed.

Solomon's voice was barely audible. "Someone's switched it..." he began.

"Ah yes, now that would have been me." At this, a small, striped sand cat sauntered out from behind the nearest rack of scrolls, whiskers sparkling, eyes gleaming, tail held high in a particularly jaunty manner. It looked inordinately pleased with itself. It strolled over the rugs and came to a halt between them. "One 'mere djinni' at your service," it said, settling itself down neatly, and winding its tail around its paws. "One 'mere djinni'"—here it paused and blinked around at them for dramatic effect—"who, while you've both been chatting away like fishwives, has got himself a ring."

30

I made it look easy, didn't I? But it wasn't *quite* as straightforward as all that.

True, getting *into* the chamber wasn't so hard—there weren't any traps or sentinels, and Solomon had his back to me when I peeked around the door. And nipping over to the rack beside the window was a doddle too, since he and the girl were absorbed by their rather tense "discussion," and were hardly likely to notice a discreetly passing fly.[1]

From then on though, things got trickier—mainly because of the nature of the Ring.

It was so *bright* for starters. On the first plane the room was adequately lit by several flickering oil lamps,[2] but on the higher ones the aura of that little golden speck leached everything whiter and brighter than the Egyptian sands at noon. It was so overwhelming that it actually made me sick to use my inner eyes. Except in briefest snatches, I stuck with the first plane from then on.

The actual sleight-of-hand stuff—putting a quick Illusion on

---

[1] The fly was an optional extra right then. They were so preoccupied I don't think they'd have noticed me if I'd turned into a flatulent unicorn and pirouetted gently across the room.

[2] Tatty, chipped ones, they were, no doubt chosen especially by Solomon for his humble little whitewashed bedroom, to go with the earthen plates and the rough wood furniture. I bet going there after the day's luxuries were over made him feel all virtuous and austere . . . and therefore, paradoxically, even more superior to the rest of us than before.

a squid ring and substituting it for the real Ring on the plate —*that* was easy too, at least in principle. Stealing stuff is second-nature to djinn—always has been, mainly because it's all we're ever asked to do.[3] So the sand cat tiptoed up behind Solomon's chair, and waited until one of the girl's spasms of righteous outrage coincided with one of the king's. No sooner were they both rolling their eyes and huffing loudly than I stuck out my paw, made my switch faster than blinking, and retreated in haste toward the window.

Which was when I hit the real snag.

How that Ring hurt me.

Of course, the silver dish that Solomon had plonked it on for safekeeping hadn't done my essence any good at all. If it had been any normal object sitting there, I'd have been most reluctant to go anywhere near it. But to steal the Ring of Solomon? I could cope with a little bit of blistering for that. So I girded my furry loins and did the deed, and it was only when I was moving away from the silver's baleful chill that I realized the Ring I held lightly between my teeth was *also* causing problems.

It wasn't a cold burning sensation like silver (or iron, or any of the other substances that are anathema to spirits). It was hotter than that, and at first not so troublesome. It began as the faintest prickling of my essence around where I held the Ring. The feeling was curiously familiar—painful, but also pleasant—and quickly grew to become a sharp, insistent *tugging*. By the time the sand cat had made it back into concealment behind the rack of scrolls, I felt almost as if I was being pulled in two. I spat the

---

[3] My very first job, in fact, when I arrived on Earth fresh-faced and dewy-eyed, was nicking a fertility statue from the love goddess's sanctuary in Ur. Morally speaking, this pretty much set the tone for my next two thousand years.

Ring down onto the floor and regarded it (on the first plane) in consternation.

Philocretes hadn't lied. The energies of the Other Place pulsed furiously in this little golden ring. It had been created as an instant portal between the dimensions, and even while closed, there was something of a draft coming under the door. The tugging sensation was exactly the same thing I experienced whenever I was released from service in this world. *Then*, of course, it was welcome, because I could give in to it; now, trapped as I was on Earth, it didn't half sting. Even after a bare few moments holding the Ring, my essence felt oddly out of kilter, pulled out of shape by the forces it contained. I dreaded to think what would have happened if I'd actually put it on.[4]

Putting it on, needless to say, was what Solomon did every single day.

I still hadn't seen his face, but even from behind I could tell he didn't look exactly as he had on the building site. His hair was gray, for one thing, and there was something ominously thin about the arms and hands. In a flash I understood something of the price he paid.

I thought about this while I sat quiet, eyeing the Ring dubiously and recovering from its touch. Beyond the rack, meanwhile, the argument was in full flow, both girl and king working themselves up into paroxysms of fury. Part of me still hoped Big Sol might lose it, produce an afrit from somewhere, and blast the girl to smithereens, so that I could just leave the Ring lying and

---

[4] Not to mention trying to *use* it. Turning the Ring would have been equivalent to opening the door to the Other Place and subjecting one's essence to the full power of its pull. Any Earth-tethered spirit who tried such a thing would surely soon be torn in two. Here was an irony which Philocretes, Azul, and the other restless spirits who desired the Ring had not lived to discover.

head off home. But my hopes weren't high. Clearly he didn't like having spirits (or humans) of any kind in his apartments at night. He relied on Illusions—such as the many-tentacled monster—and his fearsome reputation to keep his enemies at bay.

Likewise, if the girl had been a *real* assassin, she'd have scissor-kicked suddenly through the air, done a fancy twirl, and snapped his neck between her thighs before doing the splits on landing. I'd have paid good money to see that. But instead she just got red-faced and a bit shouty, and then decided to end it all in a kind of futile grump.[5]

Cue Solomon grimly turning the Ring upon his finger.

Cue his discovery that all wasn't as it seemed.

Cue my sudden entrance, casual as you like, and their consequent stupefaction.[6]

I've had worse moments in my career.

"Hello, *Asmira*," I said pleasantly. "Hello, Solomon." I smoothed out my whiskers with a paw. "First one to recover gets a prize."

The girl gave a strangled gasp. "I thought you were dead."

"Nope."

"I thought that giant demon—"

"Wasn't one. It was an Illusion. Solomon seems to specialize in them."

She scowled indignantly at the king. "You said you saved me from it!"

"You can't believe anything *anyone* says, can you?" I winked

---

[5] Actually, I couldn't help being impressed by her all-around feistiness in defying Solomon, despite the threat of the "Ring." Though I suppose hopeless last stands always look best viewed from the outside.

[6] Stupefaction's putting it mildly. Two blocks of limestone crudely daubed with cartoon faces would have been more animated than Solomon and the girl right then.

at Solomon, who was staring at me in blankest incomprehension. "We meet again, O King. In rather different circumstances from last time."

There was a pause. Well, give him his due, he hadn't seen my cat getup before. Plus he was probably still in shock.

I laughed lightly. "That's right, my friend. Bartimaeus of Uruk, at your service."

"Who?"

The tip of the cat's tail kinked slightly with annoyance. "Bartimaeus. Of *Uruk*. Surely you recall...? Oh, Great Marduk on high." With the swiftness of thought, the cat became a pygmy hippo in a skirt, plump forearms lodged indignantly on hips. "Well, perhaps you remember *this*?"

Asmira blinked at me. "Is this one of your usual guises?"

"No. Well, not often. Look, it's a long story."

Solomon gave a sudden start. "I recall you! You are one of Khaba's djinn!" He glared at the girl. "So, then...it was the *Egyptian* who sent you here...."

I shook my head pityingly. "Hardly! I am Khaba's slave no longer! Bartimaeus of Uruk has ways of escaping the harshest bondage. No magician holds *me* long! Time and again I—"

"Khaba trapped him in a bottle," the girl interrupted. "I got him out. He's *my* slave now."

"Technically speaking"—I scowled—"that may be true. But it won't be the case for long. I've learned your birthname, *Asmira*, and that puts you at a sudden disadvantage. If you want to live much longer, I suggest you dismiss me right away."

The girl ignored me. She stepped across to Solomon and plucked the silver dagger from his lap. He made no move to stop her. She stood close beside his chair, with the weapon held toward him.

"Give me the Ring, Bartimaeus," she said abruptly. "We're going."

I cleared my throat. "Wait a minute. Didn't you hear what I said? I know your name. I can deflect any Ward you throw."

"You still have to do what I say, don't you? Where's the Ring?"

"Dismiss me, and I'll tell you as I go."

"What? Like I'm going to agree to that!"

King Solomon of Israel had been sitting in his chair, watching us both intently. Suddenly he spoke; frail as he seemed, his voice still carried its note of assured command. "Bartimaeus of Uruk, did you carry out the charge I gave you?"

"What charge?" The hippo stared. "You mean sorting out the bandits in the desert? Yes, I did, as it happens, but that's not really what we're talking about right now. Listen, Asmira—"

"Tell me of these bandits," Solomon persisted. "Who were they? Who was their leader?"

"Er, they were sent by the king of the Edomites, who's annoyed with you for this massive yearly tribute you keep demanding. But you'll agree this isn't really the time—"

"*Tribute*? What tribute is this? I've never demanded one!"

"The king of the Edomites thinks you have," I said. "Just as the Queen of Sheba thinks you're after her frankincense. All rather puzzling, isn't it? Someone's up to no good behind your back. But forgive me, O great Solomon, you don't seem to quite realize the situation you're in. You're powerless. I've stolen your Ring."

"Correction: *I've* stolen it," the girl said. "I'm his master."

"Nominally," the hippo growled. "But not for long."

"Give me the Ring, Bartimaeus!"

"No! What about my Dismissal?"

"Come on, Bartimaeus," Solomon said suddenly. "Why *don't* you give her the Ring?"

The girl and I both hesitated. We broke off our argument and stared at him.

King Solomon stretched in his chair, took a piece of smoked mackerel and popped it in his mouth.[7] It had to be said he didn't seem quite as perturbed by events as might have been expected. "Give her the Ring," he said again. "Why not? Why the reluctance? You should ask yourself, Asmira of Sheba, why your servant hesitates in this very simple matter. Surely he should wish to carry out his charge so that you let him go. Can it be," Solomon went on, looking between us, one to the other, with his tired eyes, "that the djinni has understood something about the Ring that *you* don't yet realize? Can it be he wants to get far from here before you find it out?"

The hippo blew out its cheeks resignedly. He was right, of course. I flicked a forefoot toward the nearest rack of scrolls. "You want the Ring?" I sighed. "It's under the rack, on the far side."

The girl frowned at me. "Keep watch on Solomon," she said.

She stalked past me to the rack, crouched low. There was a pause as her fingers quested, then a little gasp of triumph. I screwed my eyes up tight and waited.

A scream; the sound of a ring rolling back upon the floor. When I looked across, the girl was tightly clasping her hand beneath her arm.

"It *burns!*" she cried. "What have you *done* to it, demon?"

"Me?"

"You've put some cursed magic on it!" With her good

---

[7] Not a calamari ring, note: he seemed to have gone off them.

312

hand, she waved the silver dagger. "Take it off this instant, or I swear—"

It was at that moment King Solomon stood up; and though (speaking frankly) he was in his nightie, though his frame was thin, though his face, without its cloak of Illusion, was lined and aged, he nevertheless projected a sudden severe authority, so that the girl and I fell instantly quiet. "The djinni speaks truly," he said. "The Ring of Solomon brings pain. That is its nature. If you wish for proof, look here." And he held up his hand, with the livid mark upon its finger.

The girl stared at it. "I—I don't understand," she stammered. "No. This is a trick. I'm not listening to you." But though her eyes returned to the little fleck of gold and obsidian lying on the floor beside her feet, she did not pick it up, nor make any move to do so.

"It's not a trick," I said. "It burned me, too." Note that I'd just changed from the beskirted hippo into the dark-haired young Sumerian boy, who, while less adorably curvy, better reflected the gravity of the moment. I felt that something important was approaching fast, and I didn't know which way it was going to go.

"But why *should* it burn?" the girl said, plaintively. "How will my queen—? I thought the Ring—"

Solomon said quietly: "Let me tell you what *I* know of the Ring, Asmira. After that you can do what you like with it—and with me."

She hesitated, looking toward the door, then back at the object at her feet. She stared at Solomon, and at the dagger in her hand. She swore under her breath. "Quickly, then. And no tricks."

"When I was young," King Solomon said at once, "my

313

interest was in treasures of the past—a passion that remains with me still.[8] I journeyed far in search of them, bartering in the bazaars of Thebes and Babylon for relics of the ancient days. I also visited the ruins of yet older cities, places whose names are lost to men. One such site lay on the desert's edge beside the Tigris River. It is nothing now but a few worn mounds covered with earth and sand. No doubt, over the centuries, most of its secrets had been steadily plundered, but the greatest—and most terrible—still lay undisturbed."

He paused, ostensibly to cough, but probably (given he was such an old ham) to build up the tension. I noticed that he was standing in such a way that the lantern light cast a golden, rather celestial, halo about his head. He was a good performer, Solomon, even without his power.

I watched the girl too. She was frowning (as usual), but the shock of the Ring's touch was still upon her, and she seemed willing to wait and listen.

"When I came to these ruins," Solomon continued, "a recent earth tremor had split the surface of one of the smaller mounds. The soil had collapsed, revealing a stretch of mud-brick wall, a half-collapsed archway and—beyond—a flight of stairs leading into the ground. You can well imagine that my curiosity was aflame! I made a light, crept down into the depths and, after an incalculable descent, arrived at a broken door. Some ancient rock-fall had split it open, and whatever magic might have been upon it had long been spent. I squeezed through into the blackness—"

"You were *so-o-o-o* lucky!" I cried. "Sumerian well-rooms

---

[8] In other words, he was a typical magician, wanting old-time freebies to supplement his power.

are notorious for traps! Ordinarily there'd have been any amount of hexes and things in there."

"Whether I was *lucky*," King Solomon said irritably, "I will leave to you to judge. Do not interrupt again. I squeezed inside, as I say, and found myself in a small chamber. In its center"—he shuddered, as at an oft-remembered horror—"in its center was an iron chair, and on that chair, strapped there with ancient fastenings of rope and wire, sat the mummified body of—I cannot say whether it was a man or woman, for great terror had seized me, and all I longed for was escape. As I turned to go, I caught sight of a glint of gold upon one papery finger. In my avarice I snatched at it: the finger broke away, the Ring was in my hand. I put it on"—he held up his hand, so that the red weal upon the finger shone bright and raw—"and instantly such pain came over me that I collapsed and knew no more."

Solomon took a drink of wine. We stood silent. Even I didn't try to butt in this time.[9]

"I was awoken in the darkness of that fearful place," the king went on, "by the burning pain. My one thought was to remove the Ring. As I fumbled at it, it twisted on my finger; at once a soft voice at my shoulder asked me what I desired. You may be sure I wished, with what I assumed to be my dying breath, to be home again. A moment passed, my head spun—when I awoke I was on the roof of my house in Jerusalem, with the sun shining warm upon me."

"You were transported in an instant?" Despite herself, the

---

[9] I was thinking about the unknown corpse, that person who had been bound to the chair with the Ring upon their finger, then carefully buried alive. All that power (and pain) literally at their fingertips, yet forced to endure a helpless death! It was a terrible end. It was also striking how keen the ancient executioners were to rid themselves of the allegedly wondrous Ring.

girl's face was slack with wonder. Even the handsome young Sumerian, who had seen and heard a fair bit in his time, was grudgingly impressed.[10]

"It was even so," Solomon said. "Well, I shall be brief, for you can guess the rest. Soon I learned two things about the Ring. First, with it on my finger, I had power undreamed of. The Spirit of the Ring, who is very great, provides innumerable slaves to do my bidding. By simply touching the stone, I summon them; by *turning* the Ring, the Spirit himself appears. Thus I can instantly realize my heart's desires. Second, and less pleasant"—here he closed his eyes a moment—"there is the pain the Ring exerts. This never slackens. Not only that: each time I use it, my personal strength diminishes. In the early years, when I was strong, I used it daily—I built this palace, I made my empire, I forced the kings around me to down their swords and sue for peace. I began to use the Ring to help those peoples most in need. Recently"—he gave a sigh—"this has become . . . more difficult. Even the slightest use wearies me, and I must rest long to recover. Which is regrettable, since hundreds come daily to my gates, begging for my aid! More and more I must rely on my squabbling magicians to do this work for me." He broke off and coughed again.

"You *do* know," I said, and I spoke quite sympathetically, for Solomon's story had made a favorable impression on me,[11] "that

---

[10] Spontaneous matter transfer is very, *very* tricky. I can't do it. No one I know can do it. The only time a spirit shifts instantaneously from one place to another is when it's being summoned, and *we're* made of essence. Moving a great fat heavy human (like you) in this fashion is even harder.

[11] I too understand a little about being trapped by circumstances, about enduring pain.

some of your magicians are not quite as . . . scrupulous as you. In fact, they're downright bad. Take Khaba, for instance—"

"I know this," Solomon said. "By instinct, many of the Seventeen are wicked as well as strong. I keep them near me, and I keep them nervous by threatening to use the Ring on them. That is good policy. Better this than have them conspiring against me far away. Meanwhile, I use their power."

"Yeah, fine, but I don't think you know the full extent—"

And then the girl was suddenly between us, with the dagger pointing at the king's throat. "Bartimaeus," she hissed, "stop talking with him as if he were your ally! Pick up the Ring. We have to go."

"Asmira," King Solomon said. He did not flinch from the dagger blade. "You have heard my story. Now look at my face. Would you want your queen to look like this?"

She shook her head. "She wouldn't do so. She wouldn't wear it as you have done."

"Ah, but she *would*. She would have to. Or else it would be stolen! Nothing on Earth," King Solomon said, "is desired as much as this Ring. She would be forced to wear it, and it would madden her, for the pain when you touch it, Asmira, is *nothing* to what you feel when you put it on. Try it. Put it on your finger. See for yourself."

Asmira was still holding her dagger outstretched. She did not answer.

"No?" Solomon said. "I am not surprised. I would not wish the Ring on anyone." He sat down abruptly, an old and shrunken man. "Well, you have your choice. Kill me if you must, and take the Ring to Sheba. Then a dozen magicians will fight for it and there will be war in the world. Or leave it here, and go. Leave me to my burden. I will keep the Ring safe, and with it do what good I can. I will not hinder your departure, that I swear."

I'd been uncharacteristically quiet for a bit, giving Solomon space to make his pitch, but now I took a tentative step forward. "That sounds like fine good sense to me," I said. "Give him the Ring back, Asmira, and let's g—ow!"

She had swung the dagger around, pointing it toward me, so its aura bit my essence. I jumped back with a cry. Still she didn't speak. Her face was set, her eyes staring. She didn't seem to see me or Solomon any longer, but something far away.

I tried again. "Listen," I said. "Ditch the Ring and I'll give you a lift home. How's that for a deal? True, I haven't got a nice big carpet like Khaba, but I'm sure we could find you a towel or napkin or something. You can see that Solomon's right, can't you? The Ring is nothing but trouble. Even the ancients didn't use it. They sealed it in a tomb."

Still the girl said nothing. The king sat quiet in his chair, maintaining his attitude of meek acceptance, but I knew that he was watching her closely, hanging on her word.

She looked up; her eyes focused on me at last. "Bartimaeus—"

"Yes, Asmira."

Surely she would see sense now after all she'd been told and seen. *Surely*, after feeling the Ring's power for herself, she would know what she had to do.

"Bartimaeus," she said, "fetch me the Ring."

"To give to Solomon?"

"To take to Sheba." Her face was hard, expressionless. She turned away from me. Without looking at the king, she sheathed her dagger in her belt and walked out through the door.

31

Transporting an object as potent as the Ring of Solomon is a ticklish task, particularly if you're keen to avoid being toasted as you do so.

In an ideal world I'd have put it in a lead-lined box, put the box inside a sack, and pulled the sack behind me on the end of a mile-long chain, so that neither my essence nor my sight suffered in any way from its emanations. Instead I had to make do with wrapping it in a crumpled ball made from the parchments found on Solomon's writing table.[1] This solution shielded the worst of the heat quite well, but even through the thick, coarse layers its aura remained uncomfortable. I could feel my fingers tingling.

The girl had already gone. Holding the ball of parchment gingerly like the unwilling slave I was, I followed in her wake. At the door I paused, looked back. The king was still in his chair, his chin lowered almost to his chest. He seemed older, more hunched, and far more shrunken than before. He did not look at me, nor seek to prevent my theft. He knew that I couldn't have returned the Ring to him, even if I'd wanted to.

There was nothing to say. I set off slowly down the corridor, leaving King Solomon sitting silent in his little whitewashed room.

★   ★   ★

---

[1] At a rough glance they seemed to be inscribed with some songs he was writing. I didn't bother reading any. They were unlikely to be much good.

Out into the main chamber I went, past the pool, past the doors that led to the observatory and the storeroom, past the golden tables in all their Glamour, and so through the drapes, the nexus, and the arch, and onto the balcony again.

Above me, the stars were still spread out in splendid cold array. Below me, the lights of the palace gleamed beyond the gardens.

The girl waited at the balustrade, gazing to the south. Her arms were crossed, the breeze flicked at her long, dark hair.

Without looking at me, she said: "You've got the Ring?"

"Oh, I've got it."

"Take me and it to Sheba. I don't care how we go. Turn into a bird, or a bat, or whatever monstrosity you please. Get me there quickly and I'll dismiss you when we arrive." For someone who had just carried out her impossible quest, she didn't seem exactly buoyant. More taut with anger, if truth be told.

She wasn't the only one.

I said, "We'll get to that in a moment. I want to ask you something first."

She pointed down to the distant southern gardens, where several lights still flitted like a storm of wasps. "No time for talking. What if Solomon alerts the guards?"

"We've got *this* now," I said coldly, holding up the parchment ball. "That gives us all the time we need. If they spot us, you can simply put the Ring on, can't you? That'll send them packing."

She shook her head, shuddering at the memory of its touch. "Don't be stupid. I couldn't do that."

"No? That's what you expect your precious queen to do, though, isn't it? Think *she'll* be able to cope with the pain?"

"Queen Balkis," the girl said in a toneless voice, "will know what to do."

"Will she, though?" I stepped closer now. "Perhaps you didn't understand what Solomon was telling you back there," I said. "He wasn't lying. You've felt the Ring's power for yourself, Asmira. You've heard what it does. Do you truly *want* that unleashed upon the world?"

Her anger burst forth then, just a little. "Solomon already unleashes it! Nothing's going to change."

"Well now, I'm not Solomon's biggest fan," I said, "but I'd say he was doing his best *not* to unleash it. He keeps the Ring cooped up in here, and uses it as little as possible."

The girl made a loud, unladylike, scoffing noise. "Wrong! He threatens Sheba!"

"Oh, come *on!*" My scoffing noise was louder still. "You don't *really* believe that any more, do you? I was listening to you both back there. Why should he deny responsibility? He was holding you captive—he didn't need to lie. It's obvious to anyone with half a brain that there's some other conspiracy going on, which—"

"Which is irrelevant!" the girl cried. "I don't care either way. My queen has given me a task, and I am carrying it out. That's all there is to it. I *have* to obey her!"

"Spoken like the slave you are," I sneered. "You *don't* have to obey her, and that's the point. For all I know, Balkis is normally a paragon of virtue, but she's made the wrong call here. Solomon wasn't your enemy until you crept into his bedroom with that dagger. Even now I think he'd let you off if you just took it back and— Oh, swan off all you like, young madam, but that doesn't change the obvious!"

The girl had spun on her heels with a squeak of rage, and

had stalked away along the balcony—but at my words, as if she were doing some primitive Arabian dance, she spun again and jabbed her finger at me. "Unlike a faithless demon, who has to be coerced into everything he does, *I* have sacred bonds," she said. "I hold true to the duty placed in me. I faithfully serve my queen."

"Which doesn't stop you both messing things up," I said. "How old's Balkis, exactly? Thirty? Forty, tops? Well, listen, I've got two thousand years of accumulated wisdom here, and even *I* get it wrong sometimes. For instance, I thought you had something to you when I met you in the gorge. Intelligence, flexibility of mind...Ha! How misinformed was I?"

"It's not *about* intelligence," the girl snapped, proving her point precisely. "It's about trust. I trust my queen and obey her in everything."

"In everything?"

"Yes."

"In that case"—this was a good one; I'd been saving it for a while—"why didn't you kill Solomon?"

There was a silence. I placed the ball of parchment on the balustrade, the better to fold my arms in a decisive, calmly superior sort of way. The girl hesitated; her hands gave little tremors of uncertainty. "Well, I didn't need to. He's powerless without the Ring."

"But you were ordered to kill him. In fact, that was the top priority, if I recall. The Ring came second."

"Without his Ring, he'll soon be dead," the girl said. "The other magicians will finish him off as soon as they find—"

"That's still not answering my question. Why didn't *you* kill him? You had the dagger. Or you could have gotten me to do it. I've killed kings before now, oodles of them.[2] But no, we just slipped away without giving him so much as a dead arm or Chinese burn. One more time for luck: *Why didn't you kill him?*"

"I couldn't do it!" the girl cried suddenly. "All right? I couldn't do it, with him just sitting there. I was going to, when I went over with the knife, but he was helpless. And that just made me—" She gave a curse. "I couldn't do it out of hand! Solomon didn't kill me when he had me in his power, did he? He should have, but he held back. And just like him, I failed."

"Failed?" I gazed at her. "That's one way of putting it. Another way might be—"

"But it doesn't matter," she said. "I'm going back to Sheba with the Ring." Her face gleamed at me in the darkness like a fierce, pale star. "I'm not going to fail in *that*."

I drew myself up. It was time to go for the jugular now. Her self-assurance, though still vigorously expressed, was failing her; perhaps it had already failed. If I got it right, I figured I could cut things short, save myself a painful journey back to Sheba carrying that burning Ring. Who knows, it might also save the girl. "Let me hazard a guess here," I said, and again it was good that I was in the form of the Sumerian spear-bearer, and not one of my more unusual guises. Home truths are difficult enough to swallow without having them delivered by a pop-eyed imp, a winged serpent, a miasma of poison gas, or a four-faced

---

[2] Four, in fact: three of them ultra-cool, deliberate acts of political assassination, and one an unfortunate mishap involving a barking dog, a child's toy chariot, a slippery corridor, a short, steep ramp, and a cauldron of boiling beef-fat. That one had to be seen to be believed.

demon,[3] to mention but a few. "You couldn't kill Solomon," I said, "because, in your heart, you know he was telling you the truth about Sheba and the Ring. No—shut up a moment, and listen. And that, in turn, means you know your precious queen got it wrong. You don't like that revelation. You don't like it because that means she sent you here mistakenly, and everything you risked was for nothing. You don't like it because, if your queen's not infallible, it calls into question the whole purpose of your sad little life, doing what she says, sacrificing yourself for her. Doesn't it? Oh yes, and just maybe it calls into question your *mother's* sacrifice too."

The girl gave a start. Her voice was very faint. "You know *nothing* about my mother."

"I know what you told me. She died for her queen."

The girl's eyes closed. "Yes. And I watched her die."

"Just as you expected to die on this mission too. Part of you even hoped for it." Something crumpled in the girl's face here. I waited and drew back a little. "So, when was it?" I said. "Recently?"

"Long ago." The girl looked at me. The fury was still there, but it was cracked and broken now, and there were tears in her eyes. "I was six years old. Men of the hill-tribes, angered about taxes. They tried to kill the queen."

"Mm," I said musingly. "Assassins attacking a head of state. Sound familiar?"

The girl didn't seem to have heard. "My mother stopped

---

[3] *Four-faced demon*: a guise used occasionally to guard important crossroads in ancient Mesopotamia. The faces were a griffin, a bull, a lion, and a cobra, each more terrifying than the last. I sat on a pillar, a picture of noble gravitas, gazing implacably in all directions. The problems started when I had to get up and run after someone. Then I just got confused and tripped over my feet, which made the passing urchins laugh.

them," she said. "And they . . ." She looked off into the gardens. It was still very quiet out there, no sign of any trouble. On sudden impulse, I took the ball of parchment down off the balustrade. It struck me its muffled aura might be visible from afar.

Asmira leaned back against the stone, hands resting at her sides. For the first time in our association she was truly still. Of course, I'd seen her not moving before, but always as an interlude amid swift action. Now, whether it was my words, or her memories, or something else entirely, she seemed suddenly slowed, deflated, uncertain what to do.

"If I don't take the Ring," she said in a hollow voice, "what will I have achieved? Nothing. I'll still be as empty as I am now."

Empty? The spear-bearer scratched his manly chin. Humans and their problems. It's not my strongest suit. Oh sure, it was pretty clear to me that the girl had been seeking to emulate her mother all these years, only to find—at the moment of her triumph—that she didn't quite believe in what she was doing. I saw that well enough. But in the face of her sudden desolation, I was unsure where to go next. Probing psychological analysis is one thing,[4] *constructive* suggestions quite another.

"Now listen," I began, "there's still time to take the Ring back to Solomon. He wouldn't take revenge on you. He gave his word. Plus he'd be too relieved, I think. Or, another alternative, which you may not have considered, is for us to chuck the Ring into the sea. Get rid of it forever. *That* would solve the problem big time—no more threat to Sheba, no pain for your queen—plus it would save a lot of inconvenience for a host of spirits too."

---

[4] Namely, impartial observation liberally spiced with sarcasm and personal abuse. Let's face it, I'm *good* at all that.

The girl neither agreed nor disagreed with this sensible suggestion. She remained slumped, shoulders sagging, staring into the dark.

I tried again. "This 'emptiness' you talk about," I said. "I think you're getting too worked up about it. Your trouble, Asmira, is you've got something of an issue with your—" I broke off in sudden alarm. My handsome nose twitched. It twitched again. I sniffed about me intently.

That woke her up a bit. She stirred indignantly. "You're saying I smell? Great Sheba, that was one thing I *wasn't* worrying about."

"No. Not you." My eyes narrowed. I looked along the walkway. Pillars, statues, scattered chairs—all seemed quiet enough. But somewhere close . . . Uh-oh. "Can you smell anything?" I asked.

"Rotten eggs," the girl said. "I thought that was you."

"It isn't me."

Spurred on by sudden intuition, I stole away from her on silent feet and padded up the center of the aisle. I stopped, sniffed, listened, went a little farther, sniffed again. I took another step—then spun around and blew the nearest statue to pieces with a Detonation.

The girl gave a cry; the spear-bearer gave a spring. Even as the glowing shards of stone were still tumbling, rolling, pattering down upon the tower's dome, I landed in their midst, brushed aside a few remaining filaments of lilac cloud, and seized the blackened foliot from his hiding place behind the shattered plinth. I grabbed him by his green and sinewy neck and lifted him aloft.

"*Gezeri,*" I snarled. "I *thought* as much. Spying again! Well, this time I'm going to finish you before you get a chance to—"

The foliot slowly stuck out his tongue at me and grinned. He pointed to the south.

Oh no.

I turned, looked. Far off above the palace roofs a small black cloud rose vertically into the night, a rushing cone of wind and fire. It was far away at first, but not for long. Slender bolts of lighting sprang from its sides; it boiled, churned, spun with avenging fury, and shot above the gardens toward the tower.

32

The appearance of the cloud came at exactly the wrong time for Asmira, at the precise moment when her resolve had fallen clean away.

She stood on the balcony and watched it grow: a tornado of whirling flames, lighting the trees and lawns as it passed above them, staining them red like blood. She heard the screaming of the air, heard the laughter of the little demon, heard the urgent cries of Bartimaeus as he ran toward her. . . .

She heard and saw it all, but she did not act.

Throughout the tribulations of the journey Asmira had maintained an iron discipline learned over many solitary years. The dangers of the palace, the interview with Solomon, even being brought face-to-face with the Spirit of the Ring—none of this had entirely daunted her. She understood the sacrifice she was prepared to make, and she understood why she did so. Her clarity gave her purpose and her purpose gave her clarity. From the beginning she moved toward her likely death in a mood of fierce serenity.

But death, in the end, had *not* come—Bartimaeus had instead. And suddenly the king was at her mercy, the Ring was in her grasp, and she was still alive. Everything was possible that she had long desired. . . . And now Asmira found, quite suddenly, that she was no longer certain what to do.

Even before she fled from Solomon's room, she had been struggling to come to terms with what had happened. The king's story, his helplessness, his denial of his guilt, the way he crumpled in his chair... None of this had been expected; all of it jarred with her preconceptions. And then there'd been the Ring itself, the Ring that supposedly made its wearer the luckiest of men. Except that it burned him and made him old before his time.... She thought of Solomon's ravaged face, of the pain she'd felt when she too had picked it up. Nothing made sense. Everything was upside-down.

At first Asmira had sought to ignore the conflict in her mind and to complete her mission as best she could. But then, thanks to Bartimaeus, she found her deepest doubts and motivations laid bare beneath the stars.

Much of what he said she had always known, secretly, deep down, ever since the moment when her mother had collapsed upon the lap of the impassive, indifferent queen. For years she had denied that knowledge, cloaked it beneath her angry dedication and her pleasure in her skill. But now, with the cold night's clarity, she found she no longer trusted what she was and what she had aspired to be. Her energy and self-belief were gone, and the accumulated weariness of the previous two weeks descended abruptly on her back. She felt both very heavy—and hollow, like a shell.

Onward came the rushing cloud. Asmira did nothing.

The djinni ran toward her, grasping the little green demon by the neck. In his other hand, he had the ball of parchment, held outstretched. "Here," he shouted. "The Ring! Take it! Put it on!"

"What?" Asmira frowned dully. "I—I can't do that."

"Can't you see? Khaba's coming!" Bartimaeus was right beside her now, still in his dark youth guise. He was wide-eyed with agitation. He thrust the ball into her hands. "Put it on, quick! It's our only chance."

Even through the crumpled parcel Asmira could feel the intense heat of the Ring. She fumbled it, almost dropped it to the floor. "*Me?* No . . . I can't. Why don't you—"

"Well, *I* can't do it, can I?" the djinni cried. "The pull of the Other Place will tear my essence in two! Do it! Use it! We've got barely seconds!" The young man gave a spring, hopped onto the balustrade and, tucking the foliot beneath his arm, sent a succession of scarlet bolts shooting through the night toward the cloud. None got near: all exploded against an invisible obstruction, sending plumes of dying magic high into the air, or down in fizzing arcs to set the cypress trees aflame.

Asmira picked hesitantly at the edges of the parchment. Put it on? But this was a royal treasure, worn by kings and queens. Who was she to dare to use it? She was nothing, not even a proper guard. . . . And besides—she thought of Solomon's ravaged face—the Ring *burned.*

"Do you *want* Khaba the Cruel to get it?" Bartimaeus shouted down at her. "Put the thing on! Ah, what kind of master *are* you? This is your chance to do something *right!*"

From the crook of his arm the little green demon gave a rich and fruity chuckle. Asmira recognized it now; it was Khaba's creature. She had glimpsed it in the gorge. "You've got a dud one there, Barty," the foliot remarked. "Useless. Was it her who put that package in plain sight on the balustrade? I saw that a mile off."

The djinni made no answer but spoke a word. The foliot froze with its mouth open, engulfed in a web of smoke. Still firing bolts toward the cloud with his other hand, Bartimaeus tossed the demon high, caught it by a solid ear, and with a mighty rotation of the arm, hurled it out into the dark.

Beyond, in the midst of the oncoming cloud, a bright blue pulse of light flared once.

"*Asmira*—" Bartimaeus said.

Blue fire struck the balustrade, blew it asunder, sent the djinni flying backward in a mass of sapphire flames. Across the walkway he went, through the nearest statue, smashing into the tower's dome in a tangle of bent limbs. The flames licked across him, flared, went out.

His body rolled slowly down the slope, over and over, then stopped at last amid a scattering of stone.

Asmira stared at the slumped body, stared at the package in her hands. She gave a sudden curse; her hesitation left her. She scrabbled at the parchment pieces, tearing them apart, feeling the heat of the Ring inside growing hotter, hotter. . . . She reached out a trembling hand—

Lightning flashed; the storm-cloud plunged down upon the balcony. Statues toppled, pieces of parapet warped, snapped, fell outward into the night. The storm burst upon the walkway, projecting a circular buffet of air that sent Asmira tumbling against the stone, spinning around upon her back. The ball of parchment was flung from her hands, dropped upon the parapet. A small fleck of gold and black bounced free.

The gale winked out; the storm had vanished. Standing in the middle of a broad ring of scorched black stonework, the magician Khaba looked balefully around.

At his back, something darker, taller, raised its head. Paper-thin arms that had held the magician in a tight embrace unfolded. Fingers long and sharp as needles stretched, flexed, pointed in Asmira's direction.

"Over there," a soft voice said.

Asmira had hit her head upon the stonework; the parapet

swam before her eyes. Nevertheless, she struggled to a sitting position and looked about her for the Ring.

There it was—right at the edge, beside the yawning gulf. Head reeling, Asmira rolled herself forward, began to crawl toward the Ring.

Soft footsteps nearing, the swishing of a long black robe.

Asmira crawled faster. Now she felt the Ring's heat upon her face. She stretched out to pick it up—

A black sandal came down, crushed her fingers to the stone. Asmira gasped, jerked her hand away.

"No, Cyrine," the magician said. "No. It's not for you."

He kicked out at her, catching her sharply on the side of the face. She rolled backward with the blow, sprang to her feet. Before she could reach for her belt, something like claws had grasped her waist, yanked her upward and away. For some moments she saw nothing but starlight twisting and the whirling dark, then she found herself summarily deposited back upon the stone, halfway along the ruined balcony. The sharp clasp about her did not slacken; her arms were gripped fast, pressed against her sides. There was a presence at her back.

The Egyptian was still standing over the Ring, staring at it in disbelief. He wore the same tunic as at the banquet so many hours before. His face looked haggard, and there were little purple stains at the corners of his lips, testimony to his night's consumption, but his eyes glistened with high excitement, and his voice trembled as he spoke.

"It *is*. It truly is.... I cannot believe it!" He bent down swiftly, only to pause in doubt as he sensed the emanations of the Ring.

Somewhere above Asmira, a soft voice gave a warning call.

"Master! Beware! The energies burn me even at a distance. Dear Master, you must take care!"

The magician made a noise that was half laugh, half groan. "You—you know me, dear Ammet. I—I like a little pain." His fingers plunged upon the Ring. Asmira flinched in expectation of his cry.

Instead: a gasp, a muttered curse; with staring eyes and teeth locked tight together, Khaba stood. The Ring rested on his palm.

"Master! Are you hurt?" Asmira looked up and saw, framed against the stars, a shadow-thing, Khaba's duplicate in silhouette. Her teeth parted in horror, she struggled in the monster's grip.

The Egyptian flicked his eyes toward her. "Keep the girl secure," he said. "But do—do not harm her yet. I need—I need to talk with her. Ah!" He gave a bellow. "How did the old man *stomach* it so?"

The grip around Asmira's waist tightened so that she cried out. At the same time she felt her captor make a sudden, sinewy movement to pick up something behind them.

The soft voice spoke again. "Master, I have Bartimaeus too. He lives."

Asmira moved her head a little, saw the handsome youth hanging limp beside her, suspended like a clutch of rags in a great gray fist. Yellow steam rose from many wounds upon his body. The sight gave her a sudden pang.

"Not dead? All the better." Khaba shuffled toward them, holding his right hand close against his chest. "We have our first occupant for the new essence-cages, Ammet. But first—this girl..."

He came to a halt in front of Asmira and stood regarding

her. His face was wracked with pain; his teeth champed silently against his upper lip. Still he did not put the Ring on.

"How did you do it?" he demanded. "What level magician are you?"

Asmira shrugged. She shook her head.

"Do you *want* Ammet to tear you in two?" Khaba said. "He itches to do so. Speak!"

"It was easy enough."

"What of Solomon's defenses?"

"I avoided them."

"The Ring: how did you get it off his finger? While he slept?"

"No. He was awake."

"Then how in the name of Ra—?" Khaba broke off, staring at his rigid, clutching hand. A wave of pain passed over him; he seemed to lose his train of thought. "Well, you shall tell me the details later at my leisure, whether you wish to or not. But one thing now: How did Solomon die?"

Asmira thought of the frail king sitting in his chair. She wondered what he would be doing now. Summoning his guards, perhaps, or fleeing the tower. She found she hoped he'd had time to do so. "Bartimaeus strangled him," she said.

"Ah. Good, good. No more than he deserved. Now, Cyrine —but of course, that's not *really* your name, is it? I wonder what..." Khaba gave her a twisted grin. "Well, we'll find out, won't we, in time. Whoever you are," he went on, "I'm greatly obliged to you. I have been eager to carry out such an act myself for years. So have the rest of the Seventeen—we have spoken about it often. Ah, but we were fearful! We dared not act! The terror of the Ring was upon us. Yet you, in the company of this ...this very *ordinary* djinni have managed it!" Khaba shook his head in wonder. "It is truly quite remarkable. I assume it was you who caused the kerfuffle around the treasury?"

"Yes."

"That was a good tactic. Most of my colleagues are still engaged down there. If it was left to them, you'd have gotten away."

"How did you find us?" Asmira said. "How did that green demon—"

"Gezeri, Ammet, and I have been looking for you half the night, ever since you robbed me. Gezeri has the sharpest eyes. He saw a glimmer high up on the balcony. He came to investigate. I kept watch on him with this." The magician held up a polished stone that hung about his neck. "Imagine my surprise when we discovered it was *you.*"

At that moment there was a moan behind them. A small, bedraggled cloud rose fitfully from the gulf, proceeding in sorry jerks and starts. On the cloud sprawled the small green foliot, in a state of great discomposure, with a bump the size of a stork's egg on its head. "Ohhh, me essence," it groaned. "That Bartimaeus! Got me with a Petrifaction before chucking me off the edge!"

Khaba scowled. "Be still, Gezeri! I have an important task to do."

"I'm numb all over. Go on, give my tail a tweak. I won't feel it."

"You won't *have* a tail much longer if you don't stay quiet and keep watch."

"*Aren't* we tetchy?" the foliot said. "But *you'd* better be careful too, chum. The explosions up here haven't gone unnoticed, nor that horrid aura spilling from your hand. Better look sharp. There's company coming."

It pointed: far off to the south, many points of light were fast approaching, and with them slim silhouettes, dark, rectangular, like silent doorways to the stars. Khaba grimaced. "My friends and colleagues, come to check on Solomon. Little do they guess who holds the Ring now!"

"All very fine," Asmira said suddenly, "but I notice you've not yet put it on."

She cried out; the demon had squeezed her waist vindictively. Khaba said: "It *is* slightly . . . harder to endure than I would have expected. Who would have thought that Solomon had such strength of will? But do not think to criticize me, girl. I am a man of power. You are nothing, a nameless thief."

Asmira gritted her teeth; rage filled her. "*Wrong*," she said. "My name is Asmira, and my mother was First Guard of the Queen of Sheba. I came to seek the Ring because my country was in peril, and though I may have failed, at least I acted with more honorable intent than *you*."

She finished with her chin jutting, her eyes blazing, ferocious satisfaction surging through her. There was a resounding silence.

Then Khaba laughed, a high-pitched, squealing sound, and from the shadow-thing that held her came a laugh that echoed it pitch for pitch. The unconscious djinni, hanging alongside, twitched and shivered at the noise.

With an effort Khaba calmed himself. "They come, Ammet," he said shortly. "Be ready. My dear Asmira—what a pretty name, to be sure; I much prefer it to Cyrine. So you have been sent from Sheba? How amusing."

He opened his hand, stared at the Ring of Solomon.

"Hurry, boss," the foliot said. "There's old Hiram. He looks mad."

Asmira could see the magician's fingers shaking as they hovered above the Ring. "What do you mean, 'amusing'?" she said. "Because I know why you have come. I know why Balkis sent you." The big moist eyes flashed up at her; there was glee in them, as well as fear. "And because I know you killed Solomon for nothing."

Asmira's stomach lurched. "But the threat . . ."

"Was not made by Solomon."

"The messenger . . ."

"Wasn't sent by him." Khaba gave a gasp as his fingers closed upon the Ring. "The—the rest of the Seventeen and I have long engaged in certain private transactions, taking advantage of Solomon's reputation. The petty kings of Edom, Moab, Syria, and others have all eagerly paid ransoms to avoid fictitious disaster. Balkis is just the latest in this line. She—like the rest—is rich, and can easily pay. It is no great loss to her, and it swells our coffers. If Solomon didn't notice, where was the harm in it? It's the kind of thing the fool should have been doing anyway, of course. What's the point of power if you don't get something for yourself?"

The shadow spoke above Asmira's head. "Master . . . you must make haste."

"Khaba!" A peevish cry came from the darkness. "Khaba —what are you doing?"

The magician ignored the voice. "Dear Ammet, I know I talk too much. I talk to blunt the pain. I must steel myself to put it on. I will not be long."

Asmira was staring at the Egyptian. "Your messenger attacked Marib. People died. Which magician sent him?"

Sweat ran across Khaba's gleaming head. He held the Ring between thumb and forefinger, moved it toward his finger. "In point of fact it was me. Don't take it personally. It might have been any one of us. And the messenger was Ammet, who holds you now. It is ironic, don't you think, that Balkis's petulant gesture should end by causing the death of the one king who would *not* abuse the power of the Ring? I will not be so restrained, I can assure you."

"Khaba!" Rushing down toward the parapet, resplendent in his long white robes, the vizier Hiram looked upon the scene with eyes of fury. He stood, arms folded, upon a small, square carpet that was held aloft by a man-shaped demon of great size. It had long, flowing golden hair, and feathered white wings that beat the air with the crack of war drums. Its face was beautiful, terrible, remote, but its eyes were emerald green. Without them, Asmira would not have recognized the small white mouse.

Behind stood other magicians, other demons, hovering in darkness.

"Khaba!" the vizier cried again. "What do you do here? Where is Solomon? And what—*what* is that you hold?"

The Egyptian did not look up. He was still steeling himself, holding the Ring with shaking hands.

"At least my queen—like me—acted with honor," Asmira said. "She will never bend her neck before you, no matter what you threaten!"

Khaba laughed. "On the contrary, she has already done so. Yesterday she had the sacks of frankincense piled ready for collection in the Marib courtyard. You were nothing but a side-gambit, child, a throwaway gesture your queen could easily afford to make. Since she now presumes you dead, she gets her payment ready at the last. It's what they always do."

Asmira's head spun; blood pounded in her ears.

"Khaba!" Hiram called. "Put down the Ring! *I* am the most senior of the Seventeen! I forbid you to put it on. We *all* must share in this."

Khaba's head was bowed, his face was hidden. "Ammet, I need a moment. If you would...?"

Asmira looked up. Through her tears she saw the shadow's mouth curl open, showing ranks of slender teeth—then she was tossed sideways through the air and caught again; now she hung next to Bartimaeus, tight beneath the shadow's arm.

"Khaba!" Hiram cried in a voice of thunder. "Attend, or we attack!"

Still holding Asmira and the djinni, the shadow extended across the balcony. Its free arm was held outstretched, its fingers long and curled. The arm shot forth, flashing like a whip. A slice, a snick. Hiram's head fell one way, his body fell the other. Both toppled silently from the carpet and plunged into the dark.

Hiram's white-winged demon gave a shout of joy and vanished. The carpet, suddenly unattended, spiraled swiftly out of sight.

Somewhere in the air above the garden, one of the other magicians screamed.

The shadow drew back upon the balcony and turned in keen attention to its master, who, bent double, had uttered a long, low cry.

"Dear Master, are you hurt? What can I do?"

Khaba did not answer at first; he was locked in upon himself, head lowered to his knees. Suddenly his head jerked up. His body slowly rose. His face was contorted, his mouth spread in a ghastly rictus smile.

"Nothing, dear Ammet. You need do nothing more."

He held up his hand. Upon its finger was a glint of gold.

Beside her, Asmira heard Bartimaeus give a groan. "Oh great," he said. "I would happen to wake up *now.*"

33

The Egyptian turned away to face the night. Beyond him, several magicians were visible in the starlight, standing stiff and hesitant on their carpets above the void. One called out a challenge, but Khaba did not respond. Instead he held his hand aloft and, with a slow, deliberate movement, turned the Ring upon his finger.

As in Solomon's chamber, Asmira felt her ears pop, as if she had fallen into deep water. At her side Bartimaeus drew breath in through his teeth. Even the shadow that held them took a slow step back.

A Presence stood in the air beside the balcony, man-sized but not a man, darker than the sky.

"You are not Solomon."

The voice was neither loud, nor angry, but mild and calm. Yet it seemed slightly resentful. At its sound Asmira jerked back as if she had been struck. She felt blood trickling from her nose.

Khaba gave an anguished yelp that might have been laughter. "No indeed, *slave*! You have another master now. Here is my first command. Protect me from all magical attack."

"It is done," the Presence said.

"So then..." Khaba swallowed hard; he drew himself up straight. "It is time to show the world that things have changed," he cried, "that there is a new power in Jerusalem. There shall be no more of Solomon's indolence! The Ring shall be *used*!"

At this, several of the hovering magicians acted: gleaming

shafts of magic darted across the gulf to strike the Egyptian down. As the bolts converged upon the parapet they broke asunder; each became a delicate drift of colored sparks that dispersed like grass-seeds on the wind.

"Slave of the Ring!" Khaba cried. "I notice that my colleagues Elbesh and Nisroch were particularly swift to strike. Let them be the swiftest to be punished!"

Two carpets, two magicians exploded in balls of bright green flame; smoking twists of debris fell toward the trees.

"It is done."

"Slave of the Ring!" Khaba's voice was louder now; he seemed to be mastering his pain. "Bring forth for me a multitude as great as when Tuthmosis marched on Nimrud! Greater! Let the heavens open and my army come forth at my command! Let them rain down destruction on all those in this palace who dared to raise their hands against me! Let—" He broke off with a gasp, looked into the sky.

"It is done," the figure said, and vanished.

Asmira's ears had popped again; aside from this, she scarcely noticed the Presence go. She, like Khaba, like all the magicians on their carpets, like the spirits who kept them suspended there, was gazing up at a point east of the gardens, high above the palace wall. Here a hole had opened in the sky, a fissure like a fiery wheel tilted on its side. The fires extended like spokes toward its center and burned with great ferocity, yet no sound of the inferno descended to the Earth, and nor was its fearsome brightness reflected on any of the domes or trees below. The hole was there, and yet not there—near, yet very distant, a window on another world.

Through it now flew a swarm of little specks, black and silent and moving very fast. Like a plague of bees or flies they came, like a curl of smoke, growing thick, then thin, then thick again, and always twisting, spiraling down toward the ground; and though the distance they traveled did not *appear* to be so very great, it seemed to Asmira to take an age. And all at once, as if an unseen barrier had suddenly been penetrated, there broke upon her a rush of sound like a sea of sand poured down upon the Earth: it was the whispering of the demons' wings.

The specks grew large, and starlight shone upon their teeth and claws and beaks, and on jagged weapons held in tails and hands, until the sky above the palace gardens was black with hovering forms and the stars themselves were utterly blocked out.

The army waited. There was a sudden silence.

Asmira felt a tapping on her shoulder.

She looked—straight into the eyes of the handsome youth who hung beside her in the shadow's grip.

"*Now* see what you've done?" he said reproachfully.

Grief and shame engulfed her. "Bartimaeus—I'm so sorry."

"Oh, well, that makes everything all right, doesn't it?" the youth said. "The legions of the Other Place unleashed, death and destruction about to rain down in great profusion on this portion of the Earth, Khaba the Cruel enthroned in bloody glory, and Bartimaeus of Uruk soon to meet some dismal end or other—but hey, at least you're sorry. I thought for a moment it was going to be a bad day."

"I'm *sorry*," she said again. "Please, I never thought it would end like this." She stared up at the solid mass of demons over-head. "And...Bartimaeus, I'm frightened."

"Surely not. You? You're a bold, bad guard."

"I never thought—"

"Doesn't matter now, does it, one way or the other? Oh,

look—the madman's giving orders. Who do you think's going to get it first? I bet the magicians. Yep. Look at them go."

Standing atop the broken parapet, with his spindly arms outstretched, Khaba had uttered a shrill command. At once a break opened in the layer of demons covering the sky; a coil of rushing forms descended in a great slow spiral. Below, in the shrouded darkness of the gardens, the magicians' slaves flung themselves into action. Carpets zigzagged in all directions, breaking toward the palace walls in an effort to make the open ground beyond. But the descending demons were too fast. The spiral fractured —black shapes exploded left and right, swooped down upon the fugitives, who, with desperate cries, summoned their own demons to the fight.

"Here come the palace guards," Bartimaeus remarked. "Bit late, but I suppose they don't *really* want to die."

Bright flashes of magic—mauves, yellows, pinks, and blues —exploded all across the gardens and the palace roofs as the assembled defenders of the palace engaged with Khaba's horde. Magicians screamed, carpets vanished in balls of light; demons dropped like fiery stones, crashed through domes and rooftops, and tumbled, grappling in twos or threes, into the fiery waters of the lakes.

On the parapet Khaba gave an exultant cry. "So it must begin! Solomon's works are ended! Destroy the palace! Jerusalem will fall! Soon Karnak will rise anew, and become again the capital of the world!"

Far above Asmira the shadow's mouth was open in exultant parody of its master. "Yes, great Khaba, yes!" it called. "Let the city burn!"

It seemed to Asmira that the grip upon her waist had loosened markedly. The shadow was no longer focused on the prisoners in its care. She stared at Khaba's back with sudden fixed attention. How far away *was* he? Ten feet, maybe twelve. Certainly no more.

A sudden calm detachment came over her. She took a slow, deep breath. Her arm shifted stealthily upward; her hand quested for her belt.

"Bartimaeus—" she said.

"I wish I had some popcorn," the djinni said. "It's a good show, this, if you forget we're going to be part of the second act. Hey—not the jade tower! I bloody built that!"

"Bartimaeus," Asmira said again.

"No, you don't have to say anything, remember? You're sorry. You're *really* sorry. You couldn't *be* more sorry. We've established that."

"Shut up," she snarled. "We can fix this. Look, see how close he is? We can—"

The youth shrugged. "Uh-uh. I can't touch Khaba. No magical attacks, remember? Plus he's got the Ring."

"Oh, who *cares* about that?" Her arm rose. Pressed tight against her wrist, which shielded its telltale chill from the shadow's slackening grip—her final silver dagger.

The djinni's eyes widened. It glanced up at the shadow, which was still whooping and cooing at the destruction below. It looked at Asmira, then at Khaba's back.

"From here?" Bartimaeus whispered. "You reckon?"

"No problem."

"I don't know.... It'll have to be a good one."

"It will be. Shut up. You're disturbing my concentration."

She adjusted her position slowly, keeping her eyes fixed on the magician. Breathe slowly, just as her mother used to do. Aim for the heart. Don't think about it. Just relax....

The djinni gave a gasp. "Ooh, he keeps moving. I can't bear it."

"*Will* you be quiet?"

A riderless carpet swathed in purple flames carved diagonally through the air straight in front of Khaba, who jumped aside. The carpet struck the tower somewhere below; a plume of smoke rose like a pillar before them. Asmira cursed silently, gathered herself, assessed the angles to his new position, moved her wrist back . . .

Now she had him.

"Master—watch out!" The foliot Gezeri, hovering in his cloud beside the parapet, had glanced across; he gave a sudden warning cry. Khaba turned, his arms outstretched, his fingers spread. Asmira made an instant adjustment. She threw the dagger. Silver flashed, sliced across Khaba's moving hand. Blood showered; something like a bent twig fell away. Gold glinted at its ragged end.

All across the sky the demon horde winked out. Stars shone.

The severed finger bounced upon the stone.

Khaba opened his mouth and screamed.

"*Go,* Bartimaeus!" Asmira cried. "Catch it! Drop it in the sea!"

The youth at her side was gone. A small brown bird thrust itself clear of the shadow's grasp.

Khaba screamed, clutching at his hand. Blood gouted from his finger stump.

The shadow's scream was identical to its master's. The grip about Asmira's waist was broken; she was abruptly tossed aside.

The little bird swooped low, seized the finger in its beak, and disappeared over the edge of the parapet—

Asmira landed hard upon her back.

—A mighty bird of flame and fire shot upward into view, a fleck of gold held in its beak. Turning to the west, it disappeared amid the rising smoke.

"Ammet!" Khaba howled. "Kill it! Kill it! Bring it back!"

The shadow flitted forward, jumped from the parapet. Long black wings sprouted from its sides. They rose and fell with a noise like thunder. It too was gone into the smoke. Its wingbeats faded. Silence fell upon the House of Solomon.

Asmira got unsteadily to her feet.

A haze of spent magic drifted like dark fog beyond the parapet. The palace and its gardens could not be glimpsed, save here and there where colored fires were burning. Somewhere perhaps she heard faint voices, but they were far away and far below, and might as well have been calling from another world. The walkway was all there was, a mess of fractured stone and blackened wood.

And she was not alone upon it.

The magician stood there, six feet away, cradling his maimed hand and staring into the dark. It seemed to Asmira that the lines upon his face had deepened, and that delicate new ones clustered on his skin. He staggered a little as he stood.

He was very close to the edge. A single shove was all it needed. . . .

Asmira stepped silently toward him.

A rush of air, a smell of rotten eggs. Asmira threw herself flat upon the ground, so that the swiping claws of the foliot Gezeri sliced just above her neck. She felt a tingling as the lilac cloud passed over her, then she was up upon her feet again. The foliot spun around upon his rushing cloud, reversed its direction, came hastening back. His eyes were slits of hatred, his mouth gaped wide. The barb on his twirling tail curled like a scimitar. His indolent posture and bright red cheeks were gone; he had become a crouching thing of claws and teeth.

Asmira grasped the silver pendant at her neck, stood ready. With a cry, the foliot sent a thin green spear of light shooting at her chest. Asmira leaped aside, uttered a Ward that deflected the attack, sent it harmlessly out into the void. She uttered another. Yellow disks rained down upon the lilac cloud, peppering it with smoking blisters. The cloud veered sideways, collapsed to the parapet; Gezeri, jumping free as it fell, skittered with horrid speed across the stonework and sprang at Asmira's face. She jerked backward; its teeth clashed on empty air. Asmira caught the foliot by the neck and held it outstretched, ignoring the snapping mouth and flailing claws and whiplash tail, which with each stroke bit into her arms.

Gezeri frothed and fought, and with sinewy strength began to tear free of her grip. Asmira felt her strength waning. She tore the silver pendant from around her neck and shoved it with full force into the open mouth.

The foliot's eyes bulged. It made a low, hoarse gargling sound, half-lost among the steam and vapors gushing from its jaws. Its body swelled; its thrashing limbs grew stiff. Asmira flung it to the ground, where it fizzed and jerked and popped, and presently became a blackened husk that subsided and was gone.

She turned to the Egyptian, but he had moved away from the edge, and with bloodied hands was scrabbling at his belt, where hung a whip of many thongs. He cracked it—a movement both weak and perfunctory. Yellow coils of magic burst feebly at the flail's end, scoring lines in stone, but they did not reach Asmira, who jumped back out of range.

The magician gazed at her; his eyes were misty with pain and hate. "Leap and scamper all you like, girl. I have other servants. I will bring them here. And when Ammet is back..." He made as if to strike again, but was distracted by his wounded hand, from which the blood was flowing. He sought to staunch it on the fabric of his robes.

Asmira thought of Bartimaeus fleeing with the shadow at his back. If it was a marid, as Bartimaeus had said, the djinni could not withstand it long. Soon, very soon, he would be caught and killed, and the Ring returned to Khaba. Unless...

If she were quick enough, she might save her djinni yet, and after him, Jerusalem.

But all her knives were gone. She needed help. She needed—

There, behind her: the arch that led to the royal chambers.

Asmira turned and ran.

"Yes, flee! Flee as far as you like!" Khaba called. "I will attend to you as soon as I call my slaves. Beyzer! Chosroes! Nimshik! Where are you? Come to me!"

After all the turmoil and the darkness and the smoke outside, the placid, sparkling interior of the golden room felt strange, unreal. As before, the plunge-pool steamed, the enchanted foodstuffs glistened on their plates, and the crystal globe's surface swam with milky light. Asmira was about to edge past without looking at the Glamour, when she came to a dead halt.

A man stood watching her from the far side of the room.

"Having a little trouble, are we?" King Solomon of Israel said.

34

Throw it in the sea. Throw it in the sea. Sounds simple, doesn't it? And like all the girl's commands it *was* simple, at least in concept. It was doing it alive that was the problem.

Forty miles separates Jerusalem from the coast. Not far. Ordinarily a phoenix can manage that in twenty minutes, and still have time for occasional picnic stops and diversions to inspect the views.[1] But circumstances *weren't* ordinary here. Not in the slightest. The palace was burning, the planes were still quivering from the eruption of the spirit hordes, the fate of the world hung in the balance—oh, and I was holding the Ring of Solomon in my beak.

Actually, to be precise, I was holding Khaba's severed finger, with the Ring still on it. To spare the feelings of squeamish readers I won't go into any further details.

Except to say that it was like smoking a cigar. A small, slightly wonky cigar, with a gold band wedged near the lit end. There. Picture it now? Good.

It was still warm as well, and had just stopped dripping, but I'm not going to mention that.

Suffice it to say, all things considered, it wasn't the nicest body part I've ever had to carry,[2] but even so it had a very useful

---

[1] It's the fiery tailwind that provides the jet-propulsion, making a phoenix one of the fastest aerial guises around. Lightning bolts are faster, admittedly, but tough to direct. You usually end up wedged headfirst in a tree.

[2] Nor the nastiest, either. Not by a long shot.

function. It meant I didn't have to touch the Ring, and so was spared that particular dose of pain.

There was plenty more on offer, though. I had Ammet close behind.

Through the ruins of Solomon's palace the phoenix sped, keeping to the areas that had seen most devastation in Khaba's brief attack. Half the place seemed to be on fire, while the remainder was swathed in a heavy smog of drifting magic. It was gray, but still shimmering with potent traces; my plumage stung as I flew among them, weaving and bobbing to avoid thicker knots of lingering spells. Many such clumps hung close about the shattered domes and turrets, distorting them into softly melting dreamscapes, and they might well have done the same with me, given half a chance. All in all it would have been much more comfy to head up to the clearer skies above, but I resisted this for now. The smog offered concealment, and perhaps helped muffle the aura of the Ring.[3]

Both these qualities were essential if I was to survive for any length of time.

I hadn't seen the shadow yet, but could hear the beating of his wings advancing through the smoke. I had to shake him off. The phoenix darted between two tumbling walls to a place where the smog was thickest, ducked sideways through a ruined window, shot along the length of a burning gallery, and hung high against the rafters, listening.

Nothing but the creak of roof timbers. Ancient statues

---

[3] I say *perhaps*. The Ring was so close to me I could not open my eyes to any of the higher planes for fear of being blinded. And this wasn't my only problem. Even though I wasn't touching the thing, its power was hurting me. Small drips of essence were already running off my beak.

—heroes, goddesses, animals, and djinn—stood blackening amid the flames.

The phoenix cocked its head hopefully. Perhaps I'd lost him. With luck Ammet had blundered onward through the smog and set off westward to the coast, following my assumed trajectory. Maybe if I left the palace to the north, then veered west over the cedar forests, I might yet get to the sea.

I dropped down, flitted along the hall, keeping as close as possible to the fires and smoke. At the end of the gallery I made a right into the Sumerian Annex, flanked by long, cold stony lines of ancient priest-kings that I'd known and served.[4] There at the end was a vast squared window, from which I could break out to the north. The phoenix put on a sudden spurt—

—and thus narrowly avoided being struck by the Detonation that destroyed the floor behind me. One of the statues suddenly shifted, unfolded itself; the Illusion that hid the shadow was cast off like a cloak. Clawing hands reached out, tore my burning tail-feathers loose as I twisted in midair. I accelerated away along the hall in a plume of orange flame, zigzagging desperately between the swiping ribbon arms.

"Bartimaeus!" the soft voice called behind me. "Give up! Throw down the Ring and I will spare your life!"

I didn't answer, which was impolite, I know. But then again, my beak *was* full. A moment later I burst through the window and shot out into the dark.

★　★　★

---

[4] Akurgal the Unsmiling was present, and Lugalanda the Stern; also Shulgi the Desolate, black-browed Rimush, Shar-kali-sharri (commonly known as Shar-kali-sharri of the Shriveled Heart), and Sargon the Great, a.k.a. Old Scowler. Yep, all my dear old masters from the morning of the world. What happy days.

How do you spend *your* life-or-death chases? In a state of numb bewilderment? Perhaps in continuous toe-tightening panic, or with occasional outbursts of gibbering fear? Reasonable responses, all. Personally, I use them to think. They're good that way. Everything's quiet, you're on your own, and all your other little problems helpfully fade from view as you ponder the essentials. Staying alive is top of the list, of course, but it's not the only thing. Sometimes you get a bit of perspective on other matters too.

So, as I raced west through the dying minutes of the night, with the hills and valleys rolling in waves beneath me, and Khaba's shadow speeding at my heels, I ran through the situation I was in.

Here's how it looked, mid-flight.

Ammet was going to catch me, and he was going to catch me soon. Fast as a phoenix is, you can't keep up the pace forever. This is doubly true when you've recently been knocked out by a Convulsion, and triply true when you're holding an object of such power that your beak is well and truly melting.[5] The marid —bigger than me and dense with magic—had lost ground at the start of the chase, but he was making it up now as I began to tire. Whenever I looked over my shoulder I could see his ragged knot of dark-on-darkness, half a valley back and gaining.

It was safe to assume I wasn't going to reach the sea.

Once Ammet caught up with me, the consequences would be terrible. First, and most important, I'd be dead. Second, Khaba would have the Ring again. He'd only had it for about five minutes so far, and already Solomon's palace lay in ruins, which gave you a clue to his proposed governmental style. Given

---

[5] It had *really* begun to droop by now. I looked like a depressed macaw.

time and opportunity, like an angry infant in a cake shop, Khaba was going to systematically wreak untold destruction on all the wailing peoples of the Earth. More importantly, I'd be dead. Perhaps I already mentioned that.

The phoenix flew on. Periodically, bright flashes lit up the rushing landscape as Ammet unleashed magical attacks behind me; I veered to the side, dropped low, performed aeronautical contortions as the Spasms and Fluxes whizzed past, blowing trees and hillsides into tumbling rubble.

It was all the girl's fault, of course. If she'd taken my advice and just put the Ring on, none of this would have happened. Instead she could have destroyed Ammet, killed Khaba, traveled in a twinkling to Sheba, booted out her queen, and installed herself in opulence and splendor on the throne. She could have done all this and been sitting back, watching a belly dancing floor show, before breakfast.

That was what *all* my previous masters would have done.[6] But not the girl.

She was an odd mix, all right. On the one hand determined and resolute, with more courage in one of her shapely eyebrows than any conventional magician I'd ever met. On the other, confused, contrary, and utterly unsure of herself, and with an all-time gift for making the wrong decisions. She'd gotten me into possibly the worst night I'd experienced in two thousand years, yet had stood by my side while we pinched the Ring of Solomon. She had fluffed the chance to wear the Ring herself, but had chopped off Khaba's finger without a moment's

---

[6] Except Lugalanda the Stern. He'd have skipped the belly dancing bit in favor of some executions.

hesitation. She'd probably condemned me to my death, but had apologized as well. An odd mix. An infuriating one.

By rights I should have been seeking a way to countermand her order, skip the sea bit, and chuck the Ring to Ammet. Then I could have left the girl and her world to Khaba's gentle care. Faquarl would have figured out a way to do exactly this before he'd left the palace, and chuckled in the doing. That didn't work for me.

Partly it was because of my loathing for my enemies. I wished to foil them if I could. Partly it was because of my inherent tidiness. It had been *my* skill and judgment that got us the Ring; it had been *me* who suggested chucking it in the sea. In short, I'd started this in style, and I wanted to finish it on my terms.

Partly it was because I wanted to save the girl.

But first, before any of that, I had to reach the coast in one piece, and do so well ahead of Ammet. If he was right behind me when I threw the Ring into the deep, the whole plan would come unstuck. He'd just fish the thing straight out, probably using my perforated corpse as a net, and set off back to Khaba. Somehow I had to deal with him.

Ammet was a marid. It would be death to fight him hand-to-hand. But perhaps there *was* a way to slow him down.

Over a hilltop the phoenix flew, beak gently bubbling with the aura of the Ring. Behind came the shadow on black wings. Beyond was a wooded valley, thick with pines. Here and there, in the half-light before morning, were little glades, places where woodcutters had been felling trees. The phoenix's eyes gleamed. I abruptly descended into the wood, and my tell-tale fires went out.

Ammet, the shadow, had crested the rise just in time to see

me disappear. He too dropped down beneath the canopy and hung in resin-scented blackness, listening.

"Where are you, Bartimaeus?" he whispered. "Come out, come out."

Silence in the forest.

The shadow wove his way between the trunks, slowly, slowly, sinuous as a snake.

"I smell you, Bartimaeus! I smell your fear!"[7]

Answer came there none, as might have been expected. Down between the trees he glided, following the steep curve of the hill.

Then, someway up ahead, a little noise: *Frrt, frrt, frrt.*

"I hear you, Bartimaeus. I hear you! Is that your knees knocking together?"

Frrt, frrt, frrt.

On came the shadow, just a little faster. "Is that the chattering of your teeth?"

Actually, it was neither, as any spirit who'd spent any time outdoors would know.[8] It was me using a claw to whittle the ends of two tree trunks I'd found beside a logging camp. I was making two nice long pointy stakes.

"Last chance, Bartimaeus. Throw down the Ring! I can see

---

[7] Which was, needless to say, a downright fib. Aside from the occasional whiff of brimstone, which I save for really special occasions, I never extrude a smell of *anything*—fear least of all.

[8] Since only the very strongest magicians ever summon them, and since these magicians are invariably based in cities at the hubs of power, marids like Ammet don't have any experience of the lives and lore of simple country folk, those gentle webbed-toed woodsmen who wash but once a year, and sit about their dung-fires of an evening comparing warts and counting out their remaining teeth. Yes, marids really miss out on all this.

its aura glinting in the trees. You cannot keep it from me. Run away now, and I will let you live!"

Down through the forest stole the shadow, listening to the sound. By and by the whittling ceased; the shadow paused. But he could see the aura of the Ring of Solomon gleaming brightly up ahead.

Quickly now he came, silent as black snow, tracing the aura to its source.

Which turned out to be a tree stump on the far side of a glade. There on the stump, propped provocatively against a pine-cone, was Khaba's finger, with the Ring pulsing merrily at the end.

Now, any ordinary spirit—those of us regularly sent delving into ancient Sumerian temples, for example—would have instantly smelled a rat. We'd have all had far too much experience of booby traps not to be extremely wary of innocent tree stumps bearing gifts. But Ammet, Khaba's lapdog, probably hadn't done a decent day's work in twenty years, and had forgotten, if he ever knew, the importance of extreme caution. Also, secure in his arrogance and power, and with his own ultimatum ringing in his ears, he clearly thought I'd legged it. So, with a hiss of satisfaction, he darted forth, lengthening a little in his eagerness, stretching for his prize.

Behind him came a whirl of movement—something massive thrown with force. Before Ammet could react, before he could reach the Ring, a medium-sized tree trunk, its end sharpened to the keenest point, shot down diagonally from the slope above. It struck the shadow precisely in the center of his elongated back, pierced him through, and embedded deeply in the forest mold below. The shadow was pinioned through his middle; he emitted a shrill and horrid cry.

The young Sumerian spear-bearer hopped into view above, brandishing a second stake. "Morning, Ammet," I chirruped. "Having a rest? I suppose it *has* been a taxing night. Uh-uh, naughty—not for you." One of the shadow's arms was still stretching for the Ring; the other was wound about the tree trunk and was slowly, effortfully, forcing it upward. I bounded over and scooped up the finger. "*I'll* take that, I think," I said. "But don't worry, I believe in sharing. I'll give you something else."

So saying, I leaped back, hefted the second stake and hurled it unerringly toward the shadow's head.

Ammet acted with frantic speed; ripping the first stake clear of the ground, and regardless of the gaping rent now showing in his midriff, he swung the tree trunk like a club, struck my missile aside and sent it crashing off among the trees.

"Not bad," I said. The spear-bearer had shifted, become the phoenix once again. "But how fast are you in the *air*, with a hole right through you? I'm betting not very."

With that I was up above the pines again and heading westward in a blaze of fire.

After a while I looked back. The shadow had risen above the trees and was following me doggedly. As I'd hoped, his injury had temporarily inconvenienced him—his outline was somewhat more ragged than before. He'd slowed a little too, and, though keeping pace, was no longer gaining. That was the good part. I was going to reach the sea.

Trouble was—none of this would be enough to save me in the end.

Ammet still had me in his sights. The moment I threw the Ring into the ocean, he would simply hasten forward, dive down, and get it out. Nor was there any hope of tricking him again, for I was weakening swiftly now. The chase, and my injuries, and the coruscating power of the Ring, which continued to burn small holes in my poor beak—all of this was overpowering me. My fires were almost spent. Though I could hear the roaring of the waves, they promised me nothing much except a more than usually damp demise.

35

King Solomon wore a long embroidered gown of gold, and there was a circlet of silver in his hair. He stood very straight and still. Shorn of the simplicity of his plain white robe, he seemed taller and more magnificent than when Asmira had last seen him, though certainly no less frail.

Her face colored with shame. "Please," she stammered. "I'm sorry. You were right. The Ring...the Ring has..." She gathered herself: she had no time, and there was nothing easy to be said. "I need a weapon," she began. "I need it now. Something to kill Khaba with."

The king gazed at her. "I would have thought," he said quietly, "you'd have had enough of killing."

"But you don't know what Khaba's done! He's—"

"I know what he's done full well." The dark eyes flashed in the ravaged face; he gestured at the crystal orb beside him. "My scrying globe is not for show and I don't need the Ring to use it. The war in the world has begun, I see, with my own palace the first to go."

The orb's surface swirled, the milky colors cleared. Asmira glimpsed the palace burning, people milling in the gardens, spirits hurrying from the lakes with vats and buckets, hurling water on the flames. She bit her lip.

She said: "Lord, my servant has the Ring. Khaba's demon chases him. If I can destroy the magician, Bartimaeus will be saved, and your Ring—"

"Will be thrown into the ocean." Solomon regarded her

pointedly from beneath raised eyebrows. "I know. I heard and saw it all."

He moved his hand across the crystal. The scene shifted: now it showed Khaba on the balcony, silhouetted against the smoke. He was speaking an incantation of some kind, and his words sounded faintly from the orb. As they listened, the words faltered: the magician broke off with a curse, took a breath and began again.

"He has overstepped himself," Solomon remarked, "as all fools do. The Ring steals your strength in proportion to your acts. By trying to do too much, Khaba has become weakened, and his mind wanders. He can scarcely remember the words of Transference. Ah . . . but now he has them."

Asmira looked at the arch behind her, where six dull flashes in quick succession illuminated the fabric of the drapes. In the orb, the magician's body was blocked out by dark and rising shapes. "He's bringing his demons!" she cried. "They're arriving now! Please! Haven't you *anything* we can use against them?"

"Not by my own powers." The king was silent for a moment. "It has been a long while since I did anything for myself. . . . But there may be something in my treasure room. Come then, quickly. Cross the hall. Keep your eyes averted from the Glamour. But when you pass the table on the left, open its middle drawer. Take out all the things you find inside and bring them to me."

Asmira did as she was told, quick as she could. From the orb she heard Khaba uttering shrill commands, and guttural voices raised in answer.

The drawer contained several golden necklaces, strung with precious stones; many of these were inscribed with mystic, arcane signs. She ran across to Solomon, who took them in silence. With strides of stately haste, he set off toward an arch that Asmira had not previously entered. As he went, he bent his head stiffly and put on the necklaces.

"What powers do they have?" she asked, pattering alongside.

"None at all. But they look nice, don't you think? If I'm going to die," King Solomon said, turning in at the arch, "I intend to look the part. And now—here is my little collection."

Asmira surveyed the storeroom, its shelves and chests and boxes, all overflowing with artifacts of a hundred shapes and kinds. The profusion bewildered her. "What should I use?" she said. "What do they do?"

"No idea," Solomon said blandly, "for most of them. For years I have been searching for something that might equal the power of the Ring, but at rather less personal cost. My quest has been in vain, of course. Meanwhile my servants have acquired so many objects that I've quite run out of time and energy to investigate them. They're all magical, but some are just mere trinkets, and others quite impossible to fathom."

A crashing sound came from the far end of the golden room. Asmira winced. "Well, any rapid tips would be most welcome. Do you have some silver knives?"

"No."

"Throwing stars?"

"I don't think so."

"Right. Well, I'll have that sword, for a start."

"I wouldn't." Solomon knocked aside her outstretched hand. "Once picked up, it can't be put down. Notice those yellowed finger-bones fixed to the hilt?"

"That shield, then?"

"Too heavy for any normal arm. It is said to have been King

Gilgamesh's. We might try *these*, however." He passed her two silvery metal eggs, the size of a man's closed fist.

"What are they?" Asmira said.

"Something aggressive, we hope. What about these?" He indicated three short wood sticks, each with a bulb of glass at the end. Things inside the bulbs moved restlessly.

Asmira heard stealthy sounds beyond the arch. She took the sticks. "Keep looking," she said. "Don't go anywhere near the door. I'll try to hold them off."

Flitting to the arch, she stood with her back flat against the wall and peeped around into the enchanted room. There they were: six of Khaba's demons from the gorge, fanning out among the chairs and tables. As before, they wore men's bodies; this time their heads were those of beasts—a wolf, a bear, two eagles, a hideous grinning ape, and, worst of all, a locust, gray-green and glistening, with quivering antennae. Despite the ferocity of their guises, they went slowly, with evident hesitation; behind came Khaba, urging them onward with feeble strokes of his essence-flail. His wounded hand had been bandaged in black cloth ripped from his robe; his steps were those of an invalid. Asmira saw him look repeatedly toward the balcony in expectation. He was holding back, keeping out of range—waiting for his chief servant to return once more.

Asmira pressed her head back against the wall and closed her eyes. She imagined Bartimaeus flying, desperate and alone. She imagined the shadow-demon close behind, stretching out its clawing fingers to engulf him and the Ring. . . .

She took a deep breath.

Skipping sideways from the arch, she gave a carefree yell. "Over here!"

The bestial heads looked up. "That is the girl who maimed

your master!" Khaba cried. "Tear her to pieces! He who kills her wins his freedom!"

As one, the demons sprang, smashing through tables, hurling chairs sideways into the walls, leaping the pool in single bounds, converging on the place where Asmira stood her ground.

When they were fifteen feet away, she threw the eggs and bulb-sticks, one after the other, at great speed.

The two eggs hit the eagle-demons head on and exploded violently, blowing holes clean through the center of their midriffs. They raised their beaks, uttered plangent cries, became vapor, and were gone.

Two of the bulb-sticks missed their targets by inches and landed on the marble floor, shattering like eggshells. Vertical fountains of green fire rose up, sending nearby demons somersaulting backward to the accompaniment of whoops and cries. The final stick struck the demon with the locust head just above its foot. The spur of fire ignited the upper regions of its leg. With a scream, it leaped into the plunge-pool and disappeared in a cloud of steam.

Asmira stepped calmly back inside the arch, where Solomon was rummaging through the shelves. "Two down," she said. "One wounded. What else have you got?"

The king had rolled up his sleeves, and his gray hair was disordered about his face. "I should have sorted this out years ago. . . . It's so hard to tell. . . ."

"Give me anything."

"Well, try these." He tossed her a clay cylinder, stamped with stars, and a sealed terra-cotta jar.

Asmira darted back to the arch. The golden room was filled with smoke. Through it moved four hulking forms.

She hurled the cylinder at the nearest; it struck, broke to dust, did nothing.

She threw the jar: upon landing, it opened and emitted a soft, sad sighing, then a trill of raucous laughter. The demons, which had jumped back in doubt, came on at faster speed.

Behind them, the Egyptian gave a ragged oath. "You idiots! A child could deal with this! Hit her with magic from a distance!"

Asmira moved back into the room, just in time to escape the vaporization of the floor outside. Several Detonations struck the wall, sending blocks half through the plaster into the storeroom. Dust rained down upon her hair.

The king was methodically scanning the shelves. "Any joy?" he said.

"Not this time."

"Here." Solomon flipped open the lid of a small oak casket. Inside, neatly stacked, were six glass spheres.

As he handed her the casket, a bolt of magic ricocheted through the arch, shot over her head, and blew the storeroom roof asunder. Stonework melted, lumps of wood and rubble fell. With a cry, Solomon collapsed upon the floor.

Asmira dropped to his side. "Are you hurt?"

His face was gray. "No . . . no. Do not worry about me. But the demons—"

"Yes." Asmira got to her feet, ran through a rain of little falling stones, and threw three spheres out through the ruined arch. Explosions followed, and plumes of green fire, then shrill, indignant sounds.

She crouched in the shadows, brushed her hair out of her eyes, and put her hand in the casket again. At that moment something struck the other side of the wall with such force that she was knocked off her feet. The casket fell from her grasp; the three spheres rolled out of it, bounced gently on the floor.

Asmira froze, staring at them, at the little cracks spreading on their surface.

She flung herself back into the room just as the arch erupted with green fire.

Flames poured through; heat buffeted Asmira as she jumped, lifting her up and forward with great speed. She crashed into the shelves in the middle of the room, and fell awkwardly among the mess of upturned chests. A tide of artifacts cascaded on her head.

When she opened her eyes, she saw Solomon gazing down at her.

He extended a slow hand. Asmira took it, allowed herself to be helped to her feet. Her arms and legs were bleeding, her robe was singed. Solomon was in a scarcely better state. His robes were torn and he had plaster in his hair.

Asmira stood silent for a heartbeat, looking at him. Then she said suddenly, all in a rush: "I'm sorry, Master. I'm sorry for what I've done to you."

"Sorry?" the king said. He smiled. "In some ways I should be *thanking* you."

"I don't understand." She glanced toward the arch, where the green witch-fires were slowly fading.

"You have awoken me from sleep," King Solomon said. "For too many years I've been trapped up here, enslaved by pain, obsessed with my burden, keeping the Ring safe. And what was the result? Just that I grew ever weaker and more complacent—and blind to the deeds of my own magicians, who have been busily extorting riches from my empire! Yes, thanks to you, the Ring is gone—but the result is that I feel more alive than at any recent time. I see things clearly now. And, if I'm going to die, I intend to do it fighting on my own terms."

He reached out to the tumbled treasures on the floor and picked up an ornate serpent. It was made of gold, with ruby eyes, and had several little hinges hidden on its feet. "This," the king said, "is evidently a weapon, controlled by the studs here. Come, we'll use it now."

"You wait here," Asmira said. "I'll do it."

Solomon ignored her outstretched hand. "Not just you this time. Come."

At the archway the fires were gone. "One other thing, Asmira," Solomon said as they stepped through. "I'm not your master. If this should be the last hour of your life, try not to need one."

They walked out into the central chamber, stepping over steaming holes and gashes in the floor, and almost collided with three of the demons, which, in the form of macaque monkeys, had been sidling cautiously toward the arch. At the sight of Solomon, the monkeys yelled and bounded away across the room. The magician Khaba, leaning dourly against an upturned couch beside the pool, also jerked bolt upright in consternation.

"Wretch!" Solomon cried, in a voice of thunder. "Bow down before me!"

Khaba's face had sagged in horror. He wavered; his legs began to buckle. Then he controlled himself, his thin lips tightened. Gesticulating at the cowering monkeys on the far side of the hall, he sprang forward with an oath. "So what if the tyrant lives?" he cried. "He doesn't have the Ring!"

Solomon strode forth. He flourished the golden serpent. "Dismiss your slaves! Bow down!"

The Egyptian paid no heed. "Do not fear that golden trinket!" he shouted at the monkeys. "Come, slaves, rise up and kill him!"

"O Khaba..."

"Wretch!" Solomon said, again. "Bow down!"

"He is helpless, you fools! Helpless! Kill him! Kill them both!"

"Oh no...." Asmira said softly. *"Look."*

"Dear Khaba..."

The voice came from behind the magician, from the direction of the balcony. Khaba heard it. He froze. He turned. All eyes turned, looked with him.

The shadow floated in the entrance, its essence faint and flickering. It still had the magician's silhouette, only softer, rougher than before, the edges melting like a candle. "I have been over land and ocean," its faint voice said. "I am very weary. The djinni led me a long and merry dance, but I caught him at the last." The shadow gave a heavy sigh. "How he fought! Fifty djinn together could not have done better. But it is over. I did it for you, Master. Only you."

Khaba's voice cracked with emotion. "Sweet Ammet! You are the best of slaves! And...and you have it?"

"Look what it has done to me," the shadow said wistfully. "Burning, burning, all these long, dark miles homeward...Yes, Master, I have it in my hand."

It unfurled five steaming fingers. A ring of gold sat in its palm.

"Then my first act will be the destruction of the cursed Solomon!" Khaba said. "Ammet—I shall relieve you of your burden. I am ready. Give it to me."

"Dear Khaba, I shall."

Solomon gave a cry; he lifted the golden serpent. Asmira began to run. But the shadow paid no heed to either. Unfurling its long, thin fingers, it swept forward with the Ring.

36

Here's how it finished.

Beyond the western forests, beyond the old coast road running north toward Damascus, beyond the little villages strung along the cliffs, Israel peters out abruptly on the shores of the Great Sea.[1] By the time the phoenix reached it, I was petering out too.

Out over the empty beaches I went, flying erratically, one or two fiery feathers dropping into the waves with each beat of my wings. My noble beak had largely melted, and it was only with a small, sparrow-sized nub that I maintained my hold on Khaba's drooping finger. My eyes were misting too, thanks to weariness and the proximity of the Ring, but when I glanced back I could see the shadow still in sight, drawing ever nearer.

I was almost at my limits. The chase was almost done.

Westward I went a little longer, straight out to sea, and for the first half-mile there was still no light save for the little red-and-orange glow that clung about my body and leaped and danced below me on the rushing waves. And all at once the night grew

---

[1] *Great Sea*: later (by the Romans) called the Mediterranean. In Rome's day this body of water would become a commercial playground, its waves flecked with brightly colored galley sails, its aerial lanes dark with spirits hurrying to and fro. In Solomon's time, however, when even skillful Phoenician sailors preferred to hug the coasts, the Great Sea was left blank and desolate, a primeval embodiment of chaos. Personally speaking, whatever the epoch, I always find seas the same: big, cold, and unnecessarily wet.

gray and, looking back, beyond the shadow, I saw a pink fringe above the distant shore that announced the arrival of the dawn.

Good. I hadn't wanted to finish things in the dark. I wanted the sun upon my essence one last time.

The phoenix dropped low, skimmed close to the water's surface. Then, jerking my head upward, I spat the finger high into the air. It rose, rose, caught the first rays of the sun, began to fall—and was caught in the center of a lean, dark hand.

A short distance away the rushing shadow slowed. He halted, hovering just above the waves on his tapered, pinpoint legs, and looked at me.

I stared back as the Sumerian spear-bearer, curly haired and tousled. Wave flecks wet my bare feet; dawn light broadened in my somber eyes. With a rapid movement I removed the Ring from Khaba's finger, which I tossed into the sea. Then I raised one arm. In my hand the Ring of Solomon was held outstretched, poised above the gulf.

Ammet and I stood in silence, the cold deeps below us tugging at our essence.

"So, Bartimaeus," the shadow said at last. "You have led me a merry dance, and fought well. Five djinn together could not have done better. But this is the end."

"Too right it is." I raised my arm a little higher. Where the Ring rested between my finger and thumb, my essence fizzed; the steam drifted gently up into the pink dawn light. "If you dare to drift so much as a single wave-length nearer," I said, "it's going in. Right to the bottom, down where it's dark and oozy, and things with too many legs will guard it for eternity. Think carefully, Ammet! Your master wouldn't want to lose it forever, would he?"

The shadow gave an indifferent shrug. Dawn light drifted

through the ragged hole in the middle of his chest. "You're bluffing, Bartimaeus," he whispered. "Even with your minuscule intelligence you must see that if you drop the Ring, I shall become a fish and retrieve it before it sinks a dozen yards. Besides which, its aura is bright enough to be seen even in the remotest depths. I would find it even if you stuffed it in a whale. Throw me the Ring and, on my honor, despite the retribution I so sorely owe you, I promise I will kill you quickly. But keep it from me a moment more, and I swear that I shall do such things to you that even Khaba would weep to look on your remains."[2]

I stood quietly above the water a moment. Below my feet and the shadow's pin-sharp tapers, the blue-pink wave crests rose and fell, sloshing and sucking gently. The sun rose in the east, prising open the lid of the dark blue sky. After all the fire and fury of the night just gone, everything was, for a moment, calm. I saw things clearly once again.

Ammet was right. It was pointless to throw it into the deep.

"Give it up," the shadow said. "Look at the damage it's doing to you! You've been holding it far too long."

I considered my melting hand.

"Has it burned away your wit, Bartimaeus?" The shadow flitted toward me across the sea. "No more of this. Give me the Ring."

---

[2] As newly invented threats go, that was a pretty good one, particularly after such a long chase. Ammet clearly subscribed to the Egyptian curse tradition: keep it succinct and keep it scary. As opposed to (say) those long-winded Sumerian curses that waffle on endlessly about boils, sores, and painful bouts of wind, while you, the intended victim, softly slip away.

I smiled, came to a decsion. Without a word, I changed my form. Solomon the Wise stood there.[3]

The shadow drifted to an uncertain halt.

"What do you think?" I said. "Do I look the part? I'm betting I do. I've got the slightly pear-shaped hips and everything. Even the voice is pretty good, wouldn't you say? But there's one thing missing." I showed both hands, palms outward, waved them side to side. "Let's see now... Where is it?" I patted my robes all over in a show of mild concern; then, like a backstreet conjurer, pulled a small gold band from out of my ear. "Ta-da! The Ring! Recognize this?"

I held it up, grinning, so that it caught the bright dawn light. Ammet's outline had sagged a little, grown gauzy with anxiety. "What are you doing?" he hissed. "Put it down!"

"You know, Ammet," I said. "I agree with you. Holding the Ring's really been messing up my essence. So much so, it seems to me I'm not going to lose anything right now by going one step further...."

The shadow took a swift step forward. "It'll kill you. You wouldn't dare."

"Oh, wouldn't I?"

I put the Ring upon my finger.

It was a nice fit.

A nice fit that happened to come with the excruciating sensation of being violently pulled in two directions at once. The

---

[3] I went for the fully rigged-up "official" Solomon here—handsome, healthy, saturnine, dolled out in flashy, jewel-decked clothes—not the "private," crinkly, white-robed version the girl and I had met. Partly this was to avoid having to copy all his many creasy bits (which would have taken an *age*), and partly because, at this do-or-die moment of supreme truth, I was blowed if I was going to wear the guise of an old bloke in his pajamas.

Ring, as I may have said before, was a gateway. Holding it was like feeling the breeze passing under the gate. Putting it on? That was the gate blowing open, with the full hurricane coming roaring in, and you being caught there, small and helpless.[4] It was like a Dismissal in full flow, dragging me back toward the Other Place—and yet my essence was unable to obey it. I felt my essence tearing as I stood there in the silence on the calm, unruffled water, and knew I didn't have long.

Perhaps, in those first moments, while I was reeling, Ammet might yet have acted. But he was too stupefied by my audacity. He hung beside me like a greasy stain wiped on the morning. He seemed transfixed. He didn't move.

I mastered the pain, spoke over it as best I could. "Now then, Ammet," I said in an agreeable voice, "you've been talking a lot recently about punishments and retribution. You've been quite vocal on the subject. I quite agree we should look into that in some considerable detail. Just hold on a mo."

"No, Bartimaeus! No! I beg you—"

This, then, was the terror the Ring induced. This was its power. This was what the magicians fought for, why Philocretes and Azul and the rest had risked everything to get it in their hands. It wasn't very pleasant. Still, I was going to see it to the end.

I turned the Ring about my finger. The pain fluxed and twisted; my essence tore. I gasped aloud at the rising sun.

All about me the seven planes warped. The dark Presence hung beside me in the air. The dawn light did not illuminate its shape at all, but passed right through it, leaving it as deep and black as if a hole had been cut in the day. It cast no shadow.

---

[4] And naked. Just to make the analogy extra chilly.

Speaking of which, poor old Ammet's trademark blackness looked rather gray and gauzy beside the newcomer's. He didn't know what to do with himself, exposed out there on the water. He flitted left and right with little nervous movements, shrank low, waxed long, and spun spiral trails in the water with his trailing strands.

As on the balcony, the Presence didn't beat about the bush. **"What is your wish?"**

It hadn't escaped my notice that when Khaba had summoned him, the Spirit of the Ring had sounded slightly *irritable* not to see Solomon. Hence my clever disguise. It wasn't perfect —perhaps my voice was *slightly* more squeaky than the king's, owing in part to my rampant terror and discomfort, but I did my best. I flatter myself the old king's mother wouldn't have known the difference. I spoke coolly. "Greetings, O Great Spirit."

"You can stop putting on that silly accent," the Presence said. **"I know your name and nature."**

"Oh." I swallowed. "You do? Does it matter?"

"I am bound to obey whoever wears the Ring. No exceptions ... Even you."

"Oh, good! That *is* good news. Hold on ... Where are you off to, Ammet? Can't stay around?" The shadow had turned and was speeding away across the waves. I watched him go with a light and negligent smile, then addressed the Spirit of the Ring again. "How did you guess?"

"Aside from my ability to see through all Illusions? Solomon rarely stands over open ocean. Also, you forgot the perfume."

"Two beginner's mistakes! Well, it's pleasant chatting like this, Great Spirit, but—"

"What is your wish?"

Brief and to the point. Which was good, because I could not take the pull of the Ring much longer. Where my finger passed through the band, my essence was worn and faint and thin as a thread. Portions of my strength had already been pulled through.

Ammet was very distant by now, a small diagonal blur that left a scud of foam on the sea behind him. He had almost reached the land.

I said: "There is a certain marid rapidly retreating over there. I wish him seized this moment and given a sound drubbing."

"It is done."

From nowhere, a flurry of gray shapes rose from the surf and engulfed the fugitive shadow. Sadly I couldn't see the details, because of the distance and all the spray and splashing, but the outcry was enough to send seabirds rising from their nests up and down the coast for a satisfying number of miles.

At length the racket finished. The shadow was a melancholy patch of grayness floating on the water.

The shape still waited at my side. **"Your wish?"**

If my essence had been strained before, the exertion of my will upon the Ring had worsened the pain considerably. I held back, unsure of what to do.

The Presence appeared to understand my indecision. **"That is the nature of the Ring,"** it said. **"It draws upon the energy of its user. In truth, your request was small, therefore—if you wish it—your essence could withstand a repetition."**

"In that case," I said heartily, "another sound drubbing for Ammet, please."

While the thrashing frenzy was still ongoing I said, "Great

Spirit, I require a bottle, or something similar, but I haven't one to hand. Perhaps you could assist me."

"**The sea is deep here,**" the Presence said, "**but far below lies the wreck of an Egyptian ship that sank in storms three hundred years ago. It has a cargo of amphorae that once held wine. Most are empty, but are otherwise intact and have been scattered far across the seabed. You want one?**"

"Not too big, please."

There was a bubbling and frothing beneath my feet, and a green up-current of deep cold water broke against the surface, bringing with it a great gray wine jar, covered in weed and barnacles.

"Just the job," I said. "Spirit, this will be my final request, for despite your reassurances, I think my essence will explode if I wear this Ring a moment longer. I wish the marid Ammet bound within this bottle, and the lid stoppered with lead or whatever equivalent you have to hand, and that stopper sealed with appropriate hexes and runes, and the whole returned to the bottom of the sea, where it can remain undisturbed for several thousand years, until such time as Ammet has reflected on his crimes against other spirits and, most especially, against me."

"**It is done,**" the Presence said. "**And a most appropriate penalty it is.**"

For a moment the wine jar spun with colored lights and I felt the bending of the planes. Somewhere amid it all, I fancy I heard the shadow's final cry, but it might have been the seabirds calling out across the water. The jar's neck flared bright with molten lead; saltwater hissed and steamed. Now the neck was cool, save where nine symbols of Charm and Binding still glowed upon the plug of lead. The jar began to spin, slowly at first, then faster:

fast enough to make the sea break open in a spreading cone, a dark-blue funnel winding into darkness. Down the funnel the jar went spinning, down and down beneath my feet, and the sea closed in upon it.

A little swell rose up and wet my feet. It fell away. The sea was flat again.

"Spirit," I said, "I thank you. That was my last wish. Before I remove the Ring, do you require me to break it in two, and so release you?"

"**Politely speaking,**" the Presence said, "**that is beyond your competence. The Ring cannot yet be broken.**"

"I'm sorry," I said. "That is sad to hear."

"**My freedom will occur in time,**" the Presence said. "**And what is time to us?**"

I turned to look toward the sun. "I don't know. Sometimes it feels a while."

I took off the Ring. The Presence vanished. I stood on my own above the quiet, lapping sea.

37

Even as she moved, Asmira knew that it was hopeless. She would not reach Khaba before the shadow did. There was nothing she could do to prevent him reclaiming the Ring.

Too slow, too feeble, too far away to be of use—it was a sensation she had known before. But she ran anyway. Perhaps she could distract them, give Solomon time to use his weapon, or give him space to flee. She ran—it was the right thing to do. And in those final moments Asmira was richly conscious of everything in the room: the dawn light shining through the drapes; the four demon monkeys standing huddled in a corner; the magician stumbling forward, his mouth open, his eyes gleaming, his good hand avidly outstretched...

And the shadow, Khaba's dark reflection, hastening toward him.

Despite the ravages upon its essence, the shadow still maintained its faithful mimicry of its master. Except...as it drew close to the magician, Asmira saw that its silhouette had changed. Its nose was suddenly longer than the Egyptian's, and had sprouted several enormous warts, while two vast jug-ears, resembling those of an elephant, protruded from the skull.

The shadow and its master met. Khaba held out his hand. The shadow made as if to drop the Ring into his palm, then—at the last moment—jerked it out of reach.

Khaba swiped for the Ring and missed. He hopped and danced, squeaking with annoyance, but now the shadow raised the Ring high above his head, dangling it teasingly from side to side.

"*Nearly* got it," the shadow said. "Ooh, that was a big jump. If only you were a *little* taller."

"What are you *doing*, slave?" Khaba roared. "Give me the Ring! Give it to me!"

The shadow clapped a hand against one of its outsized ears. "Sorry, ugly. I'm a bit deaf. What did you say?"

"Give it to me!"

"Nothing would give me greater pleasure."

At which the shadow drew back, swung a fist, and punched the Egyptian square on the chin, sending him bodily off the floor, whistling backward through the air, and down onto one of the golden tables, which shattered beneath his sprawling weight.

Khaba the Cruel lolled there unconscious in a mess of fruit. Purple grape juice pooled like blood around him.

Asmira stared. Her gasp mingled with the others echoing around the room.

The shadow gave a small salute. "Thank you, thank you. For my next trick, a ring to its rightful owner, followed by the immediate dismissal of a well-known djinni. Autographs available on request."

"Bartimaeus...?" Asmira began.

The shadow bowed. "Morning. I've got something for you."

"But how—? We thought you were surely—"

"I know, I know—you were probably expecting me back a little sooner. Well, I couldn't help having a chat with Ammet before I disposed of him, you see. Gave him a stern talking to, made him learn the error of his ways. Then, after that, there was all his pleading for mercy, all the inevitable wailing and begging; you know how these marids go on. . . ." For the first time the shadow appeared to notice the cluster of demons loitering in the margins of the hall. "Hello, boys," it said cheerfully. "Hope you're taking notes here. This is how to dispose of a master *properly*."

Asmira's astonishment broke into sudden urgency. "Then you still truly have—"

The shadow opened its hand. Where the Ring of Solomon lay, the djinni's essence was bubbling and spitting, sending red-hot threads of vapor into the air.

"I thought I told you to drop it in the sea?" Asmira said.

"You did. And I carried out your order to the letter. Well, I sort of let it fall in and then scooped it out again immediately. It got wet, put it that way. You have to be careful how you phrase things when you're playing at being a magician, Asmira—this is the kind of trick we naughty djinn get up to when we're not simply saving civilization. The point is," the shadow went on, "even though it *was* my idea, I don't think it's best to lose the Ring in the sea and doom its Spirit to an even longer captivity than he already endures. I wouldn't want that on my conscience. So, as per your original request and, frankly, because it bloody hurts, I'm giving it back to you now. It's up to you what you do with it, of course. Catch."

The Ring was tossed over. Asmira caught it, gasping at the pain. This time, she did not let go.

Instead, without hesitation, she turned and knelt to face the king, who stood waiting across the room. "Masterful Solomon," she began. "He whose magnificence and majesty are boundless—"

She looked up at him for the first time, to discover that the great king was gaping at her like a stranded fish. His face and shoulders were black with soot, and his hair stood on end in a frizz of spikes.

"Oh," she gasped. "What happened to you?"

Solomon blinked. "I . . . hardly know. When I thought Khaba was about to get the Ring, I aimed this golden serpent device at him, pressed a couple of buttons and—and it was like the ending of the world. I got some kind of shock, then the thing expelled a plume of tarry smoke straight in my face. I hope I don't look too discomfited."

Asmira spoke in a small voice. "Not . . . too bad."

"At least you didn't press the *third* stud," the djinni said. "That releases a really bad smell that—" He hesitated, sniffed. "Oh . . . you did."

"Great Solomon," Asmira said hastily, "I hereby return your property." She bowed her head and held up her cupped hands. They burned with the power of the Ring, but she gritted her teeth and kept them steady. "Bartimaeus and I passionately regret the wrong we have done you. We throw ourselves on your wisdom and your mercy."

The shadow gave a startled cry. "Hey, leave *me* out of it! I've been acting under duress throughout. Except just now—when I brought back his Ring."

Asmira sighed. She raised her hands still higher; as yet Solomon hadn't moved. "I take full responsibility, O King," she said, "and ask that my servant be absolved of blame for all the wickedness he committed." She scowled sidelong at the shadow. "There. *That* satisfy you?"

"All right, I suppose."

At this King Solomon stirred. He walked toward them. The shadow grew quiet. There was an anxious chittering from the four monkeys in the corner. Even the unconscious magician lying in his bed of fruit moaned and moved his head.

Silence in the hall.

Asmira waited with bent head and burning hands. She was under no illusions about her likely fate, and she knew it to be well deserved. Back in the storeroom, Solomon had expressed forgiveness—but that had been when both were on the verge of death. Now, with the Ring back in his hand and his authority restored, it would be a different matter. Beyond the tower, his palace was in ruins, his people terrorized. Most of his magicians were dead. Justice demanded retribution.

She knew all this, but it did not alarm her. She felt peaceful and calm inside.

The rustling of a golden gown drew near. Asmira did not look up.

"You have offered me the Ring and your apologies," the voice of Solomon said, "and the first of these I accept—with reluctance, for it is a fearful burden."

Asmira felt cool fingers brushing against hers, and the pain in her hands died away. When she raised her head, Solomon was placing the Ring upon his finger. A flicker of discomfort passed his ravaged features as he did so, then was gone.

"Stand up," he said. Asmira stood. Beside her the shadow gave a shimmer and changed into the handsome, dark-eyed youth. She and Bartimaeus stood before the king, waiting for his word.

"Your second offering," Solomon said, "I do not accept so readily. Too much damage has been caused. In a moment we shall come to my judgment. But first—" Closing his eyes, he touched the Ring and spoke a quiet word. A blaze of light consumed him, died away; the king stood before them all transformed. His face was clear of soot, but also of its web of lines; his hair, smoothed down once more, was dark and black and glistening with vitality. He was the youthful image of the mural on the palace wall, and it was all Asmira could do not to fall on her knees again.

"Oh come," Solomon said, "you know it's an Illusion." Grimacing a little, he turned the Ring; at once the Presence stood among them. "Uraziel," he said, "I'm back."

"I never doubted it."

"We have a little work to do."

"Where shall we begin?"

Solomon cast a glance at the magician on the floor. Khaba was groaning now, writhing a little to and fro. "You may remove this object first of all. Place him in the dungeons below the tower. I shall attend to him presently."

A blaze of light: Khaba was gone.

"His cringing slaves may be dismissed; I have no grudge against them."

More dazzlements: the four monkey demons vanished where they cowered.

King Solomon nodded. "My palace, I believe, needs some repair; we must steel ourselves, Uraziel. Survey the damage, calculate the spirits that will be required, and await my signal. I have business to attend to here."

The Presence departed, jolting the air. Asmira's ears rang; she wiped her bloody nose upon her sleeve.

She and Bartimaeus stood alone before the king.

"Now," King Solomon said, "to my judgment. Bartimaeus of Uruk, you first of all. Your crimes are legion. You have caused the deaths of dozens of my spirits, you have spread chaos and disaster across Jerusalem. It was by your advice and through your actions that this girl was able to get access to the Ring. Not only that, you have at all times displayed extraordinary insolence toward my royal person. Your hippo guise—"

"No, no, that was perfectly coincidental! It looks nothing like your wife!"

"—showed appalling disregard for the sanctity of my temple. That was what I was *going* to say."

"Oh."

"As if this were not enough," the king went on after a thoughtful pause, "you appear to have encouraged this girl to throw the Ring into the sea...."

"Only to keep it out of the clutches of your enemies!" the djinni cried. "Far better to lose it in some watery deep than have Khaba or the Queen of Sheba enjoy its power instead of you! That was my thinking. If great Solomon can't have it, I said to myself, why, let the silent coral guard it until the end of time, when—"

"Stop babbling, Bartimaeus." Solomon pursed his lips. "In all these things, you are clearly culpable. *However*, you also are a slave, forced to carry out another's will, and in truth, despite whatever temptations I may sorely have, I cannot place the blame on you."

The djinni exhaled with immense relief. "You can't? Phew. Now *that's* what I call wisdom." He gave Asmira a sharp nudge in the ribs. "So, then... over to you."

"Asmira of Sheba," King Solomon said. "In your case there is no need to recite the full list of your deeds. The harm you have caused me is very great, and to remedy that harm will weaken me even more. Not only that, you have glimpsed me in my weakness; you have seen behind the mask I wear. By all the laws of natural justice, punishment is due to you. You would agree?"

Asmira nodded. She said nothing.

"To set against this," the king went on, "there is the following. You did not kill me in my chamber. I do not know why —perhaps you already guessed your mission was ill-conceived. Then, when Khaba intervened, and the full extent of your folly was made plain to you, you struck him down and had Bartimaeus take the Ring. This act, on its own, prevented the traitor's immediate triumph. Not only this, you subsequently defended my person during Khaba's final attack, during which I would otherwise certainly have been slain. Now you hand me back the Ring. I find it hard to know what to say to you."

"She's odd that way," Bartimaeus agreed. "I have the same problem."

"I have already told you, Asmira," the king said, pointedly ignoring the interruption, "that your actions have stirred me from my slumbers. I perceive now that, bowed down by the burden of the Ring, I have neglected much, and allowed the corruption of my servants to flourish. This will change henceforward! I shall seek other ways of guarding the Ring, and wear the cursed thing less, come what may. My kingdom," Solomon said, "shall be the stronger for what has occurred."

He crossed to a surviving table, and from a stone bottle poured two glasses of bright red wine. "There is one additional fact," he said, "which needs consideration. It was not your decision to attack me, and I do not believe you had any choice in the matter. You too, Asmira, were acting under the orders of another. You are much like Bartimaeus in this regard."

The djinni nudged Asmira again. "Told you," he said.

"Consequently," King Solomon said, "the blame lies elsewhere. Uraziel."

The Presence hung beside him. "**Master.**"

386

"Bring the Queen of Sheba here."

The figure vanished. Bartimaeus whistled. Asmira's stomach gave a lurch, and the strange sense of calm that she had experienced throughout the judgment grew suddenly strained. Solomon selected a grape from a bowl of fruit and chewed it thoughtfully. He picked up the two glasses of wine and turned to face a blank space in the center of a nearby rug.

A flash of light, a smell of cream and roses: Queen Balkis stood upon the rug. She wore a long white gown with golden trim, and necklaces of gold and ivory. Her hair was piled high above a golden coronet, and earrings of twisted gold hung beside her shapely neck. Slightly detracting from her beauty and elegance was her vacant expression of numbed bewilderment, and the notably greenish quality of her skin. She swayed a little where she stood, gasping and blinking, staring all around.

The Sumerian youth leaned in close to Asmira. "Spontaneous transfer makes you nauseous," Bartimaeus whispered. "She's holding it in, though. No random vomiting. That's a sure sign of good breeding."

"Welcome to Jerusalem, my lady." Solomon casually held out a glass. "Care for some wine?"

Balkis did not answer him. Her gaze had alighted on Asmira and, after a moment's doubt, flared with recognition. She gave a little cry.

"My lady—" Asmira began.

"Wicked girl!" The queen's face turned suddenly white; red spots burned in her cheeks. "You have betrayed me!" She took a stumbling step in Asmira's direction. She raised a clawing hand.

"Not at all," Solomon said, interposing himself smoothly in between them. "In fact, quite the reverse. This is your most faithful servant. She carried out your mission. She stole the

Ring from me. She destroyed those persons who threatened you in my name. Without her, the future of Israel—and of Sheba, dear Balkis—would have been grave indeed. I am indebted to Asmira," Solomon said. "And so are you."

Queen Balkis said nothing. Her eyes, still trained on Asmira, were hard with doubt and cold hostility, her lips a single solid line. Asmira tried to recall the way the queen had looked when they'd spoken together two weeks before. She tried to recall the smiles and blandishments, the intimacy, her swell of pride...

No good. The memory was fugitive, and no longer carried power.

Balkis turned to the king. "So you say, my lord," she said at last. "I remain to be convinced of these facts."

"Indeed?" Solomon gave a courteous bow. "It is unsurprising. We *have* rather sprung this on you." He held out the wine and the full radiance of his smile bathed the queen; this time Balkis took the glass. "May I propose, then," he said, "that you accompany me for a walk about my palace, where some little work of reconstruction is going on? I can give you further details, and we can talk together about relations between our countries, which—I expect you agree—are in need of much improvement."

The queen's composure had, in small measure, returned. She bowed stiffly. "Very well."

"In the meantime, your guard—"

Balkis shook her head peremptorily. "She is no longer a guard of mine. I do not know *whom* she serves."

Just for a moment Asmira endured a keen pain, like a knife blade in the heart. Then it faded, and with it her agitation at the queen's arrival. To her surprise she felt quite calm again.

She regarded the queen levelly. Balkis took a sip of wine and turned away.

"In that case," Solomon said, smiling, "you will not mind, my lady, if I have a small suggestion. Asmira"—now all the full charm and glamour of his guise was turned on her—"I have an offer to make you. Enter *my* service, come be my guard. I have seen firsthand your many excellent qualities, and I now know —somewhat ironically after the events of last night—that I can trust you with my life. So, help me reestablish my rule here in Jerusalem. Be part of my more enlightened government! I will need all the help I can get in the days and weeks ahead, for my servants have been scattered, and if any of my magicians survive, they will need careful watching. Help me go forward, Asmira! Start a new life in Jerusalem! Be sure," he smiled, "that I will reward you richly."

At this, King Solomon put his wineglass down. "Now, it is high time that I attended to my most *important* guest. Fair Balkis, we shall take a leisurely tour, then retire to the pavilions for iced sherbet. The ice, incidentally, is brought fresh from the shoulders of Mount Lebanon; I swear you will never have tasted fresher. Please . . ."

He held out his arm; the Queen of Sheba took it. Together they moved across the room, stepping delicately around the debris on the floor. They reached an arch at the far side and passed through. The rustling of their robes dwindled, the sounds of their small talk faded. They were gone.

Asmira and the djinni looked at one another. There was a pause.

"Yep, that's kings and queens for you," Bartimaeus said.

38

Uraziel, great Spirit of the Ring, wasn't one to mess about when he had a palace to repair. Down below the tower, the work was under way. The buildings around the gardens that had sustained the most damage in the firefight had been encased in teetering bamboo scaffolding, and scores of djinn were already scurrying up and down a maze of ladders, removing rubble, pulling out burned timbers, and expunging any remaining taint of magic. From the direction of the quarry came sounds of frenzied hammering; afrits flew west toward the forests in search of logs. In the forecourts, lines of moulers[1] stood beside cement vats, stirring industriously with their tails, while in the gardens, stretching away into the blue distance, armies of imps labored to re-seed the blackened lawns.

Among it all strode Solomon, leading the Queen of Sheba by the hand.

From where I was, up on the balcony, even Solomon and Balkis's monumental self-regard seemed insignificant. They were simply two tiny figures in gold and white, almost indistinguishable from the straggling pack

---

[1] *Mouler*: an incredibly dull subtype of spirit. Imagine a small, slow, beige-colored —no, it bores me to death just describing them.

of onlookers following at their heels.[2] Balkis moved slowly, stiff-backed, the picture of brittle pride; Solomon with more of a graceful step. Now and then his arms made extravagant flourishes, no doubt as he pointed out the wonders of his gardens. On one hand there shone a little flash of gold.

It had to be said that, given the amount of power he had at his command, Solomon was, by human standards, quite admirably restrained. Most of his actions seemed more or less designed for the common good, and he was personally magnanimous too— as Asmira and I had just found out. But, all in all, he was still a king at heart, and that meant grand and flashy. Even his casual, throwaway magnanimity to us was, in its own way, grander and flashier than all his jewels. Not that you were going to hear me complaining.

But as for the Queen of Sheba... Well.

High on his lofty vantage point, the dark-eyed Sumerian youth made a rueful face. He hauled his ragged essence off the balustrade where he'd been leaning and went inside.

It was time for me to go.

I found the girl sitting on one of the golden chairs in Solomon's apartments, eating large quantities of honey cake with all the delicacy and restraint of a famished timber wolf.[3] She didn't stop when I came in, but went on scoffing. I sat in

---

[2] The usual assemblage of warriors, officials, wives, and slaves. It appeared that most categories of palace personnel, other than the magicians, had managed to survive the night with their servility intact. The indignant twittering of the wives, as they assessed the Queen of Sheba, carried through air like the calls of roosting birds. In many ways, things were back to normal.

[3] The Glamour laid upon the room had been blown apart during the night's fighting, along with several couches, carpets, murals—and Solomon's crystal orb, which now looked blank as rainwater, the spirit trapped inside having been happily released.

a chair opposite and appraised her properly for the first time since my return.

Physically she had the right number of arms and legs remaining; otherwise she was undeniably the worse for wear. Her clothes were torn and scorched, her skin bruised, her lip a little swollen; in places, her hair had been discolored green by a blast of magic fire. None of this could exactly have been considered a plus, yet it wasn't the whole story by any means. As she took a long slug of Solomon's wine, then wiped her sticky hands deliberately on one of his silken cushions, a perceptive onlooker (me) could also note that she seemed a good deal more vibrant and alive than when first I'd seen her, so stiff and cold upon her camel in the gorge that day before.

Badly as Asmira's exterior had been battered by the night's events, I guessed that a chain inside her had also been broken —and *this* breakage wasn't a bad thing.

She took a couple of grapes and an almond bun. "Still down there, are they?"

"Yes, busily doing the tour...." I narrowed my handsome eyes meditatively. "Is it me, or is your good queen Balkis something of a sour old trout?"

Asmira gave me a crooked grin. "I must say she wasn't as... generous as I'd hoped."

"That's putting it mildly."

"Well, what can you expect?" The girl flicked pastry off her lap. "She sent me out to do a nice clean assassination and steal the Ring. Now she finds me praised to the skies by Solomon, the Ring still on his finger, and herself summoned to Jerusalem like a dumb imp on a leash."

It was a fair analysis. "He'll win her over," I pointed out. "He always does."

"Oh, she'll forgive Solomon," Asmira said. "She won't forgive me."

She went back to her cakes. There was silence for a while.

"Good job you got the offer, then," I said.

She looked up, chewing. "What?"

"Solomon's offer. Richly rewarding you for helping him move forward with his new, progressive government, or whatever it was. All sounds a bit woolly to me. Still, I'm sure you'll be happy." I stared up at the ceiling.

"You seem disapproving," the girl said.

I scowled. "Well, it's just him using his Charm on you, isn't it? Hooking you with that sparkly, one-on-one eye contact stuff —all those white-toothed smiles, that business about trusting you with his life—That's all very fine, but where will it end? First you're a guard. Then a 'special adviser.' Next thing you know you'll be in his harem. All I can say is if that happens, make damn sure you don't sleep in the bunk below the wife from Moab."

"I'm not going in his harem, Bartimaeus."

"Well, you say that *now*, but—"

"I'm not taking up his offer." She took another swig of wine.

"What?" Now it was my turn to look bemused. "You're turning him down?"

"Yes."

"But he's Solomon. And...leaving aside what I just said, he *is* grateful."

"I know that," Asmira said. "But I'm not entering his service, even so. I'm not going to simply swap one master for another."

I frowned. That chain inside her had snapped, all right. "Are you *sure* about this?" I said. "Yes, he's a conceited autocrat; yes, he's got a mania for collecting wives. But he'd still make a better boss than Balkis by a long shot. For a start, you wouldn't be a sla...you wouldn't be an hereditary guard. There'd be a lot more freedom for you—and gold too, if that tickles your fancy."

"It doesn't. I don't want to stay in Jerusalem."

"Why not? Thanks to that Ring, it's the center of the world."

"But it isn't Sheba. It isn't my home." And suddenly in her eyes there was that same fire that I'd noticed the night before, burning brightly still, but with a gentler flame. All its anger, all its zealotry had gone. She smiled at me. "I wasn't lying to you —what I said last night. Being a guard, doing what I did—yes, I was serving the queen, but I was serving Sheba, too. I love its hills and forests; I love the desert glittering beyond the fields. My mother showed it all to me, Bartimaeus, when I was very small. And the thought of never going back to it, or to her—" She broke off. "You can't know what that feeling's like."

"Actually," I said, "I can. Speaking of which—"

"Yes, of course." Asmira stood up decisively. "It's time. I see that. I have to let you go."

Which just goes to prove yet again that she wasn't *really* a magician. Since the days of Uruk, all bouts of slavery have traditionally ended with a sordid argument in which my master refuses to set me free, and I become a cackling corpse or blood-clawed lamia in order to "persuade" him. But the girl, who had freed herself, was happy enough to do the same to me. And do it without a scrap. For a moment I was so surprised I said nothing.

I got slowly to my feet. The girl was looking around the hall. "We're going to need a pentacle," she said.

"Yes. Or even two. There'll be a couple somewhere."

We hunted about, and soon enough spied the edge of a summoning circle peeping out beneath one of the singed carpets. I began to throw aside the furniture that covered it, while the girl stood watching me with that same calm self-possession I'd noticed in the gorge. A question occurred to me.

"Asmira," I said, kicking an upturned table across the room, "if you head back to Sheba, what are you going to *do* there? And what about the queen? She's not going to be pleased to see you hanging about, if today's spite is anything to go by."

To my surprise the girl had her answer ready. "I won't *be* hanging about in Marib," she said. "I'll take work with the frankincense traders, help guard them on their journeys across Arabia. From what I've seen, there are plenty of dangers out there in the deserts—bandits and djinn, I mean. I think I can deal with those."

I tossed an antique couch approvingly over my shoulder. That actually wasn't a bad idea.

"It'll also give me a chance to travel," she went on. "Who knows, I might even go to Himyar one day, see that rock city you mentioned. Anyway, the incense trail will keep me well away from Marib most of the time. And if the queen *does* take exception to me..." Her expression hardened. "Then I'll have to deal with it. And her."

I wasn't a soothsayer or an augur and had no knowledge of the future, but I wondered if things might prove a little ominous for Queen Balkis. But there were other issues to attend to now. I shoved the last bits of furniture to the side, rolled up the priceless carpet, and threw it in the plunge-pool—and stood back in satisfaction. There, embedded in the floor—and quite undamaged—lay two pentacles of pinkish marble. "Slightly fey," I commented, "but they'll have to do."

"Right then," the girl said. "Get in."

We stood facing each other for a final time. "Tell me," I said, "you do *know* the words of a Dismissal, don't you? I'd hate to hang around for months while you were apprenticed out to learn them."

"Of course I know them," the girl said. She took a deep breath. "Bartimaeus—"

"Hold on a minute...." I'd just spotted something. It was a mural I hadn't seen before, just along the wall from Gilgamesh, Ramses, and all the other top despots of the past —a handsome full-length portrait of Solomon himself in all his glory. Somehow, miraculously, it had survived the carnage of the night before.

Picking up a bit of burned wood from the floor, I hopped across and made a few brisk adjustments in charcoal. "There!" I said. "Physiologically improbable, but somehow appropriate, don't you think? How long before he notices *that*, I wonder?"

The girl laughed; it was the first time in our association that she'd done so.

I glanced at her sidelong. "Shall I add Balkis as well? There's a little space."

"Go on, then."

"There we are...."

I strolled back to the circle. The girl was eyeing me in that same way Faquarl had—with a sort of detached amusement. I stared at her. "What?"

"It's funny," she said. "You make such a big deal out of the horrors of your enslavement that I almost missed the obvious. You *enjoy* it too."

I settled myself in my pentacle, fixing her with an expression of bleak disdain. "A friendly bit of advice," I said. "Unless you're *extremely* competent, it's never a good idea to insult a departing djinni. Particularly this one. In old Babylonia the priests of Ishtar forbade any magician below the ninth level to deal with me for just that reason."[4]

"Which proves my point," the girl said. "You're always boasting about your past achievements. Come on, admit it. You revel in it all. Even last night—I noticed how you stopped your moaning once we were getting near the Ring."

"Yes, well..." I clapped my hands together briskly. "I had to, didn't I? There was too much going on. Take it from me, I disliked every moment. Right, enough of this. Say the Dismissal and set me free."

She nodded and closed her eyes, a young, thin girl thinking through the incantation. I could almost hear the cogs grinding as I watched.

Her eyes opened. "Bartimaeus," she said abruptly, "thank you for what you've done."

I cleared my throat. "Pleasure, I'm sure. Look—do you truly know the words? I don't want to find myself rematerialized into a festering bog or something."

"Yes, I know the words." She smiled. "Come to Sheba some-day. You'll like it."

"Not that it's ever up to me."

"Just don't take too long. We haven't all got as much time as you."

Then she gave the Dismissal, and, sure enough, she *did* know the words. More or less. There were only three hesitations, two fluffed inflections, and one major stumble, all of which—on

---

[4] This was after a series of fatalities, my favorite of which was that of a brutish aco-lyte who'd tormented me with the Inverted Skin. However, he also suffered badly from hay fever. I thereupon brought him a massive bunch of pollen-rich lupines, at which he sneezed himself out of his circle.

this occasion—I was prepared to overlook. She wasn't very big, after all, and there wasn't that much meat on her. Besides, I *really* wanted to be gone.

The girl was of like mind. Even as my bonds broke and I was whirled free across the planes, I could see (from seven varied angles) that she had already left the circle. She was walking off, straight-backed and resolute, through Solomon's ruined chamber, looking for the steps that would lead her from the tower, and so into the waiting day.